THE TALES OF THE INFINITY STONE

WHEN DARKNESS FALLS: BOOK 1

ANGELA M. JOHNSON

THE TALES OF THE *Infinity* STONE

ANGELA M. JOHNSON

Photography by @lindeerobinsonphotography

AMJ Publishing
Prairie Grove, AR 72753

CONTENTS

DEDICATION

For those who like their MMCs dark and a couple levels below morally black: How about an FMC who makes him look like a cinnamon roll in comparison?

CONTENT WARNINGS

Some of the themes in this story may not be suitable for all, and as such, read with caution.

This telling has elements of BDSM (bondage and discipline, dominance and submission, sadism and masochism), CNC (consensual non-consent), monster intercourse, blood play, knife play, implied SA (sexual assault), suspension, dismemberment, execution, cannibalism (kinda), ritualistic intercourse, human sacrifice, torture, kidnapping, drugs & alcohol use.

Playlist

These songs inspired me as I wrote. I pictured each scene as they played in the background; scored like a movie or tv series.

Pronunciation Guide

gorget (gȯr-jət)

pteruges (pteri-yes)

Elysium (i-li-zhē-əm)

Tartarus (tär-tə-rəs)

Asphodel (as-fə-del)

Cocytus (kōk-u-tós)

Acheron (a-kə-rän)

Pyriphlegethon (pir'ə- fleg'ə-thon')

Charon (ker-ən)

Peithō (peí-thō)

apeiron (ə-pī-rän)

Asclepius (a-sklē-pē-əs)

Hecatoncheires (hek-a-tón-khei-res)

Mustéria (mys-ti-ri-a)

Kruptós (kryp-tós)

PART ONE

This tale is one of woe; of manipulation and deceit. A young maiden, a pure beauty, whose youth was stolen by lust. A promise made from a liar's lips, the terms agreed upon against her will. But she will not go quietly. She will take back that which has been stolen. She will forge her own future and write her history as she sees fit. The gods be damned!

CHAPTER I

IT ALL BEGAN WITH A FLOWER (PERSEPHONE)

The day I got married, I cried. We aren't talking about one or two subtle tears, either. They weren't a display of sweet emotion. I'm talking about giant, uncontrolled streams of distress. The kind of tears accompanied by whole body shudders, loud sobs, and a blotchy face; my terror and dismay evident for all to see.

I didn't have a grand entrance. There was no his side or her side with candles and floral arrangements decorating the space while guests turned back to look at me as I waltzed down the aisle in a glimmering gown. No, I was slung over the broad shoulder of an armor-clad Minotaur and carried from the room where I had been imprisoned for days prior to the ceremony.

The Minotaur's form, despite the beastly build, was a thing of beauty. He was all muscle and sinew; tight chiseled abs, thick forearms accentuating the chest of a god, and draped in velvety skin. Adonis, once a man, but now a beast. *Well, half of one anyway.*

Adonis had a bare chest and back, instead of crests and flanks, with luminous, tawny skin. There was an element of attractiveness about him, and perhaps he once had been beautiful, but now, with his abnormally sized head, large nostrils, and muzzle painted with a perma scowl, it's hard to imagine.

He strode forward with me over his shoulder, stretching his leather pteruges with his powerful human legs, while each footstep sounded beneath him as he bore our weight.

His gorget, made of cold steel with crossing bidents etched in the surface, clanked noisily, and the wiry hairs on his neck rubbed my arms raw as the friction and their coarseness burned me.

His scent was deep and heady, like livestock, but with a hint of rosemary and lemongrass. The contrast of scents was off-putting, as was his soft and silken voice that coaxed me into a false sense of security as he continued to apologize about the fate that had befallen me. "I'm sorry, mistress."

"You're sorry?" my voice is berating as I squeak out my reply.

"I had no choice," he explains. "My master bid me bring you to him, and so I must."

"And what choice have I? I was brought forth entirely against my will," I sob, my head lolling this way and that as he continued down the long hallway.

My soon-to-be husband didn't give me a grand gesture of love and affection where he got down on one knee and asked for my hand. No, he ripped me from everything and everyone I'd known and dragged me down, deep down, into the depths of the earth and straight to his torturous plane. A place where fires forever burned and death reigned supreme.

The sun darkened in the sky above me, and time seemed to stand still the day he took me. It's odd to say now, but I felt the world shift as I took that last breath of freedom in the ominous moments just before I became another possession of Hades.

It had been a beautiful day. One of those days where the sun danced across the sky as I frolicked through the meadows with my friends while surrounded by the essences of lilac and honeysuckle.

The moistness of the earth sifted between my toes, soothing my tired feet as I'd run my fingers along the knee-high grasses growing there; a backdrop where small white flowers dotted the landscape and the smooth reeds of the grasses tickled my calves as my feet smooshed through the sod.

I'd lay in those fields for hours, my hands folded behind my head as the bees buzzed from one bud to the next. So busy as they collected pollen to distribute from one bloom to another; the hum of their wings barely audible on the wind.

My eyes were closed while I lay there, their icy blue hidden from the sun's rays dancing across my lids, as the wispiness of my lashes tickled my cheeks. They were full, the color of copper, as were my fiery tresses that lay strewn about in every direction beneath me; each strand seeming to capture the sun as it shone down upon me.

The scorching sun kissed my skin, illuminating my cinnamon-colored freckles on the bridge of my nose and the tops of my shoulders, while the thin, soft fabric of my gown blew in the breeze. It billowed up around my waist as a gust lifted my skirts from where my long legs were outstretched bare and calling for the sun to tint their surface with the healthy glow of summer.

I'd spent hours that day walking along, dancing, and singing to myself as I collected the white, pink, and lavender wildflowers to dress my mother, Demeter's table. My arms were overflowing with my gift and offering, when in the distance I saw the most unique of blooms. I had yet to add any yellow to my bouquet, and those would have been the highlight of the arrangement. That is, if I'd ever laid my hands on them.

The yellow-belled blooms swayed in the wind, their beauty calling out to me as if begging to be picked.

The Nymphs were out of yelling distance as I'd looked back over my shoulder, so I danced toward the flowers, unaware of what treacherous part they would play in my abduction. But as I tried to pluck the first stem from where it sprung forth from the earth, the ground quaked beneath my feet.

I stepped back, attempting to avoid the chasm that broke the earth apart, but was too late. Down, down, down I fell into the abyss, the darkness surrounding me as my cries of terror echoed off the walls of the large hole swallowing me up.

Falling for what seemed like forever, I could hear wings flapping in the darkness, claws scratching along the sides of the tunnel as the pungent smell of dirt enveloped me. But just before I hit bottom, someone plucked me from whence I fell and set me on the surface below.

I looked up, my eyes attempting to adjust to the darkness, and a large being stood before me. Soft flesh took my hand, and a sultry voice asked if I was hurt.

"I... I'm fine," I muttered, squinting as I struggled to make out the man.

As I brushed the dirt from my gown, and while tending to my feet, a booming voice shouted in the distance, "Adonis! Grab the maid and bring her forth!"

"As you wish," the sultry voice answered.

Before I could protest, I was hauled up and thrown over the shoulder of the man. But he wasn't a man, he was something else.

A gruff texture covered his entire face and neck. It had a similar coarseness to the cloth of a grain sack, where the hairs on his face and neck were wiry, pokey even. Smooth as you ran your hands down them, but scratchy as you drew your hands in an upward motion; a hide of sorts. And it wasn't until we'd stepped out of the darkness, and into the light, that I made him out.

With me draped over his broad, muscular shoulders, bent at the waist, he stood upright into what little light the dim cavern afforded.

He jostled me, bouncing me against his tight backside, and with all the jarring, I struggled to focus on him. But when we'd halted, I finally saw them. He had horns, one on each side of his... head. We'll call it a head because, for one unfamiliar with the terminology of livestock, I'm not sure what the proper wording would be.

I'd heard of the Minotaur, had seen their likeness in drawings and sculptures, but had never seen one in person. To be honest, I didn't think they were real. I had seen a Centaur and a Satyr, had even frolicked across the glen with them and the Nymphs a time or two, so why wouldn't a Minotaur be real, too?

Adonis was real. He was soft skin and gruff pelt. He was flesh the color of ground Einkorn and hide the hue of cooled embers used for smudging. Not as dark as the ink that adorned parchments or berries that stained fabrics, but a rich tone, nonetheless.

His horns looked smooth as marble, with erratic striations and scrape marks along their curves; wear and tear from them bracing against something. And it wasn't until we neared Hades, reaching out with his two-pronged fork, that I realized exactly what that was.

"What took you so long?" Hades bellowed, clanging his fork across one of Adonis' horns as he knelt before the god with me still on his shoulder.

"My apologies, master," he acknowledged, genuflecting with his reply.

"Skip the apologies and give me the girl," he commanded.

Adonis rose and set me down, taking care not to injure me further after my fall but Hades stepped by him, grasping my forearm in his cinch-like grip, jerking me forward with callused and forceful hands.

"Enough wasting of my time. I have souls upon the thousands arriving every minute, and punishments to dole out." Hades huffed his dissatisfaction. "Come forth and step into the chariot."

"I'm not going anywhere with you!" I challenged.

"You'll come with me and you'll like it! It's for your own good, and I have already arranged everything. Now, come!" he seethed.

"No!" I struggled to break free, attempting to tear my arms from his grip.

"I don't have time for this," he gritted.

He jerked me by my arm, sending me hurtling forward into the back of his chariot where I landed on my palms, splinters embedding in the soft flesh as all my weight fell on my hands. No sooner had I leaned back against the side of the chariot, surveying my palms, when Hades stepped in and looked down to where I cowered at his feet.

"That's a good look for you." He smiled wickedly. "I think I like you best this way."

CHAPTER 2
LEILIA (PERSEPHONE)

"Stop your incessant weeping!" Hades rolls his eyes, standing with his arms crossed as he waits impatiently, his foot tapping at my impertinence.

As the child of a Titan, Hades is freakishly tall and dwarfs me by at least a foot and a half as I cower before him.

He stands unaffected, his dark locks curling around his face while he strokes the first stubbly growths of a beard. His features are striking: pronounced jaw, full rosy cheeks like a cherub, deep-set eyes. Storm cloud eyes that appraise me from beneath unruly brows.

A dark gown drapes across his chiseled chest, held together by a golden disc with an image of his bident stamped on the surface. And wrapping around his waist, the fabric of his skirts lie pleated, hanging down to his muscular calves.

I ignore Hades, tears streaming down my face as snot forms beneath one nostril. Spinning around, my simple cream-colored gown billows around me as I frantically scan the room, hoping someone, preferably my parents, will intervene on my behalf. But Hades claimed responsibility for arranging it all, so, most likely, that's improbable.

"Your wailing and protests change nothing. I'm unsure what you were hoping to accomplish with them?" he barks out.

He snorts in disgust, his impatience growing as he ruffles the scruff on one of Cerberus' heads where the beast stands obediently at his side.

Shifting his weight from one foot to the other, Hades says, "The only thing you have done is waste my time. You are mine, whether you like it or not."

"I don't like it," I counter, "and I don't…" I challenge, raising my chin in defiance, "want it." I step toward him, hoping to drive my statement home.

"I don't remember asking what you want." He smiles wickedly, reaching forward and grabbing the unruly strands of my coppery locks that had escaped my plait. "It's what I want. Everything down here is, or haven't you heard?" Hades then jerks strands of hair from my head, twisting them around his index finger as he glares at me.

I take a step back, my gown slipping off one shoulder as I retreat. "Oh, I've heard," I retort, rubbing the place on my scalp he pulled the hairs from. "But I don't belong here, and I don't belong to you!"

"But you do, and in a way, you always have. It has always been you, Persephone. Was meant to be you from the moment I laid eyes on you."

Hades raises his hand to his face, sniffing the strands of my hair twisting around his finger. He has long elegant fingers; the pads callused and skin wrinkled from ages spent wielding all manner of tools for torture.

His admission silences me, and thoughts overrun my mind. *How long has he been watching me? How long has someone been deciding my future without my knowledge? Why have they done it? Why have my parents allowed me to hope for a future of my making, if this was their plan all along?*

Hades takes my sudden silence as compliance, and waving his hands in the air dismissively at the priest standing anxiously before us, he commands, "Get on with it."

That poor priest, who, even in death, is forced to serve the gods. At least one of them, anyway. "Do you-"

Hades interrupts the man, holding his hand up and swatting in his direction as if shooing away a fly as he states, "You can skip that part."

"By the will of-"

"Me." Hades chuckles, once again interrupting the priest, his hands waving graciously as he mocks a bow.

"You are now joined."

Hades lifts his hand and the priest winces, lowering his head as he slowly backs away, cowering into the throne behind us.

The priest trips over Cerberus' paw, the beast yelping, and Hades chuckles at the man groveling at his feet.

He announces, "Right. And now we feast."

Grasping my wrist, he drags me from the room as not only Cerberus, but Adonis, follow behind us.

I try to make myself heavy. I try to plant my feet and make it harder for him to force me down the corridor, but he drags me across the stone floor as I struggle, my sandals scraping as he jerks me onward.

My gown catches on the jagged edge of one of the ash covered stones and the sound of ripping joins my sobs as he continues pulling me behind him because, I am no match for Hades; stand no chance against him in a battle of strength. But like my mother, who often challenges my father, I know I can win, if only in a battle of wills.

My mother, Demeter, is also the child of a Titan and as such, she has amazing power. Everything the earth produces, she commands: every blade of grass that sways in the wind, each bloom of the flowers, every stalk of wheat that feeds the faithful.

She ensures the earth remains fruitful and produces massive harvests each year for the mortals that honor her. I too have the powers of a god inside me, but it will be years before they awaken.

The floor of the hallway is slick with damp algae, the green goo coating the stones where moisture pools at their corners, and the sandstone walls seem to narrow around me with each labored step I take.

I can't breathe and as the events of the evening weigh on me, I see stars. But before I know it, everything goes dark.

Hades lets go of my wrist, and just before I slump to the floor, I feel weightless.

Someone lifts and carries me the remaining length of the hallway, and I can't see him, but I can smell Adonis all around me.

His calming presence fills me, and where panic once built, an ease sets in as the warmth of his body slows my gasping while I lay limply in his arms.

When my vision returns, I find us seated at a long wooden table: Hades to my left, Cerberus between us, Adonis in a far corner of the room.

Archways of sandstone curve above us as wall sconces line the length of the space, their light offering a dim cascade of warmth throughout the dining hall as they flicker.

Hades lounges leisurely, his head leaning back against the onyx tufted velvet of his wooden throne with gold accenting the deep grooves of the armrests as he clenches not only his jaw but his fists where they lay resting on the arms of the chair.

He glares at me over the feast filling the table before us; plates stacked high with meat and trays of intricately sliced fruits creating a colorful display down its length.

Everything smells amazing, the scent of rich spices and succulent nectars permeating the air, but I can't stomach the idea of food at a time like this.

With just the two of us seated, Hades pays me no mind as he sips wine from an ornately decorated cup made of bone. The base is a hand, fingers splayed out as if they had been squished beneath his foot, and the stem of the vessel, where it joins at the wrist bones, has an arm with gilded connective points. But because that alone isn't terrifying enough, where the gold melds the chalice together at the top, there is a skull.

Cut perfectly in half with the eye sockets and nasal cavities dripping the same gold that solidifies the base, the skull has a shining drip pattern just like a candle makes as it melts. It is ghastly in its appearance, but despite that, Hades brings the goblet to his lips, gently tracing the edge with his tongue as if a lover.

Red, pungent liquid drips from the corners of Hades' mouth with each chalice full of wine he throws back, and he wipes away the excess with the back of his hand before tossing Cerberus a piece of meat from the gilded plate set before him.

Cerberus snaps the meat out of the air greedily, one head training on Hades' movements, the middle one scanning the room as the eyes dart about warily, and the head closest to my seat has its eyes on me.

The beast's mouth gapes open, drool dripping and frothing as strands ooze from the corners before plopping down onto the hem of my gown, covering me in his goop.

The middle head shakes from side to side, ears flapping back and forth making a slapping sound against the side of his head, as Cerberus sends spittle everywhere.

I dodge most of the spray, but several globs land on the middle of my thigh closest to him, and it's revolting.

The beast is reminiscent of a shaved bear, with rat-like features and an odd tuft of hair framing his face as the folds of his skin ripple and scrunch, hanging loosely all over his body.

I don't want to touch the hound, don't want him to touch me, and I can't understand how Hades enjoys the texture of him under his fingertips because Cerberus is hideous; a thing of nightmares. A nightmare who walks beside death himself.

"You should eat something," Hades grumbles, his attention now focused on me.

"I'm not hungry," I challenge, turning my face away from him.

"With so much before us, it'd be a shame to let it go to waste," he counters.

"I said no!" I force my gaze back to him, meeting his fierce stare with one of resistance.

"Eat!" he bellows, his voice rattling the plates before us. Hades' face contorts, his teeth gritting as silvery ether flares and a pale blue light flickers behind his eyes, dancing around his pupils.

Cerberus snarls and Hades turns his head toward the beast, silencing him with one jerk of the leash.

See, that's the thing about the King of Death; he has to be in control, and as such, just like how he has to rule my every move, Hades keeps Cerberus collared.

The band of Cerberus' collar has a large, black leather strap with gleaming spikes and a center point from where the leash drapes down.

Part of the leash lies on the edge of the table, and Hades wraps its end around one of his hands where he fists it in his lap. So, when Cerberus' head, that watches me intently, bares its teeth in my direction, Hades just laughs, yanking the leash back toward him.

"Down, boy," he commands, drawing out the words. "She's all mine."

Hades ogles my body, taking in my form from my bare thigh that shines with the drool from his beast to where my full chest heaves with each breath.

He appraises me hungrily, lust gleaming in his eyes as ether sparks behind his irises, the pupils dilating with his arousal. Finally, Hades' eyes rise, meeting mine, and a wicked smirk lifts the corner of his lips.

His eyes flash, their storm cloud color shifting to a bright silver, shining brighter the longer he stares me down. "It's getting late," he says, "and we've things to attend."

He stands, tugs on the leash, and urges Cerberus to stand beside him. "Are you going to come willingly, or does Adonis need to drag you to my chambers as well? Because either outcome suits me at this point. I'd almost prefer a tussle," he hisses.

I stand, allowing every ounce of my defiance to bleed through. Because what will be the point in fighting if it's what he really wants? What good will my denial of him accomplish? If Hades wants a fight, if he enjoys it, then I will give him the opposite. I can be compliant. I can fake willingness. *Or so I think.*

CHAPTER 3

THAT STUNG A LITTLE (PERSEPHONE)

Each step toward Hades' chamber is pure torture, but still I place one foot steadily in front of the other and follow him down the wide passageway.

Torches illuminate the hallway, the smoke wafting along the ceiling, creating an ominous billowing archway throughout the corridor as Cerberus strides obediently beside Hades. One ghastly head stares back at me menacingly as Adonis follows us, mere steps behind me where his footfalls are heavy.

I hear puffs of frustration escaping Adonis' nostrils as I imagine them expanding while steam pours out, and I can't help but think, *why is he mad? He isn't the one walking to the beginning of their end. I am.*

The doors to Hades' wing are large and wooden, with rusted iron crossbars and hinges that creak angrily as he throws them open.

Wood splinters as the doors bang against the walls, and once they still, Hades steps over the threshold, standing with his back against the left door.

Dropping Cerberus' leash with a thud as he waits for me to pass, Hades stands silently as his beast takes the drop as his cue of release, casually padding across the stones of the room as his nails click with each step. The hound then lays in front of the fire roaring in a hearth along the far-left wall and momentarily, a feeling of familiarity settles over me, but quickly disappears.

I once loved a good fire. Loved sitting around a table with my mother as the timber crackled noisily, the flames burning a bright blue in the hearth while the heat filled the cold room. I would feel at ease in that space. But as I focus on the firelight now, all I feel welling up inside me is dread.

Standing, I take in my "husband" as my eyes widen with fear.

Bile rises in my throat as the realization of that word sets in, and the froth pooling in the back of my mouth burns as I choke it down. *I am married, and to Hades, no less! Hades, the torturer, the god of the Underworld, is my husband, and I... his wife.*

"I don't have all night, and my patience grows thin," he barks, motioning toward the room before me.

Slowly, hesitantly, I walk past Hades, stepping cautiously into the space where my eyes dart swiftly around the room and then fix back on him.

I look away upon meeting his smirk of satisfaction, and fear courses through me as my whole body tenses.

Adonis moves to follow, but Hades holds up his hand. "You wait here. This is the one place your presence is unnecessary." He pauses, his eyes narrowing. "Although?" he poses. His exaggerated words unnerve me, and as Hades looks at my back, the fire of his gaze sets my skin aflame. "Perhaps, another time," he states, slamming the doors behind him, shutting them in Adonis' face.

Once in the room, my feet root firmly in place. I can't move, and my eyes scan his chambers again, slowly and deliberately this time to where thick chains affix to the walls and repulsive apparatuses sit in each corner of the room. Every instrument of torture imaginable, and some unimaginable, are displayed as far as my eyes can see.

There are tables with metal pokers, knives, leather straps, and iron spikes sitting beside an enormous wooden four-poster bed where each of the bed's posts has shackles attached to them.

Faces with mouths opened wide in silent screams adorn each bedpost, intricately carved into the wood, and furs are layered, draping over the end. But the sheets, the shiny gold satiny fabric that peeks out from beneath the covers, look inviting. It is an odd mixture of gloom and decadence.

The fire, crackling wood that groans and pops sporadically, fills the room with warmth, conflicting with what feelings the room evokes from me. Dread and tension coil through my body as I stand gawking from one item to the next.

Cerberus lifts his heads from where they are resting on his outstretched paws when Hades unties the dark sash at his waist, allowing his charcoal gown to billow freely around his calves as his eyes, illuminated by the fire, appear to glow.

Seeming to sense a change in the air I can't, Cerberus salivates as the King of Death walks over to him and pats the middle head as its tongue lolls out of the corner of its mouth.

Hades unfastens the collar, and it hangs loosely from the leash as he ceremoniously wraps it around his left hand; reining in the length. Then, turning slowly, he takes purposeful steps toward me as I stand in shock. Clomp, clomp, clomp, go his sandaled feet as they announce his approach.

"Do you know what it is to be mine?" he asks.

I know he expects no answer from me, so I remain silent.

He continues, "Do you know what horrors, and perhaps what pleasures await you?"

My eyes widen, my head snapping to look at him as he continues toward me as that agonizingly slow clomping fills the air.

He stops right in front of me and says, "Do you know all the ways I plan on forcing screams from your lips? The joy those sounds will bring me?"

My mouth falls open, and just as I am about to protest, Hades slaps the collar around my neck, fastening the straps as he pulls it tight.

The coarse leather scrapes across my neck when my throat bobs, and I gulp down my fear, clenching my teeth as I try to prepare myself for the horrors he promises.

Hades doesn't look at me, he just goes about his work of yanking and jerking my head to the side as he collars me.

His left hand grips the leash and he forcefully jerks it, guiding me to look at him. "Mine," the word slips through gnashed teeth. "Hear me, girl. You are mine in every way, in any way that I want you."

A lone tear falls, trailing down my cheek, and the cool drop, as it lands on the peak of my breast, is a shock to my senses, causing my body to shudder in response.

Hades' gaze is intense, flickering with electricity, but before I know what is happening, he presses his body tightly against mine, his scent washing over me.

His aroma, a deep woodsy scent, burns as I draw in breath, and I can feel a hardness as it presses against my abdomen, begging to be acknowledged.

He places a hand firmly on the top of my head and forces me to my knees.

I lower before him, his hand still gripped firmly around the leash as he jerks it to the left. He then yanks me again, ensuring the clasp is secure, and follows with a tug to the right.

"That's better," he says.

My eyes rise slowly, fear flushing my cheeks as they redden.

"I can't describe how absolutely beautiful you are this way; on your knees before me as terror washes over you. You are perfect."

He jerks my head forward, pressing the bulge tenting his dark gown against the side of my face as I try to force my head away

I can't move far. I can't really move at all because Hades holds my head in place as he rubs himself against me.

A groan escapes his lips and, in my fear, I look up to where Hades has his head tilted back slightly, his jaw clenched as he bites down on his bottom lip.

He continues to thrust upward, the fabric of his gown rubbing harshly against the side of my cheek.

"Ow!" I cry out as the friction from the fabric burns me.

"Oh, Little One. None of that. We're just getting started."

He grips beneath my chin with his right hand and squeezes hard, his callused thumb brushing across my cheek as he taps with each squeeze.

I dare to look into his eyes, and my tears fall faster; gathering on my lashes and dripping down my cheeks.

He releases my chin and wipes my tears with the side of his hand before bringing it to his lips where his tongue darts out, swiping across the wetness he's collected.

"So sweet," he rasps, licking my tears from the bridge of his knuckle.

Smiling down at me, he lowers his right hand and grasps the fabric of his skirt, bunching it up in his fist.

Inch by excruciating inch, the dark fabric rises, and as it lifts over what he'd been rubbing against me, soft brown flesh appears.

Hades' hardness jumps toward me, the head seeping in anticipation. "Put your tongue out," he commands, jerking my head closer to it.

I do as I'm told, and once I have my tongue extended fully, he grips himself, moving toward me, where he sweeps his head across the tip of my tongue, coating its end with his essence.

It is salty, strong, but also intoxicating. *I don't like this, right? I don't like what he is forcing me to do? But if I don't like it, why is there a warmth pooling between my thighs? Why is my body tingling everywhere his eyes scan?*

His eyes look everywhere, and as they do, a heat blossoms in me, causing every inch of skin that is exposed, every curve of my body that peeks through the thin fabric of my cream-colored gown, to flush.

I can feel how heavy my ample breasts are, the nipples peaking as my chest rises and falls, and my knees ache as the stone floor beneath me leaves indentations in my skin. So, I lean back on my heels, allowing my supple ass to rest on my calves, and offer a slight reprieve from my weight.

Hades drinks in my full-figured body: my freckled shoulders, the line of my neck, my chest spilling out the top of my low-cut gown. And when he finishes surveying me, he smirks before commanding, "Now, swallow."

"What?" I squeak.

"Draw your tongue into the back of your mouth and swallow. I want to invade you, but before I do, I must claim you and you must accept me. Now, swallow!" he snaps.

Doing as I'm told, I allow the small amount of what accumulates on the tip of my tongue to slide down my throat where it oozes; the tackiness webbing across the back of my mouth. *I do like this; this element of control. But that doesn't change me not liking him.*

"Good girl," he coos. "Now, for this next part..." he pauses, "I'm going to need you to open your mouth... wide. Before you think about it, I will warn you, if you use your teeth, I will punish you. I will punish you in a way that only I will enjoy."

His eyes flash, the silver darkening to a bright cobalt, and once again I do as he instructs, opening my mouth as wide as I can, my jaw aching while I hold it so.

Hades takes himself in his hand and places his head on my lips, sliding his smooth flesh between them, and pushes forward slowly.

The leash unravels slightly, allowing his left hand the freedom to grip the side of my head, and my eyes are closed now as I feel Hades sliding between my lips, pushing forward.

Releasing his right hand from himself, he uses it to grip the other side of my head, grabbing a handful of my hair. With one hand on each side of my head, hair grasped tightly, he cups my ears in his palms as he pulses forward, guiding himself in and out of me.

He presses deeper each time until I gag. "There we go." Hades smiles when my eyes shoot open, tears streaming from their corners. "Perfection," he says, a rumble following the word.

I gag again, over and over, as he forces himself down my throat and grows bigger within me; widens. I am already so full and I don't think I can become more so as Hades' length, his power, fills my mouth leaving no room for air.

I gag once more, louder this time.

"Breathe through your nose," he chastises. I choke, the sound a mixture of gurgling and a release of suction. "That's it. You're doing so good."

He increases his pace, thrusting deeper and deeper, my lips cracking at the corners as my throat burns from his abuse.

"Had enough?" he pauses to ask, our eyes meeting.

I nod.

A wicked grin crosses his features, one that scares me, and his cobalt eyes flame to life. "Too bad," he answers, thrusting forward once more. "I'm not done using you."

Thrust after thrust, I gag, coating his length with the shiny trails my mouth forms around him, and just as I think I will black out, the rising and falling of my chest faltering from the lack of oxygen, he withdraws.

My mouth aches and I am about to reach up and see if the corner of my lips are bleeding when he moves.

Jerking on the leash, I fall forward, gasping as I draw in as many breaths as I can.

I want to speak, but my throat is on fire. His skin is so hot, and it feels as if he's been shoving a hot poker down the back of my throat.

"What should we do next?" he poses; another question he neither expects me to, nor needs an answer.

My eyes scan the room once more, widening larger each time I come across another unfamiliar fixture. And when I glance at the far-left corner closest to the fire, I gasp.

"That one? Is that what you want, Little One?" He tilts his head toward the left side of the room, turning slowly as he takes in what lies there. "I rather fancy that one," he admits.

In the corner, a wooden leather-bound chair with iron shackles at the top and bottom sits lurking, a metal collar extending from where I imagine my head will go.

"No!" I shriek, the word losing its power as he steps in that direction, pulling me behind him.

He tugs on the leash connected to my collar, forcing me across the floor as I sprawl out.

The cold stones scratch and scrape my skin, rubbing raw all the exposed places as red gashes raise on my surface. And I wrap my hands around the leash, struggling against him as he guides me to that corner.

Tired of my efforts, Hades bends down and wraps one muscular arm around me, lifting me off the floor by my hips.

I kick and scream, flailing into the air as he stomps toward the chair, and I pound on him, trying to wriggle away, but my effort goes unnoticed.

The door bursts open, and Adonis rushes inside, stopping when his eyes land on us.

"Leave! Now!" Hades' voice booms out his command and Adonis quickly steps back outside, slamming the door behind him without saying so much as a word of protest.

As I fight to break free, the skirts of my gown bunch up around my waist, exposing my backside.

Hades stands, unaffected by my efforts, and just sighs. "I really hate to do this, just as we were having some fun, but you need to learn who is in charge here, and it certainly isn't now, nor will it ever be... you."

Lying limply across Hades' forearm, pressed tightly against his hip with my lower half exposed, I give up.

Smack

The sound of the impact from his hand on my backside echoes throughout the room, the reverberations jiggling my flesh.

I am stunned into silence, the shock of what he'd done prompting my mouth to drop open, but no sound comes out.

Smack. Smack. Smack.

His palm lands forcefully, one blow after the next, blistering my pale backside, as my flesh blooms a bright crimson. "You... will... learn... your... place!" he scolds, delivering another smack with each word of warning that crosses his lips. "Do... you... understand... me?"

"Please! Stop! Yes, I understand!" the words rush from my lips, hoping to stay his hand and spare my raw bottom any further punishment.

My skin pinkens, a warmth spreading across my cheeks and down into my thighs as Hades' hand lowers one last time.

I brace myself for one more slap, but his hand smooths over me, rubbing ever so gently as he runs his palms flat across my skin, smoothing and gripping at it.

"You have a rather perky ass, and although I enjoy punishing you..." he pauses, "I'd hate to mar your beautiful skin. So, please, don't make me repeat myself."

Unable to force out the words, I just nod in response.

I surrender. I submit. I give into his whims and do so without argument. Because at that moment, I realize... no one is coming to save me. There will be no daring rescue. My father will not break down the gates to the Underworld and whisk me away to the loving embrace of my mother. The Titan's themselves can't spare me from my husband because, from this day forward, I belong to Hades. And despite his joke to the contrary, Hades doesn't like to share his toys.

I am just a toy to Hades. I am his new plaything. The new shiny doll that captures all his attention. *Not that I want it.*

Hades plays with me for what seems like an eternity that first night, but time passes differently in the Underworld. A season's passing in the Underworld could be but a few days in the mortal realm, and with that knowledge, I know Hades can do with me what he wills, as often as he wants, for as long as he wants, and there isn't a damned thing I can do about it.

I can try to fight him. I can kick and scream, ball my fists, slamming them against his chest. But what good will that do? It won't stop him. Hell, it won't even stay his hand and spare me his punishment. So, why bother? Why put forth the effort?

I'm not weak for giving in. I'm not less than for allowing it to happen. He is just stronger than I am, and in the end, the one with the strength has all the power. What use is it to fight against a god when I have no power of my own? *At least not yet.*

CHAPTER 4
TAKE ME HOME (PERSEPHONE)

Flashes of our "playtime" invade my dreams the next morning, my body aching all over as I lay in bed with my muscles tensing in response to those recollections. I can distinctly see the prints of Hades' large hand marking my skin, and as a matter of fact, it still stings.

When Hades smoothed his hands across my ass, I'd hung limply over his arm. And then Adonis barged in briefly, but scurried off once his "master" chastised him. *What was he thinking, anyway? What could he have done? Was he going to rush to my rescue, strike down Hades, and drag me to safety? No.*

The only thing Adonis' interruption accomplished was setting Hades over the edge, thus leading him to take his ire out on my backside before carrying me across the room, plopping me down in the chair, and forcing my head back where he clasped my neck into the metal collar attached to it.

He took his sweet time raising one wrist, then the next, above me where he shackled them in place, and finished by dragging his nails down the insides of my arms for effect.

It had been excruciating; the slowness of his movements as he'd dug his nails into my flesh, their jagged edges catching as they jumped from one patch of skin to the next. Now, raised red marks and crusted droplets of blood still decorate the soft skin between my elbows and armpits.

Ripping open my gown, he exposed my breasts, the thin fabric falling away and leaving me completely naked as the tattered garment gathered at my sides.

My cheeks flushed with embarrassment as my vulnerability was on full display. And then he'd pinched me, rolling one nipple then the other between his thumb and forefinger as my back arched in response.

I'd cried out in… it wasn't pain exactly, but it wasn't pleasure either. And as his mouth replaced his fingers, continuing his assault on my body, he'd circled his tongue around my nipples before blowing gently so they'd harden. Once they did, he drug his teeth across them, scraping me while a wicked smile dressed his lips.

He'd enjoyed himself; his growing length proving as much, and when I'd tried to look away, when I'd tried to close my eyes, he'd clutched my face in his hand, squeezing tightly until I'd cried out.

My eyes bulged, the pupils dilating as my normal bright icy blue irises went dark with the overstimulation.

"There she is," he said, trailing his hands down my chest and along my ribcage while my eyes trained on him. "Stay with me, Little One. Stay with me and I'll take you home."

He'd take me home? I hadn't understood his meaning. To be honest, the next day, I still don't. Because what type of home is it when the man who is supposed to protect you is the one causing you harm? That's what husbands are, aren't they; your home, your safe place? Or at least, in my limited experience, that's what I thought they were meant to be. But Hades is far from it.

Hades isn't my protector, he isn't my savior, and he doesn't look after me, seeing to my wellbeing.

He holds the title of husband, but doesn't offer any of the advantages I think a husband should provide. I feel so many things about Hades the day following our marriage, but safe is not among them.

My recollection continues with Hades' hands pressed down on the tops of my thighs, my ankles still shackled to the corners of the chair, as he pried my legs apart, soothing, "Relax, Little One. Relax."

"I..." I stammered, "I can't." I breathed out heavily.

"You can," he insisted.

He'd caressed the side of my face, running the pad of his thumb across my lips before trailing his tongue around the corners of my mouth as his hot breath and heady scent enveloped me.

His arousal peaked with his exploration and he uttered a gentle, "Just let go. Let me in and I promise you'll thank me once you do."

I'd parted my lips, and Hades invaded my mouth with his tongue where I tasted the faint remnants of the wine he'd had with dinner; sweet and tangy.

The edges of my tongue tingled as he'd caressed it with his own, and I allowed him to explore me, causing the wetness between my legs to increase.

There'd been a burning in the pit of my stomach and my head fell back as the sensation of Hades digging his nails underneath my thighs consumed me.

Rough and powerful hands pushed my knees wider for him as he'd knelt before me. And from where I sat on the chair, which was on a small riser, his face aligned with the moistened cushion beneath me. "Almost ready for me, aren't you, Little One?"

I remained silent. I didn't know what to say, didn't know what he'd meant. *Was I ready? Was my body somehow telling him so? And ready for what?*

He'd placed his face between my thighs, his hands forcing my knees apart when I tried to slam them shut. "Tsk, tsk, tsk," he'd scolded, slapping the inside of my thigh. "We've talked about this, haven't we?"

I cried out in response to the contact. *Had we? I don't remember us having a conversation at all, and not one regarding me keeping my legs opened. I think I would have remembered that.*

My mind became muddled; everything fuzzy. It was as if I'd no longer been in my body, but stood nearby, a mere bystander, gawking as Hades pawed at me. And it was from that vantage point I'd seen what he did next.

Once again, still knelt in front of me, his hands pressed my thighs apart and he moved his face between my legs where he inhaled deeply, taking in my scent.

"See, I knew it. That's my girl," he'd said, before placing his mouth on me.

My ass lifted off the seat, my lower back arching as the heat of his mouth washed over me. And then Hades kissed me. At least, I thought it was a kiss. But then his tongue swept up and started making small circles around a sensitive piece of me, drawing my flesh into his mouth; suckling and nibbling, scraping with his teeth as he had with my nipples.

It didn't hurt this time, not really. But it didn't not hurt, either. It's hard to describe, and as the pit of my stomach coiled, something snapped.

Before I knew it, sounds escaped my lips I didn't know I could make. Because I had never heard the strained sounds before, and I'm not sure I was even the one who made them.

Shaky, labored, an almost purring sound escaped my lips, and in between the sloppy sounds of his sucking and lapping away with his tongue, there was a deep growl. *That couldn't be me? There's no way I made that sound.*

I hadn't. It had been Hades; he'd made that sound.

Hades held my gaze, his face between my thighs with his tongue buried deeply within me, and his hands, that had been underneath me, lifted me off the chair and pulled me forward against him.

I tried to back up against the chair, tried to pull away, but I couldn't. I wanted to get away, but wanted to hold him tighter against me. I wanted him to stop, but also didn't. I wanted him to go away, and also never wanted him to leave my side; especially if he continued doing to me what he had been at that moment. I knew nothing, but at that moment, I knew only that I wanted.

Hades' mouth on me, in that way, was positively electric; sending tiny shocks coursing across my body in waves.

The heat of his breath caused me to flush from head to toe, and a white, fiery light shot through me, trying to escape from every tip: fingers, toes, ends of my hair.

Static filled the air and my coppery tresses, heavy with the sweat that trickled from my forehead and down my spine, rose from my shoulders all around me as I lost myself in it all: the sight of Hades devouring me, his fingers pressed inside me, the smell of his arousal permeating the air. It was sensory overload, and my head felt like it was about to explode.

I did explode, but it had nothing to do with my head.

My skull was tight with the pressure, but no explosion came from above as every overwhelming sensation, each excruciating moment, all seemed to derive from what Hades was doing between my thighs.

His manipulations, his movements, caused a dam to break wide open, and once it did, I was undone; my dam flooding him.

My satisfaction splashed across his lips and dripped down the side of his neck, and despite him drowning in the floodwaters, he lifted his head above the surface.

Hades looked positively primal as a guttural sound escaped his lips, and his silver eyes, that had been coursing with electricity, now burned a bright blue. He quickly released my ankles from their shackles as an inferno blazed beneath his skin.

He rose, stood above me and admired his handiwork before tearing his gown over his head and tossing it to the side. He was a sight to behold- a god, obviously, but in that moment, he'd been so much more than that.

Hades was ravenous, the muscles in his neck constricting, as his chest rose and fell with each ragged breath.

His abdomen tensed, the lines accentuating his form as each ripple became oh so prominent, and he clenched his fists as his anticipation grew.

The veins in his forearms popped out as he flexed each finger, and he showed an enormous amount of restraint. But soon he faltered, and with the fire inside Hades burning out of control, there was no halting what happened next.

He scooped me off the chair, one butt cheek squeezed in each hand as he settled his knees on the cushion I had been seated on.

My arms were still shackled above me, my neck remaining restrained by the collar of the chair.

"Now you're ready," he said, his pupils dilating as he looked down upon me.

He lined himself up with my opening, my floodwaters still dripping from where the dam had broken, and let out a hiss as he pulsed forward.

"That's it," he cooed, looking deep into my fear filled widening eyes. "Almost," he whispered.

It was as if he'd been fulfilling a promise; something unspoken that lingered between us. And the longer he held himself back, the longer he made me wait, the more my anticipation grew.

"Steady," he muttered.

I couldn't tell if the things he'd been saying were for my benefit or his own, but it hadn't mattered. None of it did. The only thing that mattered was he had shown me something.

Hades had awakened something in me; something that had lain dormant. A power hidden deep beneath the surface, desperate to be set free from its gilded cage. Now, there was no putting it back, and I would not be tamed.

The man, the god, who always had all the control, the one who thought he had all the power... would soon realize he didn't, and no matter how hard he tried to take it back, Hades would have to accept he'd lost the power forever.

I grin wickedly, rolling away from Hades and sneaking out of his bed the next morning.

I am going to like it here, and if Hades thought playtime last night was fun… well, then he is in for one hell of a ride, because I am about to take him on one he never saw coming.

Tiptoeing from the room, I sneak into the hallway, where, just outside the door, Adonis leans against the far wall.

He straightens as I turn to face him, closing the door quietly behind me, and he reaches out, turning my face side to side as he surveys the darkened marks on my neck. "Are you okay?" he asks.

"Never better," I say, stepping toward him.

With each step I take forward, he retreats until he is pinned back against the far wall.

"What… what are you doing?" he questions.

I lift my gown over my head, throwing it to the floor, and Adonis doesn't know what to do, doesn't know what to say. He just stands there staring at me, his eyes widening while he takes in my form as I run my hand down his chest.

My fingertips dance through his abdominal hairs as they tickle their way to his waistline. I snake my hand lower, gripping him, and he spins me around, pressing me against the wall I had previously trapped him against.

His hand grips my throat, his enormous eyes shining with so many questions, but he speaks only one. "What do you want?" he sneers, a puff of air escaping his nostrils in frustration.

Reaching down between his legs, I cup him as I rub my hand up and down his impressive length, and a snort battles to escape, getting trapped in his throat as he chokes, barely containing himself as he awaits my reply.

I turn around, pressing my chest against the wall as I arch my back, rubbing my ass from side to side against his thickness as I gently rub against him.

He hardens with each pass, and I press back into him as my anticipation builds. But once I feel him place both hands on me, one on each side of my hips, I answer his question with my plea, "Take me home."

CHAPTER 5

TIME IS IRRELEVANT (PERSEPHONE)

My marriage lacks public displays of affection if anyone other than Adonis is present, and there are no warm embraces or cherished looks filled with longing for all to see. But in his chambers lust fuels our interludes, desire and need steering the course as Hades rarely leaves my side.

He has gotten lost in me; gotten lost in our fire. And somewhere along the way I found something I never thought possible; I found my power.

Weeks had passed since Hades took me from the mortal realm, and I enjoyed Adonis every chance I could. But as I descended into the depths of the Underworld, I got lost in the darkness, finally awakening my true self. Because something festers just beneath my surface, something dark, just waiting to be unleashed.

It isn't all pain and torture with Hades. And despite what he wants everyone to think there are tender touches and quiet moments as we lay in one another's arms, the sheer exhaustion of our efforts rendering us silent.

When we are alone in the privacy of his chambers, when I'm not crying out in ecstasy, he is sweet; gentle, even. And it is in those moments I really see him. Breathing heavily beside me, my head on his chest, and his fingertips brushing through my hair; Hades is tender.

I bring him something he hadn't been searching for and something he'd never imagined possible for himself; I bring Hades peace. Or at least as much peace as the ruler of the Underworld can experience, anyway.

One day after the meal, Hades having finally coaxed me to eat, he grabs my wrist and drags me down the hall. "What? Now?" I ask, an almost irritation setting in.

"No. Not that I'd be opposed. I just thought you'd want to see."

I cross my arms, popping my hip out for effect. "See what?"

"Our dominion. I may rule here, but this is just as much your home as it is mine." He tickles the underneath of my palm with his middle finger, swirling it in circles.

"If you keep doing that..." I raise my brow, "I may just find something else to occupy your hands."

He drops my wrist and says, "There is plenty of time for all that. I promise I won't deny you for long. I can't."

"You can't?" I saunter up next to him, pressing my body firmly against his as I feel him harden.

His response to my body makes his true feelings clear as he presses himself into me.

"Can't," he admits, grabbing handfuls of my hair at my temples and pressing a firm kiss to my lips as he forces me back against the cold stone wall.

My hands grasp his chest through his gown, digging my nails in as I bite his bottom lip, and Hades growls into my mouth before a throat clears behind us.

Adonis asks, "Are you ready, master?"

"Yes, quite," Hades replies. "After you, Little One."

Hades motions in front of him and I shoot a smirk at Adonis before turning and walking ahead of them.

I sway my hips as I walk, running my fingers along the wall to feel its coolness as my locks trail down my back tickling my bare shoulders where the fiery strands cascade over them.

Wearing a lavender gown, the almost translucent gauzy fabric flowing around me, I smile to myself as I remember exactly how that wall had felt as Adonis forced me up against it.

It had taken little, breaking his resolve. All I'd had to do was bare my ass and offer it to him. All I'd had to say were those three words.

My cheeks flush as the memory of Adonis' hands gripping my hips tightly, pulling me back against him as he rubbed himself against my ass, lingers.

The fabric of his covering was thin and gauzy and he'd already been hard since I had set to teasing him. So, when I offered myself, he was more than willing; uncontrollably so. And he'd lifted his covering, sliding himself between my still wet thighs.

What had been his thoughts in that moment? Had he known? Had he felt Hades' seed as it still dripped from me? Had he hoped to replace it with his own? It didn't matter, really. None of it did; his thoughts, his feelings. Or Hades' for that matter.

All that matters is I want him. Both of them, actually. And I will have what I want. I will take what I want, whenever and however I want it, and no one will deny me. Because, as I said, I am now the one with all the power. *Or so I think.*

Adonis walks from the stables, leading a large black stallion behind him by their reins.

The beast has large hooves and a broad back, with flames tipping the end of his mane and tail; the horse, not Adonis.

"Do you stay quartered in the stables as well?" I joke. "You smell like you do." I tilt my head toward Adonis, scrunching my nose as I infer he's merely livestock.

"Persephone!" Hades chastises, shaking his head from side to side. "That was unnecessary, don't you think?"

"Was it?" I feign ignorance, scowling over at Adonis. "I hadn't noticed."

Adonis grips the reins tighter in his fist, his jaw clenching as I grin in his direction.

"Cruelty doesn't suit you. Perhaps you should leave the sideways remarks to me?"

Hades doesn't know me. Not really. He doesn't know what wicked things go through my mind or how I enjoy the discomfort I bring to Adonis with my little retorts. Also, if I'm lucky, how Adonis will make me pay for it later.

Hades lifts me onto the steed, then mounts it himself, taking his place behind me.

I settle back against his firm chest, leaning my head against his bare shoulder, and I hear Adonis snort from where he walks behind us, obediently trailing his master.

Our horse trots forward, sending my body bobbing up and down in the saddle, and I moan; a breathy sound escaping my lips.

Hades releases the reins clutched in his right hand and cups me firmly between my thighs. "Just can't get enough, can you?" he whispers, pressing beneath me as his long, elegant fingers twist and curve, brushing playfully across my center.

"Why does he have to come?" I whine, tilting my head upward as I pout.

"What's wrong with Adonis?" he poses, looking down into my face.

"Nothing," I reply, meeting his gaze. "He just always seems to lurk around. What if I wanted to stop and enjoy you?" I smirk, my lip curling up in one corner as I stare deep into his eyes.

Hades hooks his fingers, moving them back and forth against my center as he answers, "Then we'd stop, and I'd enjoy you."

"With him here? With him watching?" I feign revulsion.

"Yes," he states matter-of-factly.

My lip curls up in disgust. "But he's a monster."

"That he is. But he's my monster, and he does what he's told."

"Really?" I ask, amused. "Like what?"

"Whatever I ask of him."

"Make him do something," I goad, grinning up at Hades.

"What? Now?" his voice carries his agitation.

"Yes, now."

"Would you like him to watch us?" Hades bites down on the crook of my neck. "Would you like that?" he asks, eyebrows wiggling

"What? No!" my voice pitches up in repugnance.

"Then, what?"

"I don't know? Something," I plead.

"Well, think about it, and when you've decided, tell me what it is you'd most like me to command Adonis to do." He kisses my temple and then grips me tighter between my legs. "But until then, why don't you just enjoy the ride?"

I arch back against his chest when Hades bunches my skirt and penetrates me with one finger as we continue forward. My entire body feels like it is on fire, my legs tingling from the tops of my hips to the tips of my toes.

Soft mewls escape my lips as Hades brings me closer to the edge, and just as I think he is going to drive me over, he stops. "That's enough for now, Little One. There's plenty of time to play once we get back to the palace."

"Ugh!" I sigh in frustration, tapping my head back on his chest before sitting up. "You're no fun."

"You just wait. I look forward to showing you just how fun I can be."

We ride on for some time, Hades pointing out and educating me on all the different parts of the realm and the souls that reside in each.

I know the basics, all the Greeks do, but it is something else to see it in person, though. There are few that have gotten to explore the wonders of the Underworld and lived to tell about them. And those that have, well, they never leave this realm, thus losing their opportunity to do so.

We tour the Elysian Fields and Asphodel Meadows, which make me miss my mother terribly. And I wonder if she misses me? Wonder if she cried when my father broke the news? *How did he do it? Did he just say it was his will, and that was that? Or did they agree to it jointly?*

I had so many questions, but none of them really matter now, do they? What difference does their answer make? My fate is sealed. I belong to Hades now, and neither of them can alter what has been done.

Pushing the thoughts of my mother and father from my mind, as we dismount at the end of our tour I look over at Adonis and huff.

Hades asks, "What is it, Little One?"

"Nothing," I give a quick reply.

"That scowl says otherwise. Tell me," he commands.

"What did you give up?"

"What?"

"To have me? What did my father ask for? What was the price for my freedom?" I ask harshly.

I am angry, but why shouldn't I be? No one asked me for my opinion on the matter. Hell, no one even informed me it was going to happen. One day I was minding my own business, going about my life, and the next thing I knew, bam, forever chained to Hades.

Hades remains silent.

"There had to have been something? Something he required?"

"I'm sorry to disappoint you, but no. There wasn't," Hades admits.

"No tithes or promises? No outstanding agreement?" I question, my anger bubbling to the surface. "Then why? Why did he do it?"

Hades steps forward, lording over me with his face inches from mine. "Because I wanted it," he sneers, gripping my arms as his nails dig in.

"You're hurting me!" I cry out, wrenching my arms from him as I step back. "I hate you!"

"Fine! Hate me, for all I care. Loathe me. Despise me. It matters not. Here you are and HERE you will stay!" his voice booms out the reality; I will never go home, will never see my mother again. I thought as much, but Hades' words confirm it.

I turn away from him, racing back toward the palace as he calls after me, "Where are you going?"

"To my room," I yell back.

"You mean our room?" he corrects.

"No. My room!" I assert.

"You don't have a room." Hades chuckles, shaking his head.

"I do now!" I shout, pushing my legs to run faster.

Not making it as far as I hope, Hades catches up with me before I reach the main hall, scooping me up and throwing me over his shoulder.

"Let go of me!" I scream, pounding my fists on his back as he laughs with amusement. "Put me down. You, you... monster," I shriek.

"Monster? I'm no monster. Adonis is a monster. You said so yourself. You're nothing but an entitled little selfish brat!"

Hades stomps down the hall toward his chambers, Adonis following not far behind him.

"No! No!" I wail, continuing to batter my fists against his back.

Hades kicks open his door and marches over, tossing me on the bed.

I try to get away from him, scurrying across the bed to flee, but I get caught in the covers and he's on me.

He grabs my wrist, jerking me up the length of the bed, where he shackles me at the left post. He then crawls over me, grabbing my right wrist, and shackles it to the opposite post.

The shackles rub against my wrists as I fight, and I try to kick him, flailing my legs toward his head as he pins my ankles down. "Stop... fighting me," he growls, shackling one ankle and then the next at the end of the bed.

"No! No!" I huff, arching my back as my frustration fuels my fit. "Let me go. Let me leave. I don't want to be here. I don't want you!"

"You don't want me?" His eyes spark to life, the electricity brimming behind his irises. "Are you sure? Because not long ago you pressed back against me, grinding that wet pussy of yours into my hand, and I'm certain your body told a different tale."

"That was then," I grit, arching again.

"Was it, Little One? Was it, really?"

He grabs my ankle and lowers his face, nipping at my skin as he bares his teeth and drags them across my calf, biting down just behind my knee.

I growl my frustration. "Ugh!"

"How is it different?" he asks, trailing kisses over the fleshy part of my inner thigh.

He tosses my skirt up, exposing me, and my coppery curls shift as he breathes over me. I can feel his hot breath as he speaks the next words toward my center, "Tell me?" He nips, trailing one kiss at the joint of my hip before moving toward the other, and asks, "How is it different?"

Biting down, he leaves teeth marks on me as I arch my back and I can't speak. Even if I could, I don't know what I would say, because what words will make a bit of difference?

Hades left the door open, and now Adonis stands in the doorway, taking in the scene before him.

"Adonis!" I turn my head to the side, embarrassed he is witnessing my shame, my weakness. "Make him leave," I command.

"No, no, no," Hades teases. "I distinctly remember you calling him a monster."

I don't respond.

"Did you not?"

I still don't respond.

"Did you not?" he yells out.

"Yes!" I cry out, the tears beginning to fall.

"You were mean to him, weren't you? Cruel, even?"

"Yes," I answer flatly.

"Yes. Yes, you were, and he didn't deserve that, did he?"

I remain silent.

"Did he⁉" he screeches.

"No!" I shout my reply.

"No, he didn't. Now, how are you going to make it up to him?"

"What?" I yawp, ceasing my movements to get away.

"I know..." he exaggerates, an evil smile crossing his face as his eyes darken, a storm brewing behind them. "Adonis?" Hades holds up his hand. "Come here," he insists.

"Master, I ..." Adonis trails off.

"Come HERE!" he commands. Adonis walks sullenly toward the bed and stands just at its edge. "You were mean to my creature and for that... you must pay."

Hades rips my gown off me, the sound of the torn fabric deafening as he leaves me exposed to them both and Adonis takes a step back, his nostrils flaring as he attempts to look away.

"Ah, ah, ah. None of that," Hades snarls. "You need to be broken, Little One, and to do that, oh, to do that... I think Adonis is the key."

Hades crawls back to the end of the bed and lifts his black gown over his head.

Taking himself in his hand, he tugs roughly at first and then lets go. He spits into his palm and then once again begins circling his length as he grits out, "You need to know what it is to be broken. Need to feel what it is to be powerless."

"Please..." I plead, "no."

"Yes," Hades draws out the word, never taking his eyes off me as he strokes himself. "You were all but begging me to ravish you before. Your whore mouth was salivating as I shoved my fingers into you."

He places one knee on the bed, his powerful muscles bracing against his weight, and looks over at Adonis. "Undress," he instructs him.

"Master?"

"Now!" he bellows.

Adonis removes his pteruges, unwraps his coverlet, and exposes his hard cock, already begging for attention.

"Here's how this is going to go, Persephone. I am going to fuck you until you can barely breathe and, as I do, I want you to look at Adonis. I want you to see and appreciate him: every curve, every muscle. I want you to atone for your mistreatment of him, and as I have my way with you, I want you to get it through that thick skull of yours... that I am in charge. Not you!"

Hades releases his hold on his cock and crawls up the bed toward me.

My legs are spread so far apart, it's pointless to squeeze my thighs together. I can't move. I can't fight, and screaming will only satisfy him more.

Hades buries his head between my thighs, his teeth scraping across my clit as he bites down.

I cry out, "Ow!"

He rubs his nose up and down across me, circling my clit with his tongue, and when he gets to the top, he pauses, looking over his shoulder at Adonis. "Well, what are you waiting for?"

"Master?" Adonis asks, the question forming on his features.

"I give you permission to pleasure yourself," he announces.

"Sir?"

"Now, Adonis!" he shouts.

Adonis flinches and then places his large palm around his thick head, beginning to rotate in circles. His palm moves up and down, shuttling his shaft as he twists and turns over tawny flesh.

Hades smiles wickedly, uttering a satisfied, "There you go. Was that so hard?"

Adonis meets my gaze, and I look away.

"Now, Persephone. That wasn't part of the deal," Hades grouses.

"Deal?" I question, looking to where Hades kneels between my thighs, my juices dripping from his chin.

"Fine, punishment. That wasn't part of your punishment. You are meant to look at him. Do you understand?"

"But-"

"Do you understand?" he roars.

"Yes." I squeeze my eyes tight; the tears falling faster now.

When I open my eyes again, I meet Adonis' gaze where he stands at the side of the bed, looking at me apologetically.

Adonis continues to stroke himself, not gripping as hard or being as rough as Hades had been with his own cock as his movements are slow and steady, but there is no meaning behind them; no need.

Hades rises from the bed, the muscles of his ass tensing with each step, and walks toward the nightstand on my left side.

My eyes follow him, my curiosity getting the better of me, and he chastises, "Eyes back on Adonis, Persephone."

I slowly turn my gaze back to Adonis, where he hasn't stopped his movements, but his eyes are closed and his head is tilted to the side as one solitary tear trails down his cheek.

When Adonis finally opens his eyes, turning his gaze back to me, and before Hades makes his way back to the bed, I mouth out quietly, "Take me home."

CHAPTER 6
I HAVE COME UNDONE (PERSEPHONE)

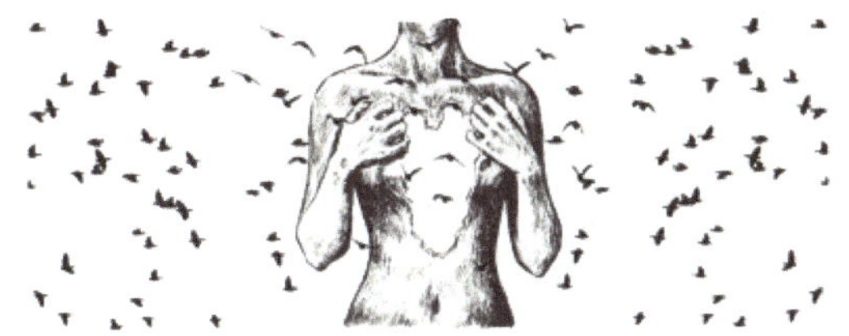

I want to turn off everything once I look at Adonis. I want to pretend I'm not the one responsible for his pain. What we are being forced to do is tearing him apart.

I did this and accept it is my fault. If I'd just ignored him, if I'd just tempered my anger and remained silent, none of this would be happening now. But I hadn't, and it was, and there is no way to turn back the clock and do it over again.

Hades stands before the nightstand, collecting his playthings, and when he turns back around, he has items in both hands and a blade between his teeth. He walks to the end of the bed, places a cone-shaped object to his right and another item with a leather strap to his left.

Taking the blade from between his teeth, he sets it next to the cone shaped item.

"Wha-?"

Hades interrupts, "Nuh uh, Persephone. Look at him, not at me."

I look over at Adonis, whose eyes widen because he knows what Hades has in his possession; knows the use for each item laying at my feet.

He's scared, and if they scare him, then I should be terrified; and I am.

Hades grabs the item with the leather strap and makes his way around Adonis toward the head of the bed. He leans down, grabbing the sides of my face in one hand, and instructs, "Open." Doing as I'm told, I part my lips, opening my mouth. "Wider," he sings. I open wider, my jaw clicking as my lips stretch. "Good girl," Hades praises.

He places a wooden bit in my mouth, between my teeth, and lifts my head, fastening the leather straps around the back.

"That should keep you quiet... enough," he says, gripping my cheeks, shaking my head from side to side before letting go.

I let my eyes fall back to Adonis, not wanting to experience Hades' rage once more, and stare into his eyes as he continues the slow movements in front of him.

It can't feel good, can't be bringing him pleasure, and he has to be raw, his skin chaffing as he rubs callused palms over soft flesh with no barrier or protection: no oils, no spit, none of me. *I should have offered. Should have said something before...*

My eyes widen, a scream trapped behind what Hades has shoved in my mouth. A garbled sound escapes me as I choke on the saliva pooling in the back of my throat.

Looking at Adonis, I hadn't been paying attention to what Hades was doing between my legs, hadn't wondered why he was so quiet, until it was too late.

There was no warning, no casing of his movements, and he wasn't slow or gentle when he shoved something inside me; something hard and pointy. *The cone? It wasn't the knife. Couldn't be the knife? A knife wouldn't feel like... this.*

I was so full and there was an odd pressure; an uncomfortable pressure. I tense around the thing in my ass, my hips lifting off the bed in protest.

"Relax," Hades says, his unexpected touch on the inside of my thigh causing me to jump. "Easy. Stay still," he insists.

I continue to cry out, keep trying to speak, but there are no words, only unintelligible mumbles.

"You're okay, Persephone. Relax. You're okay."

Hades taps the inside of my thigh with the knife, and I stop moving. I want to look down, want to see what he is doing, but I don't dare look away; don't dare allow my gaze to stray from Adonis.

Adonis' eyes plead with me, beg me to be still; warn me to as Hades trails the tip of the knife up my leg, the cold metal causing my skin to pebble beneath it as the hairs on my arms rise and tears fall.

I do my best not to shake, but it's too much: Adonis, his eyes, the cone, the knife, Hades.

My vision flickers as a dull ache sets in just behind my eyes. *Shut it off*, I yell in my head. *Just shut it off!* And I do.

I don't feel the first slice, don't feel Hades' tongue as he licks up the blood trickling from the small cut he made on my inner thigh. I just keep looking at Adonis, his pained face the only thing I focus on. There can be nothing else.

The knife digs into my flesh once, twice, three times more on the left side, and Hades looks over at Adonis from where his face lies between my thighs.

Setting down the blade, the cold metal rests against my outer thigh, and Hades calls out, "Adonis?"

Adonis turns his head slowly in Hades' direction, the pain clear on his face as he strokes himself up and down.

"Adonis, stop," Hades orders.

Adonis stops, his eyes trained on Hades as he awaits his next command.

"Come here, my beautiful boy," he coos. "I'm sorry. This was her punishment, not yours."

A tear slides down Adonis' cheek as he strides toward Hades, stopping at the foot of the bed.

Hades runs his hands through the slick pooling between my legs and then through the blood oozing from each cut. Collecting a mixture of my blood and juices, he reaches out and strokes the length of Adonis' cock with it.

"There," Hades says, looking up into Adonis' eyes, his hand still circling the creature's length. "Is that better?"

"Yes," Adonis chokes out. "Yes." Adonis' head falls back as he gives in to the feeling.

"More?" Hades asks, placing his hand back between my thighs.

"Yes," rasps Adonis.

Hades shoves his fingers deep inside me, circling around as he gathers more of my moisture to use on Adonis, wiping everything he collects all around the head of Adonis' thick length.

"Thank you, Master," Adonis chokes out.

"Of course," Hades says, smacking Adonis on the ass before he walks back to the side of the bed, his eyes wide. "Now, as you were, Adonis. You too, Persephone."

Adonis takes back up his stance, rubbing up and down his cock with my juices coating him as he looks down into my eyes. The pained look that had been on his face is now one of pleasure, his lip curling as he attempts to restrain himself.

I was so focused on Adonis I didn't feel Hades shift at my feet, didn't feel the bed dip down as he positions himself at my entrance. But there is no ignoring when he thrusts himself inside me, driving forward fast and hard, bottoming out as he fills me.

Crying out into my gag, the leather strap pulls tightly as I jerk my head toward Hades.

He leans forward, reaching underneath my arm as he grabs the back of my neck, and turns my head back toward Adonis, forcing to me look at him as he continues his assault between my folds.

My insides ache; quivering and quaking around Hades' cock as I subconsciously squeeze and constrict with each of his thrusts.

"That's it, Little One," Hades breathes heavily. "Almost there." He grabs a handful of hair at the base of my neck and pulls it as he pulses into me. "There you are," he says as my floodgates open. "So, good," he purrs.

He grips the sides of my neck with his other hand, never slowing his pace as he thrusts into me violently, and I can't stop it. I can't stop myself as the dam breaks, and as I look up at Adonis, my vision blurring from the orgasm rocking me, I come all over Hades' length.

Hades comes inside me hard, his breaths shallow as he slows, eventually falling on top of me while I hold Adonis' gaze.

With Hades' seed dripping down my thighs, and his weight crushing me into the bed, Adonis strokes himself one last time, reaching his limit. His head falls back, and he calls out, "Take me home."

The words escape his lips before he even knows what he's done, and his seed spills onto the bed, the remaining strands looping across his palm as it drips down his wrist. When he finally opens his eyes, his body shaking, his knees buckle beneath him and Hades sees me looking apologetically at Adonis, as he, too, looks longingly at me.

Trapped in Adonis' gaze, I don't see Hades coming, and he lifts me off the bed by my hair, as far as my shackles allow, and backhands me.

I fall to the bed, my eyes fluttering closed, the realization of how screwed we are hitting me just before I completely black out. *In short, we are fucked!*

CHAPTER 7

MAY HE REST IN PEACE (PERSEPHONE)

My eyelids flutter open, the light of the roaring fire blinding me as my pupils widen, and I flail, my feet kicking out as I struggle to move. The gag is gone from my mouth, and my hands are now shackled, one to each corner of the end of the bedposts at the foot of the bed.

Hades lords over me, and bending down, he pushes the hairs that have fallen over my face back behind my ear.

His fingertips run under my chin, forcing me to look up at him, and I shut my eyes, jerking my head away from his touch.

"Aw, Little One. Why so upset? I haven't even done anything yet."

"Please," I plead. "Please, let me go," my voice quivers.

"Let you go?" he shouts. "Now, why would I do that?"

"Because..." I whimper. "Because I don't want to be here."

"You don't want to be here? But Persephone, you're my wife. Where else should you be than by my side?"

"I want to go home." I snivel.

"You want to go home? Oh, my love. But you are home. I'm the only one who can take you home. Adonis may have tried, an offense that he will soon pay for, but I... I am the only one who can deliver the sweet bliss you crave." Hades grabs my chin, squeezing my face in his hand as he forces me to look into his eyes as he says, "I'm the one who can quench the fire burning uncontrollably inside you. I'm the only one who can bring you not just the pain but the pleasure you seek. It is me, Persephone. No one else. Not now, not ever."

Froth from his seething lands on my cheek as Hades stares me down and I cry out, "Why?"

"Why⁈ Because I can! Because I can, and because I want to."

Hades releases his hold on my chin, tossing it to the side as he paces back and forth. He walks behind me, his fingers brushing through my hair.

"Now, tell me, my love. How do you plan to make it right?"

"Make it right?" I whimper, looking around, searching for some way to escape.

His footsteps sound as he paces. "Yes, my dear. You have wronged me, and I want to know how you plan to make it right?"

My voice quivers, "What... what do you want?"

He rushes to my side.

"What do I want⁈" he screams, his hand wrapping around my throat, squeezing the sides. His face is so close to mine that spittle lands on the side of my face as he seethes, "What I want, wife... is for you to show me the respect I deserve. Is that so much to ask? Is it⁈" His voice booms, the sound piercing my ears as I flinch.

"I can do it," I whisper, the words falling from my lips against my will.

He grabs my hair at the base of my neck, yanking it back. "I can't hear you," he sings.

"I can do it!" I yell out, meeting his fiery gaze with my own.

"Can you?" his sing song voice questions. "By all means, tell me, Little One, how do you plan to make it up to me?" His head tilts with curiosity.

The words rush out, "Whatever you want."

"Whatever I want? Oh, how generous of you, my love. Are you sure?"

"Yes," I insist. "Yes, I swear it."

"Good," Hades says, letting go of my hair. He steps over my shoulder as I bend forward in defeat. "Let's begin, shall we?"

His footsteps sound as he steps away from me, and then he grabs the gold silken ropes tied to the side of the bedposts.

The thick, black curtains closing off the bed from the rest of the room fall to the floor, and on the other side, Adonis hangs from the ceiling, suspended by hooks affixed through the muscles of his back. Dark blood pools on the floor beneath him, and his head hangs forward as he wheezes.

I cry out, "No!"

"I'm sorry," Adonis whimpers, failing in his attempt to raise his head to look at me. He is naked, and where hooks pierce his skin, bright red blood drips from his shoulder blades and down his ribs.

"Don't speak," I call out. "Just be still," I soothe.

"How sweet," Hades coos. "The way you speak to your lover. A better man could let this go." Hades walks over to Adonis. Grabbing the creature by his horn, he lifts his head up and asks, "But I am not a better man, am I, Adonis?"

"Master?" Adonis groans.

"Don't Master me, you beast!" Hades knees Adonis in the face, sending blood flying across the room where it splatters on the floor.

The sound of the droplets as they splash on the stone is deafening, and the dripping echoes as Adonis' labored breaths come out in pants.

My blood pumps loudly, my eyesight blurring as the scene of all the horrors Hades promised unfolds before me.

"To answer your question, dear Persephone. What I want is for you to witness every torturous moment that is the few remaining of Adonis' life."

"No!" I scream, my voice cracking as I slump in defeat at the end of the bed.

"But you promised. You said I could have whatever I wanted, Persephone, and I want this. I want you to witness as I take every offense you have acted out against me... on him." He tilts his head toward Adonis and then walks over to the side of the bed, taking two metal gloves with knife points for nails off the nightstand.

Putting on one, Hades fastens the leather strap around his wrist and then puts on the other, tightening it with his teeth.

His bare footsteps clap against the stones as he strides back toward me, and when he leans into my peripheral, he asks, "Where should I start, Persephone? The back or the chest?"

I shake my head in disbelief, my chin pressing tightly against my chest as I refuse to meet his gaze.

"Back or the chest⁈ I won't ask again!" he roars.

"Back!"

Body shaking, I raise my eyes from the floor as I feel a fire burning behind my eyes. My blood feels like it is boiling as it pumps through my veins, the Adrenaline coursing through me, and I promise myself that Hades will not win.

I had shut it off before because I had been weak, but Hades will not break me. Not now. Not ever.

Adonis screams out as Hades digs the nails of his gloves into his back, the knife points slicing effortlessly through his flesh as blood gushes from the wounds. He pants, wincing as Hades languidly cuts him, his arms twitching as pain consumes him, and I can't face it. I can't face the agony I know marks those soft features I care for, so I close my eyes.

"Look at him, Persephone! Don't look away. See what you have done. All of this is of your own making." The pain is audible in Hades' voice as he speaks the truth I don't want to hear, "You think I wanted this? That I choose it? I loved him, Persephone. You took that from me, and now I will take him from you."

Adonis, still suspended above the end of the bed, the fibers of his muscles jagged over his ribs where the gloves have torn all the way to the bone and pearlescent pieces show through, sobs.

Hades pushes Adonis, and he sways back and forth, the muscles stretching where the hooks pierce through his skin while his tortured screams fill the room as his body sways. "Ahhhhh!"

Hades slices his nails across Adonis' ass, a lone tear trailing down his cheek as moisture pools at the edge of his lashes, and he says, "Tell me to stop, Persephone. Tell me to stop and it'll all be over." He pants.

"Please, stop!" I plead, my tears falling so fast now they pool in my cleavage and run down my stomach.

His words are pained as they cross his lips, "Do you want it to end?"

"Yes," I cry out.

"What about you, Adonis? Do you want it to end?" he asks pleadingly.

Adonis lifts his head, his eyes devoid of emotion as he surrenders to Hades. "Yes, Master," he answers coldly.

"Yes. Very well. I will take your request into consideration. But until then, I don't think I have quite driven my point home."

Hades takes off his gloves, dropping them at his feet as Adonis' blood trickles off each fingertip. He unties the leather strap from his biceps, withdrawing the knife from where he'd concealed it and twirls the blade in his fingers, spinning it around before grasping it in his palm.

Walking behind Adonis, he places the knife between his teeth, and as he wipes his hand across Adonis' ass, Hades collects the blood.

Splaying his fingers as the blood drips down his palm, he then faces me, lowering his chin and tilting his head to the left as he closes his eyes. He makes small circles with his head, and slowly, flames ignite up his spine.

The blaze spreads, the searing embers glowing a dark cobalt as they leave nothing but a gilded skull while the ashes of Hades' flesh float through the air.

The remainder of his flesh melts away before my eyes, and he takes the knife, now glowing like a forge, from between his teeth, dropping it to the floor. Then he presses his hips out and grabs his shaft with the hand coated in Adonis' blood.

I cringe, the sight of blood coating Hades' cock causing bile to rise in my throat.

The sound of his inferno whooshes, and flames lick Hades' dark sockets as he reaches out with his other hand, grabbing Adonis and pulling him back. Aligning himself behind Adonis, he slides forward between his cheeks ever so slowly, and moans, "There we go. That's what we needed, isn't it, Adonis?"

"Yes, master!" Adonis cries out.

"Yes. That's it. Right there." Hades pulses forward, ramming his cock into Adonis' ass. "Is this good, Persephone? Does this please you?"

"Yes," I mumble.

"I can't hear you, Persephone!"

I scream, "Yes!"

"Good. It is good, isn't it, Adonis?"

"Yes, master," Adonis groans.

He continues to fuck Adonis, his balls slapping as he thrusts forward. "Almost there, my loves. Almost there," he grits.

Hades releases in Adonis' ass: his loathing, his frustrations, his love. And leaning forward, Hades' body pulls on the muscles from which Adonis is hanging as he sighs. His breath is coming out in pants as the rising and falling of his chest slows. But just when I think Adonis' torture has ended, Hades removes his cock from where it seeps out of Adonis and walks forward, picking up the knife.

Standing beside Adonis, his fiery gaze fixed on me as he lifts Adonis' head from where it hangs down in defeat, Hades says, "I have considered your pleas. I have heard your words and have decided. I will end your suffering. I will release you, and in doing so, will fulfill my obligation to my wife. Does that please you, Adonis?"

Adonis struggles to move his head to look up at Hades. "Yes, mas-"

Hades slits Adonis' throat before he can finish his sentence, and his blood spurts everywhere as his body shakes, swinging as his legs flail beneath him.

Eventually stilling, Adonis' life's blood pools bright red at Hades' feet, and I shriek, "You killed him!"

"I did as he asked. As he pleaded with me to do. I released him, Persephone. Released him from his mortal coil."

My lip quivers. "But... how?"

"How‽ What do you mean, how‽"

I am panicking now. "He was... dead!"

Hades scowls at me, shaking his head when he says, "No, he wasn't. He was only half dead."

"So, you killed him?" I whimper.

"He wanted me to. He begged for it. You heard him."

"I would have never-"

"You would never have what, Persephone? You would have never accepted it if you had known he was alive? Too late for that, don't you think‽"

"You're a monster!" I howl, kicking my feet as hot tears stream down my cheeks.

The flames that engulf Hades' skull subside, and slowly his flesh rematerializes, his face and hair returning to their previous state.

His eyes once again shine silver, and as he looks down upon me, sadness dresses his features. "Yeah. Yeah, I'm the monster. I'm the 'big bad god' who only likes pain and torture. Isn't that right, Persephone? Isn't that how you see me?"

I glower; my teeth gritted as I stare up at him. "Yes."

"Perhaps you should look inward, my love. Because your actions, your deceit, have brought this upon you both."

I arch, my arms pulling taut as I fight against my shackles. "I hate you!"

"You hate me? Oh, Little One. Hate is such a strong word. So final. You may not love me now, Persephone, but you will. Mark my words.

One day you will love me, and on that day you will have to accept that this..." he points over to Adonis as he continues, "This was all you."

Hades drops the knife and steps toward the door.

"I will never love you!" I challenge.

Hades turns, running toward me, and closes the space between us. He squats down just outside my reach, clasping his hands between his knees as he insists, "Oh, but you will, Little One. You will. Maybe not now, maybe not in one hundred years, but we have all the time in the world. One day you will love me. I just hope that when that day comes... I still have love for you."

CHAPTER 8

YOU DON'T OWN ME (PERSEPHONE)

"How long do you intend on sulking?" Hades asks, placing another bite of meat in his mouth as I stare across the table at him.

My eyes linger for but a moment on Adonis' head, where it lies on a golden platter in the center of the table.

"What? Do you not like my centerpiece?" he taunts.

I look away, refusing to look in Hades' direction a second longer.

"So, I'm to receive the silent treatment, then? Very well. I have nothing to say to you." Hades goes about eating his meal, tossing scraps to Cerberus, who waits patiently as he gushes, "At least you know your placc. Don't you, boy? Ycs, you do."

He is talking nonsense. No more than gibberish and baby talk as he infantilizes the beast before him. But Cerberus doesn't care, because all he wants is another bite; a morsel tossed in his direction from the hands of his master.

"You know, Persephone, I'm not quite sure why you are so upset. I am the one who was wronged here." He points his knife at me to make his point.

"You?" I jerk my head toward him in shock.

"Yes, me. Do you suppose you should be painted the victim in this?" He stabs his knife into the table before clasping his hands on the surface, leaning forward.

"I'm nobody's victim," I sneer, looking away.

"But you are my wife!" Hades yells, banging his fist on the table. The platter in front of him clangs, his goblet teetering as the reverberations from his anger shakes the table. "And there are certain expectations that come with that honor."

"Honor?" I scoff. "What honor? Should I find myself fortunate that you have chosen me? That you have seen fit to trap me here with you for all time?"

I shift in my seat, trying to lean as far away from him as I can without falling off my chair.

"Fortunate? No, Little One. I do not expect you to find yourself fortunate. But it wouldn't hurt for you to be at least the slightest bit grateful." He points at me again, shaking his index finger in admonishment.

I motion around the room as I counter, "What about this life should I feel grateful to have?"

Hades leans back in his chair and begins playing with the stubble on his chin before he continues, "Well, for starters, you have a husband that loves and cherishes you."

I remain silent while Hades picks fibers of meat from between his teeth with his fingernail, looking bored as he tilts his head back against his chair.

Dark locks frame his face and stray hairs cling to the velvety fabric tufted behind his head. He's so beautiful, but I hate him, so I look away.

"I do love you, Persephone. You know that, don't you?" Hades leans forward, resting his elbows on the table as he looks over at me. "Look at me, Persephone," Hades pleads. I keep my eyes trained on the wall on the other side of the room. "Look at me!"

Looking toward Hades, tears of anger flood my cheeks, the hotness streaming down and pooling on my chin. "It is not love. It is ownership," I whimper, my lower lip quivering, as I hold back a snarl.

"Ownership⁈" Hades stands and walks toward me. "I have asked nothing of you." He reaches out and brushes his fingers along the side of my cheek, his hand trembling as I glare at him. "The only thing I required was for you to be mine and mine alone. But you just couldn't do it, could you?"

I don't answer him, pulling away from his touch as his thumb trails through my tears.

"Could you⁈" Hades yells in my face, gripping my arms as he seethes. "All I wanted was to love you. I wanted to give you your heart's desire. I would have done anything to see you happy, and now..." Hades trails off, shaking me as his clutch loosens. Hades lets go of my arms and turns his back on me. "And now I can't bear the sight of you."

"You can't bear the sight of me⁈ I despise you! I can't bear to be in your presence, and I dread every minute I am forced to be so!"

"Dread? You don't know the meaning of the word. If dread is the feeling you seek, then by all means, I will deliver it to you."

Hades stomps back to the table, grabs the platter off the center, and tosses it in my lap.

I jump up, Adonis' head falling to the floor where his clouded over eyes stare up at the ceiling, his tongue hanging out of the corner of his mouth.

The head rolls to a stop underneath the table and Cerberus lurches forward, stopping when Hades grabs hold of the leash and jerks it back.

Hades controls the beast, two hands grasping the tether as he says, "I dreaded the action I knew I must take. I hated every moment of it. Killing Adonis brought me no pleasure. I don't expect you to believe me, nor to understand, but I loved him..." his voice quivers as he finishes, "and my heart broke as the life drained from his eyes."

He slacks the leash, releasing Cerberus, and the beast lunges forward, grabbing the tattered flesh at the base of Adonis' severed head.

Cerberus shakes Adonis' head several times, drops it, and then laps at the dried blood, nibbling the soft skin of Adonis' ear before ripping it off.

"You had a choice," I whimper, bile rising in the back of my throat as the pain of Adonis' death washes over me.

"Choice? What choice?" Hades points down at my feet, where Cerberus feasts upon Adonis' remains. "To allow that monster, as you so called him, to mount you whenever my back was turned?"

The deafening sound of tearing flesh and gnashing teeth sets me over the edge as I accuse, "You're the monster!"

My lip trembles as I stand with my fists curled, my fingernails digging into my palms. I back away, refusing to look down as the sound of ripping continues.

Hades turns his back on me and drops Cerberus' leash to the floor, his shoulders slumping forward as he whispers, "If I'm such a monster, then why don't you just go?"

"What?" I pause, trembling as the blood rushes to my ears, thumping loudly.

"Go!" he bellows.

I run from the dining hall, turning the corner when I reach the end of the corridor.

My feet slip to a stop as I come to a long hallway with rows of doors on each side as torches flicker along the ceiling. I continue on, shaking and rattling the handles of each door, tugging frantically on each one until I find one unlocked.

Jerking the door open, the bottom scrapes across the stones as I heave, and then I slide inside, closing the door behind me.

As I turn, I find myself in a large room filled with row after row of chests; some wooden and some metal.

Hades is sure to follow me, stomping down the hallway as the big bad ruler of the Underworld and tear me out of the room in which I am hiding.

I still, my ear against the door as I stand listening to any sounds of him coming down the hall but it is deathly silent. There's nothing, and the image of him coming to find me, tearing me from the room... well, that never comes to pass.

Sliding down the door, the intricate designs carved in the wood scrape across my back as the weight of my sorrow bears down on me.

My head falls to the side and I sob, shedding tears of loss, tears of regret, but most of all, tears of frustration. I seethe with anger, and unable to contain my emotions, my body shivers and quakes.

I feel so powerless, and despite my best effort, I don't have the strength, nor the will, to fight him forever. At some point, I will give in. At some point, my resolve will break, and when it does, I will be forced to accept him because he is my husband. There is no getting around it, and I can tolerate him, but I don't have to like him. I certainly will never love him, despite his claims I one day will. But maybe, just maybe, if I try hard enough, I can kill the love he has for me, and then he will have to let me go. *Or so I hope.*

I sit on the floor of that room for what seems like forever, my knees pulled into my chest, and my backside numb from the coolness of the stone floor rising through me.

My legs creak when I finally stand, my muscles aching as I walk throughout the room appraising my surroundings.

The air is dry, and dust billows up with each step as dim torchlight illuminates the space.

No one has been in this room for quite some time and walking to the far wall where the chests sit, I run my fingers along their lids, the metal and wood tickling my fingertips.

There are symbols on the handles of each chest, and leather placards with the type of items found within stamped into them.

As I reach a smaller chest at the end of the room, the contents read precious jewels.

Jewels? What need is there for such finery within the Underworld? What purpose does Hades have to keep such extravagant items?

I open the chest, my eyes taking in all the sparkling gems within. There are rich crimson rubies, dark shining emeralds, and other stones I have never seen their like. Some change color as they shift, turning from teal to purple as they shine in my hand.

There are small parchments under each stone cataloging their name: the Kingmaker Emerald, the Aurora Sapphire, the Renascence Ruby. But the color changing stone, the parchment beneath has no markings; no text as its name remains a mystery.

If Hades doesn't know the name of the stone, then why did he place it among the rest? Why did he see the need to hide it away in his palace where none but he can access it?

It has to be important. There has to be a reason it's here, and I will do everything in my power to find out what that is. So, I tuck the stone into my braids, twisted and tied at the base of my neck, hiding it away so I can steal it without Hades' knowledge.

I will ask questions. I will find the answer as to the power the stone holds. But for now, I will carry the stone with me until I can find a proper place in which to conceal it.

It will be my little secret, and if I am to be trapped in the Underworld with Hades for all eternity, I'm sure it will be the first of many.

CHAPTER 9
NO STONE UNTURNED
(PERSEPHONE)

"Hades! Hades!" Zeus bellows as he stands in the corridor outside the dining hall, his golden robes billowing behind him when he steps forward.

The doors open and Hades greets my father coldly, "To what do I owe this... intrusion, brother?" Hades snickers.

I exit the room with the chests upon first hearing the voice of my father, running quietly to the end of the hall where I peer around the corner.

Something is happening. My father is angry. He hates the Underworld and vowed never to step foot here willingly, so why has he done so now? What is so important that he left his mighty perch on Olympus and drug himself into the depths of Hades' domain?

"This has gone on long enough!" Zeus roars, his hands fisting at his hips.

Hades looks at my father with indifference. "Really? Has it now, brother?"

My father flails his arms in the air as he turns away. "Demeter is beside herself and I have been the focus of her rage ever since she found out."

"And that is my problem, how?" Hades asks, ignoring my father as he turns and strides back through the dining hall, his hands clasped behind his back.

Stepping forward slowly, I cower in the doorway as I watch my father stomping forward, his radiating power forcing Hades to look at him.

He takes Hades' hands within his own and stares into those storm cloud eyes rimmed with ether as he pleads, "The crops have ceased to grow, the land lays barren, and the mortal world is in turmoil. Famine and hardship have struck, and our people are dying."

"Our people?" Hades scoffs. "You mean your worshippers, don't you? What business is that of mine? You deal with the land of the living and I oversee that of the dead. Or have you forgotten?"

Hades jerks his hands from my father's grasp and walks back to the table, where he takes another piece of meat and tosses it to Cerberus.

He picks up another and offers it to my father, "Would you like a sample? I'm trying something new. The spices are overwhelming, but you will like it."

Zeus takes the jagged piece of meat and, eyeing it warily, he pops it in his mouth, chewing slowly. After he swallows, my father asks, "It's fatty, and has a rich flavor, but what is it?"

Hades picks up a slice and places it on his tongue, his eyes closed as he savors it. A smile graces his lips and the next words he speaks sends my stomach to churning. "Minotaur. Adonis, to be exact. Not quite a steer and yet still not a man."

My father's eyes fall to the floor, eyeing the remains of Adonis' head Cerberus has finished savoring. He retches, spilling the contents of his mouth on the floor as he spits it out. "You are sick, Hades. And to think I entrusted my daughter to you?" he sputters, wiping his mouth on the sleeve of his robe.

I stride in the room, my anger getting the best of me as I accuse, "And why did you do that? Why did you curse me to this existence?" I point accusingly at my father.

"Persephone?" My father's eyes go wide as he takes me in.

My gown is covered in soot from where I sat in a pile of ashes in that room, and my eyes are still puffy from all the tears of frustration I'd shed.

"I didn't know you were here." He takes a step back.

"You didn't know I was here⁈ Wasn't it you who allowed this to come to pass⁈ Weren't you the one who approved this union⁈" I step toward my father slowly.

"Well, yes," Zeus stammers, backing up another step. "I just thought you would be elsewhere during this confrontation."

"I'm not going anywhere," I challenge, stomping my foot. "I will no longer be a bystander as my fate is decided."

"You have no say in this," Hades asserts, crossing his arms as he stands in defiance of the entire scene.

"Hades is right. This is between him and I. You should depart." My father waves his hand toward me and turns to face Hades.

"I should depart⁈" I yell. "Where shall I go, father⁈ Shall I go to Elysium or to Tartarus⁈ No. I can go to neither because I am not dead! I am a prisoner in Hades' palace and your decree has made me thus!" My arms flail about as I rant.

"A prisoner? Really, Persephone?" Hades laughs. "Is being here so bad?"

"Yes!" I scream, my voice echoing across the room.

"I'll not have this discussion with you, daughter. Go to your room and let Hades and I speak."

My father doesn't face me and takes another step toward Hades. I am dismissed, my father shooing me away as if I am a nuisance; an irritation he sees fit to silence.

With no say, I once again am powerless to decide my fate. And feeling defeated, I walk down the long hall back to Hades' room as I sulk, realizing I am utterly alone. My one comfort, one confidant, is now a meal for the beasts: my father, Cerberus, the man I am forced to regard as my husband.

Anger sends me from the palace and out the front gates, my feet carrying me to the stables.

Hurried steps turn to a run as I sprint toward the only freedom I can claim at this moment, and I mount one of the terrifying stallions, riding out to where I know not, and I don't care.

I gallop across the scorched earth at the edge of Tartarus and toward where I think I will find the Elysian Fields. None of the guards stop me as I ride by, kicking up ash with each hoofbeat that sounds beneath my retreat. And even though I have no clue where I am going, the amber glow of the setting sun guides me toward Asphodel Meadows.

When I finally reach Elysium, the smell of fresh lilac and freesia greets me as I dismount, stepping into the lush grasses at the meadow's edge. I sigh when their soft tendrils caress my calves and I walk through the wildflowers in a daze, wandering about as I take in all the beauty surrounding me.

Suddenly, I find myself at the base of a large oak where dozens gather, listening as an elderly woman tells a tale of love. Her gentle voice echoes, tinkling harmoniously as she speaks of two souls whose burgeoning love was ended too soon by death.

She regales the group with the heartbreaking account, and when it ends, a tear trickles down my cheek as the loss she'd spoken of moves me.

The story was beautiful; a handsome young man and an equally alluring young woman had a torrent love affair, only to be separated by her father. I have no love of my own, but I know the sentiment all… too… well, as I too am living a life not my own.

As the story ends, the group departs, milling away slowly, and I approach the woman, slowly advancing because there are so many questions about the tale plaguing me. "Was it fate?" I ask, my voice pleading.

"Fate, my child? No. Fate had nothing to do with this," she answers, the creases and wrinkles from a life well lived adorning the corners of her kind eyes.

She is old, older than most I have seen, and she wears lilac colored robes as she carries a gnarled walking stick at her side.

"Then what?"

"Sometimes lives just end and there is no rhyme or reason to it," she offers, turning away.

I raise my voice, "I can't and won't accept that!" My body quivers as the frustration from my situation, and the realization that some things just are as they are, hits me hard.

"Then don't," the woman says matter-of-factly, stopping mid-step.

I look to her, a pleat forming between my brows. "What?"

"You possess the power to choose exactly what it is you desire," she insists, pointing in my direction with her stick.

I look around me and then back at her as I ask, "Me? But how?" My legs shake when I finally step toward her.

She holds up her hand, halting my approach as she continues, "It will not come from within, my child. But trust me, you have it. You keep it hidden, but it's yours." She sets her stick down and leans into it, allowing her weight to brace against it as she rocks forward. "I should go," she mumbles.

As the woman turns and walks away, her stick tapping against the stones on her path; I move toward the tree, placing my palms on the bark.

I need to feel life; something alive that even Hades can't control. But is it? Is this tree alive? Does it thrive outside of his reign, or is it just another aspect of the Underworld in which his sovereignty remains supreme?

I slide down, my gown catching on the bark as I lean back against the base of the tree and ponder her words. *I have it hidden, but I possess the power.*

I reach up and retrieve the stone from where it's nestled in my braids, and as the remaining sun hits the surface of the stone, it shimmers.

A blinding light sends sparks into the sky above me, and I squeeze my eyes shut, waiting for the radiance to subside. When I again open them, a figure stands before me.

Looking up at the glowing figure, I stammer, "Who… are you?"

"I am Erymanthe," the figure before me speaks, her glow dissipating as her lavender gown billows in the breeze.

The gauzy fabric sways as the scent of pungent flowers envelopes me; jasmine and yarrow. It is sweet and earthy, with spicy undertones.

"Why have you come?" I ask, a sense of calm washing over me.

"The light of the Infinity Stone has called me to you," her delicate and airy ethereal voice acknowledges.

"The Infinity Stone?" I question, holding up the stone.

"The very same," she affirms. "This stone is a vessel. A place where you can shroud your secrets, depositing a piece of yourself within."

She turns, walking away, and I call after her, "Why would I do that?" I rise from the tree, raising my hand and reaching for her.

She stops and once again turns to face me as she says, "To make a life of your choosing. To hide what you may not want to share. The Underworld has many wonders, but there are also many terrors. Terrors thrust upon you and others of your own making. Either way, lock away the knowledge of both. And if you should ever decide to leave this place… the stone will be the path to your freedom." She clasps her hands in front of her and again turns.

"But I can never leave. Hades will never let me go." I scowl, my brows pleating as she turns back to me again.

With a defiance in her tone, she says, "Nothing is certain. There is always a way, and now you have the power to make your own choice." Walking toward the horizon, she calls out, "So, what will it be, Persephone?"

A blinding light again fractures the space before me and the oracle is gone. So, I tuck the Infinity Stone back in my braids and walk back to the edge of the Elysian Fields. Looking back only once, the memory of all that transpired dances across my periphery.

Finally turning away, my eyes adjust to the dimness of dusk, and Hades is on the outskirts of Elysium, sitting atop one of his stallions. He clutches the reins of my stallion as the setting sun illuminates his imposing form.

Sitting on his mount, he calls out, "Did you have a pleasant visit?"

"I did," I reply, smiling at him as a sense of accomplishment washes over me. I step out of the grasses and stand beside his horse as he looks around warily.

His horse stomps as it shifts beside me, and he asks, "Were you alone?"

"For some time, yes," I answer, looking up.

He seems anxious, terrified even. Frowning, his eyes stare back toward the hills in the distance as he bristles, "You can visit whenever you wish, Persephone. But only if I escort you."

I answer flatly, "Duly noted."

Hades offers me his hand, and taking it, he hauls me up onto his horse, his body wrapping around me as I take my seat in front of him.

I look back once more, to the hills in the distance as the sun drops below the horizon, and we depart.

We ride back in silence with no mention of my father's visit or my trip to Elysium. And when we reach the stables, Hades lowers me from the steed.

My feet land on the hardness beneath me with a crunch as the skirts of my gown rustle amongst the billowing ash.

He dismounts, sending a cloud of ash into the air as he looks down into my eyes, and a stable hand takes the horses inside.

Clutching my shoulders tightly, Hades leans his forehead toward mine and his scent envelopes me when our skin touches.

I think he is going to kiss me, and I prepare myself for it, but he just stands there with his eyes closed, breathing me in.

He sighs heavily and then says, "We need to talk." His eyes remain closed as a pained look crosses his features.

"Okay," I answer curtly.

"But maybe in the morning. It's been a long day." He breathes out, finally opening his eyes.

"It has," I say, gulping as I look into his silvery gaze.

He releases me, stepping aside, and we walk back to the palace without a single word or glance passing between us.

Hades looks defeated; sullen even. The whole Underworld seems to weigh on him as we continue on, our arms casually brushing against one another. And despite our proximity, there seems to be miles between us.

We have almost reached his chambers when Hades stops and pushes open a door. It creaks open, a wail escaping as the hinges groan out in resistance, and I step through, walking toward the bed.

I take a seat on its edge, staring at my feet when I realize he didn't follow me in. Looking up, Hades' back is to me with his shoulders drawn forward.

As he retreats with labored steps, I call out to him, "Where are you going?"

"I'll be just down the hall in our chambers," he says sullenly. "This is your room. Just as you requested."

Hades leaves me speechless, the door closing behind him. His footsteps echo down the hall, and as I fling myself back on the bed, the weariness overtaking me, I hear his door creak open and then shut.

CHAPTER 10

MY MOTHER'S CHILD (HADES)

Persephone wasn't what I'd expected. She wasn't the peace I thought I would find. She wasn't the frail being I presumed her to be, and that in and of itself vexed me.

For months, I watched her; sneaking glimpses of her through my peering stone as I sat in my throne room, with Cerberus at my feet. Other times, I would sneak up to the mortal realm to spy on her as she frolicked through the fields without a care in the world. But I had been reckless, and someone took notice of my attentions; an old foe waiting for the right time to strike.

Slithering as quietly as a viper, she waited. Aphrodite had found out about my fixation on the girl, and despite the time that had passed since I wronged her, she still sought her vengeance.

I'd wanted to wait, but the longer I did, the more vulnerable Persephone became.

I'd wanted to take time, get to know her, and earn her affection, but I also had to save her from the one that would take from me what I craved.

Knowing the danger lurking around every corner, just waiting to lash out, I acted. I took her, but perhaps too soon.

I hadn't desired something in a long time, but I wanted Persephone; needed to make her mine and have her by my side. She stoked a fire I thought had been all but extinguished, and I wanted to cherish her, to love her. I wanted her in a way I can't explain.

Persephone seemed soft, she'd seemed innocent, and watching her innocence, the carefree life she lived, I felt something I hadn't in a long time. I again felt hope.

I had once been as she was; a wide-eyed, loving child with a genteel nature. At least that is what my mother, Rhea, had said.

She'd told me she loved all her children, but I was her favorite.

Zeus had been the seeker of power, Hera the protector of others, Demeter the lover of creation and causing things to flourish, and Hestia really wasn't known for anything. And let's not forget Poseidon, who only liked to create chaos and wreak havoc. Even so, she'd said I held a special place in her heart.

No, not all the stories about my siblings and me are true. Then again, there are some that are.

Like the tales of our father, who devoured us out of paranoia about being overthrown. That holds truth, but we were not mere infants, we were children.

The children of Titans, who were raised by a loving mother until she, too, became fraught with the fear of being overcome. It was then her loving nature shifted, and she stood by our father's side as he swallowed us whole. But if I was her favorite, why was it only Zeus that had been spared?

If it hadn't been for Zeus, the years he remained hidden in order to set us free, we would have been snuffed out of existence as our mother stood idly by.

There was a time I'd been kind. I have memories of the distant version of me I'd once been. But striking down and trapping your parents for all eternity, fighting the Titans ruling the world, does something to you. It changed the very fabric of my being, and once I was forced to become the ruler of the Underworld, the purveyor of death and the overseer of damnation, that too altered me.

I had been lenient once. I had been blinded by my belief in another, trusting that their nature was not as the scales weighed and measured.

Cocytus had stepped on the scales, his soul being judged unworthy, and I'd thought different, ignoring what was right in front of me. His pleading eyes and cries played to the part of me that remained hopeful, and to my detriment, I let him pass into Elysium when I should have drowned him in the waters of Acheron, watching his soul burn as it flowed into Pyriphlegethon.

I didn't, though, and it wasn't until he'd stained the grasses of the Elysian Fields in blood that I saw how egregious of an error I'd made.

Cocytus turned what was meant to be a peaceful afterlife into something of nightmares, and I wouldn't forget my misjudgment. I would never again allow my naivety to overrule what the scales read, and so I named the wailing river after him.

I never again repeated that mistake, and with him, my cruelty was born. Because I took pleasure in his punishment, going out of my way to see to his penance.

Daily I would make my way into Tartarus with the sole purpose of taking out my frustrations on him. And bit by bit, I chipped away at my innocence, replacing it with a tenacity for torture.

I developed a penchant for inflicting pain and suffering, and I liked it. *No, I loved it.* The Hades I'd once been was gone, and in his place the king of torment remained.

I thought Persephone could change all that. I thought maybe, just maybe, this woman could bring back the parts of me my mother once loved. That I could love her and, in time, earn her love in return.

No, Persephone wasn't the only love I'd had in this cursed life. With her wasn't the first time I'd been hopeful. But as I watch her depart the underworld, not looking back even once as she strides into the abyss that is the labyrinth, I sigh.

"How many times must you do this?" Charon asks, standing with me at the edge of the River Styx as his dark gray robes billow behind him, and the ferry floats just beyond.

"As many as it takes," I say, not taking my eyes off Persephone until she steps forth into the darkness beyond the gates at the entrance to the labyrinth.

Charon grasps my shoulder, forcing me to turn and face him. "To what end?" he asks. His steel-gray eyes are pleading as he awaits my response, his knobby fingers clutching my shoulders tightly.

I pull away, shrugging him off as I look back at the darkened cavern in the distance. "If this is the price I must pay for a chance at love, then I will gladly pay it."

Earlier that morning, as Persephone and I had sat for the meal, I explained to her the agreement Zeus and I had reached.

Persephone had just plopped a handful of pomegranate seeds in her mouth when I divulged everything.

Demeter refused to go through eternity without her, and I would allow her to return to the realm of mortals to be with her once more.

I told her once the seasons changed she would return to me and we could begin again. I would welcome her back with loving arms and the knowledge I had been generous in my allowance of such.

Persephone crosses her arms, her head cocked to the side. "I don't understand?"

"It's simple. Half the time with your mother, when the sun is highest in the sky and the world is alive, and the remaining, when all that is lush and green begins its slumber, with me."

She scoffs, "But why do I have to return at all?"

"Because I will it so! It is by my grace alone you are allowed to leave at all. Remember that, Persephone. Remember that, while you are in your mother's embrace and laying back amongst the wildflowers, it was my will and nothing more that has allowed it to be so."

A hollow forms in the pit of my stomach as she departs, and I know the woman who returns to me will not be the same girl I watched all those months ago.

Persephone's time with me changed her; hardened her. But if she can instill hope in me, then perhaps I can plant the seeds of love that will blossom within her.

I will be better, can be better. I will be a version of me she can find comfort in. I will be the man she deserves, and the man she willingly returns to when the first frost hardens the ground at the turning of the seasons.

With me she will feel at home, safe. *Or so I hope.*

CHAPTER 11
HALF OF FOREVER
(PERSEPHONE)

The smell of lilies blooming outside the open window in the kitchen stirs me awake the third day following my return from the Underworld on an unseasonably cool summer morning.

My mother has been up for hours, wielding her power to set right all that has gone wrong in the realm since my disappearance. But as the sunlight filters into my room through the gauzy curtains, I just lay here. I lay here curled in a ball, my knees drawn into my chest like a caterpillar, cocooned in the warmth of my bedding.

I missed this: this bed, these sheets, this home. Never during my time in the Underworld had it felt like this. It had never felt this calm, inviting, or right. And I only have a short while to feel this way until, once again, I will have to return to that place; the place that haunts my sleeping hours, and the place that shattered me, leaving me forever changed.

I am no longer the girl I once was, have nothing that is just mine. I am only his now. But I can claim these moments for myself, if only to cherish the memories once this place is but a daydream.

Demeter spent the first two days after my return at my bedside, holding me as I cried. She begged me to unburden myself, pleading I let go and let her in. But I couldn't.

I can't allow her a glimpse into what life is like with him because I'm no longer the same. I'm no longer the same girl who walked barefoot through the meadow as the Nymphs frolicked beside me. Not the girl who allowed the soil to ground me, sifting between my toes as the sun warmed me inside and out. I am now cold inside; a shuddering feeling ever present.

This world is vibrant and alive, the buzzing and whispered wings of the insects on the wind a constant reminder that, in many ways, I no longer am.

I feel dead inside, and outside, if I'm being honest. Like those lost souls; those souls cursed to forever drift away in the River Styx. The tortured Nevermore.

Nevermore will they see the sun, nevermore will they feel its warmth, and nevermore will they feel anything other than endless sorrow. Their deaths are repetitive; an endless loop of cyclical torment with no escape.

Like them, this is my life now. Forever I will walk hand in hand with this feeling. *Or at least half of forever.*

Hearing my mother as she enters bustling about the house as I sit in my bed, I stare at the ceiling, and my eyes shift in and out of focus, darting this way and that.

I should take in all this life, and enjoy my time here as much as I can, but as the midday sun blankets the world outside, I just mope in my room with the curtains drawn.

"Are we planning to stay in bed all day again?" My mother shuffles her feet as she walks across the room, pulling back the curtains to filter in the light. "You haven't touched your breakfast," she says, running her fingers along the tray at my bedside. "Or washed." She surveys the pitcher and basin where it sits untouched on the table in the corner near my dressing gown, still laid out on the back of the chair. She scowls. "Today's the day, my love."

"What day is that?" I ask, tilting my head in her direction.

"The day you leave this room." She saunters over to the chair, lifts my dressing gown and shakes it about as the pale pink fabric sways to and fro, the skirts drifting with her movements. "Some sun would do you good. And the fresh air..." she breathes, closing her eyes.

"Maybe," I say, looking away. I look at the window, trying to will myself to move. I urge myself to pull back the pale-yellow sheets and stand, but all I can muster is falling back against the soft pillows as I sink deeper into my bed. "Or, maybe not," I mutter.

"Persephone!" my mother chastises, her agitation washing over me. She stands with her hands on her hips, cinching in her simple gown, as her honey-colored hair cascades down her back, and her crown of grain rests atop her head.

One sandaled foot taps impatiently as she glowers at me and I answer, "I know. I can. I mean... I will." I lift my chin and meet her gaze, insisting, "I promise."

"Indeed," she replies, pursing her lips as her eyebrows furrow.

My mother means well. She wants what's best for me, and fought for my return, after all. So, the least I can do is get up, make myself presentable, and attempt to return to the land of the living. But I just can't.

I can't leave this room, can't leave this house. Because once I do, I know I won't be able to bring myself to go back there, and back to him.

I hate myself. Hate how trapped I feel. Hate knowing that each day that passes here, in this house with my mother, is one day closer to returning to Hades. It is a life sentence hanging over my head; reminded each morning as the sun rises high in the sky, I am one day closer to months without its rays. One day nearer to his hands upon my flesh and mouth pressed to mine.

The revelation should motivate me, the approaching deadline propelling me into action. It should allow me to enjoy these moments, but it doesn't. Because it is that ever present inevitability that has me cemented in place, unwilling to step outside.

I longed for his touch once, had welcomed it. But that was before Adonis. Before what he did to him, and to me.

"I won't beg, Persephone. I have a lot of work to do and can't very well do it in this room. You can either come with me or stay as you are. The choice is yours. But if what I surmise is true, this is the one place where you do, in fact, have one. Yours alone and without consequence. So, what will it be? Will you allow him to control what happens to you, or will your time here be of your own making?"

My mother wrings her hands in her skirts, pleading with me. Her eyes glass over, and she turns and walks from the room, her footsteps echoing down the hall.

Those sandaled steps grow fainter as they trail into the kitchen, and then the front door creaks open, slamming shut behind her.

She pauses after exiting the house, then all I hear is her feet crunching across the gravel path, and her low voice muttering to herself as she leaves the yard.

Tears well in my eyes and I squeeze them shut, letting out a labored huff of frustration. I scream as loudly as I can, beating my fists into the bed at my sides as I kick my feet like a toddler throwing a tantrum; having a fit prompted by being told I can't do something I want to. But that isn't the case, because the only one not allowing me to have what I want... is me.

I've had enough. No one is going to tell me what I can or can't do. Not now, not ever. Not my father, not my mother, but most of all, not Hades.

I will no longer stand, well lay, by and let this happen. If I have any chance at all, any chance of surviving this, my will to live has to be stronger than my acceptance of death.

If death is going to be my unwelcome companion for half of what is left of the remainder of my life, then I sure as the Underworld better get to enjoying the half without him.

Getting up and dressing, I pull my pale pink gown over my head after using the basin to freshen up, and then wrap the silken chord around my waist, cinching it tight. I tie the ends loosely in a knot and take a seat in the chair beside the table, fastening my sandals before turning to grab my ivory comb off the vanity.

Tearing through my locks, I attempt to tame my unruly copper curls, fashioning them in a loose plait down my back before standing to survey my room.

I take in everything I have to be thankful for: this realm, this home, this space. My space and the one thing that is truly mine, and mine alone.

It is a simple space with plain white curtains and pale-yellow bedding. There is no finery to be found; no tufted furniture, jeweled mirrors, or gilded chalices. It's a far cry from the decadence of Hades' palace, but at least here there is no oversized bed, no restraints, or wandering hands I don't dare deny. I am free here of his jealousy, his outrage, and his control; even if only for a time.

Here I am, free to be myself. Or, more accurately, I am free to explore who I am now. Like, what are my thoughts, my feelings? What do I want to do with my time? Who is this Persephone, and more importantly, how do I become a Persephone Hades no longer desires?

CHAPTER 12

WHO DOESN'T LIKE BREAD? (PERSEPHONE)

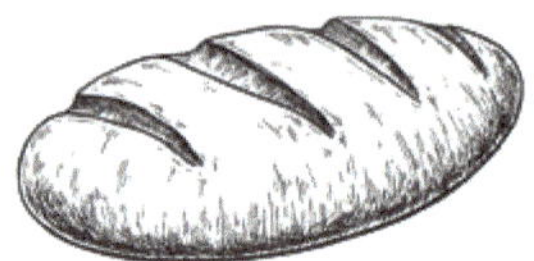

The sounds of living things overwhelm my senses as I walk out of my mother's house. There is no death here; no shrieking and moaning or sounds of torture and dismay. Only the sounds of birds chirping, and the stream that runs at the edge of the property bubbling.

It is serene, calm, and mostly quiet. All the things I once loved, but now are boring, if I'm being entirely honest. So much happened in my short time away, so much chaos, that this quaint life no longer seems peaceful as it once had. Instead, I now find it to be rather... dull.

I need some action, some excitement. I need to do something that makes me feel alive. But picking flowers or listening to the Nymphs play a tune on their lute just won't cut it anymore.

I want to be thrilled. I want to be exhilarated. In all frankness, I want sex with slick bodies and backs arching in ecstasy. I want rocking hips while nails dig into my thighs. And I yearn to be bound, being feasted upon by someone, anyone, other than Hades.

It's not like sex with Hades isn't enjoyable. Our trysts had some very memorable moments. But there are way more awful ones overshadowing the good that I just can't get past them.

With Hades, the act was primitive. It was mostly him forcing himself upon me as I took whatever he gave me. And with Adonis, it was sweet; almost slow at times. Because sex with Adonis didn't spurn a deep need. He was always too considerate of my pleasure. Actions that, while I appreciated them, I wanted to feel like he was battling against his willpower to have me.

I want to feel an urgency. I want to feel like someone needs me so badly they just can't control themselves.

What I want is a combination of those two things. Someone who can tease and tantalize me with their fingers and tongue, driving us both to the edge. But also someone who, when the need becomes too great, gives in to the primal being holding them at bay and just ravages me.

I want someone who worships between my thighs, taking in their fill before flipping me onto my stomach, grabbing the back of my hair, and pulling me against them as they plunge into me deeply. Someone who, when we are both satisfied, caresses me slowly, and holds me tightly so I know, with them, I am safe.

But mostly I want my field plowed thoroughly, and soon.

I find my mother in the far field on the outskirts of the village, watching from afar as the farmers tend their wheat. I walk up beside her, wrapping my arms around her waist.

"I think I'm going to make my way into the village. Do you need anything?" I ask her.

"There's a new baker in town. He and his son, Kairos, make some of the most amazing bread. Grab a loaf on your way home? We'll have some with the meal."

She doesn't turn to look at me, she just looks on lovingly as the farmers work, her power of creation radiating from her with a golden glow.

Grasping her arm, I squeeze my affection before I say, "There are very few things I love more than fresh bread." I smile over at her and then turn, walking toward the village.

I wander along the perimeter of the fields where the farmers stop and watch as I go by. I can feel their eyes on me, those men; old and young alike. I think to myself, *what must they make of me? What do they envision as I slowly run my fingers through the wheat when I pass, longingly caressing the beards as the kernels sift through my fingers? Does the image of me stoke their desire and make them yearn to feel my touch? Can they see themselves between my thighs as I arch back into the leaves and stems we've trampled, our slick bodies moving rhythmically?*

Crimson paints my cheeks as a flush sets in. I hope they do, and gods, how I wish they would. At least one of them, anyway.

Intently watching as I stroll, a dark-haired man with cunning eyes and tanned skin surveys me. He wears the evidence of the toiling and laboring he's done in those fields displayed on his bulging, veinous forearms and sculpted shoulders. His muscles glisten with perspiration from his exertions as I drink in the sight of him.

Despite the mischievous grin adorning his face as his eyes follow me, he wears nothing but a loincloth; a length of thin fabric twisted and knotted expertly, but nowhere near enough to hide the reaction his body has to his thoughts.

He is barefoot, and his sickle stills as he holds my gaze.

I toss my head back and laugh, playfully swishing my hips as I continue on.

His eyes follow me, his efforts halting as he licks his lips with thirst.

"You look positively parched," I call out. "Perhaps you would care for a drink?" I stop walking, my skirts swishing against my calves.

He steps forward, his sickle thudding to the ground as he stops working. "That I could," he replies, the smooth tenor of his voice trailing on the last word.

"It shouldn't take me long," I reply, turning to walk toward the village.

"Nonsense," he says, "I shall join you. I have some things to tend to in town, anyway."

"You do?" I ask., looking up and down him. "Like that?"

"I do, miss?" he asks, wiping his hands on the back of his loincloth.

He walks over to a wheat bag and grabs a robe and sandals. He slides on the sandals and then dons the robe, wrapping it around him. He then cinches the sash at his waist, tying it tight.

I shake my head, pulling my thoughts back to the present.

"Persephone," I finally answer. "Just Persephone."

"Well, just Persephone, if it's not an imposition, I would like to accompany you?" He stands with his hands on his hips, awaiting my reply.

I smile charmingly, clutching my hands together as I sway side to side. "As you wish."

He drags his fingers through his mussed hair, his shoulder muscles popping as he smooths down the sides. "I'm Kairos. My father and I have a bakery in the village."

"And you work in the fields?" I place my attention on his lips, pulling my gaze from his fingers.

He grins at me, noticing the flush creeping up my neck.

We walk through a row of wheat, weaving in between the stalks as we talk.

"There is something gratifying about being responsible for the entire process. From tilling the land and tending the crop through harvest," Kairos says, snapping off a stem and tickling my cheek with the head. "To the milling, and then turning all that hard work into something for all to enjoy." Kairos places the stem in his mouth, chewing as it rests at the corner of his lips.

"You make it sound like an art form," I respond, my eyes trained on his lips again.

"It is," he insists, licking his lips, and then pursing them.

"How so?" I gulp.

He reaches for my hand. "Allow me to show you?"

I place my hand in his, and he squeezes it reassuringly. "I don't see why not. I was planning to visit the bakery on my way home."

Kairos blabs for the entire walk to the bakery, and I tune out most of what he says, having no actual interest in his thoughts. His thoughts are of no consequence to me because I am only interested in what pleasures he can afford me; how his body can join with mine, replacing any thoughts I have of Hades and Adonis.

I want this man. I want to feel his hardness deep inside me. I want to feel his hands, those fingers, as they trace every inch of my skin, his essence erasing whatever claim Hades has on me. I want his scent, that masculine musk, to mix with my own, and when we are done, as we lay satiated within one another's arms, I want him to do it all again; over and over, for as long as he can manage.

The bakery is teeming with shoppers, making it noisy and crowded. There is the hustle and bustle of orders being placed, conversations of those milling about, and the overpowering scent of yeast filling the air.

Several dozen loaves bake in the ovens, the heat billowing through the doorway, and several more are rising in the sun. Flour is being poured in the back room, causing dust to hang thickly in the air, while feet shuffle about as patrons place their orders, and workers rush off to fill them.

I can't focus. There is just so much going on and I am lost in my thoughts as I stare at a ray of sunshine dancing across the floor.

Meanwhile, sandals kick up dust as they cross the threshold, and the heat of the space has my skin beading with sweat.

"Persephone?" Kairos calls out, touching my arm to gain my attention.

"I'm sorry. You were saying?" I blink twice, shaking off the thoughts I am lost in, and my gaze goes straight back to those lips.

As if in slow motion, his lips part and he says, "Sweet or tangy?"

The words seem to ooze from his mouth, inking across the distance between us where the tendrils caress my skin.

When it finally registers he'd asked a question, I reply, "Sweet or tangy, what?"

"The bread. Are you wanting something sweet, like a dessert, or something savory to serve with a main dish?"

"Can't I have both?" I flutter my lashes; the words dripping off my tongue like honey.

"You can have whatever you want," Kairos answers, his smile widening with the inference.

I ask coyly, "Is that so?"

"It is," he insists.

Kairos tears a sweet roll in half, the butter and sugar melting off the edge as they gum his fingers. He licks the tackiness from his palm, savoring the decadence as he trails his tongue up to his fingertip. His gaze never leaves my face, and as I reach out and grab his wrist, his eyes widen.

Pulling his hand toward me, I lean forward and place his index finger in my mouth where I suck gently, tasting of the sweetness coating his digit. "Mmmm," I groan, twirling my tongue around the tip of his finger. I release his hand, and it falls to his side, bouncing off his thigh as he stands with his mouth agape. "Delicious," I coo, wiping my thumb across my bottom lip and then sucking it clean. "Can I have more?"

"As much as you want, whenever you want," he whispers, stepping into me.

"Not here," I reply, stepping back with mock surprise as I look around for any that may have taken notice.

"Where?" his question carries a need that I feel in my core; a yearning that I, too, share.

Reaching forward and placing my hand on his cheek, I say, "Soon."

"Soon? As in, how soon?" he implores, placing his hand on mine.

"Soon enough," I chortle. "Why? Are you in a hurry?" I tease, lowering our hands and brushing past his shoulder as I approach the counter.

"Get her anything she desires," Kairos says, tapping the countertop as he addresses the clerk. "Until next time," he whispers in my ear as he brushes past me. "I'm headed back to the fields."

He turns to leave and I reach out and grab his wrist, stopping him. "What about that drink?"

"My thirst can wait," he answers, raising our hands and kissing my wrist.

I pull free of him, dropping my hand to my side. "Is that so?"

"For now," he replies. "But as you said, soon enough. Besides, I have no doubt it's worth the wait." He gazes at me.

"Indeed," I say, biting my lip as his eyes lock with mine. "Well worth it."

"Can't wait," Kairos confirms, turning for the door once more.

"Soon," I repeat, smiling as he walks to the door.

Kairos stops in the doorway, taps the frame twice, and smiles before he says, "I'll hold you to that." He then points in my direction, winks, and walks out the door.

I collect my purchases and make my way back to the house, my mind filled with vulgar thoughts of Kairos.

I imagine him sucking the buttery sugar mixture from the sweet rolls off my toes as he caresses my ankle, him between my thighs as my honey drips from his lips, and his hard cock filling me as my coated lips wrap around his shaft.

I can hear his cries, and my moans, filling the air as I imagine him contorting me into a myriad of positions as he drives deeply within me while the evidence of our efforts coat his skin and it glistens. The same glistening he had when working in the fields, but exertions where our scents commingle on the wind.

He may not have a sickle between those muscular thighs, but he can plow my field as hard and as deep as he dares. He can attempt to sow his seeds, his cock immersed within the chasm that is my center; the velvety warmth of my core where he will swell from his satisfaction as he releases mine.

CHAPTER 13
I SEE YOU (HADES)

I let her go. It was against my better judgement and contrary to all the reasons I brought Persephone down to the Underworld in the first place, and yet, I still did it. I did it because I had to, but mostly I did it because she needed it.

It tore me apart, watching her walk away. And the dangers she might face by letting her go, unnerved me as well. But what other choice did I have? I certainly didn't want to face Demeter's wrath, and I sure as shit didn't want Zeus poking around in my affairs. Simple fact is, it is out of my control. It shouldn't be, but it is.

The first week after she left, it was agonizing seeing how she struggled. I just wanted to scoop her up in my arms and breathe in her scent while I rocked her. But I couldn't. I can't interfere, can't interact, and won't bring any more unnecessary attention to her. I have already done enough.

The look in her eyes after Adonis, the terror and the hatred, haunts me.

It would have been one thing if it had just been the change in how she looked at me, but the loathing that spewed from her lips, the way she recoiled from my touch, and the way she iced me out. It was all so unbearable.

My actions with Adonis had scarred her, and I knew as much.

If only I could tell her. If I could just explain it so she could see. But I couldn't do that, either. I won't chance her safety by sharing my truth, my shame.

I am ashamed. I am downright embarrassed. Everything that has happened, and why it is happening in this manner, I am to blame.

If I hadn't been such a shit in the past, none of this would have been necessary. I mean, sure, Aphrodite is the real villain, but I am the one being painted as such. I am the one she dreads coming back to. I am the one she ran from. Not Aphrodite. Me.

If she had just remained a little longer, she would have seen, and he could have explained. Adonis would have walked through that labyrinth, crossed the River Styx, and shown her the truth. But now, all she knows is he is dead and she is heartbroken.

She is unaware that his place in Elysium is secure. She is unaware he is no longer a prisoner, if he had ever been one at all. She is unaware that, in more ways than just the one, I set him free: free of his mortal coil, free from Aphrodite's ire, if he wished it, free of me.

Three days after Persephone left, Adonis entered the Underworld. It took some doing, getting his remains to the mortal realm and seeing to his rite, but I did it. I did it not only for him, because he deserves as much, but I did it for her. And not to seem completely selfless, but most importantly, I did it for myself. I'd promised, after all. And I'm selfish. I am aware of that fact. But the steps I took to care for Adonis, during and after his life, I took out of love.

I didn't lie when I said I loved him. Didn't hide the pain I felt at his passing. It wrecked me, and he was my friend. *No, he was more than that.*

Adonis helped me heal, and bringing Persephone to the Underworld to protect her was his idea.

He knew just how ruthless Aphrodite could be. He knew just what lengths she would go to for revenge, and that she would take all her frustrations for not being able to get to me out on Persephone.

Ultimately, I know I'm the one at fault for all of it: Aphrodite's anger, Adonis' death, all the wrongs committed against Persephone. Despite that, can't a god get an ounce of understanding when everything I've done was to protect them both?

Ugh, I just can't get into that now. I need to focus. Where was I? Oh, yes. Persephone.

I watch through my peering stone as Persephone wallows in her misery. She spends day in and day out buried beneath her covers as she sulks in her room at her mother's home. But the day she crawled out of bed, pulled herself together, and finally left that room, I was ecstatic.

"That's my girl," I mutter to myself as Cerberus' snores fill the air from where he's sprawled at my feet. "See that, boy? She's up."

Cerberus just opens one eye, shifts at my feet, and then goes back to dozing.

"Well, I care, even if you don't. Mangy beast." I chuckle. I rub my boot along the underside of Cerberus' belly and he rolls to his side.

As Persephone walks through the small gate of her mother's cottage, I can't help but stare at her. With the sun catching in the loose hairs framing her face as the rest of her hair lies neatly plaited and cascading down her back, she has a glow about her; a radiance. A light that, while hidden away in the Underworld, is blazing in the mortal realm.

Persephone was jovial, her steps unburdened as she greets her mother. They speak, and then she makes her way through the fields toward the village.

"No, Persephone. Don't… don't do that." I grimace as I watch her flirting with a man in the field. "She's going to test my patience, isn't she?" I ask to no one in particular.

She transfixes the man. He is smitten. How could he not be?

Persephone is all innuendos and smiles, and for this... this undeserving nothing!

I feel my blood boiling, my skin tingling as the flames of my rage combust just beneath the surface. I am ready to explode, and my flesh sloughs off as ash surrounds me.

"Settle, Hades. Settle," I urge myself, attempting to temper the fury begging to overtake me. "It's just some harmless flirting. He's handsome, right? Why not let her have her fun?" I talk myself down, my skin reforming as my vision that had darkened over clears.

The man leads Persephone into the village, and their interaction is innocent enough. Until it isn't.

"Why? Do you see? Do you see what she's doing? She never did that for me." I shift in my seat, leaning forward as I rest my chin on my fist, while Persephone sucks sugar off the man's finger. "Kairos, is it? I've got a special place for you, son of the baker. Do you like it hot, Kairos? Do you? I hope you do!" I seethe.

Cerberus' heads lift, his hackles raising when he senses my anger, and he nudges my shin.

"Okay, boy. Okay. It's fine, see? I'm fine. It's nothing." I calm once again, pat Cerberus' head, and he lays back down at my feet. "I can do this," I assure myself. "It's just a couple of months. What's the worst she can do in a couple of months, right?"

Cerberus snuffs, shaking his head once.

"Who am I kidding? If she keeps this shit up, I won't make it a month before I'm charging up there and turning her over my knee."

Cerberus seems to chuckle at me, his haphazard teeth showing as he grins.

"Alright, boy. I get it. That's enough for now," I say, standing and stepping down from my throne.

Cerberus rises and follows behind me as I leave the throne room and make my way to the dining hall.

"Are you hungry?" I ask him as he trots beside me, his claws clicking on the stone floor, their sound echoing down the corridor.

CHAPTER 14
ETERNITY AWAITS (HADES)

Over the next months, I check on Persephone sparingly, saving myself from any scenes that might set me over the edge. I give her space, holding my urge to enter the mortal realm at bay. Because it is for the best... for us both.

I visit Adonis in Elysium, after a long day of handling the punishments in Tartarus, filling him in on all I know of her; most of it, anyway. He is at peace, and I want him to remain that way. I don't want to drag him into the middle of... whatever it is going on between Persephone and I.

He has already been in the middle and I don't want to revisit the unpleasantness. I don't want to worry him, but more importantly, she isn't his burden to bear. That responsibility falls to me.

"How's our girl?" Adonis' tone is teasing, and yet, the inference rubs me the wrong way.

I tilt my head toward him. "Our girl?"

"Oh, fuck, Hades! You know what I meant."

I do, but that doesn't lessen my unease with his word choice.

The tension in my shoulders lessens, and I smile in his direction, sighing. "I missed that."

"What?" Adonis asks.

"You calling me Hades, instead of master."

His eyes plead with me. "It was necessary."

My eyebrows shoot up in surprise. "Was it?"

"Familiarity would have been a mistake, and you know it," Adonis insists. His feet shift, his discomfort evident.

"I'm not so sure. Much of Persephone's opinion of me stemmed from you referring to me in that manner; from you being subservient to me."

He smiles widely. "But I am subservient to you."

"Were," I point out. "You were subservient to me."

"Was. Am. Same difference."

I lean back, shooting him a quizzical look. "Is it?"

Adonis bumps my shoulder as we watch the sun set over Asphodel Meadows. "As far as I'm concerned, it is, master," he teases. "But you know what I missed?"

I focus on his face, his eyes wide with wonder. "What?"

He points out at the horizon where the sun seems to melt before our eyes. "This. I took it for granted before. Who knew something as simple as the setting sun, and a good friend, could warm your soul?"

I grin, gripping his shoulder. "I like the sound of that."

"You are my friend, Hades. What happened with Persephone-"

"Please don't." I stop him, my fingertips digging in slightly as he turns to face me.

"Let me finish." His eyes plead as he places his hand on mine. "I know why you did it."

I push his hand from mine and drop my hands to my side. "Do you?"

"You love her." He worries his lip.

I sigh, stepping into him. "I love you," I insist. I place my palm on his cheek, turning his face to mine. "There is no excuse for my behavior. I can't apologize enough for letting my need to possess her, the jealousy, to control me." I search his eyes for understanding.

"I know you love me. I know it with every fiber of my existence. But I also know the feelings you have for her, the possessiveness, result from a deep need to be accepted. Admit it, you are battling with some major mommy issues, and saw her as a way to capture some of what you lost with Rhea."

"Don't say her name," I grit, dropping my hand and turning away.

He reaches out and touches my arm. "She is a part of you, and always will be. Her choosing your father over you, that broke something inside you." Adonis trails his fingers up my arm and places his hand on my chest. "You envisioned Persephone being the bandage to heal that wound; that open, festering, putrid flesh encasing what remains of your delicate heart. A heart that beats fiercely." He pats and then pushes me back gently.

I roll my eyes, turning my head to once again gaze at the sunset. "How did you get to be so perceptive?"

There is silence as Adonis considers his words carefully. "Years and years of watching. I was pretty, so Aphrodite didn't need me to speak to fulfill her needs."

"I'm still sorry it took me so long." I reach for him, and he brushes my hand away.

"It was a lifetime ago." Adonis gazes up at the sky above us, where the stars twinkle overhead. "Besides, you came when you could."

"Still, I should have come sooner."

"I don't think you give yourself enough credit," Adonis says.

"For?"

"All of it. The sun, the stars, everything in this realm. It's a kindness, really."

"I'm the god of the Underworld, not just the ruler of Tartarus. I owe it to the souls here in Elysium. They deserve tranquility just as much as those in Tartarus deserve punishment."

"I know. But it takes a kind heart indeed to produce such beauty. To provide us with some comforts from our mortal life."

"You deserve nothing less," I urge. "And I will do everything in my power to ensure your forever is everything you dreamed it would be."

Adonis and I part ways after a brief hug, and I slowly trudge through the high grasses at the edge of Elysium before mounting my steed and riding back toward the palace.

I halt once along the way, peering back at Elysium as I long for Adonis' companionship. The palace is lonely without him, and with Persephone in the mortal realm, I have nothing but time with the person I hate most, myself.

A deafening silence awaits me back at the palace, and I know, in the silence, my mind will compel me to overthink. I will punish myself with memories of my actions, and the look on Persephone's face. I will fight sleep and every painful cry that escaped Adonis' lips as he died will torture me.

Tomorrow. She returns tomorrow and I am on edge.

I am pacing, burning footprints into the floor as I fight against my need to see her. The flames flicker up and down my legs, my gilded bones peeking through the exposed flesh at my calves as I walk back and forth in front of the steps to the dais.

If I can just hold out one more day, one more night of solitude, and then she will once again be in my arms.

The Peering Stone beckons me from where it sits on the stone pedestal near my throne. Its power hums, a melodic strumming that pulls at my heartstrings.

Persephone has behaved, as far as I know, and has been helping her mother as she wields her power. There is no reason for me to spy on her now. No reason for me to once again look into the stone and upset myself with the visions I might see. And yet, I can't take my eyes from the stone as it reflects the light.

The light refracts through the stone; a crystalline orb gilded and beset by the bones of a Titan. There are human remains atop the fixture and the glass sends prisms dancing above me where Persephone's face projects on the ceiling.

I falter, halting mid-step, and turn away from the stone's resting place. I say aloud, "No. I can't."

I turn toward the stone again. "I shouldn't," I tell myself as I take one labored step forward. I am fighting against my better judgement, but I already know who will win. It is a lose-lose situation, really.

I will lose the battle with my will and, in turn, a piece of myself. I will lose that piece because I already suspect, no, I know, what I will see.

Trudging up the steps of the dais, I plop back into my throne and look over to where the stone lies. The prism shines upon me, and Persephone's face materializes again, right before my eyes.

I sigh. It is a sigh of relief, and one of disappointment because there she is, my heart's song, half naked as her yellow gown rests at her waist. Her full, beautiful breasts bounce up and down, breathy moans escaping her lips as she's straddling him, her skirts bunched up along her thighs while her skin's slick with sweat.

My fury peaks and indigo-colored flames engulf me as my skin sizzles.

The ash from my burning flesh rises into the air, and my gilded bones burn white-hot, creaking when I clench my fists.

Ether courses through me and I go full on god as I become consumed by my rage.

The growl that escapes my lips is positively primal as I grit out, "Mine!"

I watch as that... that nothing runs his filthy hands all over her, grasping and groping MY WIFE!

Kairos' body quakes, his moan cut short as the sound catches in his throat. He comes, spilling his seed within her as she leans back in ecstasy.

Persephone dismounts Kairos, walks back to her satchel and

crouches down as she collects something; a bladder of wine. She hides something behind her back and then takes a large gulp from the bladder, sashaying topless back to Kairos as her gown gathers at her hips.

Her skirts swish as she walks seductively toward him. "Care for another round?" she asks, handing the bladder to Kairos as he lays propped up on his elbows in the grass, reveling in his post coital bliss. She remains standing above him.

"Don't mind if I do," he states suggestively, taking the bladder from her. He takes a swig and then lays the bladder at his side.

Persephone pulls a dagger from behind her back, and then with the other hand, unties the sash at her waist. Once her gown lays at her feet, she steps over the fabric and straddles Kairos.

He sits up, taken aback by the sight of the dagger in her hands. "What's that for?" he asks, his unease evident.

Persephone raises her hand with the dagger, and Kairos grasps her wrist, stopping her. "Not to worry," she purrs. "Just adds to the excitement," she assures him.

Kairos looks at her warily, but still releases Persephone's wrist. His hands fall to her thighs, where he grips them tightly. "As you wish, my Aphrodite."

I seethe, "Don't fucking call her that!" My voice echoes across the throne room, the doors shaking on the other side of the space.

Persephone lays the dagger beside them and then gathers her sash. She takes Kairos' hands from where they rest on her thighs and binds them in front of him. She then raises his arms above his head, slowly laying him back into the grass.

Raising her hips, she places his length at her opening before sliding down his shaft and a hiss escapes his lips.

"Gods," he draws out the word.

Persephone rocks back and forth, slowly tilting her pelvis as she grinds into him. She leans down, placing her weight on his chest as she reaches for the dagger.

Kairos raises off the grass, his muscles tensing with each movement, and she pushes him back down.

"Just trust me," she soothes, placing a kiss on his lips. Persephone takes the knife and slowly moves toward Kairos, placing it at his lips. "Open," she commands. He does and then she says, "That's it. Now, bite down." Kairos bites down on the blade, careful not to nick the corners of his mouth. "Good," she praises.

Persephone sits up, leaning back as she gyrates once again. Placing her hands on his chest, she pushes off him as she fucks him. She covers him in her slick, the moisture pooling beneath her as sloppy sounds fill the night while her pussy devours him.

"Titans be damned," Kairos mumbles.

"Yes," Persephone moans. "Almost there, my loves. Almost there."

I shift to the edge of my throne. "What did she fucking say?"

I know those words, know what they preceded. I hear them ringing in my ears each night as I lay restless.

Persephone leans forward, resting her swollen breasts on Kairos' chest, as her pebbled nipples brush against him. She reaches above him, urging him up as she grabs his bound hands.

They both rise, Kairos placing his hands over Persephone's head as he holds her to him.

She circles her hips, his cock sliding in and out of her effortlessly.

Kairos' head falls back, the feeling overtaking him, and he is so caught up in the moment, his eyes closed as he gives in to her, that he doesn't see her face change. But I do.

Persephone moves quickly, pulling the dagger from between Kairos' teeth. She slices the corners of his lips as she withdraws, and his eyes shoot open as shock dresses his features. Then, quickly, effortlessly, Persephone slits Kairos' throat.

She bathes in Kairos' blood, relishing in the feeling as his life force spurts out with every heartbeat, escaping from the gash across his carotid.

The warmth drips off Persephone's nipples and cascades down her abdomen, and still, she continues to ride him. "That's it," she mutters. "That's what we needed. It's good, isn't it? So good," she moans.

That bitch is using my words as she fucks the man to death. "Fuck you! You... you... FUCK!"

I don't realize I've been grasping my chalice, and the bones crack. It falls to pieces, and the skull shatters at my feet.

Kairos' eyes close, his head going limp, and Persephone finally comes, her body shaking as her thighs quiver while she pants noisily.

With Kairos still inside her, she raises his arms over her head and pushes him back to where his body thuds on the ground, bouncing slightly as he lands.

Looking down at him, Persephone's chest rises and falls quickly. She laughs, one brief chuckle at first, but then she cackles maniacally, the sound filling the night.

She doesn't stop, she just looks at the dagger in her hand, raising it into the moonlight before setting it on the ground beside Kairos' still body.

The sight of Persephone, in those moments following Kairos' death, will haunt me for all time. It will replace the images of Adonis as the life left his eyes, and I will never look at her the same way again.

When she finally stops laughing, Persephone leans forward, catching her breath as she lies on Kairos' still chest. His blood has become sticky, its tackiness making eerie sounds as she shifts against him.

She rises slightly, taking Kairos' chin in her hands, and shakes his head from side to side. "You know what, Kairos?" she asks aloud. "I think I like you best this way."

~

The next morning, I watch as Persephone is readying for the day. She acts as if nothing has changed. She acts as if she hadn't snuffed out the light of a man the night before, leaving his body in the field to be found the following day.

Demeter is in the kitchen, readying the meal, when Persephone walks in. "Are you ready?" she asks.

Persephone raises a brow. "Ready? Ready for what?"

"To go back... to Hades? Your husband?" she asks, her tone filled with bewilderment.

Persephone announces, "Oh, him. Yeah, I don't think I'm going to go."

My head pounds as she utters those words. The audacity of that girl. After all that I have done for her? All I've sacrificed?

"You're not going?" Demeter asks.

"No," Persephone answers pointedly. She sits unaffected as her mother places a plate before her.

Demeter wants to say something, but refrains and they eat their meal in silence. When they finish, Persephone becomes ill and Demeter rushes from the table, grabbing a towel from beside the waste bin.

She returns and hands it to Persephone. "Are you alright?" she asks.

Persephone smiles up at her mother and then wipes the vomit from the corner of her mouth. "I'll be fine," she assures her.

She gathers the pile from the table and is walking to the bin when she throws up again, dropping the towel at her feet.

Demeter walks over and picks up the rag, toweling the mess off the floor. She takes it to the bin and is about to toss it in when she stops. She opens the towel and is looking at the contents within. "Persephone?" she calls out.

"What?" Persephone asks.

"Did you eat while in the Underworld?"

"Well, yeah," Persephone answers, taking a drink of water.

Demeter walks toward her. "What was the last thing you ate?"

"Oh, I don't know. The last day was weird, and I-"

"What did you eat?" Demeter is frantic, taking and shaking Persephone's shoulders.

"Pomegranate. Why?" Persephone looks worried as her mother stands silently, her eyes wide. "Why, mother?"

"You have to go back."

She shakes out of her mother's grasp. "Wha... no!"

Then Persephone becomes violently ill, retching all down the front of her gown.

Demeter demands, "You have to. This will continue until you do."

CHAPTER 15
SHADOW OF MY FORMER
SELF (PERSEPHONE)

It's ruined! Pomegranate juice soaks my gown, the seeds clinging to the bustline as I look at myself in the mirror. There are crimson splotches dying the soft crepe-like fabric, so I pull it over my head and throw it to the floor in anger, kicking it away with my foot.

I stand naked in front of the mirror, surveying my features as my hands trail up my neck. I stop. *I have to go back to him. Have to return to the man, the god, whose hands will replace my own.*

My face hardens, and I squeeze, encircling my throat with my hand. I cut off my airway, my face turning colors as my image flickers and my vision darkens. Just before I black out, I release my hold.

I won't do it. Won't give up this feeling, this power. I will not return to Hades... and that is that.

Wiping off the sickness still clinging to my skin, I use the basin sitting on the table next to the mirror and freshen up, dropping my cloth in it.

I dress in a simple ivory gown, tying the sash at my waist as I cinch it in. I smooth the skirts and then look at myself in the mirror again, where I can practically see Hades' silvery eyes staring back at me. I can feel his hands as they caress my arms, the nails trailing down them.

Walking back down the hallway and into the kitchen where my mother sits at the table worrying her lip, she looks up when I enter.

"Perse-"

I hold up my hand. "I don't want to hear it, mother. It's like you said. This is the one place where I do indeed have a choice. I'm not giving that up."

My mother opens her mouth to respond, but says nothing. She closes her mouth and then stands, crossing her arms as she stares at me.

"I'm fine, see. No more sickness, and before you speak, know this: my life in the Underworld is not a pleasant one."

"But Hades loves you," she says, reaching for me. "I would have never allowed this, this... arrangement, if your father didn't believe as much." She drops her arms when I step back.

"My father?" I grit out, placing my hands on my hips. "He would not even allow me to speak when they were arranging it. He dismissed me and said that it was no concern of mine." My hands flail about as I rant.

"No concern?" She fists her hands. "How is the matter of your life of no concern?" She speaks with her hands, pointing at me as her anger builds, "The nerve of those two, two..."

"Assholes!" I blurt out, motioning toward the door.

"That is not the word I was leaning toward, but yes. Those assholes!"

I laugh aloud, my mother's anger warming my heart. That is why I love her so. Even though it will be a losing battle, for me, she will fight Hades and my father all the same.

Just then, a knock comes at the door, startling my mother.

I step back, unsure of what or who waits on the other side as she opens the door.

A man speaks to her and they exchange words for some time before she thanks him. He bows, turning to leave and she shuts the door on him, turning around to face me; the color drained from her face.

"I'm only going to ask you this once," she says. She pauses, wringing her hands in her skirt as she looks over her shoulder at the door and then at me. "Where were you last night?"

"Last night? Out, why?" I stand looking at my nails, picking the jagged skin on one of them. It bleeds and I place it in my mouth, sucking it clean.

"Out where, Persephone? And with whom?" she asks.

I remove my finger from my mouth. "Just visiting friends. Nothing special," I answer nonchalantly, wiping the finger on my skirt.

"Which friends?"

I don't answer. I just plop down in the chair, crossing my legs as I lean back. "What's the big deal? I just went out for a couple of hours. Besides, I was back in my bed well before dawn."

"What's the big deal? What's the big deal?" her voice rises as her anger builds.

My mother stomps across the room, grabs me by the neckline of my gown, and hauls me up. She stares down into my face, the skin around her eyes crinkling as she narrows her gaze on me.

"A man is dead, Persephone, and you want to know what the big deal is?" She searches my face, but I give nothing away, standing unaffected.

"So what? A man is dead. What business is that of mine?"

"Not just any man, Persephone. It is the same man you've been strutting around with for months. Everyone saw you two together. Everyone knew you two were doing the Titans know what until all hours of the night. And now, someone found that very man brutally murdered the morning you are set to return to the ruler of death. His father is beside himself and the finger is being pointed at you."

"They think I killed him?" I huff in astonishment, falling into my chair. "Why would I-"

"No, Persephone, they don't think you killed him. But their

assumptions that your husband played a hand in his death are not too far of a stretch, now, are they?"

"Hades? They think Hades did it?" I chuckle, leaning back in my chair.

"This is no laughing matter, Persephone. I am the goddess of creation and, despite that, they are holding me at fault for this loss. The villagers are raging outside my temple, asking that I deliver you to answer for this."

"Mother, no!" I wail.

"Yes. I will have no choice." She walks past me, sinking into her chair, defeated. "I have until midday."

I jump to my feet. "You can't!"

"I must! More importantly, you have to go willingly."

I step toward my mother. "I won't. I did nothing wrong."

She holds up her hand, stopping me. She looks toward the window and says forlornly, "It is done."

"Mother, this is lunacy. Asking me to answer for a wrong I haven't committed. What justice is this?"

She looks over her shoulder at me. "They don't seek justice, Persephone. They seek vengeance." Her jaw clenches, and she shakes her head. "You now have no choice. You must return to Hades or face their reckoning."

"And these are the people you hold in high regard? You are a god, mother. If I was you-"

"But you're not me!" She stands, stepping toward me. "You're not me and you do not hold the responsibility to these people as I do. You don't care about them. You don't need them."

"Need them? They need you, not the other way around," I implore.

"You're wrong!" She shakes her head. "I need them. Without their support, their love, my power dwindles. It's give and take, Persephone."

"The harvest is over, the world will soon slumber, and you have time."

Frantically, she reaches out, shaking my arms. "Time for what?"

"Time for them to forget. By the time they need you once again, all of this will be in the past." I pull free of her.

"This will not go away, Persephone. If at midday I do not deliver you to the temple, they will, in fact, come for you. You can't stay here." Her face falls.

"Where will I go?" my voice shakes, and I wrap my arms around myself.

Placing her hands on my arms, she says, "The one place they will not dare set foot." She rubs up and down to soothe me.

I look pleadingly in her eyes. "Do you know what you're saying? What you ask of me?"

"I'm not asking you; I'm telling you. Go now and don't return." She drops her arms, turning her back on me.

"But mother?" I step toward her, and she pushes me away, turning toward the window.

"This is the way it must be. It's for your own good." She sniffles, not turning to look at me.

I sulk back to my room and pack a small satchel, not forgetting the dagger Erymanthe delivered to me while walking through the fields several days past, when she gave me the instructions for its use. Then I return to the kitchen where my mother is standing by the window, looking blankly at the world outside.

"If I leave... I'm never coming back. You know that, right? Once I step out that door, this is no longer my home," I assert.

"Your home is with Hades now," she states coldly.

My mother doesn't meet my gaze. She doesn't turn and watch as I walk toward the door. She just stares out that damned window.

Stepping over the threshold, I turn, shutting the door behind me. I place my palm on the wood, tracing the floral designs on the door one last time, committing them to memory, before turning and walking away.

I am stepping through the gate at the edge of the garden when he appears. He's just standing there with his arms crossed, veins popping, and midnight-colored robes cinched with a golden cord.

"Trouble in paradise?" Hades asks.

I snarl, "What are you doing here?"

"Is that any way to greet your husband?" He opens his arms to me.

"I was just leaving," I say, not stepping into his invitation to embrace. "You're free to stay, though I'm not sure you'd be all too welcome." I push past him, leaving him standing with his arms wide.

He drops his arms. "And why is that?"

I stop, turning to face him. "It seems there is some unrest in the village."

"Is there, now?" He grins. "And what business is that of mine?"

"I suppose it's not. Just like my comings and goings are no business of yours," I say flippantly.

He steps toward me. "That is where you are wrong, my love. Your wellbeing is of my highest concern."

"My wellbeing? Really?" I take a step back, not taking my eyes off of him. I stare him down; the silence growing between us. "Tell that to Adonis." I snort my disgust.

His face twists, and Hades stomps toward me.

Picking me up, he throws me over his shoulder, slamming the gate behind us. He trudges up the hill, and once we are some distance from the house, he throws me down.

I land on my ass; the impact sending pain coursing up my spine, and I fall backward into the grass. "What now?" I huff as I prop myself up on my elbows.

Hades lords over me. "I wanted you to come peacefully, but seeing as you chose to be a little brat about it, this will have to do."

He stomps his foot, breaking the ground apart beneath us, and then we fall. We fall through the darkness, the screeching of the night creatures surrounding us as we do.

Hades lands first, his colossal frame sending up dust as the force of his feet impact the ground beneath him before he catches me in his arms. He throws me over his shoulder once again, beginning his trek through the elaborate cave system.

The twisting and winding rock walls narrow in around us, as torches illuminate the way ahead. When the narrowing ends, the system opens up into a large cave where stalagmites and stalactites have formed along the far left of the space, jutting up from the cave floor and haphazardly seeming to drip from the ceiling above the sinter pools.

Columns appear the farther into the system we go, and as we step through the last set, large pyres sit burning on each side of the path.

Mumbling echoes fill the cave, the voices of the departed bouncing off the flower-like crystals formed above the pools as they wander slowly through the labyrinth that leads to the Underworld. Their muffled cries of confusion fill my ears and the whoosh of flames greet us as we reach the end.

Hades sets me down once we reach the gates, the opening at the end of the labyrinth near the River Styx where hundreds of souls mill about as his horsemen, the guardians of the Underworld, and Charon, go about their duties; dividing and ferrying the souls to the other side.

Several of the departed cry out as they reach the Ferryman because with no tithe or offering, no coins to buy their passage, the guards corral them, their horses stomping toward them as they're driven into the river.

Hades walks through the throng, striding up the planks onto the boat waiting at the river's edge as Charon holds up his hand, halting all those wanting to board.

Charon finally steps onto the vessel so we can depart, and as I hang from Hades' shoulder, the blood rushing to my head, I look into the river and see those souls; the departed who'd been driven to the river when they'd had no payment for their passage.

Their gnarled, decrepit hands rise from the water, as their ghastly faces remain trapped beneath the surface; the tortured Nevermore.

They call out to me, their muffled screams beckoning me to save them. But I can't save them. Underworld, I can't even save myself.

Now, here I am, back in the grasp of the one person, the one god, I'd hoped to escape, once again the Queen of Death.

~

I spend the next days in my room, Hades allowing me my space and time to "reflect."

Reflect? I snort. *As if I need to reflect on anything. I am the Queen of Death, right? So, I did as my title requires. What's the big deal, anyway?*

Why hadn't it worked, the stone? Why hadn't I been able to wield the power and hide my deeds? A piece of my soul was supposed to entwine with his upon his death, but it hadn't. The woman had said..., oh, forget it. It is too late for that, anyway. I won't sit here and keep dwelling on what should have happened, but on what did. On how what happened had made me feel. *That's right, feel.*

I didn't think I could feel again after Adonis. Didn't think I could muster anything other than anger or helplessness. But somehow, I coaxed something from myself. Somehow, the acts I carried out in the field that night with Kairos had awakened something. Albeit, something primal and vicious, but something spawned to life the minute that blade carved through flesh. And when his blood blanketed my skin, the warmth, the life that glazed over my entirety, I knew that was what it was like to truly feel alive.

I long for that feeling. I yearn for it. I want to dance my fingers through the tacky remnants of another's life force as it slips through my fingers because there is power in it; taking a life. A power that fed a part of me that had been ravenous.

I need to feed that piece of me again, but I know it will be months before I have the opportunity, nay, the pleasure. So, that hunger will remain unsatisfied until then.

As I lay back on my bed, fantasizing about that feeling, the revelation hits me: *maybe there is something else residing within the chest that can give me the power I crave?*

Sneaking from my room, my bare feet pad down the corridor. I pass the dining hall, not bothering to peek inside because Hades will be at the docks tending to the arrivals and managing his responsibilities in Tartarus before he ever graces me with his presence, so I have time.

The dampness of the stone floor coats my feet, the soles turning black from the ash scattered beneath the torches as I turn the corner and there it is; the door to the treasure room. At least that's what I call it, because what other name befits a room full of magical gems and trinkets?

I push open the heavy door, the hinges creaking as I muscle my way inside and shut it behind me, the bottom scraping against the floor in opposition as it rakes against the uneven ground.

Once inside, I walk toward the chest. It is just where I'd left it, nestled against the far wall, cloaked in shadows.

I raise the lid and, knowing I have more time to nose around, pull the top tray out and place it at my feet. I have already memorized the stones in the top tray, so now to see what lies beneath it.

The second tray contains nothing of note, just your standard diamonds and miscellaneous gems. But the third tray, as I paw my way through it, has one stone that sparks my interest. One item whose sheen solidifies that it will be in my possession once I leave; an iridescent jewel the size of a grape with black and gold striations snaking across the surface.

I lift the stone from its placement, take it and the scrap of paper beneath it, and walk toward the torch affixed to the far wall. I unfold the paper, and the words *Subjugation Stone* appear.

"Subjugation Stone?" I whisper, and as the words leave my lips, text appears on the parchment in gold glowing letters; a hidden text only those words spoken aloud reveal.

I am confused. It's a word, yes, but also a person. A person I know, and if saying her name aloud unlocks the power of the stone, then I know exactly how I can use this stone for my benefit.

"Peithō," I say aloud, more hidden text appearing on the parchment; instructions guiding me through the use and purpose of the stone.

I didn't have the parchment when I said the name of the Infinity Stone and it appeared to come to life, so maybe I hadn't, in fact, unlocked its power.

My eyebrows rise in astonishment, and looking back over my shoulder at the door, I pace back toward the chest.

I pick up the stray parchment, the one I assume is for the Infinity Stone, tuck it in my cleavage, place the trays back inside, paying particular attention to their order, and then leave the room.

Discretely nestling the stone between my breasts, snuggled up to the parchment, the edges of both dig into my flesh as I walk down the corridor and back to my room.

Once inside, I hide the stone in a small scrap of fabric. I then take a candle from beside my bed and drip some wax on the scrap. After the fabric is tacky with the wax, I kneel, pressing it underneath my bedside table, affixing it. Another stone to add to my collection.

The Infinity Stone is also hidden beneath that same table, and I reach underneath, retrieving it.

While holding the stone in one hand, and the parchment in the other, I say the name, "Infinity Stone."

The Infinity Stone glows, and just like the parchment of the Subjugation Stone, hidden golden text appears. The words are fainter than the others, but I am certain I can still read it.

"Apeiron," I call out, and the stone heats up.

The stone brands the infinite symbol in the center of my palm, and I drop it to the floor, shaking my hand to ease the pain.

"What in the Titans was that?" I ask to no one in particular.

I look down at my hand, my other bracing my wrist as I breathe through the burning. I'm panting now, hoping that soon this agony will end.

I open my hand, and there, in the middle, an angry, red infinity symbol flickers. "So much for it being hidden," I curse the old woman. "How do I go about hiding this?"

I lift my hand in the air and no sooner had I voiced my thought of hiding the mark, had a wind rushed through my room, blowing a healing breeze across my raised palm.

I lower my hand and the symbol is gone.

I call out, "How... how is this possible?" I look around for some wielder of magic to step forth and claim responsibility, but no one does, and nothing happens. *Or so I think.*

CHAPTER 16
QUEEN OF DEATH
(PERSEPHONE)

I take my meals in my room, doing my best to avoid Hades at all costs. He knocks on my door, asks if I need anything, and then leaves a tray outside. The sound of his footsteps fade and then I sneak out and retrieve the tray, bringing it inside. I eat alone and then place the empty tray outside my door. He will eventually retrieve it, not bothering to announce himself before taking it away.

This can work, this indifferent existence. He can go about his life, seeing to his responsibilities, and I can go about mine.

I'd been back for what seemed like only a handful of days, when Hades enters my room for the first time since my return.

He says gruffly, "I need you to come with me."

"You need me-"

"It's not up for discussion. Make yourself presentable and come with me," he commands.

"Presentable? Presentable as in...?"

"As in clothed. As in, something other than the disheveled state you find yourself in now. Presentable," he asserts.

I cross my arms. "What's wrong with how I am now?"

"Oh, I don't know, let's see? You haven't bathed, your hair is a mess, and your gown…" he trails off.

I look down at my sheath. "What's wrong with my gown?"

"It's transparent," he says matter-of-factly.

I cock my hip in frustration. "And?"

"And I'll not have you by my side looking like-"

"Looking like what? Your harlot? Isn't that what I am?" I grab my gown and tear it from my body. I then ball it up in my fist and throw it at his feet. "How about this? Is this better? Why don't we show them how I really am, how you prefer me?" I seethe, my face contorting as my whole body shakes.

"I-"

"You what?" I challenge. "Are you saying this isn't how you prefer me?" I saunter up to him, standing within arm's reach, disgust dressing my features as I glare up into his face. I take his hand and place it around my throat. "Say it!"

Hades drops his hand, his face wearing the shock his body evidently doesn't share. He steps away from me, turns and leaves the room, closing the door behind him.

Through the door I hear him plead, "Could you just make yourself presentable? That's all I ask. Can you just do one thing I ask? Please?"

He is begging me? Me! Where was this restraint when I begged him to spare Adonis? Where was it when I pleaded for him to let me go? Where?

Sitting at my vanity fuming, I tear through my hair. I create one braid on each side of my temples and then fasten them at the back of the crown of my head.

I leave the rest of my hair down, cascading across my shoulders. Then I pick out a simple black gown and put it on, tying it at the waist.

I smudge a dark liner around my eyes and look in the mirror. "Too clean," I say as I appraise my reflection. So, I rub the liner, smoking it out above and below my eyes. "That's better." I sigh and rise from my chair.

Hades is just outside my door, leaning against the wall, when I exit. "Was that so hard? Now you're presentable."

"Yeah, well, I'm still missing something," I say, pointing at my head.

"What?" Hades' look of confusion is a foreign sight to me.

"What queen do you know that doesn't have a crown?" I cross my arms.

"How about the kind that doesn't fucking need one? The kind that walks beside a king who also doesn't fucking need one."

"Well... I want one!" I assert.

"Too fucking bad," he scoffs.

I plant my feet. "I want one... or I am not moving another inch."

"You can come of your own free will or I will fucking drag you from the palace kicking and screaming!"

"You wouldn't dare!" I provoke, stepping into him.

"Fucking watch me!"

Hades hauls me up and tosses me over his shoulder like it is nothing, and I do just as I'd threatened; kicking and screaming every step of the journey.

He walks out of the palace with me screaming and banging my fists against his back, and makes his way to the docks where the souls are arriving. They stand in line by the hundreds on this side, with more being ferried over by the boatload. They just stare at me, draped over his back and flailing about, but the scene I am making doesn't faze a single one of them.

As we reach the scales, Hades sets me down beside him. I huff, straighten my gown, and scowl in his direction.

He motions toward a dais positioned beside the scales and I take the two steps up to the platform, standing beside a large throne made of bones fused together with gold as he ascends. Dozens of gilded skulls frame the tufted back of the chair, and mounted guards sit posted on each side, riding the same imposing steeds from the stables;

stallions with manes the color of midnight, tipped with glowing red flames.

Hades sits down and calls out, "Proceed!"

One by one, souls step onto the scales and Hades measures each one, making his judgement before sending them either to Elysium or Tartarus.

It had been hours standing there while Hades passed his judgment, leaning back in his chair, propped up on one elbow as he waved two fingers in the direction to which the scales determined.

I am getting restless, and am about to ask if I can leave, when Hades sits straight in his chair. His eyes scan the line, stopping when they land on a familiar face.

Oh, please gods, no!

Hades points at the line. "That one. Bring him to the front," he instructs.

The guard does as Hades commands, his horse nudging the man forward with its muzzle. And as I look on in horror, Kairos steps to the front, taking his place on the platform.

I watch the pointer, holding my breath as the scales read in his favor, and I exhale, breathing a sigh of relief as Kairos steps down.

Hades holds up one finger, causing the guards to place a spear at Kairos' back before forcing him back onto the scales. Once again, the scales determine a reckoning in his favor, but they won't let him leave.

Hades, who had been ignoring me this entire time, turns toward me. "You asked, 'what queen do I know that doesn't have a crown,' and I counter with what queen do you know that doesn't rule?" His eyes blaze a bright silver, the ether sparking in his irises. "Well, Queen of Death, what say you?"

"It's obvious," I say. "The scales rule in his favor."

"True." Hades strokes his chin, his fingernails bouncing along the growth of stubble. "But still..." he trails off, "I want to hear it from your lips." His canines flash as he smiles.

"Elysium," I say, looking away, refusing to give him the satisfaction.

He snarls, "Wrong."

"Wrong‽ How is it wrong‽" I counter.

"In many kingdoms..." he says, "the king may choose to overrule the queen. It just so happens that I reserve that right."

"You reserve that right‽" I fume.

"I do!" he seethes. "And also, I do so just to show you I can."

"Stop!" I plead, grabbing ahold of Hades' arm as the guards drag Kairos toward Tartarus. "I get it! I get it." I concede.

Hades holds up his hand, and the guards halt. "What exactly do you get, Persephone?" Hades looks down at me. "Do you understand the importance of one's life, or are you just coming to realize how selfish you've been?"

I mumble, "Both."

"Say it so I can hear you, so everyone can hear from you. Say it so you understand," he directs.

The words rush from my lips, "I do. I understand!"

"What is it you understand?" he coaxes me to continue.

I look out at everyone standing witness to the discourse between Hades and I. I step forward, wringing my hands as I worry my lip. My chin raises and I call out, "I understand how precious and how valuable every life is and acknowledge how selfish I have been in the taking of such." I step back, lowering my gaze as I wait.

"Well, Kairos..." Hades calls out, looking where Kairos stands on the scales. "Do you have anything to add? Anything in your defense?"

Kairos, who had been staring intently at me, looks at his feet.

"Nothing? Nothing at all?" Hades pauses, lifting his gaze toward me. "I think I will err on the side of caution," he announces.

I cry out, "Wha-? No! Please, no!"

Hades looks at Kairos once again. "I will allow this one mercy," he states. "Persephone will be the one responsible for your punishment.

One of her choosing. She will start every day doling it out. Perhaps then she will grasp the importance of the decisions she's made, and in doing such, will act in a manner more befitting of her title."

Kairos hangs his head.

"She may be the Queen of Death, but she is MY WIFE!" Hades clenches his jaw as he finalizes his ruling, pointing one finger toward Tartarus.

I fall to my knees, sobbing as the guards haul Kairos away to the gates and Hades motions to the guards at my side. "Take the queen back to the palace." As they are escorting me down from the dais, he calls out, "And Persephone…"

I look up, my tear-streaked face red and blotchy. "Yes?" I grit.

"Do see you find yourself in our chambers this evening. A king is no good without his queen by his side."

The guards pull me away, and as I fight against them, I turn, spitting on the ground at my feet.

Once back in the palace, and secured in my room, I unravel. I stand before my vanity, taking in my state, and a fit of laughter engulfs me.

Mussing my hair, I walk over to my bed, falling back against the soft coverlet. I grip the sheets at my side, laughing again.

"Gods, that was exhausting!" I sigh. "My WIFE!" I mock, in my best Hades impersonation. "More like your accessory."

The fatigue from feigning all that emotion weighs on me.

"No! Please, no!" I mimic my earlier performance. "And to think he's going to grant Kairos mercy? Him? I'll show him mercy. If he thinks I'm going to take it easy on Kairos, that I regret my actions? Well, HUSBAND…" I sneer, "you will find out tomorrow just how wrong you are."

I sink into my bedding, imagining all the ways I can show Hades just how depraved I can be. Will I flay the skin from Kairos' bones and feed them to Cerberus as he had with Adonis, or will I slice into him, over and over, reveling in the blood as it spills at my feet? What will do it? What will make the god of death fear the woman he's forced to be by his side?

What if it backfires? What if everything I do, everything I choose to do, only stokes the embers of his passion for me?

But then again, what if it doesn't?

I know what is coming. I know where I should go. But I also know that once Hades makes his way into the palace for the night, he expects me to be in OUR room. So, I make my way to the dining hall, and for the first time since my return, sit down for a proper meal.

Finding peace in the silence, the only sounds invading the space are the torches blazing along the walls, so I eat my meal and then go back to my room to clean up and change.

Once inside, I change out of my flowing black gown and don a deep purple silk one; thin and sheer.

I can see my darkened areolas and the peaks of my nipples as they press against the fabric as a high slit rises to my hips, gold braiding along the seams to where the neckline plunges.

Walking over to my vanity, I sit before it, my eyes fixing on the face that stares back at me. I grin because I have an idea; a wicked, sinful idea. Maybe an awful idea, but only time will tell.

I arrange my hair loosely atop my head and pin curls at the crown while leaving some strands loose on one side of my face. I then open the top drawer and pull out a small container of body paint, setting it aside. I collect my cloth from atop the table and begin wiping away the excess liner around my eyes.

"Soft and subtle," I say to myself. That is the look I am going for. Something demure and alluring.

Applying a rouge to my cheeks that complements my cinnamon freckles, I select a darker berry to stain my lips. I then take the container of paint and lift the lid before taking a small brush from off the table.

I dip the brush in the gold paint and create elaborate swirling designs that start at each finger, trailing upwards where they conclude at the base of my throat. I then intricately decorate the tops of my full breasts, where they spill out the top of the gown and start on my legs. When I finish, I have gilded myself from head to toe in tiny vines and leaves.

I am a thing of beauty. Irresistible. Not that I think it will matter. So, after I complete fixing myself up, I walk down the hall to Hades' chamber.

I won't call it OUR room. It isn't OUR anything. It is his. Everything is; even me. And I hate knowing that. Hate that I have no say.

One day that will change, but for tonight, I can be his whore. He can use me, and if nothing else comes from it, at least I can satisfy my body.

CHAPTER 17

LOVE INTO A WEAPON
(HADES)

"If she wants a crown, then I'll give her one," I snarl as I finish weighing the souls, sending them off to their afterlife. I then make my way into Tartarus because I have unfinished business and I won't be leaving empty-handed.

Placing the finishing touches on Persephone's crown, I wipe my hands clean of the blood that remains.

It had been no easy feat; bending, breaking, and gilding all the pieces in place. But after a couple of hours, I finish the task. Even so, it is still missing something.

Making my way back to the palace, I pass Persephone's and then our room before continuing down the corridor. I pass the dining hall, turn the corner, and head straight toward my archives where I sling open the door, the bottom scratching against the uneven stones at the threshold.

"I have to remember to fix those," I fuss aloud, closing the door behind me as the latch clanks in place.

As I walk over to the chest in the far corner, the dim lighting hardly illuminates my path; another thing I should remedy, but that is a problem for another time. For now, my goal is to finish the piece in my hands.

I look down to where the crown rests in my left hand, droplets of blood still crusting the corners. I think about wiping it clean, but stop myself.

"She'll take what I offer and she'll like it." I stiffen, dropping my left hand, and the crown dangles from my grip at my side.

I lift the lid on the last chest lined along the wall and begin sifting through the contents. Each gem I pick up seems wrong; isn't befitting of a crown for the Queen of Death.

Which should it be? Which one is intended for her? As I lift the Kingmaker Emerald, I know I have found the last piece; the last element to adorn the crown of my queen.

The Kingmaker Emerald sits in the crease of my palm where its cushion cut and faceted design draws in what little light shines in the room.

I hold the gem, turning it over as the faint firelight from the torches glints across the surface. I toss it up and fist it into my palm.

"That's the one," I say, slamming the lid of the chest. Then, straightening, I place the stone in the discrete pocket of my gown and turn, walking from the room, and closing the door behind me.

I pull, but the door sticks, so I jerk it again, the bottom splintering as I force it across the raised stones.

"Ugh! Just another fucking problem," I sigh.

Frustrated about the state of my palace, I stomp down the hall toward our room. I turn the corner and stop, taking a deep breath to calm myself.

It isn't Persephone's fault; the door. It is just another thing for me to handle. I crave a state of peace and I need to be different. I promised I would be. Assured Adonis of such.

I smooth my unruly hair with my right hand, still carrying the crown in my left, and step into the throne room.

Once inside, I pull out the stone and call forth my fire, sending indigo flames flicking across my fingertips as the light refracts through the enormous emerald in my palm.

The stone heats, and I hold it to the front of the crown at its center. Heat radiates into the gold connection points and soon, with some coaxing from me, I affix the stone.

Turning the crown in my hands, I send my flames away as I admire my masterpiece. "Perfect," I say.

The gold cools, and I wipe the embers from the gem where it is now placed high atop the crown. Soot from the embers now compliments the crusted blood on my fingertips, and I clean most of it off, but some remains beneath my fingernails, so that will have to do.

I walk from the throne room and make my way to our room. I open the door, and to my surprise, Persephone is waiting.

Walking through the doorway, I turn my back to her as I close the door. Still facing away from her, I walk to the far wall and place the crown in a chair. When I turn around, I see Persephone propped up in the bed, with the skirts of her gown flowing around her outstretched legs as her lips wear a menacing grin.

She is radiant. She has messily gathered her hair atop her head and several strands hang loose, framing her face. Freckles sprinkle her bare shoulders, but I can't help but notice the gold vines and leaves encircling her ankles and snaking up her thighs. The same intricate tracings adorn her hands and arms, their lines drawing my attention to her full chest.

"My king," she purrs.

I just raise a brow in her direction. "Is that so?" I ask. "To what do I owe this sudden change toward me?"

"Can't a wife be happy to see her husband?"

"Wives can, but you never have been." I cross my arms.

Persephone sits up, puffing her lips in a pout. "Is that any way to greet your queen?"

"I'm sorry, but did I miss something? Several hours ago you spat at me and this, this... change..." I motion toward her, "begs one to question."

I shake my head in disbelief, chuckling to myself as I walk over to the basin on the other side of the room where I rinse my hands, wiping the remnants of the blood and soot from them.

As I stand with my back toward Persephone, I hear the bed shift, and then bare feet padding across the stone floor toward me. Not turning around, I towel my hands dry, dropping the rag to the floor. I sigh, my shoulders dropping as my hands hang limply at my sides.

Persephone steps into me, her breasts pressing into my back as she lays her head against my shoulder. Her face feels cool against my bare skin and she traces the bottom edge of my shoulder blade, her soft lips trailing kisses down my spine. Her hands grip my arms, and I freeze.

I pull away, stepping to the side. "Not that I don't appreciate... whatever this is." I motion toward her, my eyes catching on the peaks of her breasts. I glance up, shaking my head to release myself from the sight of her.

She steps toward me. "I just thought..."

I hold up my hand, halting her. "Let me decompress. I've had a long day, and you were quite the spectacle earlier."

"Me‽ And what of you, huh? Forcing me up in front of everyone while you passed your judgement?"

"That's my job, Persephone. It's what I do," I announce.

She scoffs, "It's what you do? Is making a fool out of me also what you do?"

"I did no such thing," I offer, walking toward the bed and sitting down to remove my sandals.

"You sure as shit did." She walks toward me. "And what's worse, you enjoyed every minute," she proclaims.

"I took no pleasure in forcing the truth from your lips."

"The truth? Whose truth? Certainly not mine." She walks around to the other side of the bed, sitting on the edge with her back facing me.

Rising from the bed, I walk around it to stand in front of her.

"Would you like me to apologize?"

She pouts, looking up at me. "Yes."

I reach down, cupping Persephone's face in my hands. I rub my thumbs across her cheeks and then lean down, placing a soft kiss on her lips. While still at eye level, I tilt her chin up, surveying her features as she stares back at me, a fire burning in her eyes.

This is what I want. The way she's looking at me is everything I hoped for: the need, the fire. Her look has my breath catching in my throat.

"I'm sorry," I say, meeting her stare. "I could have handled the situation better," I admit.

"Or let things unfold as intended," she refutes.

"And what, let Kairos dance into Elysium after he ravaged MY WIFE for the Titans know how many months?" I tense, readying for her opposition. Persephone moves to stand, and I push her back. "Sit the fuck back down," I command. "This conversation is not over." My hands remain on her shoulders as she looks up at me in shock. "Do you think I enjoyed watching him as he groped and pawed at you? Do you think it pleased me that MY WIFE gave herself to some... some baker?"

"You're hurting me," she whimpers, pulling away. "And why do you always say it like that, MY WIFE?"

"Because you are MY WIFE! Have been for over half a year. That fact didn't suddenly change when you stepped foot in the mortal realm."

"Why does it even matter? You don't love me, you said it yourself," she accuses.

"I said no such thing." I sit down on the edge of the bed next to her. "What I said was the day you deign to love me, hope that at that time I still have love for you. Those were my exact words," I oppose.

"Exactly! Because if you truly loved me, it wouldn't matter what I've done." She looks away.

"Well, that's a convoluted version of love if I've ever heard of one. Actions have consequences, Persephone. Love can grow, but it can also dwindle. And at the rate you're going, it'll be snuffed out entirely," I parry.

"Fuck you!"

She rears back to slap me, and I catch her hand.

"Fuck me‽ Well, why didn't you say so? We could have skipped all the chitchat and gotten right to it."

CHAPTER 18

DOWNWARD SPIRAL (PERSEPHONE)

Hades moves so fast, crowding me. One minute he's lording over me as I sit defiantly on the edge of the bed, and the next he's forcing me back as he pins me down with his full weight.

He anticipates the fight coming, sprawling out as he pins my arms; one on each side of my head. His scent washes over me, purely masculine, with its woodsy and creamy undertones.

The musk is rich and powerful. It is decadent, exotic and earthy, even. Sandalwood, and something else. Cedar, maybe? It wafts through the air like the rising of incense as it burns in the temples while worshippers pray before a dais. But I won't pray to him. I won't grovel and worship at his feet. And I'll be damned if he thinks I will cower before him, either.

I arch my back, raising my hips off the bed as I attempt to buck him off me.

He barely lifts an inch, a smile dressing his lips as his eyes gleam that bright silver. The ether flashes, sparking as his pupils enlarge and he presses into me, his body reacting to the wriggling as my frustration builds.

"Get off me!"

"What's wrong, my love? I thought you wanted this?" he goads.

"And what gave you that impression?" I grit.

"Oh, I don't know. Maybe it was the fact you begged me to fuck you? That might have had something to do with it."

"I did no such thing. I-"

Hades crushes a kiss to my lips, halting my retort. His tongue leisurely darts out and traces my mouth as he seeks entrance, his nostrils flaring and breath heavy as he pants.

Caught in a lust spiral, Hades' hunger flames to life as his indigo flames fight to burst forth.

I want to get away, want to put as much distance between us as I can, but with each swipe of his tongue across my creases, he is pulling me down with him; drowning in his essence as his buttery scent marks my skin.

Hades is claiming me. Again. I am already his, have been for some time. I have been his since the priest proclaimed it as such, and yet, he still feels the need. He isn't of my choosing and I've never had a say. Even so, at this moment, he is the only thing I want.

Or what my body wants, anyway.

I open my mouth, and Hades graciously accepts my invitation. His forceful kisses turn to soft, passionate caresses, our tongues inter-twining as I drink him in.

My body reacts to him, my nipples pebbling beneath the gauzy fabric of my gown, and each time his chest heaves, the movement of him above me sends tiny shockwaves through me as the friction sends my senses into overdrive.

I yearn for him; a fire burning deep in my belly as my passion blooms deep within my core.

Hades pulls away slightly, stopping his exploration of my mouth.

"Hades," I plead breathlessly.

"I..." He just stares down at me, his eyes darting back and forth as he reins himself in. "I just need a minute." He lifts off me, one hand on each side of my head as he extends his arms and he rises slightly, a question in his eyes while he stares down at me. "What... what is this?"

"What is, what?"

"This!" He sits back on his heels, his arms raising as he gestures at me. "You're hot, you're cold, you loathe me, you don't. To be honest, I never know which Persephone is going to grace me with her presence," he argues.

I rise on my elbows, a look of disgust washing over me. "What did you expect? You have had my head twisted so far around I feel like an owl. Honestly, I don't know which way is up half the time. And I'm hot and cold? What about you?" I accuse.

"What about me?"

"Oh, no. You don't get to do that. You don't get to put all the blame on me for, as you said, 'whatever this is!'"

"Okay. So, talk to me!" he pleads.

"Talk to you‽ Are you serious, right now‽" I glower up at him.

Hades turns to the side and plops onto the bed beside me. He fists his hands, covering his eyes as he lets out an exaggerated growl. Once he settles, he lowers his hands to his sides and lets out a loud sigh.

"Just fucking talk to me, Persephone. What am I doing wrong here? Throw me a bone, a fucking lifeline for Titan's sake," he begs.

"You want me to talk to you‽ Now? Of all the times when we should have talked, you choose now as the opportune time?" My frustration seeps out of me. "Why now? Why is this the moment you choose to ask and hear what I have to say? It never mattered before."

I lower my head to the bed, my arms flattening at my sides. I fist the coverlet in my hands and we don't speak for some time, our breathing the only sound breaking the silence between us.

When Hades finally speaks, it is barely above a whisper. "You have always mattered."

I don't know what to do. Don't know what to say. This is a side of Hades I have never seen before. He had been gentle and sweet before, sure. But never had he been as raw and exposed as he seems now.

Staring at the draping above the bed, I ask, "Why do I matter?"

Hades rolls his head to look over at me. He raises his left hand toward me, his fingers brushing through the errant strands of my hair loose at my shoulder. "I don't know how to do this, Persephone. I'm no good at it."

I turn my face to look at him. "Yeah, no shit." I smirk.

Hades chuckles beside me, his fingers playfully tugging at my strands. "Ugh," he groans. "Do you have any idea how hard this is for me?"

"For you? And what, this is just a leisurely stroll across Asphodel for me?" I snicker.

We both laugh and then slowly, Hades rolls over onto his stomach. He leans his head against my ribs, and instinctively I run my fingers through his hair. His breathing slows, and we just lay in silence as our bodies relax into one another.

Hades clears his throat and then utters, "My mother didn't choose me."

My voice pitches up in confusion, "What?"

He nuzzles his head against my breast and lets out a huff. "Apparently, or so I've been told, I have mommy issues." He doesn't elaborate further.

"Mommy issues?" My brows furrow. "You have... mommy issues?" I clarify.

He offers a short, "Uh-huh."

"Now I'm gonna need a lifeline because I have no idea what that has to do with any of this."

Hades and I talk for what seems like hours. Volleying back-and-forth stories about our past and how we think those experiences molded us into the fucked-up beings we've become. He speaks about Rhea and his siblings, being open and honest about his fears and insecurities.

I am forthcoming about what happened with Kairos, the parts he didn't witness anyway, and how I felt in the moments following what I did.

He doesn't chastise or judge me, he just listens. He listens and seeks to understand.

To be honest, I am still trying to do the same.

He nestles up against me, listening to the sound of my voice as I gently run my fingers through his hair when he shifts.

"Wait." He grabs my hand, halting my affections. "You did all that to feel in control?"

I think about it for a moment. "Yeah. Something like that. At least that's why I think I did it."

"And the way in which you did it, and the things you said, was just to get back at me and take back the control you felt you lost... with me?"

"You make it sound so simple."

"Isn't it?" He rolls to the side, looking up at me for confirmation.

"I mean, I guess. I'd always thought my life would tick all the boxes. That I would live it as I'd imagined it," I offer.

He's confounded by my answer. "And it's not?"

I scowl down at Hades. "How could it be? How could this ever have been in anyone's plan? Let alone mine?"

"So, you never planned to get married and have a husband?"

I shift uneasily beside him. "I never planned for all of this," I gesture around us. "I never planned for you, a throne, the Underworld. I mean, come on. Who dreams about their future life and sees this as the end result?"

Hades looks insulted. Sitting up so fast I don't expect it, I freeze, my body tightening since I have no clue what his next move will be.

"What if I could give it back? Some of it, anyway?" he poses.

I sit up, scooting away slightly. "Give what back?"

He rushes through his next responses, "The control. What if you had a say? What if you had a choice?"

My eyebrows rise. "In being your wife?"

He answers curtly, "No. Not that. I'm sorry, my love, but I have already decided that."

Exasperated, I ask, "Well, then, what are we talking about?"

"What if I allowed you control… of me?" His eyes plead, his hands wringing in his lap.

"Control? Of you?" I burst out laughing so hard I am on the edge of hysteria.

Hades doesn't join in on my laughter. He just stares at me with wide eyes. His hands stop moving, and he shifts toward the end of the bed.

"Wait. Stop. Come back," I urge him, reaching out. "I'm sorry."

Hades sits at the edge of the foot of the bed.

"I was being serious, Persephone." He looks away.

"I see that." I choose my next words carefully. "Please, elaborate?"

Hades explains, perching on the edge of the bed, his eyes trained on me as he talks through what my control will look like.

It will start with little things; choosing the foods to be prepared, the styling of our room, and obligations to the realm. He outlines his vision for us as the king and queen.

He persuades me, "And there would be other ways, of course."

I stare deeply into his eyes, reach for his hands and ask, "What about in here?"

His face twists, not understanding my meaning. "In here?"

"What about… in here?" I string out the words.

I gesture towards the room, pointing out the apparatuses along the walls, and then stop at the table beside the bed where all his "toys" lie.

"Oh!" His eyes widen. "In here," his voice pitches up. "I see. So, you don't like the way things have been?" He drops his head, staring at his hands.

"I didn't say that. What I mean is, when can I be in charge… in here?"

"You want to… you want to be in charge?"

I nod my head to clarify. "Uh-huh."

"In... in here?" Again, his eyes widen as my meaning becomes clear.

"In here. Yes. I want to be in charge in here." I scoot across the bed until our hips touch. Looking up into his eyes, I ask, "Would that be so bad?"

I run my hand up his thigh, my fingertips caressing to the dip of his hip. I trace my fingers through his curls and then grip his already hardening length.

He sits as stiff as a teenage boy being groped for the first time by a hand other than their own and inhales deeply, gritting back a groan as I stroke him slowly, rotating my hand as it rises to his tip.

I squeeze hard, and he gasps. "You didn't answer my question," my voice is breathy as I circle my fisted palm around his tip once more. "Would that be so bad?" I click my tongue on the last word.

Hades doesn't answer, he just allows his head to fall back as his throat works a swallow.

"Hmmm?" I stop, pulling my hand away.

He chokes out the words, "That could be..." He clears his throat. "That could be good."

CHAPTER 19

THE HEART OF THINGS
(PERSEPHONE)

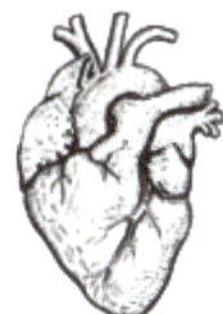

Hades sits ramrod straight at the end of the bed, and slowly I drape my leg across him. I straddle his lap, raising my skirts so that the softest parts of me brush against the softest (well, not so softest at the moment) parts of him.

As I ease down, a hiss escapes his lips. "I like control," he moans out. "Control is good."

I lick Hades' neck, stopping at the juncture where his crook meets the shoulder. I bite down and grind my hips into him. I then lean back, arching away from him as he holds my hips in place. I rock, allowing my juices to pool between us.

"Control is good, isn't it?" I coo, tilting my hips.

"So good." He pants, his nails digging into my flesh as he thrusts up against me. "So fucking good."

I moan, the friction of our bodies stoking a fire within me. I reach up and grab his jaw, applying a slight pressure to his throat as my nails dig in.

"Who's in control?" I ask.

"You," he grits out. "You're in control." He mouths a silent oh, as I scrape my nails down his Adam's apple.

Leaning forward, I draw his ear lobe into my mouth. I suckle and then nibble his soft flesh, nipping and tugging as my tongue darts across the smooth surface. I release his ear from between my teeth, whispering huskily, "Good boy."

Hades' hardened length throbs between us, jumping and pulsing with need.

I roll off him, throwing my leg over as I dismount. I get up from the bed and take a step toward the head of it when he reaches out and grabs my wrist. "Wait. Where do you think you're going?"

I wrap my hand around his, holding my wrist. Leaning toward him, I smile before I say, "I was planning to exercise some of the control you've allowed me. Unless, of course, you've taken it back?"

He releases my hand, shaking his head. "No. No, I have not."

"Good," I say, sauntering away. "Then lay back, close your eyes, and let me."

Hades falls back to the bed, his body sinking into the soft down of the mattress. He smiles, his canines in full view as he lays there with his eyes closed.

I walk over to the table displaying all of his "toys," grabbing two things; a leather strap and his knife. I can hear him shifting on the bed as he waits for me, and I untie the strings keeping my gown together, allowing it to fall to the floor. I then pad back to the edge of the bed and set my toys on the coverlet beside him.

Slowly I unfasten the leather band, holding his covering up, and throw the fabric of his gown open, exposing his impressive length to me. "Well," I exaggerate. "What have we here? Is all this for me?"

A rumble escapes Hades as his hearty laugh fills the air. "Really?"

"That's enough out of you, my king. I'm in charge, remember?" I tease.

"Fair enough," he says. "You're in jcharge."

"Good," I say, picking up the strap. "And you'll do well to remember that." I bring the strap down on Hades' inner thigh, just above the knee, and he grits out, a low growl escaping his lips.

Without moving another inch, and without opening his eyes, he answers, "Yes, my queen."

"That's more like it," I chirp, trailing the leather strap across his flesh, brushing it up and down him as if painting a canvas. "You know..." I pause, "you are a work of art, and your body is a fucking masterpiece."

Once again I deliver a lash, the leather strap streaking his skin with a welt where it slaps his outer thigh and ass.

Hades winces, his teeth gritting, and I walk toward the other side of him, dragging the leather across his abdomen as I do.

Once on the other side, I rear back and deliver a complimenting lash to that cheek and a mark twinning the one on his left side blooms.

My core tightens when he groans, so I ask, "How are we doing?"

Hades opens one eye to look at me, shifting his head. He moves without permission, and when he does, I strike again on the same side. This time he attempts to jerk away. But he is too late and now two lashes pinken his entire outer right thigh.

I toss the strap on the bed. "I don't remember giving you permission to move," I sing. Hades immediately closes his eye, a low grumble escaping, and lays back in his previous position. "That's better. Now, just relax."

Using my left hand to grab the knife, I crawl up the bed, positioning myself at Hades' hips by tossing my right leg over him. I lift my ass and grab his cock with my right hand, positioning it at my entrance. I slide down onto him, his head breaching my lips and filling me.

"You're so hard," I moan, lifting and lowering myself as I coat his shaft with my wanting.

Hades raises his hands, gripping underneath my thighs. I slap one away. "Uh-uh," I express my disdain, tsking at him as I stop moving. "No hands. No words. No control. I give and you receive. Understood?" Hades doesn't answer, so I press the knife in my left hand under his chin. "Do... you... understand?" I speak each word. "You can answer."

"Yes, my queen."

I move the knife away but don't lay it down. "Good. Shall we continue?"

"Yes."

"Yes, what?" I ask, running the knife down his ribs; bouncing over each protrusion.

"Yes, my queen."

"Excellent," I purr, squeezing my core around him.

Hades arches his back, his hips lifting slightly as he pulses inside me.

I place both hands on Hades' chest, one still gripping the knife, and begin rocking onto him again. His shaft slides in and out of my center, his head rubbing against my bundle of nerves when he withdraws.

I draw him out, his tip rubbing across my lips, and then slam back down on him, taking him as deep inside me as I can. Over and over, I bear down and coax the most glorious moans from his lips.

I beckon, "Come to me." And Hades rises to a seated position, not withdrawing from inside me as I curl my legs behind his back.

I place one hand on his shoulder and slice a small gash across the right side of his chest with my left hand. He grunts, and the ichor trickles down from where I made my cut; his god's blood seeping, its golden color pulsing with power.

"Now, fuck me within an inch of my life," I command.

His eyes spark, the ether pulsing in time with the throbbing of his cock inside me. His pupils dilate and I can see his indigo flames begging to be set free.

"Let go," I beg. "Let go and fall with me."

Hades grips my hips, his hold fierce and powerful. He pulls me farther onto him and then pushes me back before slamming into me again. He unleashes his power; the flames sloughing the skin from his gilded skull as the fire consumes him.

Burnt flesh from his face and head rises into the air as ash drifts away with our movements, and my hands cling to the remaining skin on his shoulders. But soon, it too will drift away as we burn.

Lowering my head to his chest, I trail my tongue through his god's blood, and he moans as I suck, taking his power into me.

His blood is thick and tangy, coating the back of my throat like vanilla and honey as I suck it down. The essence is intoxicating, and I can feel the power of the ichor as it amplifies my own.

I am drunk on the feeling, my body swaying as euphoria washes over me. Ichor, the golden essence of the gods, is invading me and making me whole as I burn inside and out; my skin feeling like his flames are licking across my skin.

I am melting deep down to my core as I too wait to turn to ash. And feeling him inside me, throbbing and wanting as his movements become more erratic, more urgent, my insides tighten.

I coil around him and he doesn't hold back. He does just as I commanded and lets go.

"Persephone," he moans. "You're... you're so hot."

I open my eyes, wanting to gaze upon his gilded bones as the indigo flames dance across the surface, but dark orbs stare back at me and his jaw slacks, gaping open.

I freeze. "What? What is it?"

"You're... you're on fire," he remarks.

I lean back, catching my breath as he stills, and I breathe, "I know."

"No, Persephone. You're actually on fire," he proclaims.

I look down and sure enough, deep purple flames dance across my chest, spreading down my torso. "That's new." I chuckle.

"It must be the ichor," he states. "My power must be... inside you." His dark sockets dim as the indigo flames subside from his skull.

"Is this... bad?"

"Not bad." He shakes his head. "Just different. I don't know."

"Well, then if it's not bad...," I say, shifting my hips, pressing against him, "then let's not waste what we've already started."

His cock stirs within me and he flips me onto my back, grabbing my hips in his hands as he plows into me once more. Then Hades does as I asked and fucks me until my vision blurs and my breath comes out in rasps.

My gasps and moans fill the air as he penetrates me over and over until he can take no more. I wrap my legs behind his back and hold him to me as we both reach release, our bodies quaking and quivering as our muscles tense.

His flames subside, his skin reforming, and mine are now a lavender hue as they extinguish as well. Then Hades rolls off me, plopping down beside me on the bed as we lay in silence, and our breathing slows.

He reaches for me, our fingers intertwining as he holds my hand. "That was…," he breathes.

"That was," I answer. "To be honest, I'm not sure what that was, but I can't wait to do it again."

Hades rolls toward me, his hand rising to caress my face. "My queen," he relishes.

"My king," I answer, looking longingly into his eyes that are now back to their storm cloud gray.

He sits up, his eyes twinkling as he says, "That reminds me." He then gets up from the bed, his glorious backside on full display as he strides across the room to where he picks something up from a chair in the corner.

He turns around, his hands behind his back, and waltzes back to the foot of the bed, where he stops. "I have something for you."

I prop up on my elbows, my neck craning as I look up at him. "A gift?" I ask. "For me?"

"For my queen," he proclaims, bringing his hands around in front of him and presenting me with a crown.

Two skeletal hands adorn the crown with the Kingmaker Emerald gilded at the center. He extends it toward me and I sit up.

My expression shifts to one of disgust as I utter, "What is that?"

"You wanted a crown, so I made you one."

"You expect me to wear that... that thing? On my head?" I glower at him.

"Don't you like it?" his tone is rough and cold. "I thought this was what you wanted?"

"You thought... that I would want to wear the remains of some poor soul on my head!"

Hades rests on the edge of the bed, staring at me expectantly, the crown still extended toward me. When I don't take it, Hades' face shifts, and he drops the crown on the bed.

"Everything I have done is for you!" he churns. "Every action, every decision, and this is the thanks I get? Anger and disappointment?"

"Excuse me if I don't jump for joy at the idea of wearing bones on my head! And those... those things would touch my skin!" I shout, pointing at the two skeletal hands encircling the stone at its center.

"You bitched and moaned about not being a queen without a crown, so I fucking made you one, and now even that effort to please you isn't good enough?"

"Fuck you!"

"Oh, my love, we already did that and now... now you're going to fucking wear what I give you and you're going to fucking like it!"

Hades grabs the crown off the bed and lunges toward me. He pins me down on the bed, his knees holding my arms down as he places that ghastly thing on my head.

"Stop! No! Let me go!" I fight beneath him, wriggling and writhing in anger. "Get that fucking filthy thing off me!"

Hades grips my shoulders, pushing me into the bed as he yells in my face, "You are MY WIFE, Persephone! The fucking Queen of Death! And now you will wear a crown befitting of that title!"

"So much for having a say, huh?" I challenge.

"You have a say, just not in this."

"Then what's the fucking point? And whose fucking bones are those, anyway?"

He grins wickedly. "That answer will reveal itself in due time, my love."

"Don't fucking call me that. I'm not YOUR fucking anything!" I yell out my frustration, still fighting to get him off me.

Hades releases me, and when he does, I yank the crown from my head and toss it across the bed. "I fucking hate you!"

"Well, I see the old Persephone is back," he snarls. "Didn't even give me time to miss her." He springs up from the bed, tears a robe from his cabinet on the other side of the room, and then stomps toward the door. "I'm going to grab something to eat. I'm assuming you'll be gone when I return?"

"You're fucking right I will," I assert.

"Right. Well, this was nice. Let's do it again sometime. Shall we? Hades then turns and stalks from the room, leaving the door ajar as he exits.

CHAPTER 20
PENANCE (PERSEPHONE)

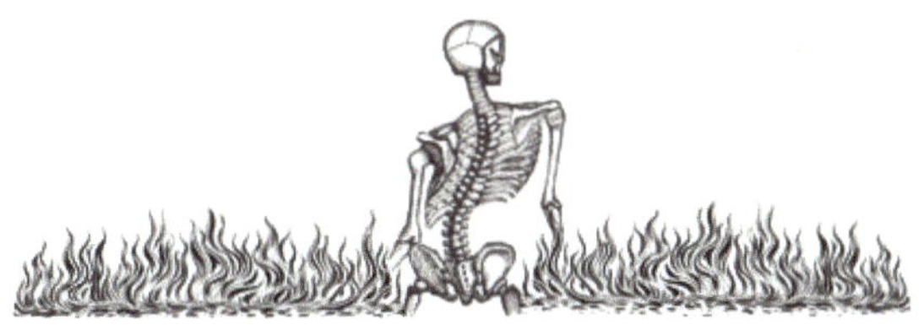

The next morning, I awake in my bed when Hades plops down beside me. I open one eye to see his face smiling mischievously down at me. I huff, "Ugh! Not you again."

"Afraid so," he beams. "Get up. Duty calls."

With a quizzical brow, I ask, "Duty? What duty?"

He frowns. "Yours, of course."

I open my other eye and sit up in my bed.

Hades taps the bed. "Come on. It's best not to keep the guards of Tartarus waiting."

"Tartarus?"

He scowls. "Yes, Tartarus. Today is the first day of your punishment. Or have you forgotten, already?"

My voice pitches up, "You're serious? I'm not going into Tartarus. Not one step."

"Well, seeing as I proclaimed it for all to hear, you are. Now, in fact." His voice is still cheerful as he announces, "Get up, get dressed, and meet me in the dining hall. You can eat before we go." Hades stands and walks for the door, stopping just before reaching the threshold.

"On second thought..." he pauses, "better wait to eat until after. Not sure you have the stomach for what is coming."

I groan, pulling the covers over my head as Hades leaves the room, closing the door behind him.

Moving around a bit, I stretch my legs as I whimper. I am sore, my body objecting to what I put it through the night before, but my core still feels heated and I don't know why.

Then I remember; the ichor. I tasted of the god's blood. I'd devoured it, actually. And now, who knows what the aftermath of that decision might be?

Pulling myself from the comfort of my sheets, I plant my feet on the cool stone floor, and the ground sizzles beneath me.

"What the-?" I say aloud, halting as I look down at where steam rises from my feet. *This can't be happening, right? I can't be burning foot-prints into the stone beneath me?*

I lift one foot, and, sure enough, scorch marks in the imprint of my foot mark the ground.

"Get ahold of yourself, girl. Now is not the time to lose your shit." I take a deep breath, settling myself as I stand silently with my eyes closed. *It was just a little blood. Just a little more power than you had before. Nothing to freak out about.*

But I am freaking out. I am practically beside myself. My heart and mind race with all the possibilities. *Child of a god (two, in fact), check. Power thrumming through my veins, double check.*

This makes little sense, though. I'm not to come into my powers for some time- years, in fact. But maybe, just maybe, the ichor sped up that process. *So I am what now, a goddess?*

Great! Add that to the list of things I have to worry about this morning. First, I have to summon up the courage, no, the patience, to deal with Hades; and oh, just that little thing about heading into Tartarus. That too, I grimace.

Getting up, I dress in a billowy purple gown, and fashion my hair simply; half up and half down, with loose strands cascading down my back.

I am just about to get up and leave to meet Hades in the dining hall when I stop. *If he wants a spectacle, and this is all a show, then I'll give them all something to gawk at.*

I reach for the paint, again decorating my visible flesh with gold vines snaking up and around each arm. I take my time, drawing an intricate burning heart just above my cleavage, the flames lifting to the base of my throat where the curves and tendrils twist across my collarbones. I then paint my lips a deep crimson and add a dark liner around my eyes, extending out to a perfectly tipped wing. "That should do it," I announce.

I leave my room and walk down the corridor to the dining hall. When I enter, Hades is standing at the end of the long table, leaning against it, with that ghastly crown dangling from his left hand. Irritated, I ask, "Seriously?"

He extends it out to me, his face displaying all the smugness of an oppositional child as he states, "Our kingdom awaits, my queen."

Stomping forward, I snatch the crown from his hand and turn, walking away without offering a single word of challenge. My sandaled footsteps echo down the hallway as we walk toward the exit; Hades merely steps behind me.

I step outside the palace and turn toward the stables when Hades stops me. "Not that way," he announces. "Only we may walk into Tartarus. The horses must not enter."

"Why?" I glare.

"Only guards and souls may enter. And of course the king and queen. But no others."

"Well, that's just dumb. Can't we at least ride to the gates and then dismount?"

"Why? Are you missing my body pressed tightly against you already?" he teases.

I mutter, "Forget it." I then turn, place that stupid crown atop my head, lift my chin defiantly, and march toward the gates of Tartarus.

The gates of Tartarus are massive; an impenetrable wall of gilded bones rising as far as I can see.

I crane my neck, looking up into the abyss of gleaming skeletal remains. They seem to writhe together in agony- twisted remnants of limbs, torsos, and misshapen hands; fingers grasping as they attempt to claw their way free of the structure.

As I look back and forth along the wall, I can see the jaw bones of skulls peeking through the golden connective sludge; twitching and moving, their mouths agape as they scream out. Despite there being no words spoken, I can hear their bones clicking together like thousands of beetles, their hardened exoskeletons rubbing against one another as they skitter.

Adorning the locking mechanism of the gates, snakes coil, their bodies poised to strike. They are enormous, their pronounced scales the size of a shield, and one head extends toward us, its fangs dripping an opalescent venom.

"I hate snakes," I squeak, recoiling from it.

Hades caresses the head of the snake, its slitted eyes closing in acceptance of his touch. "They were a gift."

With my repulsion evident, I ask, "Any chance we can re-gift them? They creep me out."

"One does not re-gift an offering from Asclepius." Hades snorts. "Besides, Anástasia, is like family."

"My father IS family, and you had no problem sending him away," I retort.

"She stays," Hades answers. "She and her sisters are the guardians of the gate. No one enters without appeasing them."

I point to the snake, still nuzzling his hand. "And just how does one appease Anástasia?"

Hades turns his palm upward, cocking his hand out toward the snake. Anástasia recoils, her serpentine locomotion almost rhythmic as she sways, transfixing Hades with her ether sparked gaze.

She strikes, her fangs penetrating the soft flesh of his wrist, her nostrils flaring when the ichor beads from the puncture marks. Then the snake's forked tongue lengthens, lapping up his essence.

Once Anástasia has her fill, her silvery ether laced vertical pupils replaced by the golden translucence of his ichor, she retracts. She holds her mouth open and Hades reaches out, gliding his thumb across the end of one fang.

He accumulates the opalescent venom and swipes it across his puncture wounds and they seal instantly. Hades again caresses the head of the snake.

He coos, "Until next time, my lovely."

Anástasia turns her head away from us, nodding toward the other snakes. It is then she and her sisters slither into a large outcropping of rocks at the base of the gate.

The bolted latch of the gate clanks, and Hades, straining, hauls the barrel out of the groove in the wall. He grasps the handle, a gilded skull with the spine still attached, and places his foot against the wall. Heaving, he forces the gate opened and a gust of ashes billows out.

The hinges groan as he muscles it wider, the inferno within Tartarus enveloping me with its intense heat as I step inside and my stomach roils.

As we walk on, me trudging beside Hades, the sound of whips cracking, chains clanking, and agonized screaming echoes. I pause, eyes widening in horror as I take everything in.

Hades chuckles as he motions about. "Now, do you see why I said to wait for your meal?"

I grasp Hades' forearm, bracing myself as nausea overtakes me. I wretch what little I have in my stomach, the brimstone burning my eyes as the winds of Tartarus rush past.

Their gusts carry wailing from the tormented souls undergoing punishment from their misdeeds in life, and somewhere, Kairos awaits me with the expectation I will deliver the same.

Tartarus is much larger than I anticipated, and tortured souls span the distance like a dense forest filled with trees, while masked guards with chains crisscrossing their chests shout out commands.

Emaciated, disfigured, and sometimes burned bodies toil along our path as we walk for the better part of an hour, each scene we come upon more horrific than the last when Hades finally halts.

He asks, "Are you ready?"

"That depends," I say, my eyes trained on Hades. "What exactly is it you expect of me?"

Hades doesn't answer, he just stands there, his body tense and face unreadable.

I continue, "I suppose the better question is, what punishment do you think he should receive?"

"Oh, no. It won't be that easy, my love. His penance is for you to decide. There is no right or wrong in determining what it should be."

"Is there a standard measure? Perhaps an example of what is… customary in this situation?"

"Standard? Customary? Use of those terms will only stifle your creativity. Nothing is off the table, Persephone. His reckoning will be of your making. Whatever your dark heart desires."

I stand my ground. "And if my dark heart, as you say, desires to forgo this charade all together?"

"Again, not that easy," he announces.

"Fine." I grumble. "Where in the Underworld is he, anyway?"

Hades points to the base of a hill where one of his masked, bare-chested giant guards, with fifty heads and one hundred arms, tugs on the chains attached to a man; one resembling Kairos. The man has his build, anyway. Well, most of it, since the man being pulled forward, struggling to place one foot in front of the other, has bloody stumps where his hands should be.

I gasp. "What have you done to him?"

He frowns at me. "Only what was necessary."

"Necessary? How was that necessary?" I point to where Kairos lumbers up the hill.

"Fine. It wasn't absolutely necessary. But he had what I needed."

I glare at Hades. "And that was?"

"The makings of a crown fit for the Queen of Death."

I look at Kairos and then back at Hades. When I finally grasp his meaning, I tear the crown from my head and toss it at him, pelting him in the chest.

"You sick, sadistic, selfish asshole!"

"Selfish? You bitched and complained about not being a queen without a crown on your head. I delivered one. A finely crafted one, might I add? And I'm the selfish one?"

I motion to where the crown lays at his feet. "That is not what I meant, and you very well know it!"

"Do I?" he asks. "How so?"

"What I wanted was a crown to rival all others. What I wanted... was glittering jewels that shone so brightly I might just forget how awful this place truly is. But that... that farce of a crown you gave me is an insult. An insult to me, and an insult to queens everywhere!"

"What is an insult, my love, is that you think you can bear the title of queen, have all the perks that come with being crowned, and not shoulder any of the responsibilities a queen is expected to carry. That and that alone is an insult to queens everywhere!"

I scream, "Go to hell!"

"Where do you think you are?" he challenges.

CHAPTER 21

RETRIBUTION (HADES)

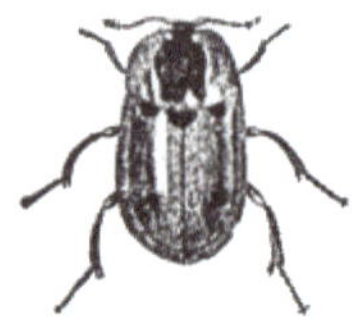

Persephone trains her fiery gaze on me as she stands defiantly, her fists clenched at her sides. Hatred and loathing seep from her, the tendrils of her rage reaching for me.

It is all-consuming, her anger. And it takes on a life of its own as a deep purple burns brightly in her irises. Hot and intense, she can barely hold it in check as the ether fights to burst forth, intensified by my ichor pumping through her veins. I know it changed her, but I wasn't aware just how much until that moment.

Sparks dance across the surface of her skin as an intensifying glow radiates from her. And the ground crackles beneath her feet; the stones fracturing as her power surges.

She is powerful. More than I ever could have hoped, and more than she should be.

"Persephone?" I softly call to her. "Persephone?" I don't reach for her. In this state, I don't dare touch her. "Persephone?"

Persephone blinks, and in an instant, there she is again. The ether quells, and my queen returns.

"What... what happened?" She looks around her and then back at me. "I..."

"It's fine. You weren't yourself. The ether-"

"The ether! You think the ether caused, whatever that was? Oh, no! That wasn't the ether's fault. It's yours!"

"Mine?" I ask incredulously.

"Yes, yours. You with your need to dominate and control... everything!" she shouts, unclenching her fists.

"If I recall, you had the reins when you consumed the ichor. You did it as freely as when you spread your legs for him." I motion toward Kairos accusingly.

Her anger is boiling again when she asks, "What upsets you more, the fact another man claimed what you consider yours, or that I wanted it?"

Persephone knows just how to stoke my rage. The look of satisfaction on her face as she squares up to me, the defiance in her eyes. The woman infuriates me. Her malcontent and malice make my blood boil as easily as her own, and I can hear it thumping angrily with each heartbeat, burning its way to the surface.

My vision goes dark, the ashes of my searing flesh rising all around me as heat scorches every inch of my remaining skin. I look down at my hands, seeing the effect she has on me; my gilded bones peeking through charred flesh.

I close my eyes, keeping my breathing even as I attempt to calm my fury.

"This is pointless!" I shout. "Your constant poking and prodding. What do you hope to accomplish with it? Do you actually think if you piss me off enough, I'll let you go? Well, my love... you'd best get comfortable because you are going nowhere."

"Well..." she challenges, "then you better get used to this version of me, because SHE is also here to stay."

Persephone stomps down the hill to where the giant guard drags Kairos behind him, and extends her hand up to the guard, bidding him to give her the chains.

The guard momentarily looks to me for permission, but before I can nod my response, Persephone reaches up and grabs the guard by one hand and jerks it toward her.

I can hear her berating him, her commanding voice echoing across the distance and over the roaring fires of Tartarus. I called her my queen, from my lips, a term of endearment, but in that moment, she is the Queen of Death.

She is the fires of Tartarus and the deliverer of torment, the wielder of pain, and bringer of sorrow. Persephone is the punisher, Kairos' anyway. *And perhaps mine if I'm not careful.*

For the better part of an hour, Persephone tortures Kairos, flaying his back and chest with rods and whips, tearing the flesh from him as blood seeps from each lash.

She eases, wiping the sweat from her brow as she deliberates the next way to break him.

Soot and ash have stained her gown and blackened her skin, leaving her looking disheveled as streaks and smudges mar the intricately painted designs that previously accentuated her beauty. And the vines, which had been golden as they snaked up each leg and across each arm, now have a reddish-brown tint with the crusted smears of Kairos' blood.

The fiery heart adorning the center of her chest now resembles a gaping hole as if ripped from her chest with each delivered blow, and she terrifies me because this is nothing like I'd pictured.

I'd imagined her sobbing as she punished him. Pictured tears streaking down a blotchy, remorseful face. But she isn't upset. She has not shed a single tear. Hell, she isn't even scowling.

Persephone is smiling; her gleaming teeth in stark contrast to the darkness surrounding her. She is loving this, and I... well, I am beside myself.

No more do I look upon a creature of unparalleled beauty. No more does frailty and innocence stand before me. The being, the creature that I gaze upon now, is nothing more than darkness; a festering, seething, and putrid thing.

I thought she would break. I thought she would beg and plead. But as her chest heaves, her arm cocking back once more, the monster she's become stands resilient. She's a beast hungry for more: more pain, more anguish, more death. She has become one with it, and now it consumes her.

I draw in a breath, attempting to clear my throat to gain her attention, but I only choke on the sound.

Persephone finally halts, and when she sees me watching, she laughs. She drops the cat-o'-nine-tails, Kairos' blood dripping off each knotted end, and begins walking toward me where I'm sitting on a boulder; the guard shadowing me as he stands with his many arms crossed as we watch her.

She reaches down, grabbing the hem of her gown, and wipes her face with the tattered fabric. She was stunning when we entered the gates, but now she is ghastly as sweat and grime cover every inch of visible skin and blood spatters speckle her face, hiding her cinnamon-colored freckles.

Climbing the hill, she stops before us as she places her hands on her hips, and says, "Well, was that what you expected?" She grins mischievously. "I tried to be thorough." She chuckles, plopping down beside me.

My tone is ambivalent as I reply, "I'd say you succeeded. And then some."

"Aww, thanks," she says. "How I'd hate to be a disappointment." She sighs. "So, are we done for the day?"

"Sufficiently," I answer.

"Oh, good. Because I am positively famished. Lunch then?" Persephone bumps my shoulder before rising to her feet, and turns to walk toward the gate, my guard staring after her.

"Are we to follow her lead, then?" the guard grumbles, half of his heads turning toward me.

I pat his shin. "Relax, Hecatoncheires Cottus. I'm the one expected to follow her lead. Do me a favor, though?"

"Yes, majesty?" his many voices ask.

"See you bring the dermestids forth to deal with Kairos."

"My king?" they question in unison.

I glower. "If she thinks I'll allow her a spectacle like that tomorrow, she's got another thing coming."

Only one answers this time, "Yes, majesty."

I get up and begin walking toward the gate, but before I am out of earshot, I call out to Cottus, "And see the beetles clean every shred of flesh from his bones, will you?"

"As you wish," his many heads reply, their voices echoing after me.

CHAPTER 22

HIDDEN AGENDA (PERSEPHONE)

Once I return to the palace, I retreat to my room. I am exhausted, and the crusted blood from my efforts still paints my skin.

I wanted to put on a performance, showing Hades just how merciless I could be, and I'd done just that. I actually made him wince. Several times when stopping to wipe my face, I saw him.

He underestimated me... again. He wanted punishment, so I gave it to him. He wanted retribution, and I more than delivered.

I held up my part, the tattered flesh and blood dripping from every surface of what remained of Kairos when I finished with him, evident of just that fact.

Not long after sitting down at my bedside, the basin beside me with fresh water, Hades enters and asks, "Doing a little post-torture cleanup?"

Dragging the cloth across my neck, I respond, "Something like that."

"I prefer a good soak to toweling off, after a day like today."

I swivel on my stool, turning to where he sits on the edge of my bed. "We have a bath?"

"An entire room, in fact. Just down the hall from my archives. It's more of a grotto, really."

"Where was this grotto all those times before when I needed to freshen up?" I ask, tossing the soiled rag at Hades.

"Don't get all pissy with me, my love. It's always been there. As I recall, you never asked," he says plainly, dropping the rag at his feet.

"I never asked?" I harrumph.

"Fine, I never offered. But I'm offering now. The cleanup you require will take more than a couple of swipes from a cloth," he says, pointing at me.

I stand, strip off my gown, and toss it at his feet. "You think?" I motion toward the door. "Lead the way."

Hades stands, kicking my gown and the cloth at his feet away before offering his hand. I begrudgingly take it, allowing him to lead me from my room and down the corridor toward the grotto.

As we walk, I peer forward, not wanting to see that smug look I'm sure dresses his features.

"So, what's in your archives?" I ask innocently.

Hades stiffens beside me. "Lots of things. Nothing of note, really. I have journals and ledgers stored within. Odds and ends, if I'm being honest. I rarely step foot in there these days. There's really been no need. Besides, the damn door sticks, and even though I keep meaning to fix it, there always seem to be so many other things needing my attention." Hades looks in my direction.

I counter, "I don't NEED your attention. You just insist upon me having it."

His tone is lighthearted when he says, "Yes, well. Be that as it may, my attention you will have, all the same."

"Yay for me." I roll my eyes, turning my attention back to the path ahead.

As we reach the end of the hallway, the temperature rises and a heat creeps across my skin as the air thickens with humidity.

Hades presses into the wall, and a large stone door pops out. He slides it back; the door scraping loudly as he muscles it into place.

Through the opening, steam escapes, billowing out in a large puff as it reaches the cool air of the corridor.

He motions for me to enter, standing beside the opening with his hand outstretched as I step past him. And as my feet cross the threshold, wall sconces flicker to life, lining the length of the cavern where vines creep up the walls, night-blooming jasmine with greenish-white tuber-like flowers, creating an otherworldly feel.

"Flowers? In a sealed cavern? How do they thrive in a place where death rules on high?" I continue along the walkway, leisurely reaching out to touch the small petals as I pass.

"She may be the lady of the night, but I see she gets everything she needs to thrive." Just then, Hades snaps his fingers, and the chamber fills with a luminous glow. "Like with Elysium..." he says, "I ensure there is life where death is so prominent."

A pool waits at the back of the chamber with chaises and seats carved out of stone along its edges. I pad to the edge of the pool, my aching feet longing to be soothed, and lower myself slowly to the edge, my feet dangling into the water.

I kick back and forth, sending ripples across the surface as the heat radiates up my calves. "This is nice," I offer, lowering myself into the pool. "Would have been nicer several months ago." I swish my arm through the water, splashing Hades where he stands at the edge, watching me. He chuckles at my playfulness and I offer, "Even so, it's nice. Thank you."

With a longing in his gaze, he says, "Anything for my queen."

Wading up to where he now sits at the edge of the pool, I tease, "Anything?" I swim between his legs, grasping his calves as I tread.

His gaze is forlorn as he says, "I would give you anything, Persephone. Anything within my power, and anything within reason."

"Within reason," I scoff. "What has reason had to do with any of this?"

He looks away as he says, "I have my reasons, Persephone. I-"

"You what? You have reasons for which you can't bother to share with your wife? A wife, might I add, who never had a say in the first place," I argue.

His gaze turns back to me. "It's not like that."

I grip his calves tightly. "Then what is it like, Hades? When will you finally tell me why?"

Hades brushes me off, rising to stand. "I should go. You can remain here as long as you'd like. A meal will be prepared for you in the hall once you're ready."

He walks toward the entrance to the cavern, but before he exits, I yell after him, "You can't keep secrets from me forever! I will find out the truth of this."

Hades steps through the opening, and I can hear his footfalls as they stomp down the corridor.

I wade to the edge of the pool, what seems like a lifetime later. I'd washed the filth of Kairos from my surface at last, but the ache of a life trapped with Hades still radiates through me.

My feet and hands are pruny from remaining in the pool for far too long, and as I towel dry, I grunt with frustration.

Why? Why me? Why now? Why forever?

Forever is a long time to be saddled to someone you can barely stomach being around, and now, with ichor flowing in my veins and a power I shouldn't have building within me, maybe it doesn't have to be. Maybe I can outsmart, outmaneuver... Underworld, maybe I can outfox the trickiest trickster that ever existed. Maybe I can outplay death, and in doing so, win at this game. But unfortunately, I don't know who all the players are, and sadly, I don't understand the rules.

Rules! Everyone is so dead set on them. But gods and goddesses don't have to abide by such trivial things. My mother doesn't, my father certainly doesn't, and I know for a fact that Hades doesn't. If he did, I wouldn't fucking be here and I wouldn't be stuck in this place with a man I despise, forced to perform the most...

Shit! I don't actually hate the things he makes me do.

The revelation has me reeling because I am obstinate to a fault, and I don't do what I don't want to. So, why am I blaming him when I could have refused... all of it?

I must stay the course because there is a light at the end of my tunnel. I have the stone and the instructions are clear; well, kinda. Now I just need to figure out that minor part about hiding my secrets within. That and that alone will be my salvation. I will achieve freedom, if he likes it or not.

After finishing my meal, I decide to take another trip to Elysium. Hades had said I may not go alone, but as I said before, I do what I want. Or I am going to start. It doesn't matter which, that's all semantics.

I am going to Elysium, and hopefully Erymanthe will appear to me once more, because she has some explaining to do.

That evening, after scouring the palace for Hades, and him being nowhere to be found, I make my way to the stables and, as before, I mount a horse and ride away, his flaming tail trailing behind us as we gallop along the ashen road.

We pass the scales where Charon and the scores of souls waiting along the banks of the river watch us as we gallop by, and finally, we arrive at the edge of Elysium; Asphodel meadows calling out to me with her swaying grasses as the sun sets behind the hills.

The meadows are beautiful, and once again, as before, they make me long for my mother. My mother, who, at last we met, no longer welcomes me into her home.

Where will I go when I once again am free to leave the Underworld and walk amongst the living? Who will I seek if not her? I have some months yet with which to plan, but the thought that she will not see me makes my heart ache. Who will I go to for loving embraces and tender words? Who will welcome me now? A life with Hades has cost me much, but the thing I miss most is Demeter.

I walk through the grasses and brush of the meadow for an hour when I once again find the lone oak. It still stands imposingly in the center of the field surrounded by wildflowers, but no one is at the base of the tree now; no people lounging as they listen to tales of love. There's only me and the sounds of the night creatures stirring to life as the day ends.

Birds flutter in their nests overhead as the crickets play a soothing tune, and I lean back against the tree, the clicking and chirping sounding as I close my eyes.

It is peaceful here. Nothing like the clamoring and clanging found within Tartarus. No mournful cries or pleading, only the wind as it rustles through the branches above.

I needed this; this respite from the chaos always seeming to find me. *Maybe it is of my own making? Maybe I am at its center, drawing it to me like a gravitational pull?* Because it always seems to find me, if I want it to or not. Just like he always seems to find me.

I need to make it stop. Need to make him stop, and the only way to do that... I think, as I pull the stone from the hiding spot within my braids, *is within my grasp.*

CHAPTER 23

UNEXPECTED VISITOR (HADES)

Finishing up for the day, I head to our room, my footsteps sounding down the hall as Cerberus lumbers at my side. I pass Persephone's door where it stands ajar, but there are no sounds from her within because she must still be in the grotto. Still lounging in its refreshing waters as they wash all the tension away.

She'd be pruny by now, her toes and fingers wrinkled and hair sticking to the side of her face or flowing out around her shoulders. But she was stunning, floating in the water as her beautiful breasts bobbed up and down in the water, droplets trickling down her neck.

That neck I long to bury my face in, that crease where her pulse beats erratically beneath my lips as I trail them along that line.

I huff, my shoulders slumping forward as I release my frustration. She doesn't want me. Not really.

She said as much, and no matter how hard I am trying, I'm not sure I'd spoken the truth; she might never love me, no matter how long I wait.

Waiting for Persephone to love me is a battle I might never win, and despite the seeds I plant, despite the efforts I make, I may never succeed. The reality saddens me.

I was lonely without her, lonely with Adonis' passing, but now with her back, she still seems so far away, and I am still alone; alone with my thoughts and self-loathing. I hate how this is playing out. Hate how she looks at me; her resentment.

Persephone resents me for all of it: the loss of her freedom, loss of her autonomy, loss of her life. I took what little from her she had, and in her eyes, offer nothing in return.

I wash off the ash and grime of Tartarus in my room with a cloth in the basin beside my bed, and then don a robe, making my way to the dining hall. Her plate lies on the table still, most of the food I'd laid out now gone, but she is nowhere to be found.

Making my way down the hall, I pass by my archives. I stop, looking down at the uneven stones at the threshold, and just sigh. *I will get to it*, I think. *One day I will pry up those impertinent stones and even them out.* But for now, I just want to see her.

Seeing Persephone smile, hearing her tinkling laugh, is the high-light of my day, and I miss it. I miss how her lips turn up at the corners, that berry stained flesh parting over her teeth.

She has no smiles for me now, only mischievous grins and scowls; evidence that wicked thoughts fill her mind, but not of me. Is she thinking of Adonis? Is she thinking of his hands trailing across her skin, caressing and pulling her into him? Or is she thinking of Kairos and the nights they'd shared out in the fields as he ravaged her body?

"My body!" I growl possessively.

I stop myself, pressing the stone on the wall and opening the grotto. She is not within, and I groan. My shoulders slump forward in defeat as I stare at the empty cavern.

This. This is the part of me she doesn't like. This is the me she doesn't love: erratic, compulsive, possessive, dominating. I have been this for so long. *How can I ever be anything but these things? How can I ever be what she desires, what she deserves?* Questions that plague me as I close the grotto once more and head back to the dining hall.

Taking a seat at the table, I make myself a plate, stacking meat high atop it. I stop, staring down at the pile. *Why had I done it? Why had I served Adonis, preparing him as if he were no more than a game hen or prize steer, ripe for slaughter?*

Bile rises in my throat and I wretch up what remains of my lunch onto the floor at my feet.

Cerberus pads across the room and begins lapping it up.

"Fucking gross, Cer," I proclaim.

Standing, I push back from my plate and leave the room where Cerberus is still enjoying my leftovers, helping himself to the food I left behind on the table, one paw pressed on either side of the tray.

"Well, at least someone is enjoying the meal," I say aloud.

I've lost my appetite, and all I want to do now is crawl beneath the cool sheets of my bed and sleep. *When was the last time I'd slept? When was the last time I'd woke up refreshed, not angered by every inconvenience?*

It had been years, maybe longer. Probably since before Aphrodite and what I'd done to wrong her. That was the last time I'd felt at peace, but I just can't get into that now. Now I needed to focus on Persephone and keeping her safe.

Safe. Had I done that? Had anything I'd done made her any safer than she'd been before, or had I just placed a target on her back? I thought taking her and bringing her to the Underworld would keep her safe, but my actions were shortsighted. They always were, and despite planning every minute detail, I could never have expected that the person to do her the most harm would be me.

Harming Persephone was unintentional, but I hadn't thought everything through. Not really. Sure, Adonis and I had plotted how it should go, and how we would do it, but the one thing we didn't plan for was Demeter's opposition.

Where was her opposition now? Where was that fight to safeguard her child she had put up in the beginning? Now all that remains is indifference. *How does a mother do that to their offspring? How do they turn their back on them all to retain their power?*

I'm not sure why I'm asking this question, seeing as my experience has shown me how easily it can be done. I had experienced it with my mother, and maybe that is why I feel bad for Persephone now. Because I was the one that led to it; through my actions or inactions, rather.

I could have stopped it. I saw where it was going and could have intervened. I could have risen from behind the peering stone, transported myself to the mortal realm, and stayed her hand, but I didn't. I didn't, and now she is feeling the loss of her mother just as acutely as I had with my own, blaming me for all of it.

I'm in bed, my covers pulled up to my chest with my legs outstretched, when panic hits me. There is a god in my realm and I can feel them. I don't know which one, or who sent them, but immediately I think of Persephone.

She wasn't in her room, wasn't in the dining hall. She wasn't in the grotto as I thought she would be and I'd just gone to bed none the wiser to her whereabouts. I had been reckless and stupid. I had been ignorant to the wellbeing of the one person whose safety I held above all others. *Some fucking husband I am.*

Dressing as quickly as I can, I sprint from the palace, making my way to the stables, where I find Persephone's saddle rack empty in the tack room. I'd told her not to wander out into the realm without me, but did she listen? Fucking, of course not.

I mount my stallion after leading him from the paddock and rush across the ashen road. She had to have gone to Elysium. Had to have wanted to feel a closeness to her mother amongst the wildflowers and grasses. That was where I would find her, I was sure of it.

But maybe she had gone to Tartarus? Maybe she had gone to see her lover once more to apologize for what she'd inflicted on him earlier that morning?

My mind races with all the possibilities, all the dangers, but there's only one way to know for sure.

Galloping down the road, I stop at Charon's temple at the edge of the river. Asleep inside, I rouse him, and he sits up in his bed, wiping the sleep from his eyes.

Charon looks up at me with a quizzical brow. "What is it? What's happened?" he mutters.

My words are frantic as they rush from my lips, "Have you seen Persephone today? Not early this morning, but after we returned from Tartarus?"

Charon's eyes widen, and then he speaks, "Not... not since she sped past toward Elysium earlier. Why? Is something wrong?"

"There is a god in this realm. I'm not sure where or why they have come, but I have felt them," I relay.

"Impossible," he says, standing, reaching for his robes. He puts them on. "No one is dumb enough to enter your domain without announcement."

My eyes widen in question. "You sure about that?"

"She'd never be that stupid," Charon insists, cinching the ties at his waist.

I cross my arms. "Why wouldn't she? Why wouldn't she encroach upon my territory and take her vengeance? She's tried it before."

"She wasn't successful then, and if she's dumb enough to do so once more, she won't be successful now," he assures me.

"Rouse the guard and send them after me, just in case. I'd hate to be taken by surprise and lose her," I plead.

Charon reaches out, placing his steadying hands on my shoulders. "You won't."

I shrug him off, turning away. "I'm not willing to take that chance."

Stomping out of Charon's home, I slam the door behind me and once again mount my horse, riding off toward Elysium. The sun has almost set, and if I'm right, if somehow she has come to take from me what she thinks I took from her, I'll never forgive myself.

～

My stallion's nostrils flare, large puffs escaping from the exertions I put him through. I'd ridden him hard across the wastelands, his rhythmic, repeated pattern kicking up dust where it billowed behind us. With each heavy footfall, each left lead, four-beat sequence landing firmly as we'd sped along, he'd traversed without fail. Now, as we skid to a halt, he backs up naturally, reversing in that two-beat natural gait.

I dismount and pat his side, looking to the hills in the distance where the sun sets on the horizon. Nightfall approaches, and then I will struggle to find Persephone in the darkness. I can't use my fire as those flames would set the dry grasses and edge growth aflame, and then a wildfire would rage through the meadow out of control.

Panicking, I step into the meadow, the grass brushing against my calves as I run toward the center. *The oak. I had seen her there before. That must be where I will find her now? That must be where she has gone and where she will be when I once again pull her into my arms, ensuring she is safe?*

As my feet pound the earth beneath me, I can feel the essence of the god getting stronger; nearer. I will be upon them soon, and then they will pay for their encroachment on what is mine; the Underworld and Persephone.

Conversation, the mumbled voices of two women, echoes across the meadow and I struggle to listen in.

What are they saying? I hear Persephone's voice tinkling on the wind and know, at least for now, she is safe. *But who is the other woman? Whose raised voice is speaking to my wife?*

My wife, my love, my heart's song. She is so close I can almost feel her. But as I step quietly through the wildflowers, their sweetness enveloping me in their essence, I feel anything but calm.

Why has she come here, and without me, no less? I know she is still angry with me, know she is upset. But why is she speaking to a goddess in my realm, and behind my back?

It is suspicious and I creep through the grasses now, crouching low to remain undetected. But the goddess feels me and she stiffens.

Just as I jump from the shadows to the base of that tree, she vanishes before I have the chance to exact my rage. I turn about, looking all around for the one, the goddess who dared enter my realm without permission. But she is gone.

Who had it been? Where had she gone, and why was my wife meeting her in secret?

I turn on Persephone now, my anger yearning to be released. My ether is sparking, begging to be set free and unleashed upon the one who has wronged me.

Persephone backs up, cornered against the base of the tree as I step toward her. "Hades," she calls to me.

I don't hear her.

She holds out her hands in front of her. "Hades, calm down."

I step into her, her hands resting on my chest as I press against them. "Who in the fuck were you talking to?"

She pushes me back, her face wearing the fear she should very much feel. "Talking to?" she squeaks. "I... no one. I was talking to no one." She cowers.

"Lies!" the words pass through gritted teeth.

Persephone cringes, attempting to back away, but there's nowhere to go.

I wanted to keep her safe, to protect her. I had raced across the Underworld to ensure as such. But who could protect her now, keep her safe? Who could shield her from me?

Attempting to temper my rage, I choke down the flames flickering beneath the surface. I tilt my head, the bones in my neck cracking as I fight against the power thrumming through my veins. My jaw clenches as my god's power wants loose; to be set free. My power wants to wash over us both and scorch the earth on which we stand.

"I'll ask you again..." I grab her arms, branding her with my palms as they burn into her flesh, "who in the fuck were you talking to?"

She cries out, the pain of my burns washing over her. "Ow! Hades, no!" she screams, her bellows filling the air as my fury burns bright in my palms. "Please," she whimpers, "please, Hades. Please stop. Let go. Let go!" She wails again, her lips trembling as she chokes down her screams.

"Was it your mother? Was it?" I seethe, shaking her. "What have you been doing here in secret? What have you two been planning, hmmm?" I drop her wrists, her skin welted with the imprints of my hands circled around them. My voice quivers, my resolve breaking as my anger subsides, and I ask, "Have you been plotting to leave me? Is that why she was here? I'm so terrible you couldn't stomach spending another moment with me?"

I subdue my anger, quenching my flames and sending them away.

Stepping back, I finally see the fear in her eyes as tears stream down her face and her hands hang at her sides. Her back is arched as she bends away from me and she can't seem to get enough distance between us.

"I..."

I reach for her, and she flinches again, drawing her hands up to protect her face. Dropping my hands, I step back and look down at my hands, these treacherous hands that just keep causing her pain. I squeeze my eyes shut, tears threatening to spring forth and betray the shame I hide behind my anger.

Turning away, I raise my head and speak over my shoulder, "I'm sorry."

Persephone says nothing. She just leans back against that tree, allowing it to hold her up as I stand staring off into the distance.

I snivel, composing myself as a numbness washes over me.

Walking away, I leave her standing at the base of that tree, and when I reach the edge of Elysium, I don't look back to see if she follows. I know she will return when she is ready.

She will return to the palace in her own time and then we can once again attempt to speak on all that transpired at the base of that tree. But until then, I will leave her be. She will seek me out. She will walk to our chambers and spill her secrets willingly. *Or so I hope.*

CHAPTER 24

FRUITS OF MY LABOR (PERSEPHONE)

Staring down at my singed wrists after Hades leaves, I look at his fingerprints branded on the flesh there. He'd marked me before, in other ways, but this is different; visible and forever. Now, whenever I look down at my hands, he will be there. And even if I break free from him, his mark will remain permanently etched into my skin, a constant reminder of his ownership.

I don't want to be his. I never did, not from the start. But it's not like I ever had any say in the matter. Not like I'd had a choice. He'd claimed I was his from the moment he saw me, that it was always me, was meant to be, whether or not I liked it. So what point is there in refusing him?

I can't refuse him. Can't say no. Can't run, can't hide, and can't escape. That's why I needed her. That's why I needed answers.

The parchment had divulged nothing: the golden text written on that scrap, the word apeiron hidden beneath. Neither one had me any closer to understanding the full extent of the stone's power, and that frustrated me. Sure, the symbol had disappeared when I'd thought about hiding it, but how was the stone a vessel, and how did I place a piece of myself within, gaining my freedom?

I had just taken the stone from my braids, allowing the light to shine off the surface, prisms refracting the facets, when she appeared, Erymanthe.

It was just as before. Just as the last time the light fractured, and she'd materialized. It's as if the stone that called her to me and I were somehow connected.

"Still here, I see," she said indignantly.

"As if I could be anywhere else?" I bristled.

Erymanthe knelt before me, smoothing her lavender gown over her thighs as she brushed her hands across the fabric. "Well, I had hoped you'd be gone from this place, wandering amongst the living and enjoying the freedom I promised." She shrugged her shoulders, tilting her head as she pursed her lips. "But I guess you just weren't ready." She rocks back on her heels and stands, turning to walk away.

"Wait!" I called out, jumping up from the base of the tree. "I unlocked the stone. Its mark hides in my flesh, but I have no clue how to place a piece of myself inside. How is it a vessel? How do I gain the freedom you promised and assume I should already have?"

I reached for her, and she turned to face me, placing her hands on her hips.

"You haven't figured that out yet? And here I thought you were smart. You found the dagger I left you, I assume?" she condescended.

"Yeah, but-"

"But what, Persephone? Finding it too hard?" She forced a pout.

"It wasn't hard. I used the dagger, but nothing happened. Hades still knew of my misdeeds. He saw everything!" my voice pitched up.

She snickered. "Yes. I'm sure he did."

"This is no laughing matter." I grabbed her wrist, and she twisted out of my grip.

She sneered. "No. No, it's not. It's sad really."

"Sad! How in the fuck is it sad? You promised it would work and yet here I stand." I motioned around us.

She appraised her nails, looking disinterested. "Yeah, well. You obviously didn't do it right."

"Didn't do it right⁉ A man is dead, by my hand, and by way of the dagger. How is that not doing it right?" I challenged.

She pointed at me. "You fucked him before you killed him, right?"

"Yeah?" I exaggerated the question.

"Was that before or after you unlocked the stone?" She crossed her arm over her stomach, gripping her elbow as her hand rested under her chin. She tilted her hand toward me as she pointed. "It was before, wasn't it?" She rolled her eyes. "Ugh, seriously?" she groaned.

"Don't take that fucking tone with me. I did as you instructed," I grimaced.

"Yeah, but none of that matters since you hadn't unlocked the stone yet." She patted my shoulder, batting her eyelashes at me. "We'll just have to try again, won't we?" she taunted. She pushed me back, chuckling.

"Try again! Do you know how long I'll have to wait now?"

"Considering the time of year, I'd say... another six months or so." She giggled in that furiously annoying tone.

"Yeah. That's another six months trapped in this fucking place with him. I don't think I can last another day," I admitted.

"Too bad, so sad." She grinned. "Wish there was something I could do. But alas, I cannot. You're on your own," she goaded. Her eyes glimmered, ether sparking behind them. She turned her head slowly, a smile widening. "Better luck next time."

Erymanthe disappeared without a trace and Hades jumped from the shadows as she did.

He knew she'd been there, knew we'd spoken, but he didn't know who she was or what words we'd shared. And despite his torture, despite the fear and terror that washed over me, I divulged neither.

～

Later that evening, back at the palace, I tend my burns and sulk, soothing salve over my wrists and then bandaging them with a cloth. The realization of my predicament hangs over my head.

Six more fucking months! There's no way I can survive down here for a lifetime, but maybe I can tolerate six more months.

Erymanthe had said by unlocking the stone I would finally be successful; could finally be free. I will just have to try again, she'd said. There was nothing she could do, and the burden was mine alone to shoulder.

So, had Kairos been all for nothing? Had his death really served no purpose? I suppose Kairos' death serves one purpose. Taking his life proves I am capable, and willing to take the steps necessary to achieve my freedom, but will it be that easy the next time? Can I once again so callously take a life and lock them away in the Infinity Stone, wrapping a piece of myself around their soul to hide what I'd done? There's only one way to know for sure, and now, literally, only time will tell.

Hades enters my room as I sit at my table, the bandages wrapped around my wrists and hiding his marks. He takes a seat on the corner of my bed, not looking at me. He just sits sighing, wringing his hands in his lap, and his presence irritates me.

Is he sorry? Does he regret what he's done? Or is this all for show and another way to trick me?

"What do you want, Hades?" I say, not bothering to turn around, staring down at my wrists where my hands rest in my lap.

"I..." he chokes out. "I wanted to say I was sorry. About before, I mean. I wan-"

"I don't really give a fuck what you want." My anger is bubbling to the surface again, seeping out of me with every gritted word. "Because it's apparent you don't give a fuck what I want, and despite the few moments you relinquished control for pleasure's sake, it's obvious that's the extent of your ability to do so."

Despite my anger and hurtful words, he still doesn't turn. He doesn't look at me, and I don't look at him. I can't. I refuse to. I won't spend another minute in his presence, and as I am about to voice as much, I hear the bed creak as he stands before walking from my room.

I grab the bottle of gold paint off my table and turn, throwing it at the door. It shatters against the wood, the shards landing at the threshold as paint drips down the face.

The gold trickles down to the floor where it pools and I realize I can no longer paint a pretty picture on myself, pretending everything is fine when it isn't.

Turning back to my vanity, I look in the mirror, my once crystalline blue eyes filling with silvery ether before they spark with the purple flame hidden beneath. They flash, electricity sparking around my irises as they shift.

I blink slowly, and when I open them again after a long pause, they are now an emerald green. The same green as the Kingmaker Emerald adorning my crown.

The next morning, I walk into the dining hall, my queen's crown on my head as my fiery hair cascades down my back. I hold my head high; the bandages removed as I wear my burns as a badge of honor instead of the torturous reminder I had said they would be. Because this is what claiming your power is. It's taking the shitty things that happen to you and turning them into your strength.

I stand before the table and shift my deep purple gown before taking my seat, a plate already laid out for me. There are orange slices, dates and figs placed neatly on one side and a slice of meat on the other- though I'm not sure I will ever be able to eat meat again.

Hades enters the hall and walks stoically to his seat, where he fixes himself a plate. He says nothing, stacking the meat high before grabbing a roll from the center of the table. He breaks it apart as I watch him with curiosity.

Turning my attention back to my meal, I cut my fig in half, placing a piece in my mouth before reaching for my wine. It's red for me this morning, something sweet and tangy to wash down all the bitterness pooling in the back of my throat.

My hatred froths as it begs to be set free. I could easily spew my words about control, the malice dripping off them as they shoot off my tongue like daggers. But what would be the point? They could shoot across the table, embed themselves in his chest, search for his heart, the blood seeping down as evidence I had broken skin, and still come up short. Because how do you pierce the heart of a man, a god, who doesn't appear to have one?

He'd said he loved Adonis, said he loves me, but I'm not sure he's even capable of such a thing as love. Love requires faith, love requires trust, and love requires relinquishing control, something I know with every fiber of my being, Hades is incapable of.

The silence is deafening, sitting there chewing our food. The only thing shared between us is the weight of our indifference as it wafts through the air like the sulphury smell of the River Styx; putrid, like death. Our indifference, just like death, is rooted in permanence. It will walk hand in hand with us as we navigate what our life has become.

Hades clears his plate and walks from the room, leaving me alone with the silence and only my thoughts to accompany me. It's fine, the solitude. I prefer it to forcing niceties and conversation. I prefer the peace and the time to think about how I will spend the next months in this prison.

Walking down the hall later, staring at the walls that once again seem to close in all around me, Hades steps from his room and into my path. I lift my eyes, meeting his brimming with regret. They are puffy, red rimming the edges as his lashes glisten. I look down, not wanting to stare. This is all just an act after all, and I'm not falling for it. Not for a second.

"We..." he begins, "we need to talk, Persephone."

My eyes shoot up, my anger sparking the fire behind them to life. "About?"

He hesitates, and then whispers a one-word answer, "Us."

"I'm sorry?" My eyebrows pleat as I consider my next words. I shake my head, closing my eyes as I cross my arms. "There is no 'us.' There is only you and your will."

Hades reaches for my hand, but stops, dropping his to his side. He steps toward me and I hold up my hand, halting him as I train my gaze down the hall.

The angry red marks circling my wrist seem to pulse in the torchlight when I spew, "Nothing you can say will fix this."

He's silent for a moment, his feet shuffling as he transfers his weight back and forth from one foot to the other nervously. He looks back at his room and then at me. "I'm not asking for forgiveness," he offers.

"Good! Because you'll get none from me," I seethe, dropping my hand to my side.

"I know." He sighs, wringing his hands. "I..." He breathes out. "This was not how I envisioned it," he admits. "You are so different. You're nothing like the image I had of you, and we're nothing like what I had built us up to be in my mind."

"This was never going to work, Hades." My hands drift back and forth in the space between us. "You can't force a life like this on someone."

He drops his shoulders. "I know that now," he says. "But I thought I was doing a good thing. I thought I was keeping you safe."

"You and I have a different definition of that word, apparently," I state flatly.

"I know you're unhappy. I-"

"Unhappy?" I shout. "You think this is just about me being unhappy?" I walk away, mumbling my frustration, "Are you fucking kidding me?"

I make it several steps from my room when he stops me, grabbing my elbow. He spins me around, pulling me into him. Stepping forward, he forces me back against the wall.

"I wasn't finished," he grits, the ether sparking in his eyes.

I turn my head, squeezing my eyes shut as I curve my body into the wall, cowering away from him.

He breathes deeply, slowly raising his hand and I'm startled by his touch, jerking back reflexively when he caresses my cheek. He places his fingers under my chin, turning my face toward him as he lowers his face and our foreheads touch.

I open my eyes, expecting to see that fiery cobalt rage burning behind his pupils, but it's not there. They're just that simple storm cloud gray, cool and pleading for something. The same eyes that used to look at me as he ran his fingers through my hair lovingly. And the same that watched me so intently as he cupped my face before kissing me so many months ago.

"As I was saying…" He swipes his thumb across my parted lips and then trails it up my cheek. "I know you're unhappy here with me, with this life. I get it. I do. I didn't want this for you, for us. But I come with a peace offering."

"A peace offering?" I mumble, fighting the feelings his touch stirs.

"Control," he says.

Turning my head away, I roll my eyes. "We tried that already." I huff.

He turns my head back and waits for me to open my eyes before he continues, "Not like this. This time is different." He slides his other hand up my body and taps my hand. "Open," he commands.

With reluctance, I open my hand, wiggling my fingers to chase away the tingling from squeezing them into a fist.

Hades drops six drachm sized black pearls into my palm and closes it around them. "This is your control."

I look down, opening my palm, and take them in. "How are these control?" I raise my eyes, looking into his expectantly.

"Each pearl allows you to go wherever you wish, and whenever you choose to do so."

"Anywhere? Whenever I want?" skepticism fills my voice.

"Whenever and to wherever you want. You only need crush one beneath your foot and think where you want to go," he clarifies.

"What if I want to go now? Not in six months, not in six weeks, but now?" I search his eyes for deception.

Hades drops his hand from where it's twisting my hair in his fingers and steps back. "Whenever," he affirms, nodding his head toward me.

We stand there silently, staring at one another before I slide along the hall the three feet to my door. I grasp the handle behind my back and click it open.

"Okay," I say, standing at the threshold.

"Okay," he asserts.

I push back on the door and as it opens behind me; I stand looking warily at Hades. My eyes narrow and I lift my hand, looking at my fist and then back at him.

I retreat into my room, but before closing the door, I call out, "Thanks."

He doesn't respond, he just turns on his heel and walks away, his sandaled steps flopping as they depart.

Stepping into my room, I close the door and make my way to the bed. Flinging myself back, I land in the middle, finally releasing the sigh I'd been holding in. I breathe out in a huff, my arms falling to my sides and settling into the bed.

I lay there for several minutes before raising my hand into the air above my face. I open my hand, allowing the pearls to cascade onto the bed beside me. They clank as they bounce off one another, settling along the side of my neck, and I nuzzle them, allowing the warmth of the freedom they represent to soothe me.

I whisper, "Take that Erymanthe. I'll show you six fucking months. With these babies..." I grab the pearls, "I'll be free in six fucking days. Just you watch."

CHAPTER 25
THE DEATH OF MY HOPE
(HADES)

The next morning I awake and pad down the hallway to Persephone's room, Cerberus at my side. I rap on the door twice, waiting for sounds of her stirring within. But there is nothing. No movement and no reply.

In the hall, with only the silence and Cerberus' panting keeping me company, I open the door. Inside, the bed is neatly made, dirty linens are draped over a chair in the corner, and her wardrobe is open. The doors are ajar, and when I glance inside, not only are her clothes all missing, but so is her satchel that normally sits on the bottom.

Persephone wanted to leave, so I knew she'd take full advantage of the pearls, but I didn't think it'd be this soon. I thought she'd at least wait a week before she fled. My hopeful self believed that, anyway. Now, as reality sets in, my hopeful self retreats to where I shoved it deep within me for many years before her.

Silently, I walk from the room, Cerberus on my heels, his nails clicking on the stones as we enter the dining hall. We sit for the meal, my clanking glass as it slides along the plate, the only sound besides Cerberus' whining as he begs for scraps.

I push my plate to the edge of the table and call him to me. He places his paws on the table, causing it to shift under his weight, and he laps my plate clean before going for the trays in the center.

I stand, stepping around him, and leave the room. He'll be there awhile. He can't resist the opportunity to eat from so many untouched trays, and honestly, I don't give a damn. Make a mess. Tear the whole fucking room apart as far as I'm concerned. It doesn't matter. Nothing does anymore.

Leaving the dining hall, the sound of Cerberus having his fill follows me down the hallway as I head back to our room. But I can't call it our room any longer, can I?

Persephone's desire to run as fast and as far from me shows how little we actually share. She'd said, there's nothing ours, only mine and my will, and maybe she's right.

What's left of my will has me stepping indolently from the palace later that morning. I have to drag myself to my throne by the river where I sit detached and disinterested with the day's tasks as I stare numbly towards Tartarus, dreading the responsibilities awaiting me there.

The day passes, blurring by like the river current those lost souls drift away upon; murky and torturous. Am I lost like them now? Will I too be swept away without the gravity her presence provides? Will the steepness of the riverbed and the volume of flowing water batter me along the rocks and sandbars? Will the current drag me down as I struggle to break free, gasping for breath as it takes me far from here? Maybe it will. Maybe it's what I deserve.

Filled with maybes, my head pounds as I finally walk back to the palace later that evening. Vision flashing, a pain behind my eyes, the dull ache turns to a punishing pressure. It's weighing me down, this existence. I can't go through the rest of eternity without her.

I promised her control, promised her time and distance. I promised things I thought I could give. But as I walk down the hallway, the torches flickering noisily while Cerberus' snores fill the air; I realize I can't.

Cerberus lies sprawled beside my chair, high on the dais, when I enter the throne room. He doesn't rouse as I take my seat, so I lean back against the soft tufting, sinking into its velvety comfort; the only comfort I will find with her gone.

Sitting in my chair, I close my eyes, pinching the bridge of my nose. I attempt to ease the tension, but all this waiting and wondering is torture. A day hasn't passed, and already not knowing is eating me up inside.

Lowering my hand, I turn to the Peering Stone and tap on the glass. Stirring to life, the Peering Stone sends light throughout the room; the prisms dancing along the walls as it awaits my command.

"Show me Persephone," I call out.

The Peering Stone fills with black smoke, wafting through the orb as I wait. Nothing happens at first, but eventually darkness fills it to the brim and then disappears. The Peering Stone returns to its clear state, the iridescence of the exterior pulsing with power, once, twice, and then subsiding. It's like it can't find her. Like she's gone.

"Impossible!" I grit, banging my hand on the arm of my chair.

Cerberus jerks awake, his hackles raising in response to my anger coursing through the room. He growls, looking to me for confirmation of danger.

"Easy boy," I say, patting one head as another licks my open palm. "It's fine. I'm fine," I soothe.

My words calm him, but do nothing to slow my erratic heartbeat. I am panicked, the stone's inability to find her worrying me. I know she's alive in the mortal realm, but without the stone's guidance, I have no clue where.

～

From the Underworld to the mortal realm I travel, starting at the most logical place: Demeter's home. Because where else would she be? What other choice is there? Surely, I will find her at the home of her mother. But if I don't, then what? Where do you look for your wife who you've just given the freedom to transport herself anywhere, if she's not the one place you thought she would go?

I knock and wait for Demeter to answer.

She throws open her door, pulling her robe closed as she stares out with a shocked expression. "Hades? What are you doing here?" Her tone is worried as she looks past me. "Is Persephone alright?"

"I was hoping you could tell me?" I bristle.

"How in the Underworld would I know?" Her discontent fills the doorway, not permitting me to pass.

"Can I come in?" My eyes plead for admittance.

She steps outside, closing the door behind her. She seems anxious. "Now's not a great time."

"I see," I answer, taking a step back. I look around the garden and then back at her, my eyebrows pleating. "So, she really isn't here?"

"Not since the day she returned to you." She stares wide eyed at me, and with an accusatory tone, she asks, "What's going on, Hades? What's happened?"

I give a short, controlled, "Nothing I can't sort out," before turning and stepping toward the gate.

She sighs loudly behind me. "Hades, wait," she calls, stopping me. She places a reassuring hand on my forearm, clutching it. "Try Naxos. We used to spend time there when she was a child."

"Naxos?" I ask. "Why there?"

"The beaches. When she needs to think, she buries her toes in the sand and listens to the gulls calling out."

"I'll try there. Thank you, Demeter. For everything." I turn and walk through the gate, closing it behind me.

As I crest the hill, she calls out once more, "Hades!" I stop, turning to face her, realizing that perhaps it's for the last time as she continues, "She can't come back here."

"Can't?" I question, my eyebrows furrowing.

She narrows her eyes on me. "What happened last time, after you..." she trails off, shaking her head, "she can't"

"After I-"

"You know what you did!" she accuses, stepping toward me. "The village welcomes her no longer because of it." Her frustration spans the distance, slapping me in the face.

"Of course. After what I did." I lower my eyes in shame, taking responsibility for Persephone's misdeeds. "I'll trouble you no further," I answer forlornly.

"And Hades..." She wraps herself in the comfort of her arms. "See that you find her," she pleads.

"I promise. If it's the last thing I do, I will see her safe."

Turning, I walk away from Demeter, unsure if I can keep my promise. I meant what I said. I will not rest until I find her. I will not stop until she's home, even if she'd rather not be. But will she ever be safe with me?

Naxos is just as I remember with her pristine white and golden beaches, lush groves, and fertile farmland. The full moon illuminates the treetops of the cedar forests inland, their scent carried to me on the wind, while the imposing peak of Mount Zas rises in the distance.

Zeus once hid from our father in the Cave of Zas, a place with narrow passageways and outcroppings of rocks that remind me so much of the Underworld. After all the time he was forced to spend there, it's no wonder he hates my realm, and it's zemblanity Persephone has fled here now, choosing the place Zeus once hid from Chronos, now to hide from me. It's like she's taunting me.

At the edge of the village, merriment sounds; music playing and dancers moving gracefully around a bonfire. They congregate near a glistening white rock wall as I watch them enjoy themselves, unencumbered by life's external stressors

I envy their freedom as they embrace the moment, living their lives to the fullest as their laughter is the only sound to break the silence.

The slow music from an aulos and a kithara fill the air as the sound of feet shuffling on the sand nearly drowns out the conversation. Despite the soothing harmony, my ears perk up when I hear Persephone's name spoken barely above a whisper as it drifts to me above the revelry.

My ether flickers, fire sparks to life, and vision clouds over as my darkness threatens to close in and ruin their fun. All from hearing her name spoken from mortal lips.

A young, dark-haired man sitting at the fire's edge with a bladder of wine in his hand tells a somewhat older, golden-haired one about a gathering in the grove organized by none other than my wife. The pungent scent of fermented grape drifts to me as wine sloshes, spilling at their feet as he nudges the man beside him.

"She promises wine and debauchery for all in attendance, and I am contemplating heading that way," he boasts. "Join me, and if we're both lucky, she'll join with us once we get there."

What I hear about my wife's plan enrages me, but what the man infers he will do with her once he gets there tips me right over the fucking edge.

I jump from the shadows, my gilded bones encased in blue flames, and point at the dark-haired man as I go full god.

"What the fuck did you say about my wife?" I bellow, pointing my bident at the man.

The man falls from the wall, cowering on the sand as I lunge for him. He grabs for the wall behind him, pulling rocks loose as he attempts to stand. He fails to rise to his feet and instead sifts deeper into the sand beneath him as his skirts gather at his thighs.

The moonlight and my fire illuminate his face, and in his eyes all I see is terror as my blue flickers in their glassiness. Everyone else scatters, screams of terror filling the night as they flee, leaving the poor soul alone to contend with me.

"I... I meant no offense, Pluton," he whimpers, gripping his gown tighter in his fists.

"You dare use my formal name?" my voice booms, causing the man to cower in the fetal position, drawing his legs in tightly as he's rattled by the sound.

The ground before me quakes, my fire heating the sand and turning it into molten glass. On my command, it snakes toward the man, a glowing golden stream that slithers across the ground like a viper preparing to strike. It cracks and pops as its tendrils spread out like thin fingernails scratching their way toward the man.

He's backing into the wall, trying to flee from the golden flow, when the tide comes in, sending a burst of steam billowing as it cools. The glass hardens from the outside to the inside and before me is now a widened plate of hardened glass.

I take another step toward the man, the glass snapping as it cracks beneath my foot. The force of my powerful steps sends splintered shards shooting through the air, piercing the man's flesh as they embed in his abdomen.

His blood flows freely from his wounds, the shards protruding from his center.

When I finally reach him, he's holding his hands to stomach, placing pressure, as blood snakes through his fingers and pools in the sand beneath him.

"Where is she?" I demand, flames covering every inch of me as I burn out of control and my flames whoosh, their rhythmic melody singing as their eerie cries fill the night.

The man struggles to answer, his muffled reply of, "The groves," barely audible over my roaring flames.

I place my skeletal hand encased in flame on his head, enveloping him with my rage.

Blue flames sear the flesh from his bones as his agonized screams fill the night and he wails, his piercing torment barely a hum in my ears as I look down on him.

His body writhes and then becomes motionless as I release his life and essence. It drifts skyward, a mere whisper and remnant of what he once had been; a trailing of smoke toward the heavens.

My anger subsides, and as I stare down at the man, my flames vanish and my skin reforms. I remove my hand, turn it over, and just stare at it.

A muffled cry escapes my lips as sorrow fills me. This was not my intent. My purpose was only to retrieve her, not to take a life. *How can I lecture Persephone about her actions when I have now done the same?* I have been reckless, out of control, and this is the result.

I stand above the charred corpse, staring down at the crispy remains as an icy tear trails down my cheek. I produce a Charon's Obol, willing it to appear in my hand, and drop it at my feet. I then raise my voice to the sky, praying for peace in death.

I have stolen what peace he'd found when I took his life, and I now beg the forgiveness of the man whose thread I cut too soon. The man whose name I do not even know.

With his rite complete and my power finally in check, I set out toward the grove to find my wife. I look back on the destruction I caused only once, seeing what it truly is to be death.

I listen for sounds of celebration as I walk through the grove looking for Persephone. But as many people as the man had said were attending, I should have heard something by now. There should be laughter, or at least moans filling the air as those in the throes of passion cry out. But all I hear is my feet crunching through the underbrush and a faint low rumble; a distant crackling.

The farther into the woods I go, the louder the rumble becomes, eventually becoming a roar with loud cracks and pops interspersed. It's unmistakable now, the inferno blazing.

The smell of burning flesh greets me with the next gust through the trees, the scent reminding me of Tartarus. And as I step into a clearing, smoke rises into the night from a house burning out of control in the distance.

Flames engulf the structure at the edge of the trees while a faint silhouette of a woman stands watching. It has to be Persephone, those curves and skirts blowing in the wind. I'd know that outline anywhere.

Standing in the shadows, watching Persephone as she dances beyond the billowing smoke, I see someone appear. I can feel her before I can make her out clearly.

It's the goddess. The same one as before in Asphodel Meadows, I'm sure of it. She reaches out, her firm hands grasping Persephone by her forearm as she turns her about. She has on the same lavender gown as before, billowing out around her ankles as she stands with an ominous glow surrounding her.

Once they're facing one another, Persephone throws her arms around the goddess, pulling her into her embrace.

Persephone sounds happy, relieved even, as she holds the woman dearly, and I take another step toward them.

I am close to them now, still hidden in the shadows, but near enough, the goddess should have felt me. She should have fled like last time, pulled from Persephone's embrace, disappearing before her eyes, and yet she stays.

Creeping up on them, I hear Persephone speaking to her. It's faint, the conversation, and I struggle to make out the words over the sound of the roaring in the background.

"How many?" the goddess asks.

"Twelve, and this time I did everything as you instructed," she beams. Persephone's happy about whatever directives she's followed, but the goddess seems unimpressed.

"You needed fifteen." She stiffens, pushing Persephone away. "Tell me exactly," she insists.

Persephone seems unsure, but she responds, "I placed the subjugation stone in the dagger's pommel as you said, and as I... you know, I drove it into their chest, calling the stone to action."

"And when you were done?" the goddess exaggerates her question.

"Oh, yeah," she mutters excitedly, "and when I was done, I trailed the stone across their lips as the last of their essence escaped, and brought it to my own, trapping their soul with a piece of my own wrapped around it in the stone."

"Perfect," she says, reaching out and caressing Persephone's arms, rubbing up and down reassuringly. "Where are the dagger and the stone now?"

Persephone pulls from the goddess' grasp and skips to where she'd been dancing at the edge of her massacre. She leans down, picks up two items, and charges back to the goddess' side, handing them to her. "I can get the rest. I know I can. There's still time," Persephone assures her.

The goddess smiles wickedly. "I'm afraid we've run out of time."

"Out of time? But I'm so close."

Persephone seems panicked as the goddess lifts the stone, allowing the moonlight to glint off the surface. She then lowers it, fisting it in her palm, and appraises the blade.

Turning it over in her hand, the dagger clanks as it contacts the stone in her palm, and she swipes her index finger through blood. She smears it up the hilt where she wipes it on the pommel stone as she grins wickedly.

"Good. You've done so well, Persephone. Now, you're finally ready," she proclaims.

"I can't wait," Persephone squeals, bobbing up and down with excitement. "But you said I needed fifteen? I've only gathered the twelve, and you said we're out of time."

"I said you're out of time. But time remains for me to complete your task," the goddess insists.

Filled with unease, I step into the clearing, a branch snapping loudly beneath my foot.

As Persephone turns her attention toward the sound, the moonlight illuminates my face, and she sees me. She gasps, her hand going to her throat as she steps toward the goddess.

"Hurry!" she begs. "Do it, now!"

I run, my eyes going to the goddess as her hand holding the dagger raises into the air above Persephone. She brings the dagger down swiftly, impaling her, plunging through bone and imbedding it in Persephone's chest to the hilt.

Persephone smiles, eyes locked on the goddess, and gurgles, "I am free."

As blood spills from Persephone's lips, the goddess' face changes, and the golden Aphrodite stands before her now, her gilded robes flowing around them both like a cyclone.

Persephone's eyes go wide and her hands grip tightly on the neckline of Aphrodite's gown, her fingers scratching along her neck, leaving trickles of blood trailing down.

Aphrodite reaches up with her hand and presses the stone to Persephone's lips and it glows, a pulsing light filling the night.

As the life drains from Persephone's eyes, her soul escaping her mortal coil, the last of her essence is drawn into the stone in the goddess' hand.

Aphrodite looks to me, her teeth gleaming in the moonlight as a look of satisfaction crosses her features. "It is done, and now you share my pain," she cries out, chest heaving.

Pulling from my stupor, my rage engulfs me, and my fire roars to life as I lunge for Aphrodite. I close the distance between us quickly, reaching out for her with my skeletal fingers extended. And as I attempt to grasp hold of her shoulders, Aphrodite disappears right before my eyes.

She blinks out as the light fractures the space between us, taking the dagger and the stone along with her, but leaving Persephone's life-less corpse lying prone in the grass at my feet.

PART TWO

Evil destroys even itself.
-Aristotle

CHAPTER 26

DARKNESS RISES (HADES)

Persephone never came. Her soul and the souls of the twelve she massacred, despite performing the rite and placing Charon's Obols with their remains, never stepped into the labyrinth. They never milled through the gates with the others, offering their tokens to the Ferryman for passage across the river. And as such, I have spent millennia after millennia alone with just my thoughts. The monotony of my never-ending torment as the one most damned accompanies me as I alone remain awake, forced to persist in the Underworld as the last remaining member of the Greek pantheon while those once residing on Olympus slumber through the ages.

The Middle Ages were mostly uneventful. The numbers of the faithful dwindled with emerging new faiths throughout the mortal realm, and without their love and adoration, my siblings went to ground. They rest, conserving their power in hopes of one day reemerging and reclaiming all they lost, but I alone endure, for there will always be need of death. I alone maintain the balance, and so I wait. I'll wait for eternity if I have to, ushering souls of the departed into their afterlife, whatever it may be.

My numbers picked up with the invention of advanced weaponry, greed and the lust for power steering the course as mortals sought to dominate one another. Civilizations rose and fell, souls arriving by hundreds of thousands each day as they wiped one another from the face of the earth. Then came plagues and pestilence, genocide, and eventually weapons of mass destruction, to fill the labyrinth with new arrivals.

Charon is ever my faithful servant, ferrying those presenting a tithe to him across the River Styx one boat load after the next; a never-ending stream of fresh souls. He never sleeps anymore as the ferry crossings are his eternal burden. There is always work to be done and he and I stand strong, making room for all those seeking passage.

The scales are struggling now, finding it harder to gauge what misdeeds warrant an afterlife in Tartarus or Elysium. Humans have evolved and, as such, the lines of right and wrong have blurred. Mortal justice doesn't match the scales' judgment, so someone declared innocent above might find themselves judged differently here. Our judgement has become more subjective, and as such, I am ever seated on the throne at the edge of the river for the times when the scales cannot determine. It is at those times I become judge, jury, and, more often than not, executioner.

Mortals have become arrogant, vile creatures with no moral compass, and even less of them feel remorse for their wrongdoing. This has led to my guards in Tartarus being overworked and undermanned. Conditions like that have a direct correlation to much harsher punishment for the smaller crimes, so I've had to section off much of the land to ensure lesser crimes reside above and the more heinous offenses below.

We dug caverns and pits deep in the earth below Tartarus; the cells teeming with prisoners who've committed atrocities against mankind. I've found amusement with some of the worst offenders, however; like Hitler, he's a megalomaniac, sure, but he's a formidable chess opponent. We play twice a week and then afterword I allow those who lost their lives to his mania to cut off his cock and feed it to him. *Not such a big man now, are you, Adolf?*

In all seriousness, life in the Underworld is lonely, and with the workload increasing, some days it's more than I can handle. I rarely get to see Adonis anymore, and when I do, his memory seems diminished. There are days he doesn't know me, and his eyes, once bright with fondness, stare up at me with dulled indifference.

I'm not sure anyone loves me anymore, except Cerberus. That mangy beast is ever my faithful companion, but a terrible conversationalist. There is only so much one can glean from a wagging tail and lolling tongue, but at least his affection is unconditional.

On the nights when I'm feeling most vulnerable, I think of Persephone. Remembering our first nights together and all the good things about her: her warm embrace as she held me, her fingers as they ran through my hair, her intoxicating orange and honeysuckle scent. She invaded me mind, body, and soul. I haven't been the same since losing her, haven't felt whole, and perhaps I never will.

I am fast asleep when I feel it. A roiling in my gut sends me hurtling out of bed, immediately on my feet and poised to strike. My fire blazes to life, the cobalt flames searing away my flesh and exposing the gilded bones hidden beneath.

I felt... her. It was brief, but I'd know that essence anywhere.

I run from my room, my feet sizzling down the hallway as steam rises from the stones below; leaving a trail of charred footprints all the way to my archives, where I tear open the door. It catches, the jutting stones stopping the bottom of the door as I force it ajar.

"Fuck!" I yell out, kicking the bottom of the door. The wood splinters and my flames jump from me, igniting the entryway. I wait for the entire door to be engulfed in my anger and then kick the center, sending wood fragments exploding into the center of the room.

Flames consume what's left of the door, and my inferno illuminates my path as I step through the Hades sized hole in the center.

Once in the room, the lack of oxygen snuffs out my flames and slowly my skin rematerializes. I take a deep breath and run my hands through my newly formed hair, slicking it back.

I step purposefully toward the chest along the far wall and throw open the lid. I then pull out one, two trays, reaching for the third when I stop. I look down at the two trays at my feet, noticing that stones are missing: two of them. The top and the second tray each have one place-ment empty. *What were the contents of those two? Which stones had been there?*

My mind is reeling with all the questions.

"Persephone!" I yell out, the reverberations of my booming voice shaking the chest and trays at my feet. "That fucking bitch!" I seethe. That's how she did it. She found those stones and found her way free; free of the Underworld and free of me.

I kick the chest, sending it hurtling across the room where it crashes against the wall, and the trays topple, their stones skittering away like retreating cockroaches. Stones and gems scatter across the floor, and their parchments drift haphazardly about.

"She's not even here, and she's still a royal pain in my ass!" I grumble.

I settle, my shoulders slumping forward as I realize the mess I've made. I trudge forward, bending and picking up each stone, and then place them back in the trays. Having them all gathered, I look to where the chest lies splintered at the base of the wall from the destruction I caused.

"Well, now what do I do?" I wring my hands, my frustration with myself building. "This is why she left," I say aloud. "I destroy every-thing I touch."

Sadness overcomes me, and I sink to the floor, landing on my knees. I place my head in my hands and cry out, sorrowful sobs quaking through me as my whole body trembles.

I've held it in too long, my grief, and I just can't do it anymore. Giant tears stream down my face and plop onto the stones, tinkling with each drop. I look down through my tear soaked lashes to where golden pools have formed from my sadness. The ichor, my essence, my power, pools beneath me as I cry out in agony.

It hurts so much: the loneliness, the pain, the rejection. I haven't cried like this since my mother, and even then I shook it off quickly, swearing I would never allow myself to be that vulnerable again. Yet, here I am, surrounded by my misery, stripped naked and lain bare for... well, not for all to see, because I am the only fucking one left!

I close my eyes and lay on the cold stone floor, my erratic breaths breaking through my resolve like tiny hiccups, my throat bobbing as each one escapes. I curl into myself, into the fetal position, and revert to a much simpler time when only the worries of a child weighed me down. I wallow in my self-pity, a heap on the floor no longer resembling the God of Death.

Everything I'd done led me to this: this place, this life, this torment. Every decision I'd made had been wrong. I am a flawed god and it would be much simpler to be a man. At least mortals receive grace for their flaws and are forgiven for their mistakes. I wish I was a man, then maybe I could be happy. *Titan's sake, why can't it be so?*

Nails click across the stones as padded feet advance toward me. I turn my head, looking up to where six eyes stare down at me. Before I have the chance to acknowledge him, Cerberus coats me with slobbery kisses, three enormous tongues lapping salty tears off my cheeks.

"Okay, that's enough, boy," I say, hoping to ease the assault from sandpapery tongues on my flesh.

Cerberus doesn't stop, so I pull him down and curl up behind him, allowing his warmth to comfort me. He smells awful, like sulphur, but he is a hellhound after all and I run my fingers through the tufts of hair around his face as my breathing slows to an even cadence, my chest rising and falling in tune with his.

Once my panic dissipates, I shift to a seated position, pushing

Cerberus off me. A difficult feat because he is the size of a large grizzly bear, weighing close to six hundred pounds.

"Move," I say, shoving against his back. He rolls over and slowly rises to his feet. "That's better, you mangy beast." I pat his large bottom, sending him across the room.

Cerberus trots away, stopping when he reaches a stone resting next to the toppled trays. His middle head sniffs and then picks it up in his mouth. He looks over his shoulder at me and then pads in my direction.

"What do you have for me, boy?" He drops the stone in my hand, slobber coating the entire surface. "Gee, thanks," I say, shaking the drool, and then wiping what remains off on my gown. "I didn't think you cared." I chuckle, ruffling his ear and scratching behind it.

After giving Cerberus the love he deserves as the bestest boy, I look down at the stone. I have no clue which one it is, but there is only one way to know for sure.

I walk across the room to where all the parchments are strewn about, and with the stone in my hand, I pick up one and read it aloud.

A stone near one tray glows brightly, so I pick up the next one and repeat the words inked on the scrap, and again, another stone near the trays glows. I do this again, over and over, placing the parchments with their corresponding stones until only one remains.

Holding up the last one, I call out to Cerberus, "Well, buddy, wish me luck." I read the name, saying it aloud, "Mustéria Stone," and the stone glows, confirming I have the right piece. "That solves that mystery," I announce to Cerberus. "Now to see what this beauty can do."

The golden text, hidden before I spoke the name of the stone, shines brightly through the parchment in my hands. Holding it up to the light, I inspect both sides.

There is only one word, one command to bring forth the truth of the stone's power, and I toss the parchment into the air above me as I call out, "Kruptós."

A light fractures the space, and I squeeze my eyes shut to avoid the super nova-esque brilliance filling the room. When the heat from the explosion of power finally dissipates, I open my eyes and gape in wonder at what appears before me.

A massive black screech owl, with golden primary, secondary, and tail feathers and a gilded beak and talons, soars through the air, flying straight through the hole I left in the door of my archives.

He moves like an apparition, blending into the shadows of the hallway, his screech echoing as his wing flaps signal his departure.

Running for the doorway, I almost trip on the uneven stones at the threshold. I catch myself on the charred doorframe, staring down at the ground as I curse, "I will fucking destroy every damned stone in this fucking hallway, so help me..."

I enter the hall, screeching sounding down the corridor as my dark visitor keeps to the shadows. I take to a sprint, trying to keep up with his retreating silhouette as his flapping wings sound above me.

Turning the corner, my eyes train above me as my sandaled feet slide on the slick stones. I careen into the wall with a loud thud, pushing off and continuing toward the throne room.

Once in the throne room, the torches burning along the walls hide the creature. A faint outline creeps through the darkness, landing on the titan's skull at the apex of my Peering Stone, where it sits next to my throne.

Ether filled eyes glow from atop the skull and my visitor spreads its wings, his impressive plumage beckoning me with each flap. His golden feathers reflect the light, the air submitting to him as he draws them back and forth. He lets out another ear-piercing screech, settling on the skull as he bobs his head up and down. It rotates slowly, watching me warily as I approach him with caution.

My hands are out at my sides, extended into the air slightly as I try not to spook him.

"Easy boy," I soothe, taking one step and then another. "Easy. I'm just going to step toward the dais, and you're going to stay put, okay?" I bargain with the bird, his talons clicking as he shifts along the gilded skull, gripping into the eye sockets as his eyes watch me intently.

I step up the dais to my throne, lowering my hands and sliding into the seat as he tilts his head.

He blinks, bobbing his head one more time before he stills.

Still gripping the stone in my hand, I extend it toward the bird.

His eyes fix on me, his body remaining still, and electricity pulses in his gaze, the ether sparking the irises. He is power manifested, taking the form of this amazing creature.

I am about to say the words again, activating the stone in my hand, when Cerberus barrels into the room, nails clicking on the stones as he charges straight toward the bird.

My dark visitor turns his head, extends to his full height, and stretches his wings back behind him. He draws them forward, sending a gust of wind toward Cerberus and he yelps, sliding to a halt before turning and running from the room, his six eyes wide and his tail tucked between his legs.

I look at the bird as he's puffed up his body and shakes his head as he appears to chuckle.

"I think you enjoyed that a little too much," I note.

He turns his head almost upside down, peering at me from his perch.

"Let's try this again, shall we?" Holding the stone out, I speak the word, "Kruptós."

My dark visitor shakes his feathers, his head returning to its extended position before settling. He then turns to stone; a dark onyx with golden marble for wings and silver obsidian eyes.

"That's not at all what I expected," I say.

I lean back in my chair, sinking into the corner, and squeezing the bridge of my nose, I sigh.

"Now what do I do? How do I find what I don't even know I'm looking for?"

The Peering Stone glows, sending prisms dancing around me, and fills the room with rainbows. Then it hits me. *I use the Peering Stone to watch the mortal realm, but maybe this stone is to find that which I seek.*

I lift the stone, allowing the prism to shine on its surface. I know I'd felt her, however brief it might have been. Persephone's essence is somewhere, whether in the Underworld or the mortal realm. I know not which.

CHAPTER 27

WHAT IS LOST DOES NOT ALWAYS REMAIN HIDDEN (HADES)

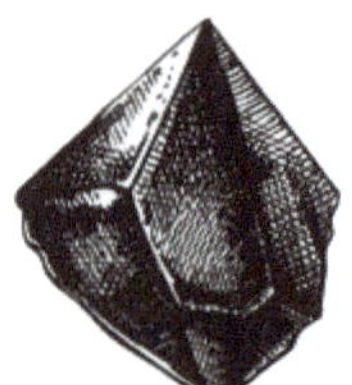

Sitting in the throne room with Cerberus lounging at my feet later that evening, I pull out the stone again, holding it up to the light. My dark visitor, now a statue, perches atop the skull with his talons gripping the sockets as they had when he transformed. There is no life in his eyes, no ether sparking there. Only his silence and Cerberus' snoring fills the surrounding emptiness.

I call the stone to life again, uttering the word as light glints off the facets. It sparks, a trail of silvery ether snaking toward the Peering Stone where it fills the orb like smoke.

Curling throughout the inside of the orb, the shining ether tendrils slither along the edges of the sphere, tapping and scratching like fingernails. It tap, tap, taps on the glass, the sound rousing Cerberus from his slumber.

Lifting his heads, Cerberus tilts them with curiosity, his six ears swiveling as he attempts to pinpoint the sound as he growls. He rumbles his protest, piloerections raising along his hackles, shoulders, and tail. He looks ridiculous, that overgrown scaredy-cat.

"Easy, big fella. Nothing to be worried about. It's just the ether, yearning to be set free," I soothe, ruffling my fingers through his scruff.

He settles once again, a chuff escaping as he lays his heads on the dais. One mouth opens, squeaking out a yawn as another snores once more, his jowls flapping as air escapes.

Once the smoke has filled my Peering Stone, swirling about the inside like the eye of a hurricane, a light flashes, and a woman appears.

The woman is petite, with dark auburn hair, and full lips tinted with a dark berry stain. She stands somewhere, a market maybe, talking to a man as a chain hangs loosely in her hand; draping across where a stone pendant rests in her palm.

The blue and purple stone flickers, its essence beckoning me. I know that stone, have seen it's like. It has been ages, but I am certain it is one I'd recently discovered missing from the chest.

The woman reaches in her bag and pulls out payment, handing it to the man.

He takes it, walks over to a box where he places it inside, and returns with a small case. He extends his hand with the case and she declines, placing the necklace over her head and draping it down her chest where it rests above her bosom. Looking at her hesitantly, the man turns and walks back to his table, where he sets the case down.

I can't tear my eyes from the stunning woman, and the stone seems to thrum with her heartbeat between small perky breasts peeking out the top of her shirt.

The stone nestles in her cleavage, and I can still see it glowing, pulsing as it rests against her toasted skin, the power caressing her flesh as it settles in place.

Picking up a card from the ground that had fallen when she pulled the parchment out for the man, I see a symbol emblazoned on its surface and letters spelling out a name.

Leaning toward the stone, I say aloud, "Hello, Melody Goins. I am Hades. We haven't been properly introduced, but just who in the Underworld might you be?"

I race back to my archives, stepping carefully over the jagged stones, and sigh as I step through the hole in the door.

Taking in all the destruction I'd caused the last time I was in that room, I look to where the chest still lies splintered along the far wall. The trays remain as I'd left them, near to the rubble, and the scent of smoke still lingers in the air as I shuffle through the ash.

I advance to one of the metal chests; the lid creaking open as I lift it up. Inside are my potions: spells of reanimation, persuasion, transfiguration.

Grabbing a bottle of the transfiguration potion, a gift from Zeus who often used it to walk amongst the mortal realm in disguise, I turn and leave the room.

I head back to the throne room and once again climb onto the dais, taking a seat in my chair. I stare at the bottle, trying to convince myself this is the only way; the only decision. *How else can I enter the mortal realm and find the answers I seek?* But it's risky, and using this potion comes with a catch.

Using the potion will transform me into whoever I wish to become, allowing me to take over their life; controlling it. But will require me to leave all my god powers behind until I return once more to the Underworld.

What else can I do? What other choice is there? If I want to find Persephone's essence, and discover who the woman is, the one the stone has shown me, then this has to be the way, right?

I reach into the pocket of my chair and pull out the stone. With the word said once again, the Peering Stone fills with the ether laced smoke and I state my demand.

As I consider the symbol on the card she had put back in her bag, I state my request, "Find me a man to inhabit. A man of that symbol who will allow me to get close to her; to know her."

The stone flickers, and a face appears. I turn to Cerberus, who tilts his heads in confusion, and removing the topper from the small bottle, I toss back the contents. But before I transform completely, I transport myself to the mortal realm, to a place called Fayetteville, where I arrive in a dwelling with two sets of stairs.

Padding up the first set of stairs, my body continues to transform as I reach the first floor.

Just as I turn the corner; I come face to face with the man I am becoming and he utters, "What the-"

"Sleep," I command, and the man slumps to the floor.

I pick him up and descend the second set of stairs, taking him into a back bedroom where I tuck him into bed. I don't need anyone coming upon him, so this is the best option; the safest option.

Walking back down the hall, I enter what I presume is his room, looking for the same card the girl had possessed.

I find it laying next to a set of keys on the bedside table and pick it up.

"Well, what have we here?" I say aloud. "It appears I am now Mr. Aaron Evans."

I walk to the bathroom and look in the mirror where an unfamiliar face with my eyes looks back at me. "Yes," I say. "This will do. This will do nicely."

CHAPTER 28

DO YOUR DREAMS TELL YOU SOMETHING? (MELODY)

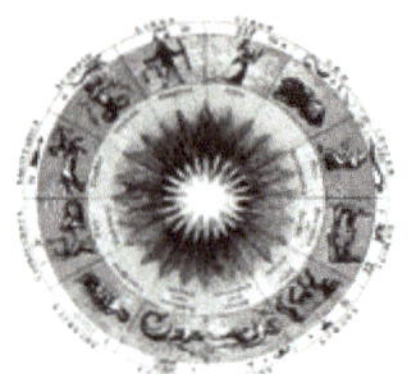

"What the fuck, Melody?" I speak aloud, my body still quaking from the nightmare I came out of.

I clutch my hand to my chest, gripping tightly to my tank top as the cool gemstone of my necklace settles between my breasts. The ribbing of the fabric I have balled in between my fist leaves a waffle pattern in my palm as my chest rises and falls in quick spasms. I attempt to catch my breath, my body slick with sweat, and my legs aching from how tightly I had them drawn into me.

Smoke trails upward from the lemon and rosemary scented candle burning on the table beside my bed, while the Virgo constellation flickers brightly as my planetarium projector illuminates the ceiling above me.

Her stick figured body glimmers as Virgo's headless form seems to fall from the heavens. *Of all the images for me to look up and see after what I experienced in my dream, why her?*

I extend my legs, untangling my feet from the blankets, my toes tingling as blood slowly flows back into my extremities.

The Maker's Market convenes in Washington County once a year, and even though I told Desire we'd go several times before, we never have. But this year was different, and we actually went, which was good because I never would have scored my new trinket from last weekend at one of the shops downtown.

I reach over to the left side of my bed, picking up my laptop from where it sits on the empty pillow at my side. I was up late, scrolling through the images of the items for sale on the vendors' webpage who sold me my necklace earlier that day.

A to Z Oddities. Where Ancient Craft Meets the Wonders of the Modern Age. The elaborate logo, A to Z with a dragon circling the letters, glows up at me from the screen when I open my laptop.

The jewelry tab is still open, and as I scroll my cursor over the screen, my necklace pops out at me. Sold Out, it says.

I was curious, and Desire had said something about the stone I purchased; had said it brought good energy. *I need some of that in my life.*

The description of the piece reads: *Wire securely wraps this healing stone, ensuring the precious gem remains secure and accessible. Embrace its energy wherever your path may take you.*

My eyebrows rise as I smirk. *Really?* I lift the pendant from where it's nestled in my cleavage, dangling it out in front of me.

"Well, here's to hoping," I say aloud, kissing the stone and then placing it back beneath my shirt.

There is a link underneath the image and as I hover over it, the words *properties for Alexandrite* rise from the page.

"Okay, you sneaky devil. I'm curious. What do you got?"

I scan the page quickly, scoffing from time to time as the thought, *okay,* echoes in my head. I roll my eyes, but just before I shut the cover of my laptop, the last line jumps out at me. *Many believe that Alexandrite, as a protective stone, brings elation, emotional balance, and strength of spirit.*

I chuckle to myself. *Really? Does it now? Well, the only thing mine has brought me has been fucked up dreams and an urge to pee.*

At the urging of my bladder, I shut my case, set it back on my pillow and crawl out of bed, making my way to the bathroom.

I finish up in the bathroom, and as I stand at the mirror washing my hands, the light overhead flickers.

"What the fu-" I curse, the words trailing off as I raise my eyes toward where my light dims above me. My vanity light glows, pulsing once, twice, and then goes out completely.

As I lower my eyes, an image appears in the mirror. A face grins back at me for a split second, and I jump back, banging into the door as I scream.

A minute later, my bedroom door flies open and Desire stands at its entrance, one of their high heels firmly clutched in their hand.

Taking in their appearance, pink silk pjs with dainty red hearts patterned across them, hair wrapped up in their bonnet, and a size 12 high heeled pump in their hands, I can't help but laugh.

"Girl!" Desire sinks to the floor beside me, dropping their shoe between their outstretched legs as they fan themselves. "You about gave me a heart attack."

"I'm sorry." I throw my head back, laughing, bashing my head on the frame of my bathroom's doorway. I grab the back of my head. "Owie," I snivel.

"That's what you get. What's wrong with you? Scaring the ever-living bejesus outta me?"

"It's nothing," I insist. "Just had a bad dream and an undeniable urge to pee."

"And?"

"And nothing," I offer.

"That scream wasn't nothin'," Desire's voice trills as they purse their lips, cocking their head sideways at me.

"Seriously. It was nothing," I assure them.

"Don't do that shit again," they warn, pushing off the floor as they stand above me.

I reach for their hand, hoping they'll lift me to my feet.

"No, ma'am," Desire says, picking up their shoe from where it lies sideways on the floor. Turning, they walk away.

I call out after them, "Door!"

"Get it your damned self," their voice trails off as they walk back to their room down the hall, slamming the door behind them.

I yell out to them, "Love you, too!"

Desire's voice echoes, the barely muffled reply escaping beneath their door, "Goodnight, Melody."

The next morning as I sit at our small kitchen table in the corner of our apartment, gulping down my second cup of coffee, Desire finally emerges from their cave.

I smile. "Nice to see you in the land of the living."

"It's too damned early for... all of that." They gesture toward me, circling their hand.

They turn away, their slippers scratching across the linoleum as they pull a box of cereal from the cupboard above them and turn, opening the refrigerator door. Desire rummages around the fridge, then huffs as they lift their hand in the air, the milk sloshing as they swirl it around.

They fume, "Could you leave some for me, just once?" They mumble under their breath as they dig through the panty, "This bitch has the nerve to keep me up all night and then her rude ass can't even leave enough damned milk for me." Their voice trails off, but I can still make out several curse words as they complain under their breath. "Could you, Mel-O-dee!" Desire stands above me, one hip cocked out to the side, both hands on their hips.

"Could I, what?" I smirk.

"See. And this is why I don't fuck with y'all." They flick their fingers in my direction.

I stand, wrap my arms around their shoulders, and kiss their cheek.

Desire pulls away quickly, wiping my affections from the side of their face as they frown at me.

Walking back toward my room, I stop in the doorway and tease,

"Don't be mad, baby. If you play your cards right, I'll do that thing with my tongue you like so much."

Desire picks up their slipper and chucks it at me. "You're fucking disgusting, you know that?"

"And that is why I don't fuck with y'all," I counter, pretending to jerk myself off.

That finally gets a smile out of them, and Desire laughs as they say, "I know that's right."

Later that day, as I sit in my office plugging away at the stack of medical records piled on the corner of my desk, my thoughts wander back to my dream from the night before.

I take my glasses off, pinching the bridge of my nose as I scrunch my face, yawning as I do. The frames have created two indentations on each side of my nose from how tightly they are pressing in, and a dull headache radiates from behind my eyes.

I reach above my head, arching my back as I stretch my arms in the air. I am so distracted, enjoying each pop of my spine as I shift in my seat, that I don't hear my door open behind me.

"Melody," Elliott whispers against my left ear, causing me to jump back.

"Jesus!" I shout, clutching my hand to my chest as I attempt to steady my racing heart.

"No. Not Jesus. But you can call me a god." Elliott grabs my hair and pulls it back as he hovers above me.

I swat his hands away, tagging him in the balls as I flail.

"Damn, Mel," Elliott grimaces. "All you had to say was, let go. Was that entirely necessary?" Elliott bends over at the waist, bracing himself on the back of my chair as he gains his bearings.

"I didn't mean to." I chuckle, turning my chair to face him. "But you had it coming."

"Remind me next time not to sneak up on you," he says.

I wink at him. "I already did."

He rubs his crotch once more. "Point taken."

"Uh, huh. I bet it was." I giggle again.

"So, I was thinking-"

"That never ends well," I interrupt.

He glowers at me. "Mel?"

"Elliott," I say mockingly, grabbing his hands for effect.

Elliott pulls his hands free, nervously running his left one through his hair as he leans back against the filing cabinet behind him. He is handsome, and he knows it. The way he carries himself proves as much.

He has icy-blue, crystalline eyes with thick wispy lashes that flutter when he speaks. His lips are full and his bright white teeth, whose prominent canines press into his lips as he smiles, gleam in the incandescent lighting of my office.

The buzzing from the lights overhead distracts me and, although he speaks with an even cadence, his voice lilting as he chats, I ignore most of what Elliott has been saying to me. I'm still thinking about something else.

"Mel?" he sings. "Earth to Mel." Elliott snaps his fingers at me. "You are somewhere else today."

"I'm sorry. Okay..." I say, leaning back in my chair as I look up at him, "tell me again?"

"As I said before, when you were so obviously tuning me out, there's a thing down on Dickson tonight. It's Thirsty Thursday and I just thought, you know, if you didn't already have any plans..." He slides his hands in his pockets, wrinkling his slacks as he crosses one ankle over the other. "Have a couple of drinks with me later?" His hands fiddle in his pockets, and he adjusts himself as he awaits my reply.

"Elliott," I draw out his name. "We've talked about this." Elliott pulls his hands from his pockets and crosses his arms as he waits for me to continue. "I don't date co-workers. It's bad business."

"It's not a date," he assures me. "It's just two friends going out for a few."

"Elliott?"

"Mel?"

"I-"

"That's not a no." He dances. "Look, it'll be fun. I promise," he assures me.

"Fine!" I exaggerate my response. "You win."

"I win?" he asks, surprised, tilting his head toward me to confirm.

"Yes."

"Woo!" he cheers. "I win. I win!" His voice echoes as he walks out of my office. "Hey, Luke? Did you hear that? I win." I can still hear him chattering away, his voice trailing off as he makes his way back to his office.

Elliott Marshall is a referral analyst at the insurance company where I work. He spends his nine to five chugging down double espressos as he clicks away at his desk, frantically typing as he closes out one requisition after another. After I compile all the medical records, review everything submitted, and ensure the file's accuracy, I send it to him for approval.

It isn't what I thought I would be doing at twenty-seven. This isn't what I pay $600 a month in student loans to do, but it pays the bills, and at this point in my life, where everything else is uncertain, it will have to do.

My mother had warned me. She had said an artist's life would be one of hardship, but I didn't listen because I knew better. At eighteen, with my entire life in front of me, and no experience to go on, of course I did. At least that's what I'd thought. But boy was I wrong.

After four years at Fulbright College, four years working at Dickson Street Bookshop, and a degree in graphic design under my belt, here I sit in a sterile office wasting my best years working for a big name medical insurance company.

I graduated five years earlier and have yet to design a single thing. Sure, I design in my spare time, or at least I used to, but I hadn't applied an ounce of creativity to anything since my final submission. Now, here I am, staring at the flickering screen of my computer, the twinkle in my eye all but extinguished by the mind numbing existence my life has become.

It won't last, the job I have now. An algorithm will eventually replace me and a program will complete the tasks I find oh so tedious. There is an elapsed timer counting down the minutes until I become obsolete. An expiration date set that will force me to make some drastic changes. And when that time comes, well, that is a problem for a different day.

As the day ends, shutting off my computer and grabbing my purse from where it lies on the top of the filing cabinet behind me, I make my way to the door of my office, closing it behind me.

I step into the hallway, my coworkers all but gone for the day, their doors closed as their unfinished work still lines their desks, ready to greet them the next day.

The imaginary clock ticks as I walk down the corridor toward the elevator, my heels clacking on the tile floor beneath my feet.

I hate heels. Hate the way I have to squeeze into them each morning, convicting my baby toes to a day of pure torture. But it isn't torture. I know torture. I have tasted it on my tongue and felt it slicing its way across my skin as I lay bare.

No. No, I don't. I correct myself, shaking my head as I attempt to clear the images from my mind as I wait for the elevator doors to open.

It is eerily quiet, and as I wait impatiently for my exit, I realize I haven't pressed the button to call the lift to our floor.

Just as I am about to reach over and depress it, someone steps beside me, our fingers reaching for the button at the same time.

"Sorry." The man chuckles, awkwardly pulling his hand back and sliding it into the pocket of his slacks.

"It's fine." I force a smile, sliding the strap of my purse back up my arm and over my shoulder from where it slipped down.

We just stand there in silence, neither one of us looking at the other, and as I rock back and forth on my heels, the silence getting the better of me; I open my mouth to speak when the man speaks first.

"Have you worked here long?" he asks.

"About a year and a half," I answer. I grin anxiously, glancing at the man briefly and then back up at the light above the doors.

"That long?"

"Yeah." I huff, fidgeting with my purse once again.

He admits, "I've never seen you before."

"No?" I ask, finally turning to the man as I look up at him.

Storm cloud eyes stare back at me as he shifts his weight from one foot to the other.

He stands facing me, and as I survey his features, I can't help but feel I have seen him before, so I ask, "Have we met?"

"No," he answers, a smirk lifting the corner of his mouth.

"Oh. Okay," I stammer. I pause a moment, but as a familiarity washes over me, the words rush out, "Are you sure because-"

"I'm positive," he interrupts me.

I roll my eyes and then face back toward the doors. "Okay," I whisper, mouthing the words to myself in agitation.

From where he stands beside me, the man states, "I would have remembered."

I blush, the blood rising from my neck and pooling in my ears as it pumps loudly.

The doors finally open and as I look over at the man, he motions with his hands for me to enter. "After you?"

I step into the elevator, turning to face the doors as he presses the button for the lobby.

We ride down in silence; me gripping tightly to my purse as he leans up against the back wall, his hand still in his pocket.

When the doors open, I jump forward, exiting quickly as my heels click on the floor.

I rush to the front doors, and as I push them open, the cool gust of that November night brushes across my face.

The man's steps sound not far behind me, and he calls out, "Goodnight, Melody."

"Goodnight," I call over my shoulder, not looking back as I hurry to my car where I unlock my doors, jerking the handle back as the hinges creak.

I plop down in my seat, the forgotten mail I'd left in my car crinkling beneath me as I slam the door to my laser blue two-door Chevy Cobalt.

As I turn the key, bringing my car to life, it hits me; I never told him my name. I never told him, and yet somehow, he knew.

Somehow, "Mr. tall, dark, and press the stop button on the elevator, rip every stitch of clothing off me, and ravish me while I scream out," knew. He knew my name, and he knew me, despite his statement to the contrary.

CHAPTER 29
IT'S JUST DRINKS (MELODY)

I sigh as I step from the shower. "That is exactly what I needed."

I had leaned against the wall, the stream of the scalding water turning my skin a blotchy crimson as it washed over me. I felt chilled, which had nothing to do with the crisp temperatures of that November night, and everything to do with the eeriness of the shadow of the stranger from the elevator as I left him standing in the parking lot of our office building.

As I showered, I imagined him pressing me back against my wall, his hands intertwined with my own as he pinned them above my head. My hands wandered over my skin, the suds from my body wash increasing the sensation as my imagination ran wild and a moan escaped my lips.

The lubrication added to the experience as my hands trailed lower where a heat blossomed across me as my fingertips brushed against my breast, then finally explored between my thighs, causing my body to surge forward.

In that moment, as my fingers circled my clit, my mind only thought of him: his eyes, his mouth, his hands. Those long, elegant fingers that caressed the lapel of his dark blue suit jacket as he leaned back against the elevator wall, those bright silvery eyes gleaming at me from under unruly brows, and those full, inviting lips. Those lips wearing a devious smile as he stared after me.

Who was this mysterious stranger? Who was this man whose image had drawn the most body rocking, mind-altering orgasm from me?

As I dry off, my wobbly legs barely hold me up as I groan. *Get ahold of yourself, Mel. Going out for drinks half-cocked never ends well.*

I bathe my legs in baby oil, allowing the lavender scent to calm me. I then wring the remaining moisture from my hair and shake it up and down several times before wrapping my towel around me.

The steam from my shower still hangs in the air, my mirror coated in its remnants, and I wipe my hand across the surface, bracing myself for the face that had stared back at me the night prior. But only my face stares back at me now: dark brown eyes with flecks of caramel, sloping nose, full pouty lips, toasted brown skin.

I smile back at my reflection. *Well, Mel, let's see what we can make of ourselves.*

I apply my makeup in the same mirror after I choose an outfit, laying it out on my bed. Looking at my clothes, I huff. *What am I doing? I don't want to go out with Elliott. Don't want the headache I know will follow.* I know he said it was only drinks amongst friends, know I can ensure it remains as such, but how he looks at me... I'm not sure he can live up to his end of the bargain.

With my face applied, I sit on the end of my bed, sliding on my boots, when Desire opens the door.

"Where are we going all tarted up?" they ask.

"Tarted up? What are we, in a period romance?"

They fan themselves. "If only I was that lucky."

"Aw, baby, one day you'll find love," I tease.

"I'd settle for a little dinner and dick," they click the last word suggestively.

"I bet you would," I goad, smiling.

"But seriously, what gives? You don't go out on a school night?" they lecture.

"Elliott," I admit.

"Oh," Desire exaggerates the word. "Mr. look at me, look at me, I'm all tall, dark, and fuck me, please. What does his ass want?" they accuse.

I roll my eyes. "Drinks."

They raise their eyebrows as they cross their arms over their chest. "Drinks?"

"Just, drinks," I assert.

"Uh-huh. I can smell 'it's just drinks' from here." They wave their hand in front of their face, wafting the air around. "Smells just like… pussy."

"Now who's fucking disgusting?" I fake gag, tossing my fuzzy pillow off the corner of my bed at them.

"I'm just saying." They turn to walk away, kicking my pillow across the floor at me.

"Say less," my words trail after them.

I arrive at the bar about thirty minutes later, showing my ID to security before walking in.

As I descend the stairs, the overwhelming scent of perfume and cologne assaults me; overpowering florals and pungent spices, as I make my way through the crowd, searching the surrounding faces while I look for Elliott.

Sitting toward the back, on the other side of the dance floor, Elliott waits at a bar height table with two high-back chairs.

He stands as I approach, looking at me from head to toe before he says, "You look… nice. You didn't get all gussied up for me, did you?"

"Gussied up? What is with everyone using antiquated terminology this evening?"

He raises a quizzical brow at me, not understanding my meaning, and then motions toward the server, taking his seat as I place my purse over the back of my chair.

The server saunters over to our table and props her elbows on the tabletop, her ample bosom spilling out of her shirt as she bends over. She has dark curls up in a ponytail, pale blue eyes, warm tanned skin, and her tight jeans accentuate her curves; round ass popping out as she bends one knee. She looks up at Elliott, capturing his attention as they both ignore me.

"What'll it be, handsome?" she flirts.

I throw up a little in my mouth.

"Long Island. Mel?" he asks, not glancing over at me as he waits.

He just sits there, making eyes at the girl, who is shamelessly biting down on her full bottom lip. *Am I getting jealous? Why am I getting jealous? It's just drinks with a friend, right?*

"Patron. And make it a double."

Elliott finally turns his attention toward me. "Wow, Mel. You aren't fucking around."

"I turn into a pumpkin at midnight," I quip.

"Well, pace yourself. We're in no hurry."

The server brushes her fingertip under Elliott's chin as she says, "Coming right up."

Elliott turns in his chair, staring at the girl's ass as she walks away.

I scoff, "Could she make it any more obvious?"

"Huh?" Elliott states, his attention still on the girl as she leans on the bar, placing our order as she flirts with the bartender.

"Somebody's thirsty."

"Isn't that why you ordered a double?" he says matter-of-factly.

I look up from where I am playing with my coaster, my eyes meeting Elliott's. "What? No," I trail off. "Absolutely not."

"You sure?" he asks, reaching for my hands.

I pull my hands back, placing them nervously in my lap, smoothing them across my thighs. "Positive."

The bar brims with twenty-some things everywhere I look. There is chatter and laughter filling the air as their voices filter through the small space. The inside of the bar is small, the patio being the largest space, but with the cool temperatures of fall, it now lays empty; save the occasional smoker, who steps outside to get a quick nicotine fix. Illuminated bottles line the back wall, while music reverberates from the speakers, making the glasses in the wells tremble.

I take in the entire scene, an odd feeling washing over me as I scan the room. Someone is watching me. Somewhere, someone has their eyes trained on me, taking in my form, and I can feel it.

I scan the room and then stop as my eyes fix to the corner of the bar where seated on a barstool, staring intently at me, is my stranger.

He swishes his glass several times and then raises it to his lips.

Those lips. Those succulent looking lips. *What I wouldn't give to be that glass, that drink? To have his tongue licking my curves as he sucks me down.*

I swallow, a flush rising from my neck and settling on my cheeks.

"What?" Elliott asks. He turns in his chair, scanning the space, and then tilts his head in acknowledgement.

When Elliott turns back to me, leaning back in his chair, I inquire, "Do you know him?"

"Who? Mr. Evans, Aaron? Yeah, he's okay. Why? You want me to ask him to join us?" He starts to turn.

"No!" I reach out and grab his hand, and he turns back around. "No. I'm good."

"Yeah?" he confirms, his smile widening.

My cheeks warm. "Yeah."

"Okay, good. Because I kind of wanted to have you all to myself." He winks.

"Is that so?" I smirk.

He confesses, "Of course. I'd hate to share your attention when it was so hard to get you here in the first place."

I tilt my head, looking away. "Not that hard."

"Mel?" he shortens my name for effect.

I turn my attention back to him. "Elliott?" I say in my best E.T. impersonation, my eyes widening.

He scoffs, "Are you serious? I have been asking you for months to have a drink with me."

"Yeah, and now I'm here," I answer with my hands, motioning around us.

"Exactly," he leans on the table, looking at me intently. "So, let me enjoy this a little."

"Seriously?" I ask skeptically, cocking a brow.

"Yes," he exaggerates. "It's not every day I get to have drinks with a beautiful woman."

I laugh out loud, my head falling back as I glare at Elliott. "I doubt that."

"Why?" he asks seriously.

"Because you're... you." I motion toward him, my hands flowing up him like a game show host. "You're Elliott. You're a confident, employed man in his late twenties," I gush.

"Hey?" he sounds offended.

"And you're handsome. So, I doubt this is a rarity for you," I say, taking another drink.

"I'm handsome?" He wiggles his eyebrows.

"Stop." I set down my glass, looking away. "You know you are."

"Do I? Do I, Mel?"

"You are, and what's worse is you know you are. So, let's quit with the coyness." I turn back to him.

"I am pretty handsome, aren't I?" He brushes his knuckle across his collarbone before blowing it off.

"Well, now that your head is too large to walk through the doorway, how about we change the subject?" I offer.

"Fine. But stay focused. I'd hate for you to get distracted by how handsome I am," he teases.

I pretend to put my finger down my throat and gag as the server returns with our drinks, once again flirting with Elliott before walking away.

"Tips must be light tonight," I joke as she takes back up her stance at the bar.

"No. It's probably because of how handsome I am." Elliott winks at me before taking a drink from his Long Island.

Frowning, I say, "Ugh. Why did I say anything? You're not gonna let it go, are you?"

"Nope," he says as he crunches the ice between his teeth. "What fun would that be?" he jests.

"Can we talk about something else, anything else?" I say as I stare over his head.

"Sure. How about we talk about how you are here with me, as handsome as I am, and yet, can't stop looking over at McSteamy over there?"

"I am not," I argue, my cheeks flushing once again as I look back at Elliott, tearing my eyes from where they had obviously been staring at Mr. Evans. "And I didn't take you for a Grey's Anatomy fan?"

He smiles. "I'm not."

The conversation shifts, moving from where we had grown up to what schools we had gone to and ending back with how I ended up at our company.

"So, wait. You have an art degree and don't have a single tattoo?" he asks.

I confirm, "Nope. Not one."

He leans back in his chair, looking at me in disbelief. "Not possible. That combination doesn't exist. How can you call yourself a proper artist without one?"

I cross my arms as I say, "Because I'm not a proper artist. And as far as the tattoo is concerned, I guess I'm just a unicorn."

Elliott spits the mouthful of drink he'd just taken on the table in front of us, choking as he tries to catch his breath.

"What the fuck, Elliott?" I grumble, wiping the stickiness from my arm with the small bar napkin I pull out from under my drink.

"I'm sorry." He laughs, handing me his napkin. "That word doesn't mean what you think it means."

He stands and walks over to the bar, grabbing more napkins, and returns with a handful.

"Control yourself or this is the last time I go on a date with you," I announce, throwing back the second round the server delivered to our table.

Elliott's eyes lock on mine. "I thought it wasn't a date?"

"It's not." I shift in my seat nervously. "It's... it's... I have to pee."

I rise from my seat and head toward the restroom, having to walk by Mr. Evans to get to the restroom. My eyes fall to the floor as I walk past, and as I wait outside the door, turning my head, our eyes meet.

I glance away, rushing into the bathroom as soon as the door opens, and a girl exits.

In the bathroom, after I pee, as I stand in front of the mirror washing my hands, I feel something; the same feeling I had when Mr. Evans had looked at me earlier that evening.

I look around the bathroom, which is crazy considering how small it is, but there is no one. I dry my hands and look in the mirror.

"Get ahold of yourself, Mel," I order, pulling my lip gloss from the inside pocket of my leggings, and sliding the smooth rollerball across my lips.

I purse them twice, smacking them together as I look at my reflection, and once again, I have that feeling.

The next thing I know, bright emerald eyes shine back at me in the mirror, but I don't scream this time. I just turn my head from side to side, those emerald eyes following my movements as I do.

My eyes are enchanting, but these eyes are mesmerizing and rimmed with something dangerous.

I blink several times, thinking the alcohol is playing with my mind and I am just seeing things. But the color of my irises never changes, remaining that deep, sparkling green.

A knock comes at the door, and when I jerk it open, a friend from the bookstore stands on the other side.

"Oh, shit, Mel. You sacred me pulling the door open so fast."

"Terrin! Oh my god, it is so good to see you. I need your help," I mumble, pulling her into the bathroom and shutting the door behind us.

"Girl, are you feeling okay?" she asks.

I ask frantically, "What color are my eyes?"

She looks at me incredulously. "What?"

"What color are my eyes?" I insist, grabbing both of Terrin's arms.

"Brown. Mel, they're brown," she asserts.

I let go of Terrin's arms and walk back to the mirror. I gaze into the eyes peering back at me, still that shining emerald color.

I shake my head in disbelief. "Are you sure?"

"I don't know what's going on with you, Mel. But maybe... maybe you should ease up on the lines," Terrin says, tapping the side of her nose as she smirks at me.

"Right," I exaggerate. I force a laugh and then exit the bathroom.

They were green. I know they were. I know what I saw.

As I step out of the restroom, I feel different; warm. I feel like my whole body is vibrating, and as I am about to walk past Mr. Evans, I stop. I stand in front of him, studying the features of his face before I ask, "What's your deal?"

CHAPTER 30
WHAT HAPPENS AT MIDNIGHT? (MELODY)

"My deal?" Mr. Evans parrots, looking all around to see if I am addressing someone else. He leans back in his chair, sliding his hands in his pockets as he glares at me. "No, deal. Why do you ask?"

"You're a liar," I challenge, turning to walk away.

He reaches out and grabs my arm, spinning me back to face him. "How so?"

"You said you had never seen me before. You said you would have remembered. For someone that acted like they didn't know me, how was it, as I was leaving, you knew my name?"

"Your name?"

"My name," I assert. "How?" I step into him, my anger bubbling to the surface as I hold my face mere inches from his.

Mr. Evans snakes his arm behind my back and pulls me closer to him. Moving his face to brush up against the side of my cheek, his lips graze across the corner of my ear. His hot breath across my lobe has me melting into him and I close my eyes as I give into the feeling of him pressed against me. He whispers, rubbing his lips over the opening of my ear, "Your ID badge was hanging out of your purse."

My eyes shoot open, and I pull back from him, smoothing my hands across my legs as I gain my bearings.

I blush. "Oh."

"Oh," he states matter-of-factly. "That wasn't the answer you were hoping for, I see. How was it you thought I knew your name, if not that?"

"I... I didn't know. It was just odd."

His eyebrows raise. "As odd as you asking someone in the bathroom what color your eyes are?"

"Are you spying on me, creeper?" I inflect.

"No. It's just that you weren't exactly quiet. I could hear you from out here."

"Oh."

I sway, my vision blurring slightly before I turn away from Mr. Evans and walk back to Elliott at our table.

Before I am out of earshot, I hear Mr. Evans state under his breath, "They're green, Little One."

As I sit back down, Elliott looks at me oddly.

Sliding over another round, he looks over his shoulder at Mr. Evans, then back at me as he asks in a jealous tone, "What was that about?"

"It's nothing," I answer nervously.

"That didn't look like nothing." He raises his eyebrows as he takes a large gulp.

"Jealous?" I jest, giggling as I try to lighten the mood.

"Should I be?" he asks flatly, looking seriously back at me.

"What? No. It's nothing. It's..." my words trail off.

"It's?" he asks.

Suddenly, my whole body tingles, my head spins, and I feel a painful pressure behind my eyes.

Elliott reaches out and touches my arm, but his words sound muffled as he asks with an almost slow-motion, "Mel? Mel, are you alright?"

"I…" my words get lost on my lips, and I blink slowly. "I have an uncontrollable urge to dance," I draw out my statement.

I hop down from the bar stool and take off my jacket, tossing it in my chair as Elliott's concerned gaze follows my movements. My body still tingles from head to toe and I can't control the movements it is making to the music as I stand on the dance floor alone, swaying to "I Wanna Be Your Slave" by Måneskin while my hands rub up and down my body.

I'm not in time with the rhythm, but it feels so good; every electric movement, every jolt of sensation my fingertips send running across my bare skin.

As I sway, my eyes closed and hands wandering, I feel someone come up behind me.

I open my eyes and the server who had been flirting with Elliott stands behind me, her hands on my hips as I lean back into her. Her fingers trail across my torso, up my ribs, and finally grip around my throat as I gasp.

"Dirty girl," she whispers in my ear.

"The dirtiest," I coo.

Elliott slides off the barstool and walks towards us, swiping a finger across his lips before he licks them. He stands in front of me, his hands in his pockets as I rub my body back against the girl.

"Like what you see?" I ask suggestively, reaching out and grabbing him around his neck as I pull him toward me.

He doesn't fight me and there is no protest because he wants this; he'd hoped for it. And despite all my previous thoughts to the contrary, in that moment, I want it to.

His hands grip my hips, pulling me against him as he stands with one of his legs pressed firmly between mine.

I grind against his leg as the sensation sends sparks up my back and my whole body vibrates.

Everywhere Elliott's hands touch feels like flames licking my skin; like I am on fire.

I burn, needing something, someone to quench the undeniable thirst scalding the back of my throat. But who will it be? The girl or Elliott?

The girl left, gone back to her work after her manager walked behind the bar, and Elliott's hands have taken up where hers left off. They're all over me; cupping my ass, and lifting my leg up as he pushes his erection that begs for attention into me.

He presses it harder against me and I practically moan out the question, "Wanna get out of here?"

"I thought it was just drinks?" he whispers in my ear, squeezing my ass tighter.

I grab Elliott's face when he tries to pull away, gripping his chin tightly.

"Last chance," I say breathlessly.

Elliott drops my leg, steps back to our table, drops a twenty-dollar bill on its surface, and then grabs my jacket and purse. He comes back to where I stand motionless on the dance floor; the speakers blasting out the next song behind me, and grips my hand, pulling me toward the front of the bar.

As we exit, I look over briefly to where Mr. Evans had been sitting at the bar, and to my shock, he is gone.

The sounds of my boots pounding on the asphalt as Elliott guides me behind him echo throughout the dark parking lot as my body continues to vibrate. *I didn't have that much to drink, right?*

After weaving through several rows of cars, Elliott spins me around and pins me up against the side of a black Range Rover. The doors unlock with a click and he grabs underneath my thighs, wrapping my legs around his waist. His hands trail up and down my legs, his nails digging into the fabric of my leggings as he moans.

Kissing me forcefully, his tongue invades my mouth and then he bites down on my bottom lip, letting out a groan of frustration. He jerks open the back driver's side door with one hand and leans me back into the seat where my legs unravel from his hips, and my lower back arches as his hands go under my thighs.

He leans down and buries his face between my legs, rubbing his nose back and forth across the seam of my pants. Taking in a deep breath, he bites the inside of my thigh.

"What do you want?" he asks, pulling his face back slightly.

I grasp his hair, gripping it in my fists as I press him harder against me, and I buck my hips up, rubbing his chin across my most sensitive parts as he laughs.

He grabs the waistband of my leggings, quickly pulling them down over my ass, and with my legs trapped in my pants, lifts them in the air.

"That is a beautiful pussy," he says before once again burying his face between my legs.

He slides his mouth from the top of my folds to my asshole, then spreads me apart as he glides that skilled tongue across my center.

I cry out, "Oh, god, Elliott!" Fisting handfuls of his hair as I hold him in place, grinding into him.

He draws back slightly and says, "That's my girl. I told you you'd be calling me a god. Didn't I?"

"Yes," I answer breathlessly.

"Yes?" Elliott confirms.

"Yes," I moan, trying to force his head back between my thighs as he pulls away, causing me to groan in frustration.

"Patience," he says, unbuckling his jeans.

As I look down, I see him releasing his cock from his pants. He is large, almost imposing, slightly terrifying, but oh so beautiful.

"You have a beautiful cock." I giggle.

"Do I?" he asks, stroking it up and down. "And what would you like me to do with my beautiful cock?"

He climbs up onto the Range Rover, the door still open and my ass exposed for all to see. He wipes his pre-cum on the inside of my thigh before positioning himself at my opening, and then trails the head of his dick up and down, collecting my juices on him as he hisses.

"Come on, Mel. I can only hold this dog off for so long. You've offered him a bone, and he wants to eat. Now, what do you want?"

I tilt my hips, and he breaches my opening, the head of his dick sliding into me.

"Fuck, Mel," he gasps through gritted teeth. "You're not playing fair."

He thrusts forward, burying his entire length inside me, and I cry out, "Yes."

"Yes?" he asks again, pulling back so his tip is barely caressing me.

"Yes!" I exclaim.

He thrusts forward again, this time gripping my thighs and lifting my ass up to meet him. He drives into me hard, pulling out painfully slowly, and then pounds back in where my ass bounces against him with each thrust as he hardens inside me.

I clench around him, my walls closing in as the rush fills me and I want to drain him. I want him to cover my insides with his pleasure and then have him lick it off the inside of my thighs, but Elliott isn't the type. He's the type of guy to be turned off by such an ask. So, when he asks me again, between the next couple of thrusts, what I want, I cry out the first thing that comes to mind.

"Take me home!"

I fall apart once those words escape my lips, and Elliott takes them as a call to action because he lifts my upper body off the seat, pressing me tightly against him as he continues to fuck me mercilessly.

I wrap my arms around him, my legs up on one of his shoulders as the door remains open, the cool air rushing in all around us as my cries fill the night, echoing across the parking lot.

Someone could see, but I don't care. Someone could hear, and I hope they'll be jealous. I hope my cries will make them stop and pleasure themselves right then and there. I even imagine as much.

I imagine him- Mr. Evans. I imagine him walking to his car, and in hearing my cries of ecstasy, coming to watch. I imagine him leaning up against a car with his hips thrust forward as he strokes his hard, throbbing cock, and not once does he take his eyes off me.

Actually, I imagine him coming to the Range Rover, tearing Elliott off of me and taking what he wants while Elliott is forced to watch.

The thought drives me over the edge, breaking open my floodgates as I soak Elliott from his balls all the way up to his navel. I come all over his dick and as my insides milk him, soft pants escape his lips.

"Wow, Mel," he mutters. "I had no idea."

I murmur breathlessly, "What?"

"I didn't know you could fuck like that," he calls out, chuckling. Elliott pulls himself from between my thighs, grabs some shop towels from under the seat, and begins wiping himself down. He then places one on my chest and says, "For you, milady."

I laugh, taking the towel and cleaning what I can of the wetness between my legs.

"And they say chivalry is dead," I tease, as I pull my leggings up over my ass and then smooth down my hair with my fingers before sitting upright.

Once I am mostly put back together, I look up at Elliott as he stands with a shit-eating grin on his face.

"I should probably go," I say.

"You could come back to my place?" he offers.

"Can't, remember? I turn into a pumpkin at midnight."

I hop down from the back seat, and he looks down at me pleadingly. "It's 11:30. We can be back at my place well before then, and if you still want to turn into a pumpkin at that point, then by all means."

"I'll see you at work tomorrow."

I step past Elliott, place a quick kiss on his cheek, and then pat his chest before walking away.

I walk toward my car, not looking back to where Elliott still stands with his hand on the side of his vehicle.

He calls after me, "See you at work?"

"Yup." I raise my hand in the air and wave back at him, not bothering to turn around.

As I pass the next row of cars, almost reaching my parked car, a figure suddenly steps out with smoke trailing from his lips as he places his vape back in his pocket, Mr. Evans now stands before me.

I look up into those silver eyes, a shiver racing up my spine as neither of us says anything, and we just stare at one another.

After an uncomfortable silence, he steps out of my way and I step toward my car, stopping at the end of the next vehicle.

I turn around, facing him, and I grumble, "What are you doing out here?"

He moves quickly, decreasing the space between us in what seems like only several steps.

"Leaving, and you? What were YOU doing out here, Melody?" he asks accusingly.

He glares down at me, an almost scowl on his lips as the words drip off them like a warning.

"I... I'm just trying to get home."

He grabs my wrist, lifts it to his lips, biting the flesh above my pulse point, and I shudder.

"And did you?" he asks, still holding my hand captive.

My voice shakes as my words spill forth, "Did I... what?"

Mr. Evans moves so fast, spinning me into the back of the car we had been standing in front of. His body presses into me, arching me back across the trunk of the car.

As he leans over me, his mouth grazes over my ear just as it had in the bar, and he asks, "Did he take you home, Little One?"

I push him off me, my boots pounding against the asphalt as I run toward my car.

I unlock the door and am about to get in when I hear him yell in the distance, "I could have done better."

I get in the car, slumping into the driver's seat and just sit there. Anger fills me as I sit with tears of frustration falling from my eyes.

I pull down the visor, slip back the mirror cover, and the light illuminates my face as I stare at my reflection. I expect to see red, puffy brown orbs, but as before, only those deep emerald eyes stare back at me.

Mr. Evans' words are still echoing in my head when I finally pull out of the parking lot. *Well, did he?*

First, he listened in on my conversation in the bathroom, and now he had been listening, at a minimum, to Elliott fuck me in the parking lot. *Why did he ask me that question? Why did he care? Even better question, why did I?*

I drive back to my apartment in a daze, a dull headache building behind my eyes again, and the last thing I remember of the night, as I sit in the parking lot of my apartment, is getting a text message from Elliott.

You turn into a pumpkin yet?

CHAPTER 31
HANGOVER (MELODY)

My head pounds, my alarm sounding beside me as my cell vibrates on the spare pillow.

"Too early," I complain, my voice muffled by the pillow as I pull it tighter over my head.

The alarm continues to sound, and I sigh as I reach over and shut it off.

"Alright. Alright, I'm up," I grumble, pulling my pillow off my head. "Ugh. I don't want to adult today."

My door opens, and Desire stands in my doorway drinking a cup of coffee, the aroma of the beans wafting across the expanse of the room, coaxing me awake.

They chuckle and say, "You don't want to adult any day."

They have a thin pink tank top and matching shorts on, with a flowing robe that has feather trim around the cuffs of the sleeves as they lean against my door frame, tapping their foot, their slippers flopping up and down each time.

"Come on, bitch. Get up. You have some explaining to do."

I roll over, pulling my pillow over my head again.

"Go away," I mumble.

My eyes sting as I squeeze them shut, the scent of alcohol still on my breath as I exhale deeply with a sigh.

"Oh, no ma'am," they say, stomping across the room and yanking my pillow off my head before slamming it down on my ass.

"Hey. What gives?" I grumble.

"What gives? What gives?" they ask, their voice raising in agitation. "I don't know, you tell me? You're the one coming in here, well past your bedtime, making all kinds of loud fucking noises, and ruining my beauty sleep."

"I did not," I refute.

"You most certainly fucking did! And your drunk ass trailed in a whole lot of mud down the hall, which you will clean up, might I add."

"Mud?"

"Yes, bitch. Mud."

"I-"

"I don't want to hear shit from you unless it's I'm sorry Desire, I should have called, or anything close to that."

"I'm sorry?" I inflect.

"You aren't sorry. No, ma'am. Not one bit, you nasty ass. Laying here in your own filth smelling like straight padussy."

I laugh. "Padussy?"

They scrunch their nose. "I can smell it all over you. You had to have bathed in it."

"Do I really smell that bad?" I pout.

"Yes, bitch. Yes." Desire gets up and walks toward the door, stopping in the doorway. "And don't you think about taking your ass back to sleep? You're gonna be late for work and, unless you became some millionaire overnight, you need that job."

"Okay. Okay," I huff. "I'm up. See?" I sit up, sliding the covers off my feet, and there is mud smeared on my sheets, caked on my feet up to my ankles. "What in the...?"

"See. Nasty bitch..." Desire pushes off the door frame, their voice trailing off as they waltz down the hallway to the kitchen.

I arrive at work an hour later, placing my coffee on the edge of my desk as I sit in my chair. The scent of the double espresso teases me as I pick up the stack of records in my inbox and begin sorting through them.

An hour passes and when Elliott doesn't come by for his morning visit, I stiffen, pulling out my phone and sending him a quick text.

> What gives?

Several minutes go by with no reply, but rather than dwell on his silence, I go about the rest of my morning.

When lunch comes, I walk by Elliott's office, and the door is still closed. The lights are off within and when I jiggle the handle; I find it locked. So, once again, I send him a text.

> Ummm… hello?

Still, I am met with nothing; left unread, with not even an *I'm good.*

This is why I don't date. This is why I don't fuck people I know, and this is exactly why the idea of a relationship has me tapping out after one or two dates.

I'm not "that girl." I'm not the type to get hung up on someone and sit there wondering why they haven't called me back or why they aren't answering my texts. And yet, here I am, checking my phone every couple of seconds, waiting to see those three little dots. *Ugh! You're pathetic, Mel.*

I return from lunch, having scarfed down a club sandwich with avocado and sprouts from the cafe around the corner, but still no Elliott. Still no sign of "Mr. Bright and Bubbly," "Mr. I'm gonna fuck you silly in the back of my car and invite you back to my place with the hopes of a cuddle afterward."

All that effort, and even a follow up text to ensure I got home safe, and now nothing? I don't get it.

Another thing I don't get is how our evening turned so fast. How one minute I was turned off by his overly flirtatious interlude with our server, and the next he had my legs pinned in the air as he shoved his cock deep inside me. The whole thing is completely out of character, and that's saying something because a busty blonde with roaming hands once fingered me in that same bar.

I am deep in thought as I sit at my desk, scrolling through the documents for the record I am working on when a text finally comes through. But it isn't from Elliott.

> C4 tonight at 8. I'm on tonight, so you better
> not bitch out on me.

I reply:

> I may be a bitch… but I'm your bitch 😘.

They don't reply, but I expect as much.

Hours go into Desire's prep routine and when I see them next, they will be the glowing goddess I remember from the first night we met.

It had been five years prior, right before graduation. Some of the crew from the bookstore had wanted to blow off some steam, so we made a night of it. The Dickson Divas were hosting a show and Drinks & Drag was what we'd all agreed upon.

Desire was on that night, dressed as Poison Ivy, their fiery red tresses cascading around their shoulders as they stomped across the stage with their knee high lace-up boots and long ombre green and red cape flowing behind them. They had intricate ivy designs stitched into their stockings and a green jewel encrusted bodice that accentuated their curves, making Desire the fiercest being I had ever beheld. So, once their number ended, I knew I had to meet them.

We hit it off right away because we share a love of art and music, can talk about the randomest shit over an overpriced frappé, and devour romance novels at an alarming speed. Plus, they were there when I needed a swift kick in the ass to get me out of a funk and back on my feet. So, of course, they were there when my mom passed away. And when she left me with no other family, they became my entire world.

Nowadays we just fill our hours trapped in pages with men who always seem to say the right thing and never miss the mark. And, sure, our relationship's had its growing pains, as all new friendships do, but I can't imagine my life without them.

I am in a daze as I stand at the copy machine later that afternoon, rubbing my neck, stiff from all the tension I carry there.

This whole thing with Elliott is getting to me. It shouldn't be, but it is. He still hasn't messaged me back, and after asking around, I find out he didn't call in today either.

Now, I'm not one to worry, and if I'm being honest, I don't know him that well. Even so, I am getting a little concerned. *Had he made it home okay? I hadn't thought he'd had that much to drink, and after our backseat gymnastics, I thought for sure he was okay to drive. But maybe I was wrong?*

Lost in my thoughts, I never hear him walk in behind me, and when Mr. Evans lightly taps on my shoulder, I jump.

"Fuck!" I call out, turning around, ready to give someone a good tongue lashing. Then I realize, once again, it's him. "Oh, I'm sorry," I declare. "You caught me off guard."

"Obviously." Mr. Evans raises an eyebrow at me. "In your own little world?" he asks, smirking.

"Something like that," I grumble, shifting nervously as I lean against the copy machine, my hands behind my back.

I feel trapped and, despite him standing a foot away, his presence crowds me.

He's not doing anything wrong, per se. But he's just standing there in that perfectly fitted indigo suit with silver detailing, his tight pants making it difficult to ignore his impressive bulge, staring at me.

Ugh! God, he's hot.

My mind shifts back to the previous evening, and I remember what he felt like pressed against me as he bent me back on the trunk of that car.

My body flushes in response to the memory: the strength of his body as it coiled around me, the length of his cock as it pressed against me.

As he adjusts his pants, I realize that I have been focusing on his crotch. *Fuck, I'm staring! Did he notice?*

I quickly avert my eyes.

"You seem... anxious," he points out. "Is something bothering you?"

"No. It's nothing," I reply quickly.

I evade looking him in the face, turning around to collect my papers. I grab them from the tray, tap them on the top of the machine to straighten the pile, and turn back around. *He's still just standing there. God, why doesn't he leave already?*

"What are you doing in here, anyway?" he inquires, looking at me with furrowed brows.

"Making copies," I string out my reply, shocked by his question.

"How does one... make copies?" he asks.

Is he being serious? I look over my shoulder, "On the copy machine." I tilt my head toward the Xerox I'm leaning against.

His eyes widen in surprise. "Really? Huh? Show me!" he exclaims, almost giddy about the prospect of making copies.

He is being so fucking serious right now, and I have no clue how to handle it. "Oh. Oh, my god. Umm, o... okay," I stammer.

I give him a quick tutorial on the wonder that is the copy machine and the biggest grin I've ever seen dresses his lips as I finish.

"It's a simple thing, really. I'm surprised you've never had to you use it yet." I pause, waiting for some sign he's joking. But he offers nothing. "How long did you say you've worked here?" I ask, pressing him.

He takes out his phone and begins scrolling through messages and without glancing up, he says, "Well, then I'll leave you to it," and turns to leave.

"See you later," I call after him, but he doesn't look back as he exits the room.

His footsteps land quietly on the carpet in the hallway as he heads back to, I presume, his office. *Which, that reminds me, where is his office anyway?*

There is something about that man. Something odd, and something I can't quite place. After a year and a half of working at the office, not once have I seen him, and now, in two days, he seems to be everywhere I am.

But I can't get into all of that now. Hell, I can't even get into whatever is going on between Elliott and I. I just need to finish out my day, go back to my office, and then get the hell home so I can be on time for once. Because if I miss Desire's act, I'll never hear the end of it.

CHAPTER 32

MISS JESSICA RABBIT (MELODY)

My feet vibrate from the EDM pumping through the speakers as I walk down the urban industrial stairs of C4 that night. And as I take each step into the downstairs venue of the Metro District building, I am greeted by the stale odor of sweat and overpowering cologne hanging in the air as swarms of people congregate below.

Descending the last rung and stepping into the club, the neon blue and green laser lights stream across the ceiling, strobing across the fluorescent walls as a disco ball shimmers from where it's hanging overhead, blinding me.

It is a small industrial venue, with exposed ductwork and visible PVC piping along the walls for the electrical dispersed throughout the lounge. There is one TV, high on the entry wall, and several behind the small length of bar along the left side, as a DJ booth sits at the end, centered on a small riser.

Bar height tables and pub chairs are spread sporadically about the space, visible only when patrons make their way to the bar; a sea of bodies parting as they step forth and order their libations.

Some performers are already milling about, their brightly colored and glittering costumes reflecting the lights as they stream by, but I don't see Desire. I don't see their sparkling red, sequined silhouette, that distinctive second skin like gown, with red flowing tresses and purple gloves that represent "Jessica Rabbit." So at least I haven't missed their introduction.

I am dressed to the nines; wearing a plunging halter micro mini sequined dress with my hair loosely curled and cascading down my back. My makeup is on point, as it usually is for this type of event, and I have already drawn admiring looks from at least three women and two men at the bar. Which is not surprising because I applied a high gloss fuchsia flair lipstick and winged out my liner; the cat eye intricately perfected to a tight point.

Red ribbon, criss-cross pleated cocktail heels are a flawless addition to my ensemble, bringing attention to my French manicured toes and slim ankles. I have freshly shaven legs, their velvety smoothness glistening with lavender baby oil and just begging to be touched as I step forward into the throng.

Everything about my look says I'm down to fuck, from the tight fitting, barely there dress, to my perfect pout. And no matter the sexual orientation: queer, straight, poly; it doesn't fucking matter because I'm in it for the satisfaction.

I step to the bar, pushing forward between two women who attempt to survey me discreetly out of the corner of their eyes, and wait to order a drink from the bare chested bar keep but he's preoccupied by a hot thing several seats down from me. *Gay*, I think. *No good for me, but perhaps Desire will give him a go.*

The woman on my left is pale with short cropped black hair, slightly spiked in the front, wearing a black long-sleeved button down and dark jeans. The one on my right, a lipstick lesbian I've seen many times before, has shoulder length honey colored locks curled at the ends, perfectly applied subtle makeup, and a low cut top with tight black pleather pants.

They are both attractive, both an option, but after Elliott, I'm not thinking of hooking up at the moment. Of course, get a couple drinks in me and that very well may change.

I finally get the bartender's attention and want to order my usual, but decide against it at the last minute, ordering a specialty drink of my own design.

"Do you have any of that salted caramel moonshine?"

"The stuff from Crystal, something or other?" he asks.

"Yeah," I acknowledge.

"Mark ordered some. I think after the last two times you came in and asked for it, he finally caved. You must have been very persuasive." He chuckles.

"Persuasive? Me?" I tease. "Surely not?" I giggle.

"Uh, huh," he mutters. "Surely not." He smiles widely as he winks. "So what'll it be?"

At this point, the two women are listening intently, no longer trying to be discrete. "A Messy Melody," I state confidently.

"And how would I go about making a Messy Melody?" he asks, bracing himself on the bar with his eyebrows raised.

I look to my left and right, and then back at him. "It's too early to tell, but you can start by adding two shots of the moonshine to a glass of ginger ale."

He chuckles and then says, "One Messy Melody, coming up."

The woman on my right leans toward me and voices, "Why is it called a Messy Melody?" She licks her lips, her wide smile showing her perfect teeth.

I turn toward her, and reaching out I pull one of her curls, making it bounce, as I answer, "Because after several of those, that's exactly what I become."

She's intrigued by the prospect and giggles at my response as she places her hand on mine, resting on the bar top. "I'm Celeste," she says. "I'm assuming you're Melody." She caresses my hand lightly.

"In the flesh," I confirm.

"And what beautiful flesh it is," she counters, squeezing my hand once.

Just as I'm about to flirt back, the DJ taps the microphone and begins his announcement, "Ladies and gents, gays and theys... you've seen them before, but never like tonight. Put your hands together, or slap those cheeks and welcome Desire as Jessica Rabbit." The DJ extends their introduction as if an MMA ring announcer, calling Desire to the center of the floor.

The lights dim, a spotlight flashes on, and Desire enters beside the DJ to the first notes of "Why Don't You Do Right." Their arms raise into the air, and then sweeping down they grasp their hips, popping one leg out for effect.

They are just as I imagined they'd be; waist cinched in tightly with impeccable contouring as they sashay through the crowd in a bejeweled ruby gown, highly slit to the right hip.

Deep purple satin gloves grace their fingers, trailing up their arms to the biceps where they run their hands up and down their bodice with each step forward as they lip sync.

Impeccably contoured silicone breast forms create the most eye-catching cleavage under their nude bodysuit, drawing whistles and jeers from onlookers as they waltz through the crowd.

Pale bluish green contacts peek out from beneath thick lashes as fire engine red lips purse and pucker throughout the number, and their eyes scan the crowd, widening when they land on me.

Their lip curls up slightly in a snarl as their beauty mark above the left side of their lip seems to dance with the sound of the bass, and then they turn, their flowing red locks sweeping outwards around them like fringe.

I lean back against the bar and Celeste tilts her head toward me as she whispers, "I take it we know, Desire?"

"Intimately," I answer.

Celeste is intrigued. "Do tell?" she requests.

"They're the love of my life," I swoon, "and I would be nothing without them."

Still leaning into me, Celeste whispers, "Color me jealous."

Because I'm such a fucking tease, and my Messy Melody flows effortlessly through my veins, I answer, "Don't be jealous, baby. If you play your cards right, I'll do that thing with my tongue you like."

"Promise?" she coos, leaning back to gauge my reaction.

I turn toward her now, answering with my signature, "Absofuck-inglutely."

Once they finish their number, Desire beelines toward me, a look of irritation on their face.

"I need a fucking drink," they announce.

I hand them my glass, and wait patiently for the line of questioning that I'm positive is about to ensue as they make eyes at Celeste, standing so closely at my side.

"And you are?" They eye her warily, raising the glass in their left hand to their lips and stopping as they await her reply.

"Celeste," she blurts out. "Can I just say that you were amazing," she gushes.

"Honey, don't I know it," they gloat, tossing their hair over their shoulder with their right hand before gulping down the remainder of my drink. Desire leans over me, tapping the glass on the bar top to get the bartender's attention. "Another. Make it a double, and how about in a big girl glass this time?" they chastise, pushing the glass toward the man.

So much for Desire giving him a go.

Turning around, Desire nudges their way in between Celeste and me, leaning back against the bar.

"So, where are we off to after this?" they ask.

"We..." I exaggerate, "are going home. But Celeste and I might make a night of it." I lean forward, peering around Desire. "Isn't that right, Celeste?"

Celeste's eyes go wide and then she answers, "Oh. I..."

Desire laughs heartily, turning their head from Celeste back to me as they say, "I don't think this one has the moxie for you, love. Now, this one behind you…" they tilt their head toward the woman with the short hair. "I'd say they've got more than enough spunk to handle your ass."

I laugh, looking around Desire to where the woman beside her lifts their glass in my direction and winks.

Not wanting to continue with whatever Desire has put me in the middle of, I excuse myself and head toward the restroom.

As I round the corner, I see Terrin in the hallway, waiting outside the door. She has her coppery red hair in a ponytail, is wearing no makeup, and is in simple clothes; a band tee and dark jeans. Not her normal Friday night look, but her self care has suffered since her breakup.

She and Miranda had been together for seven years, and now it's like she doesn't care about her appearance anymore. No longer is she trying to be cute and sexy. The way she looks now has aged her, and not in a good way.

"All full, seriously?" I grumble.

"You know how it is, Mel. They can't just bump and go. They have to primp, prod, and push up the girls," she jokes.

Just as she says this, two girls walk out giggling, their eyes glassy and pupils dilated.

"See," Terrin says, and then enters the restroom, closing the door behind her.

Standing in the hallway, waiting my turn, the hairs on the back of my neck raise. A tight pressure sets in behind my eyes and my ears ache.

I plug my nose, blowing out to relieve the pressure, and my ears pop, the release squeaking like a dolphin.

As I open my eyes, down the hall, exiting the other restroom, is none other than Mr. Evans.

I turn around and face the other direction, hoping he hasn't seen me. *Fuck! What the hell is he doing here?* I lean into the wall, leaving plenty of room for him to walk by in the hallway, hoping he will just pass by and pay me no mind. But I could be so lucky.

"Ms. Goins," he mumbles as he walks casually past, not stopping to converse.

I can see that shit-eating grin on his face as he does, and I'm not sure why, but it really irritates me.

There he is again looking fine as hell, that tight ass filling out his slacks nicely as he waltzes by with his hand in his pocket playing with what I imagine being a glorious cock, and he has the nerve to use my government name? Fuck him and the horse he rode in on.

Terrin exits the restroom and sees me glaring at him. She taps my shoulder, gaining my attention, and says, "Your turn, and I left you a little something for your troubles."

I finally look in her direction, force a smile, and walk into the restroom where I do my business.

Standing at the sink, surveying myself in the mirror, I am surprised not to see those emerald eyes staring back at me. But just as I am about to wash my hands, I see a small line of white substance on the small ledge below the mirror and a straw from the bar set beside it.

Terrin had said she left something for my troubles, and I would have to thank her for her contribution later.

Leaning over the ledge, I pick up and place the straw in my right nostril, plugging the left, and snort the line quickly, pinching my nose afterwards. I then toss the straw in the bin, wash my hands, drying them on a paper towel before I toss it too in the bin. I probably should have washed my hands first, but I didn't want to chance wetting and wasting any of the flake Terrin had left me. Waste not, want not; as the saying goes.

As I'm reaching for the door handle, a zing courses through my body, an electric sensation warming me from head to toe.

Stepping back to the mirror, I take a quick glance at my reflection to make sure my eyes aren't bugging out since they feel large as saucers.

And not only are the pupils dilated, but my irises now shine that bright emerald from the previous night. *You've got to be fucking kidding me? Not this shit again!*

I step back from the sink and the mysterious face that had flashed the first night in my bathroom peers back at me.

Deep green eyes, blinking behind wispy coppery lashes and hair to match, stare from a sun kissed face with cinnamon-colored freckles across the bridge of her nose.

"Hello, Melody," a smooth voice echoes in my ears. *"I'm sorry to do this, but I need to let loose a little. I hope you don't mind?"* The voice is sweet and ethereal with a hint of danger rimming the request.

I am fighting to voice my opposition when my whole body tenses and a severe, blinding headache overtakes me.

My vision goes cloudy, and then, then... nothing. I am an empty cask as the owner of that face takes control, forced to watch as she wills my body forward.

CHAPTER 33

MY LIFE THROUGH EMERALD EYES (MELODY)

I see my hands reaching for the door, unlocking and then opening it as we enter the dimly lit hallway outside of the restroom. I say we because there are two of us now, even if I have no control over what's happening or know who the hell this parasite is in my body.

Walking down the hall, we pass by a group congregating near the DJ and look all around us, surveying the space.

I am seeing the room as if for the first time, a feeling of elation overcoming me as the new resident of my body takes in everything around them. I could be imagining this, however, Terrin's gift laced with a little something extra and sending me on an unintended trip as we continue pushing through the crowd; a sea of slick bodies parting as they gyrate to the music booming around us.

A scan of the bar reveals Mr. Evans leaning back against the ledge with a drink pressed to his lips as he surveys the crowd. His eyes land on us and searing anger floods me, as my occupant is far from happy to see him. I think avoidance is the best option in this situation, especially considering our reaction to him, but without the ability to control my body, my uninvited guest veers straight toward him.

"What the hell are you doing? Please, stop!" I yell out in my mind, but my parasite continues moving in his direction.

We stop just outside his reach, and he glares at us. "What do you want?" he asks, wearing a look of displeasure.

"Me?" she asks unceremoniously. "I was just about to ask you the same thing." Her tone is accusatory, and Mr. Evans doesn't take too kindly to it, his weight shifting as he stands upright.

"Were you?" he asks. "I find that funny because, unlike you, I know exactly what I want, Little One." He is dismissive as he looks away.

"Don't call me that," she warns, brushing past him and stepping toward where Desire still stands chatting.

He reaches out, grasping our biceps as he spins us back around. "Did I say you could leave?" he grits.

She twists our arm from his grip and presses one perfectly mani-cured finger in his chest as she retorts, "I didn't ask for permission the first time, so why would you think I'd be asking now?" Disdain drips from her lips.

Shit, she knows him. Whoever this unwelcome guest is, I am now hosting, knows Mr. Evans.

Stepping forward into us, he snakes his arm around our back and pulls us in tight. He leans down, his lips brushing across our ear as he snarls, "I don't know what game you're playing here, but I will find out. And unlike before, I will stop you."

She laughs, not giving him the satisfaction of pulling away despite the repulsion that washes over us. "That's where you're wrong, my love. You couldn't stop me before, and you certainly won't stop me now. I'm just too close to the finish to allow you to interfere," she gloats. "Two more and I'm free of you forever. No more of this looking over my shoulder and wondering when you'll appear. No more of this cat and mouse you seem to enjoy so much." Hatred seeps through me as my visitor bristles.

Screaming out in my mind, I beg her to walk away, and she finally does.

Wrenching out of his forced embrace, we turn and he let us go. We push through the crowd until we're standing before Desire, where they're still socializing at the bar, but we can still feel the fire of Mr. Evans' gaze burning into our back.

"Relax," she says in our mind. *"He's nothing to worry about."*

"Nothing to worry about?" I argue. *"I work with this man and whatever connection you have to him, I'm the one who will suffer because of it."*

"I've suffered enough at the hands of that man," she counters. *"If this all goes according to plan, he'll be just another name in the history books."*

"Who are you?" I ask.

"Just settle the fuck down!" she voices, not realizing she's done so aloud.

"Excuse the fuck out of me!" Desire answers. "So, the restroom was not to your liking and now I'm to what... suffer your mutha-fuckin attitude? I think the hell not, miss ma'am."

"Aww, baby. It's not you. It's me." She giggles.

"You're damn right it's you. Now, how about you sit your crazy ass down and continue our previous conversation? This is Jen; like the drink, just not spelled the same," they say, motioning toward the woman with the short hair beside them.

"Is it a true 50/50 alcohol to tonic ratio, or are you more on the high side, Jen?" she asks, flirting with Jen.

Jen leans into us and says, "I'm more of a tequila drinker if I'm being honest. And my pronouns are they/them, if it matters?"

"It matters to me if it matters to you, Jen," she offers, running her fingernail under Jen's chin before tapping it on their bottom lip.

"No. Not that one. Celeste. I was flirting with Celeste," I implore them.

Beside Desire, Celeste looks perturbed. She huffs her agitation and grabs her purse from off her chair and storms off into the crowd.

"See?" Desire says. "Doesn't have the moxie."

I groan, but my uninvited guest ignores me.

"That's for damned sure," my visitor agrees, sliding in next to Desire and taking a seat on the barstool beside Jen. "So, Jen?"

"Yeah?" Jen answers, holding their shot glass as they await the follow on question.

"Where are we headed after this?" my visitor asks, reaching out and taking the shot glass from Jen's hand. She throws it back and then slams it down on the bar, smacking her lips as she lets out a satisfied, "Ah!"

Jen's eyes widen as a smirk lifts the corner of their lips. "A woman that shoots tequila like that…" Jen runs their fingers up our arm, "we can go wherever the fuck she wants."

My visitor hops off the barstool and steps into the space between Jen's widespread legs as they lean back on their barstool. "That's exactly what I was hoping for." She winks, taking Jen's hand and leads them onto the dance floor. Once amid the crowd, surrounded by bodies on all sides, Jen spins us around before pulling us against them.

We dance for hours; Desire, my visitor, and our new acquaintance, Jen. Jen has removed their button up, revealing a black ribbed tank tucked into their jeans that accentuates their taut waist and toned arms, while our micro mini wears like a second skin, clinging to the sweat from our efforts and making us slick to the touch. We are positively soaked, and despite that, Jen pulls us closer.

Trailing her hands up Jen's arms, my visitor stops and grips Jen's biceps as she admires their ink. "I'm assuming this piece has a meaning?" She taps her finger on Jen's right arm, tracing across the ghostly figure of a robed woman starting at their upper deltoid and trailing down to just above their elbow.

"Lady Death? Of course it has a meaning," Jen insists.

"And that would be?" she asks, turning and leaning back into Jen.

Jen trails their lips over the shell of our ear and whispers, "Lady Death is always with us. From our first breath until the last. As that last breath escapes, Lady Death is there to usher us into the afterlife." Jen nips our earlobe and grabs our hips, pulling us back into them.

"I'm not sure I believe in an afterlife," my visitor offers a breathy reply. "I'm not sure I believe in an after anything. Besides, I plan to live forever." She curves her ass into Jen.

"Is that so?" Jen asks, trailing their hand up and cupping our breast. "And how do you plan to accomplish such a feat?" They pinch our nipple, sending electricity sparking across our skin before letting go.

"Now, Jen, we've just met. I can't share all my secrets so soon. What would we have to talk about tomorrow as we lay naked in bed?" She turns around and faces Jen, meeting their eyes.

"Fine," Jen says, reaching up and grasping our jaw. "Keep your secrets. But if I have my way, my tongue will unlock them all before the sun rises." They trace the outline of our lips with their tongue and she opens for them.

As she allows them entrance, circling her tongue around theirs, I voice my disapproval. *"They're not even my fucking type. Seriously?"*

Still insisting on ignoring me, my visitor pulls Jen closer, gripping and groping at them as they run their hands down our body. They grip our ass and finally she pulls back as our eyes open and Mr. Evans comes into view, standing just behind us at the bar, watching us intently.

Placing her attentions back on Jen, my visitor says, "I've been wanting to get some ink. Any chance you know a place open at this hour?"

"No! Absolutely fucking not! This has gone far enough!" I counter.

Jen's eyes widen in surprise, and then a smirk lifts the corner of their lips. "Hell, yes. Come on. I know just the place."

Desire butts in, "Umm, excuse me? Did I just hear you say tattoo?" They grab our arm and turn us to face them.

"Yeah," she answers. "What of it?" She pulls back from Desire.

Desire states firmly, "You don't do tattoos."

"Who says?" she argues, crossing her arms.

"You! Many fucking times, might I add," Desire asserts, placing their hand under our chin and raising our eyes to meet theirs as they plead with us.

My visitor opposes with, "Maybe I've changed my stance. Ever think of that?" She jerks away, scowling.

"Look, you may be 'Messy Melody' at the moment. Which I'm okay with, you know me. But don't forget who the fuck you are, Mel," Desire argues, taking a step back.

My visitor rolls her eyes. "I know who the fuck I am, but do you?" she sneers.

"I guess the fuck not. Fine, do what the fuck you want, but don't come crying to me when things don't turn out." Desire turns and stomps angrily toward the bar.

"I won't!" she shouts.

"What are you fucking doing? Don't talk to them like that!" I plead.

"Well, Jen. It appears I've overstayed my welcome. Care to get out of here?" my visitor asks.

"After you." Jen motions us forward as I continue chastising this bitch of a parasite who insists on leading me down a path I'd rather not tread.

"You can't do this. I won't let you. Just who the fuck do you think you are?"

"Oh, enough already! If you don't shut the fuck up, I will silence you for good," she threatens.

"You wouldn't?" I counter.

"Watch me!"

As Jen leads us toward the exit, we look over our shoulder to where Mr. Evans is trying to follow us out discretely. I want to call out to him. Want to plead for help. But as we're led up the stairs, stepping onto the landing, my world once again goes dark.

CHAPTER 34

MY UNKINDNESS REBORN (HADES)

There is so much I don't know about this realm and about this time. I am at a disadvantage, really. This man, this mortal, is handsome, sure. At least handsome enough to catch her eye. But is he enticing enough that Ms. Melody Goins will tell me everything I need to know despite her unwelcome visitor? I need to find how the stone connects to the essence; my wife's essence. How she's come to be in this place and why. But without the knowledge of technology and the ways of this world as it is now, I will never be able to.

I walk around his apartment after I get back what is now early the next morning. I followed her after she left the bar, stopping at a tattoo shop before losing her in the chaos of traffic after she left.

I am familiarizing myself with the layout and decor to get a sense of this Mr. Evans, pacing the top floor where there are three bedrooms, one being used as an office.

In the office, there is a leather high-back chair sitting before a large desk where an illuminated box sits beside two large peering stones. At least I assume they are peering stones, but when I shift some parchments on the desk and a small orb moves, the peering stones come to life with neon lights zig-zagging across the faces of them. I place my hand on the orb and the zig-zags disappear; the stones illuminating bright white with words emblazoned on the surface. I have no idea what I am meant to see in the stones, so I attempt to coax them to life.

"Show me Melody. Where did she go?" I call out.

Nothing happens; the stones don't change, and only the name of the man remains centered on the face of one stone.

Pacing in front of the desk, I stare at the stones. They are important, and I'm certain of it, but have no clue how to convince them to show me what I desire to see. So, I walk into the bedroom across the hall and sit on the bed next to the man as he sleeps peacefully.

There is too much I need to glean, but I don't know where to begin. I only have one option, and there is only one way to catch myself up with this age. I have to go back to the Underworld, go back to my realm and back to my archives. Back to my chest of potions, where the vial of knowledge lies waiting. I will take it once I am back in this man's presence, and then I will know everything he knows as his thoughts, his memories, meld with my own. Because becoming this man in appearance alone will not suffice. I must have the knowledge trapped behind those sleeping lids. If I don't and I make another mistake like I did yesterday afternoon with the copy machine, this trip will have been for nothing.

I never recovered the remaining pearls I gifted to Persephone, so locating an entrance to the Underworld will be my only way back. And finding portals to my realm is easy enough if you know what you're looking for.

I need a grave where someone who died received their last rites and ceremony in one place, sending their soul to the afterlife, was later dug up, and their soul coaxed back into this realm as they were reinterred elsewhere. That movement would have led their soul to unrest. It would have trapped them as a shade in this realm, their new resting place fracturing the separation between the realms and allowing me to return home. In other words, off to the cemetery we go in search of evidence of such an unrest.

. . .

About an hour later as I traipse through Evergreen Cemetery, the taller grasses crunching beneath my feet as I weave in and out of the rows of gravestones, a tall obelisk-like marker beckons me in the distance. It glows ominously as the moonlight shines on its white surface, and I can hear a whispered wailing carried on the wind as it rustles through the trees.

A translucent figure wanders beneath the trees, their face obscured by their robes as their gown billows around their bare feet. Their wailing gets louder as I step toward them, and when they turn to face me, it stops completely.

The shade turns, their hand reaching out as they face me. A gravelly woman's voice asks, "Have you come to take me home?"

I'm not sure I should answer her. Not sure I should engage her in conversation. She is already so confused. What words can I offer that would change any of that? But still I answer, "I'm sorry. No. I have not."

Grabbing the sides of the hood covering her face, she pulls it tight in frustration as she cries out in anguish. "Torment. You've come with only torment." Her voice quivers and she releases her hood, her arms draping at her sides.

I step toward the grave marker, and she jumps into my path. I lift my hands, stepping back. "I don't mean to torment you. I only seek passage home."

"Home? Why can't I go home?" she pleads. She tilts her head and steps toward me, stalking forward like a predator. Her teeth clack, chattering as her jaw clenches.

She turns, stepping back into the moonlight, and looking over her shoulder, she asks, "Can't you take me home? I just want to go home." She takes several steps away from me again.

I take another step toward the white stone and again and my eyes search for cracks in the surface. I find one, but no power radiates from within, so I continue on.

My hands are wandering along the face when I smell her rancid breath as it wafts across the back of my neck. I didn't even hear her move, but I wouldn't, would I?

"You come to this place, my place, and all you offer is escape for yourself? But what about me? What about my escape?" she seethes.

I can feel her breath cold against my neck as her icy suffering washes over me, chilling me to the bone. My hands continue to search, trailing down the cold stone as I step away from her and around the stone. She follows my every movement like a shadow as I circle, my feet crunching through the leaves at the base of what I assume is her grave.

She screams in my ear, and I turn. Her ghostly face, pale and weathered in the moonlight, is mere inches from mine as puffs of frustration escape her nostrils. Spittle forms at the corner of her lips as they curl over rotted teeth in a snarl, and my hands continue tracing behind my back as I lean against the stone, tilting my head away from her death breath.

"Look, I wish there was something I could do. But I can't. I have no power-"

"You have no power?" she shrieks, jerking forward. "And I do?"

"Sophia, stop!" I call out. And she does.

A look of confusion forms on her face and her head tilts, the bones clicking as they grind against one another as she leans away from me. "Do you know me?" she asks, taking two steps back into the moonlight once again.

Uttering her name distracts her long enough for me to locate another crack in the stone, and from this one the power I had been searching for seeps out.

I trail my fingertips through the slickness of the power, and it glows. It soaks into my skin and soon, I too am glowing from head to toe. She shrieks again, jumping toward me as the power pulls me through the fractured space and sends me hurtling toward the Underworld.

I am pulled through darkness, bumping and bouncing off hard

rocks as I fall away from that realm and back into my own. I am hurtling downward, the scent of the earth enveloping as I am welcomed once again home. And when I finally land, my feet sending up dust and ash, I arrive in the labyrinth's heart amongst the souls milling through the cave system on their way to my gates.

CYNTHIA SAWYER
DIED
Feb. 22, 1851
Aged 61 Years

CHAPTER 35

LOOKING GLASS (MELODY)

There must be something wrong with me. What other explanation is there? How else can I explain the fucked up dreams I've been having? They're horrific, absolutely. But then why is it I wake up so incredibly aroused from them each time?

First, there was the dream with major BDSM vibes during a wedding night, then there was the torture scene where a beast was ravaged before being killed in the most brutal way imaginable. And now this?

I mean, the first wasn't all that bad; at the end, all parties appeared to be extremely satisfied. And who doesn't like it a little forceful some-times? I know I do. But then there was the second; a scene where terror was obviously the goal, as most of their faces showed evidence of it. Now, don't get me wrong, I'm not against a good male/male romance, even though it's not my normal go to, but the savagery of it? Nothing turns you off a romance quite like death. And the look on the beast's face? The pleading in his eyes, the anguish? I felt his loss deep within my soul.

The last dream had me shaken. The last dream had me waking up soaked in sweat, my legs and body aching like I'd run as if my life depended on it.

I had been in the grasp of a powerful being, a gleaming dagger held high above my head before she drew it down, plunging it deep into my chest. I had felt my life force waning, drifting toward the heavens when her face changed before my eyes. Terror overwhelmed me. I felt a sense of loss as my final breath escaped, and I could not stop it. But it was just a dream, right? Then why is my heart beating so erratically in my chest?

It felt so real, felt as if I was there, and felt as if blood coated my fingers. I felt the warmth as it oozed down the tips, but those weren't my fingers. They were hers; Persephone's.

I know tidbits and fragments of myth and lore, but not once have I ever heard that Persephone was a merciless killer. She's supposed to be the Goddess of Spring, Queen of the Underworld, wife of the God of Death, sure. But to commit murder of her own accord? I certainly have never heard such tales.

The tale of Hades and Persephone is supposed to be a love story, but what I am dreaming is anything but. And now, as if dreaming isn't bad enough, I am imaging things. Seeing things that can't possibly be real and losing time when I shouldn't be. Unless the coke Terrin left me was tainted, a parasite living inside me is taking over my body and sending me into the ether while it does God knows what. But that's impossible. *Or is it?*

The sun is shining through my blinds as I'm shaking off the last remnants of the dream. There is an ache in the center of my chest, and when I look down, my necklace nestles between my breasts as it bounces up and down with each beat of my heart. It feels heavy, weighted as it brushes against my skin, and the flesh it contacts warms to the touch when my chest rises and falls. It is radiating through me, and in a moment of panic, I lift the necklace off and toss it on the bed beside me.

"That's enough of that," I say, looking warily at the necklace.

I am lifting my arms over my head and stretching when pain shoots across my right shoulder. I drop my arm and look down, rolling my shoulder forward when I see a fresh tattoo sealed beneath second skin. Blood has pooled around the edges of the protectant, and for a moment, I don't think what I'm seeing is real, but then I touch it. My skin is angry, red, and irritated by the ink emblazoned on the outside of my deltoid, but I can't make out the design.

"Fucking, fuck me!" I groan.

A knock comes at my door, and I freeze. Desire doesn't knock. They just come in unannounced and plop down on my bed as they throw whatever judgment they have about my behavior at me.

I call out an anxious, "Come in."

The handle clicks, the knob turning ever so slowly before the door swings open and there stands Desire. They brace against the opening with their coffee in their hands as they wear that all too familiar look of judgment.

"Well, let's see it," they demand.

With my brows pleated, I answer, "See what?"

They glower at me. "You know damn well what." Their irritation slaps me in the face as they pad into the room and plop down on the end of the bed. "Come on, bitch. I don't got all day." They tilt their head as they eye my wrapped arm.

"Oh. You mean this?" I twist my arm, rolling my shoulder forward. I wince.

"Yes, that. You know what I fucking meant. Now's not the time to play dumb. You did plenty of that last night." They reach out, pulling my arm toward them with their coffee still in their other hand.

"I did?"

They drop my arm. "Yes. You most certainly, absofucking did." They chuckle, despite there being no humor on their face. "Look at the fucking stupidity Messy Melody done got you into, huh?" It wasn't a question, not really, anyway.

"I-"

"Yes, I. I am an idiot, Desire. I don't know what I was thinking, Desire. How 'bout maybe I'm sorry, Desire? How 'bout that?" they chastise.

I huff. "I'm sorry. Last night was so-"

"Wrong on so many fucking levels. Yes, Mel. I fucking agree. Last night was wrong. Wrong attitude. Wrong tone. Wrong fucking call." They turn away, shaking their head as they raise their cup to their lips, sipping loudly on their coffee.

"I don't know what I was thinking," I mutter.

"Thinking?" their voice pitches up. "You weren't fucking thinking!" They point at my shoulder. "Does that look like the effects of someone who was thinking?"

"No. I know. I just-"

"Just what, Mel? What the fuck has gotten into you lately?" A look of worry marks their features and I know I have some explaining to do, but there are no words of explanation I can offer.

"Things have been weird," I admit.

"Weird? Things haven't been fucking weird, Mel. You've been fucking weird. For the last week, you have been flitting around here just like that dumb as fuck hummingbird you have permanently etched in yo' skin."

I look down at my arm. "It's a hummingbird?" I try to turn it so I can see, but all I can make out is blobs beneath the congealed blood underneath the covering.

"Butterfly and some fucking flower, it seems. Hummingbirds, butterflies, and flowers? Really, Mel? That's some basic ass bitch shit, right there." They motion toward my arm before standing.

"I don't even remember getting it," I offer, looking up at them pleading.

"Oh, I know. I tried to talk some sense into you, but did you listen?" They pause, turning before they whirl back around on me. "And another thing. Did you know I called yo' ass so many times last night after you stormed off? But did you answer? Did you acknowledge me? We are supposed to be friends, bitch. But you are testing my mutha-fucking patience." They stomp their foot as they await my reply.

"It was out of character. I know." I lower my eyes.

Their voice quivers. "Out of character? More like out-of-body. Whoever that bitch was last night, she isn't the bitch I know and love."

"You still love me?" I snivel, tears streaming down my cheeks as I look up at Desire.

Desire sits on the edge of the bed, reaches over me, and sets their coffee down on my bedside table. They pull me into their embrace and soothe me, pulling me against them as they run their hand up and down my left arm reassuringly. "I do love you, Mel." They kiss the top of my head as it lies on their chest. "But we have got to get you figured out."

"I know," I sob. "I just-"

"Shh," they silence me. "Enough of that. We will get through this. It's you and me against the world, remember?"

"Come hell or high water?" I mumble.

"Fire and brimstone, or treacherous depths. Girl, you know I got you," they insist. They lean back and I look up into their eyes. Their features are calm now, but then they scrunch their nose. "But you smell like shit, so get your nasty ass in the shower and I'll make us some breakfast."

"But I forgot to grab milk," I whine.

They get up and make their way to the door, stopping at the thresh-old. "What did I say? I got you." They wink and then turn, leaving the room.

In the bathroom some time later, I wipe the steam from the mirror and brace myself for those green eyes once again, but they are absent. My normal brown stare back at me, still puffy from the tears I shed while in the shower. I have been an asshole to the one person in the world who accepts me despite my faults and I am ashamed.

Dark circles are prominent beneath my lower lashes, evident of just how shitty the sleep I have been getting, or not getting as it were, is. I look down to where the second skin bubbles slightly, and press down, attempting to see the butterfly, hummingbird, and flowers Desire described earlier. But still, all I can make out are globs of smeared ink and blood. I'll have to wait the several days of healing, and after I finally remove the second skin, to see the full extent of my stupidity. Because, for the life of me, I have no clue why I would have selected any of that imagery for a tattoo. But coke makes you do weird things. Let's hope a tattoo is the weirdest of the things I'd done during the time that I lost.

Thinking back to last night at C4, I remember seeing Mr. Evans and the response my body had to our interaction. But was any of that real, either? Had any of what I thought happened actually occurred? Or was I just imagining it all? Was I imagining a being inhabiting my body and taking control? Someone who obviously knew Mr. Evans intimately? Or had that been the coke, coaxing me into what I can only describe as an out-of-body experience where a she bitch held the reins?

I shake off my thoughts and continue drying off my body before covering my flesh in baby oil. Humidity beads on my lashes and I blink, sending the droplets falling to where they land between my cleavage. A light pink mark the size of my pendant is between my breasts and when I touch it, the skin is warm. *Maybe I am having a reaction to the stone or the wire? I'll give my skin a day's rest and see how it looks tomorrow,* I think.

I dress in a chocolate-colored ribbed tank, taupe jeans, and sneakers as the weather app says it is unseasonably warm today. I fashion my hair, half up and half down as it should be a lazy day around the apartment and I have no plans on leaving. Then I leave my room, heading down the hallway where the smell of bacon and pancakes greets me as I enter the living area.

Desire is in the kitchen, their pale blue bathrobe billowing out around them as they dance between the stove and the counter fixing our plates. They look up when I enter, smiling as they place a piece of bacon in their mouth.

"So, how's Jen this morning?" they ask around the bacon.

I frown. "Who?"

They cock their hip, pointing the spatula in their raised hand in my direction. "You know, Jen; like the liquor, just not spelled the same?" they mimic, chuckling.

I laugh with them. "Oh, them. Jen, yes. I searched my phone this morning and no Jen. So, obviously, Jen wasn't that good."

"Girl, you are such a H- to the O- to the E!" they sing.

"Is it a crime to have high standards?" I ask, offended.

Desire throws their head back and laughs heartily, then stops, their face going serious. "Is that what we're calling it now?" They plop another pancake on my plate and slide it toward me, one eyebrow cocked as they glare at me.

I grab both plates off the counter and set them on the table, turning around and grabbing the syrup before I answer, "What's a girl gotta do to have her world rocked?"

"Story of my life," Desire responds, reaching in the refrigerator and grabbing the orange juice before walking to the table.

We eat our breakfast, casually chatting about our plans for the weekend and the following week. Just as we are in the kitchen cleaning up, I remember that I have some unfinished business at work I meant to bring home, but left my laptop in my office. I tell Desire I need to pop into work real quick, but it should only be an hour or so and I'd be home. They say they will be here when I get back and tell me to be safe as I'm leaving.

After a quick twenty-minute drive to the office, I slam my car door and stride toward the entrance, noticing only one other car parked out front. I'm not sure whose it is, and don't give it a second thought as I use my key card, entering the building.

Once on the fourth floor, I step from the elevator into the eerily quiet lobby. My footsteps sound down the hallway as my sneakers creak beneath me, and after several minutes, I am standing before my office. I pull out my keys, open the door, and step inside, turning on the overhead light.

My light illuminates the carpet just outside my door, but other than my office, the only other illumination is from the emergency lights beaming over the exit door at the end of the hallway to the stairs.

I hear whirring in the distance and down the hall, something clanks in the copy room. I pad quietly down the hall and stand at the corner, peering into the copy room where none other than Mr. Evans stands before the machine. Several sheets are sliding into the tray and he picks them up, surveying them triumphantly.

I say nothing, chuckling to myself as I make my way back to my office. *If he doesn't know that I am here, then I will grab my things and leave him none the wiser. Besides, he seems quite occupied with his new fascination of making copies.*

Who'da thunk it. A man that hot overjoyed at the prospect of making copies. He was just standing there, his hands in his dark denim jeans and form fitting black tee, the muscles of his arms tensing as he braced himself on the machine while he leaned in, staring in awe at his handiwork.

I wish I could find something that made me as elated as Mr. Evans was at making copies. And to think, I was the one who taught him such a menial task. I smile as I gather my things, locking my door and pulling it quietly shut behind me.

I am walking to the elevator, my laptop case hanging over my shoulder, when I hear pounding footsteps behind me. I am attempting to turn when Mr. Evans slams into me, pushing me back against the wall, and my case slides to the ground.

"Couldn't stay away, could you, Little One?" he snarls.

"What? I-"

"Oh, come now, my love. No need to be shy." His body presses tightly against me, pinning me against the wall as I force my head away.

His scent is all around me, fresh and woodsy as he breathes puffs of frustration against my ear.

"Mr. Evans, what are you doing?" Terror washes over me and I have no clue what brought this on.

His hands begin their torturous ascent up my abdomen and to my ribs, where he clutches the fabric of my tank in his hands. He pushes me back against the wall and I turn my face to him, my eyes widening as I look into his; those storm cloud grey orbs flaring with blue at the edges of the irises.

Trailing upward ever so slowly, his other hand raises to my face and takes my jaw in his grip. He trails his thumb across my lips and I take in a breath, my words of opposition catching in my throat.

He stares at me intently, searching my eyes for something. And when he doesn't see what he was seeking, he loosens his hold on my tank and steps back slightly.

"I'm sorry," he says. "I must be mistaken. I thought you were someone else." He closes his eyes and takes a deep breath.

"Who? It doesn't matter," I quickly offer. "Why have you been following me?"

"It's not you..." he trails off. "It's nothing. I said I was sorry."

"Umm, no. I don't think so. You don't get to dismiss this," I challenge, raising my arms between us and breaking his hold. I turn to escape where he has me caged in, but his arms close in around me.

"Not so fast," he says. "There are some things we should discuss, don't you think?"

"Discuss?" I raise my voice in question. "What exactly is it you think we need to discuss, other than how inappropriate whatever this is?"

He looks offended, his head moving away slightly as he takes in my face. I lift my chin, meeting his icy stare.

"Step back," my voice challenges. He does.

I straighten, sliding down the wall and grabbing my case from where it lies at my feet. I stand slowly, never taking my eyes off him as I arise once more.

He is standing facing me with his hands hanging at his sides and then raises one toward me. I flinch, turning my head away and he runs that same hand through his hair. His muscles flex and his shirt goes taut over his chest as he runs his hand down across his body, looping his finger in the band of his jeans.

"There is much to explain," he offers, shrugging his shoulders.

I glare at him, sliding the case strap over my shoulder once more. "Is there, now?"

"Yes. But maybe elsewhere?" he asks nervously.

"You're crazy if you think I'm going anywhere with you," I glower.

"Melody, please?" he pleads. "If there was another way, I would gladly take it."

"Another way?" I question. "Another way to what?"

He steps into me again, placing his hand on my cheek as he smoothes the loose hairs behind my ear. My eyes flutter at the sensation of his fingers on my flesh, and I take in a deep breath, gulping loudly.

"Maybe a cup of coffee?" I offer. My lips are dry, so I wet them with a quick swipe of my tongue.

He stares at my lips, his tongue trailing across the crease of his mouth and settling behind his teeth. His jaw clenches and he inhales loudly, taking in my scent. "So sweet," he coos. "Jasmine and lavender. So much better than orange and honeysuckle."

The hand that had brushed the hairs behind my ear trails down the length of my neck, up and across my jaw before stilling at my lips. His eyes follow the same line his finger traces as he brushes back and forth across my lips that are partially parted as I pant.

"I thought we were going for-"

He crushes his lips on mine and a searing heat seeps through that kiss, down the back of my throat, where it blooms as it reaches my lungs, spreading out into my extremities. My insides burn and my skin pebbles as the hairs raise where I feel tiny pin pricks all across the surface of my arms as his other hand traces across my wrist, up my forearm, to where it finally grips my right biceps.

I cry out into his mouth, "Ow!"

He stops instantly. "I. I'm sorry," he mutters. "I never meant to hurt you. I-"

"No. You didn't hurt me. It just so happens that my stupidity last night led me to some unforeseen circumstances." I look up reassuringly into his eyes.

He searches mine before raising a brow at me. "Circumstances?" he questions.

He moves my arm and l roll my shoulder forward.

"A tattoo. Compliments of too much alcohol and poor decision making on my part," I confirm.

"Ah. I see," he says.

"That's what I get for having one too many and a little something extra." I chuckle, allowing my head to fall forward.

He lifts my chin and meets my gaze. His stare is intense, and his grey eyes are shining as he offers a genuine smile. "Not your fault at all. It could happen to the best of us."

Letting my head fall to the side, I laugh as I admit, "Yeah, well. It doesn't normally happen to me."

We walk to the elevator and depressing the button, Mr. Evans gazes at me. "Still on for coffee?" he asks.

"Your place or mine?" I quip.

His eyebrows raise and he asks, "I thought it was just coffee?"

I grin over at him, and as the bell dings, announcing the lift is at our floor, I offer, "We can start with coffee and see where it goes from there."

This could be a bad idea, but I can't shake the feeling I would regret not taking this opportunity. So, I take the hand he offers to me and step into the elevator. Once inside, he steps into me once again, pinning my back against the back wall of the elevator. One hand lifts slowly, his fingers splaying out once they reach my jawline, as the other snakes behind my back, and he lowers his face toward mine.

"Are you sure?" he asks.

I reply with the only thing I can think of in the moment, "Absofuckinglutely."

CHAPTER 36

ALTERED STATES (MELODY)

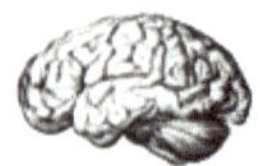

Mr. Evans, or Aaron, rather, and I walk to the only other car in the parking lot; a charcoal Mercedes SL550. We share glances back and forth at one another before he opens my door and I slide in.

Plopping down on the low seats, the leather groans beneath me as I notice mail littering the floor boards and empty energy drink cans in the center console. There is a new car air freshener hanging from the rearview mirror and he depresses the push button, the car purring to life as he clicks his seatbelt. I do the same as we pull out of the parking lot of our office building on West Center street.

Twenty-minutes later and we're turning north on I-49 off MLK and heading toward Rogers before we take the next exit and circle back around. We turn off of Wedington, onto the access road, and eventually pull into a complex with a steep entrance. His car scrapes despite the slowness of our turn and then we head up the hill where he turns right in front of a three story mid-rise.

"You live in a town home?" I ask.

"Yeah," he answers, putting his car in park before pressing the garage door opener on his visor. "It's an Airbnb, really. But it's fully furnished. So that's a plus."

He exits the vehicle and comes around to my side, opening the door.

As I struggle to get out, he offers his hand to assist me and I quip, "Saves on furniture. I get it."

"Few do. But who am I trying to impress?" He winks as he places his hand on the small of my back and ushers me inside the garage, where he presses the button beside the entry door before pulling it open.

His car honks as he locks it, and then he follows me up one set of stairs. We turn the corner and there is a bathroom on the left before we enter the living room and kitchen area. I pull out a barstool from beneath the white marble countertop and hop up onto it as he walks into the kitchen.

There is hog art everywhere, hanging up on the walls, and a throw tossed over a grey armchair in the sitting area of the living room as I look over my shoulder. I turn back around and offer the hog call, "Wooo Pig Sooie!"

He chuckles. "Something like that," he replies, opening the fridge and offering me a drink. He has beer, wine, or if I want something stronger, he offers his Don Julio 1942 Anejo.

"This isn't exactly a special occasion. But I love me some Tequila," I admit.

"Tequila it is," he says, opening a small pantry and pulling it from the cupboard before setting it on the island in front of me. He goes to the cupboard beside the sink, grabs two glasses, and then shuts the blinds before walking back to me.

I reach over the countertop, grab the bottle and pop the cork out of the top before pouring us each a generous serving.

He lifts his glass toward me and I raise mine, clinking them together as he toasts, "Here's to starting with coffee." He sniffs it before taking a swig, and I do the same, my eyes smiling at him over the rim of my glass as I savor the smell.

I sit on my barstool and he stands with his elbows pressed on the counter as he leans toward me, watching as I flick my tongue out and trace the rim of my glass. I toss back the rest of my glass, eager to get to the part where we see what happens next, and he follows suit, reaching out and taking my glass once I set it down.

I slide off my barstool while he's rinsing our glasses out in the sink and make my way to the sofa, where I plop down and prop up my feet on the coffee table. I slide off my shoes, placing them beside the table, and fall back into the cushions as Aaron walks toward where I'm lounging.

He takes a seat beside me and slides his arm behind my back as he settles into the cushions.

I pick up the remote where it's sitting on the arm of the sofa and click on the TV. It's a smart TV, all of his streaming apps popping up on the screen, and the show, "Sex Lives of College Girls", prompts him to continue watching.

I shoot him a sideways glance and he says, "What? I live in a college town. A man can be curious."

I lean into him, press the button to play the episode he was on as I offer, "There's nothing wrong with a little curiosity."

Remembering Desire, I pick up my phone, checking in with a quick text:

> met a friend for a drink. It's too early to tell…
> but don't wait up!

They reply with a simple:

> be safe bitch!

> I'm always safe.

Tell that to your arm.

I set my phone down and turn my attention back to Aaron, who is intently watching the show over my head.

"So, what's your favorite part?" I ask.

He turns his shoulders toward me, and I face him. "My favorite part of what?" he asks.

"The show?" I urge.

"Oh. Probably all the chaos," he answers.

"That simple, huh?"

He places his hands, one on each side of my face, and leans toward me. He gives a soft, "I'm a simple man," as he hovers over me before pressing a kiss to my lips.

There it is again, that slow burn creeping across my lips and flushing my face as it trails down my neck and into my chest. It spreads down my ribcage, bouncing along each one before settling in my stomach.

My body is on fire as his hands leave my face and make their way to my shoulders, where he pushes me back into the couch.

He slides off the couch, pushing the table with both hands as my feet fall to the floor. He slides across the laminate floor on his knees, where he settles between my legs. Placing his hands on the insides of my thighs, he presses them wider as he stares at me with such an intensity that I freeze. I don't dare move as he holds me with his predatory gaze, his eyes searching my face for any signs of trepidation.

I reach down and undo the button on my jeans, slowly lowering the zipper. He reaches under my ass with both hands, grabs the waistband, sliding them down, and I assist him in shimmying them off me. He pulls them off one ankle and then the next, before throwing them to the side where they land on the armchair.

Once his attention is back on me, he runs those long, elegant fingers up the inside of my legs, from my ankles, up my calves, and rests them between my thighs. His eyes take in all my exposed flesh as he tickles his way to my center, where he slides both hands under my ass once again and pulls me forward to the edge of the couch.

"Tell me how you like it."

It's not a question. It's a command, and one I'm not sure how to comply with. I'm not shy by any means. And this wouldn't be my first hookup with a stranger, but still.

He leans forward, burying his face between my thighs and I grab hold of his hair when he places his hot lips on me.

I'm already soaked, the anticipation from his kisses pooling behind my panties, and I'm sure he can smell my arousal as he takes a deep breath, filling his nostrils with my essence.

He utters a guttural, "So sweet. But how do you taste?"

Then, using one hand, he tugs my panties to the side, the cool air of the overhead fan blowing across my already sensitive center as he pulls my flesh into his mouth. He stops when tastes me, his eyes locking with mine before he draws me in further. I squeeze mine shut.

The fire courses through me again, sparking between my folds with every movement of his tongue and licking up my stomach where it settles in my chest, peaking my nipples as if a second set of hands pinches each bud.

I can feel the flames as they wash over me, the heat building as he slides his thumb across my sensitive nub with that perfect rhythm, all while he laps me up, taking in his fill.

Up, down, up, down. He thrums, a beat all his own as he plucks my strings, urging the most melodic sounds from me.

A moan escapes my lips, and I squeeze his head between my thighs, trapping his thumb beneath his nose. The instantaneous ceasing of his movements has me begging for more, and I plead with a breathy, "Don't stop."

My legs quiver as I let my thighs fall apart, releasing his head and his hand.

He starts once again with that relaxed movement of his thumb, urging me to play my sweet music once more. His tongue darts in and out of me as my heart beats erratically in my chest. And just before I fall completely apart, he reaches the crescendo.

"Yes. That's it! That's it!" I cry out.

Nudging my clit with his nose, he holds the pressure as he takes his hand that had been thrumming across me, and slides it down my thigh. He places his index finger in his mouth and then slides it inside me before placing his mouth on my clit. He continues thrumming up and down my clit with his tongue, adding a light suction while he slides his finger in and out of me.

I am so close now I am practically purring as my back arches off the cushions. One more slide of his finger and I'll reach the finale.

Finally, my hands grip tightly in his hair as I suffocate him between my thighs while my tide comes in, crashing onto the shore.

Soaking us both, my satisfaction splashes across his face and he pulls back. He growls out a, "That's a good girl," before undoing his pants and pulling himself free.

Then, yanking me forward with both hands to the edge of the couch, he lines himself up and slams inside me. Holding onto my hips, he slides out, coating himself in my slick, and presses forward, burying himself as deep as I can take him.

"You're so fucking tight," he grits, his jaw clenching as he slides forward.

My garbled cries fill the air as my hands grip his where they're grasping my hips.

His nails dig into my flesh, and my hands fall to my sides as he trails his fingers from my hips down to my cheeks, where he takes my ass in his palms.

He pulses forward slowly and thrums my clit once again with his thumb, continuing to slide effortlessly in and out of me. Keeping his digit in time with his cock, the up, down of his thumb coincides with his inward and outward movements, and soon I am cresting once more.

My insides quake, my stomach coiling tight as I tense around his hardening length, and my muscles clench and tighten around him as I draw him toward the finish line.

Groaning out with a, "Gods, Melody!" he slams into me one last time, his chest heaving before he breaks free and lets go inside me.

He falls forward, putting all his weight on me as the tendons in his neck tense. And I can feel his Adam's apple as it bobs up and down with each ragged breath he takes as his head rests between my breasts.

I am still clothed from the waist up, but I can feel his heavy pants on my arms as I circle them around him.

Absentmindedly, I circle my fingers around his ear and across his jaw before trailing them to his soft lips.

He grabs my hand and presses it to his lips and kisses each finger before running his hand up my arm. He stops when he gets to my second skin and pulls his hand back, remembering how sensitive it was before.

"It's fine," I say. "I can barely feel it."

He lifts his head from my chest, and looking up into my eyes, he says, "When I touch you, I always want you to feel it." His gaze is intense, and as he meets my own, I feel a blush creeping up my neck and settling on my cheeks. "So fucking innocent," he states, shaking his head.

I push his head back playfully. "Don't get it twisted, Aaron. I'm anything but innocent. And I would do you a disservice if I pretended to be anything than what I am."

He pushes off the couch and stands, smiling down at me as he pulls his pants up before repositioning himself. He then zips and buttons up his jeans.

I am about to reposition my panties when he walks over to the kitchen and offers me a rag, raising it in the air. I accept, and he tosses it across the living room to me.

As I clean myself up, he walks over to the armchair and picks up my pants from where they lay draped across the arm. He offers them to me and I take them, sliding them over one foot and then the next before standing and pulling them the rest of the way on.

With my pants on, I take a seat in the armchair and grab my shoes. I'm putting them on when Aaron asks, "What are you doing?"

"I just figured it was time I get home," I say.

"Why?"

"Because I don't live here," I answer matter-of-factly.

He runs his hand through his hair while the other is in his pocket. He rocks back and forth nervously as he says, "I was hoping you'd stay for dinner."

"Um, okay," I answer awkwardly. "How about after a shower, then?"

He takes his hand from his pocket and offers it to me. "We can shower. But you know if we do, it'll be some time before we get to dinner."

"I am hungry," I admit. "But I have no problem waiting."

"Yeah?" he asks, walking around the armchair and pulling me toward the second set of stairs.

We stop at the landing just below the stairs, and before he leads me up them, I answer, "Yeah."

CHAPTER 37

UNUSUAL SUSPECTS
(MELODY)

"I don't think I've ever showered so many times in one day," I admit to Aaron as he stands before the stove sautéing mushrooms with olive oil and minced garlic in the pan five hours and many orgasms later.

"What can I say? You were rather dirty, and I'd hate to send you back to your place smelling like nothing but sex. What would your roommate think?" he poses, stirring the contents of his pan with a wooden spatula as I sit on my barstool sipping a glass of Moscato.

The scent of the meal he's preparing permeates throughout the apartment, the pungency of the garlic mixed with the mushrooms lifting into the air with each puff of steam as he stirs them.

He sets down his spatula, steps to the sink where he fills a pot with water, and pours in some olive oil before salting it. He put the pot on the stove, turns on the burner to boil the water, and then goes to the sink to get the shrimp and scallops from where they're thawing in the colander. He adds them to the pan of mushrooms and garlic.

I take another sip of my wine, watching him intently as he walks around the kitchen barefoot in nothing but tight fitting boxers as he cooks us dinner. The tight muscles of his back stretch as he moves and my eyes linger on his right shoulder where my handiwork marks his skin.

Red, raised scratch marks from where I dug my nails into his back as he fucked me within an inch of my life taunt me as they bring about flashbacks of our exhausting afternoon. I smile into my wineglass and set it down with a clink on the countertop once I finish.

He turns and walks around the counter, placing a soft kiss on my lips as he takes my glass. "Care for another?"

"I'll wait for dinner," I answer, my eyes wandering up his muscled chest, across his collarbone to that succulent portion of his neck where I bit down as I muffled my screams many times that day.

"My eyes are up here," he teases, pulling me from my stupor.

I blush, raising my eyes to his as he steps into me again. He stands between my legs as I sit on the barstool and he runs his fingertips leisurely across my thighs before tracing the bottom of his t-shirt I have on. His touch is electric, and it sends little sparks dancing across the top of my thighs. My pussy pulses where she sits exposed on that wooden stool and despite a shower, I can smell our efforts wafting up and slapping me in the face. He can smell us too, and his nostrils flare as he scents my wanting.

He raises a brow. "Still?"

"Apparently," I offer. "What can I say? You make me absolutely feral."

"Feral. I like the sound of that," he admits. He bends down and speaks toward my center, "Down girl, or I'll never get dinner finished." He purses his lips, sending a teasing burst of hot air as he blows on my pussy.

I chuckle, shifting on my stool as he walks back to the stove where he places the linguine noodles in the boiling pot of water.

"Have you always liked to cook?" I ask, genuinely curious.

"No. But there's something relaxing about the process," he answers.

"I hate cooking," I state. "I wish I could just snap my fingers and have it all done for me. You know? Then I wouldn't have to deal with the aftermath because I hate doing dishes. Desire does most of the cooking, and they're an excellent cook, but there is always such a mess afterwards."

"It's not as glorious as it sounds," he says, still standing before the stove as he goes back and forth between stirring the noodles and the seafood concoction.

"How would you know? Did you have servants and maids growing up that did everything for you?" I huff.

"No. But this is nice. I like this part," he says, turning around with a spoon in his hands. He extends it toward me and I open my mouth.

I take a small bite of the mushroom and shrimp off the spoon, blowing around it so I don't burn my tongue.

As he steps back to the stove, my tastebuds come to life, the garlic tingling around the edge of my tongue as the mushroom and shrimp melt in the center. "That's so fucking good," I say around the food in my mouth.

He looks over his shoulder, still stirring in front of him as he says, "Not as good as you. But beggars can't be choosers."

I swallow and then reply coyly, "Dinner first, remember?"

Aaron finishes preparing the meal and then plates each of us a serving of his seafood Alfredo. We sit beside one another on the barstools, clearing our plates as we finish the bottle of wine. Between each bite, we share little tidbits about ourselves since we are practically strangers after all.

He grew up not far from Fayetteville, in a rural town where his parents own a Veterinarian clinic. He has no brothers or sisters, and they still live in the same house he grew up in. I ask him why he didn't follow in their footsteps, and he replies he has no problem managing a business for others, but he doesn't want to run his own.

I am just about to ask him why when my phone buzzes beside me. I lift my phone and a message from Desire shows on my lock screen.

Call. NOW.

I apologize to Aaron, telling him I have to go, and ask him if he can take me back to the office to get my car. He offers to just drive me to my place, but I decline as I have no clue what is going on yet.

We drive to the office in silence as I fervently type into my phone back and forth with Desire. They haven't told me what is going on yet, only that I need to get home and to call when I'm on my way.

After I get out of the car, I walk around to Aaron's side and give him a quick kiss through his open window. I take out my phone and get his number before I turn and step toward my own.

He calls after me, "Hope everything's okay. Text me later?"

"Okay," I call back, unlocking my door and getting in my car.

I'm driving home, about five minutes away from our apartment, when I finally call Desire. They pick up on the first ring.

"Girl! What the fuck took you so long?" they bristle. They sound anxious.

Through my speaker, I say, "I had to go back to the office and get my car."

"How long?" They sigh.

"Five minutes, maybe less."

"Okay," they say.

"What's going on?" I am worried now.

They huff. "I'll tell you when you get here. Not over the phone, okay?"

Four minutes after I hang up with Desire, I pull into our apartment complex's parking lot and find a patrol car parked in the visitor space near our door.

As I'm walking up, Desire opens the door and inside our apartment there is a uniformed and, I assume, a plain-clothes officer standing in our living room, their backs to me. I step past and look up at Desire with a *what the fuck is going on* questioning look on my face. They close the door behind me and as I step into the living room, the two officers turn around to face us.

"Ms. Goins?" the man in a suit asks.

"Yes," I answer nervously.

"I'm Detective Spence and this is Sergeant Reece." He pauses.

"What is this about?" I ask.

"We'd like to ask you some questions," he answers curtly.

I answer plainly, "Okay."

Detective Spence asks, "Do you mind if we take a seat?"

"Sure." I point toward the sofa and loveseat, taking a kitchen chair from the table and sliding it into the living room.

I take a seat and Desire remains standing in the doorway to the kitchen, leaning against the wall with their arms crossed. They look just as nervous as I feel. We have had no dealings with the police, outside of when I had to identify my mother's remains, so we are both shaken.

Detective Spence begins with, "We are looking into a missing persons case of one Elliott Marshall."

"Elliott? Yeah, I know him. We work for the same company," I offer.

"Can you tell us about the nature of your relationship?" Detective Spence asks.

"Well, we work for the same company, as I said. We're friends." I stop short, not offering anything further.

"When was the last time you saw Mr. Marshall?" Spence continues his questioning.

"Thursday? Yeah, Thursday. It was Thirsty Thursday, and we went out for drinks down on Dixon." I look over at Desire anxiously and they just shrug their shoulders, so I look back at Detective Spence.

Detective Spence is eying me warily. "And you haven't seen him since then?"

"No. We left the bar, I walked him to his vehicle, and then I came straight home."

"What time was that?"

"11:30 p.m. I know because I joked that I turn into a pumpkin at midnight." I chuckle and then stop, seeing the seriousness on his face as he purses his lips.

"11:30 p.m.?" he asks, his eyebrows raised.

"Yeah. He texted me to make sure I got home. I texted him the next day when he didn't show up for work several times. But he never answered. I can show you?" I offer.

Spence nods his head toward me and I pull my phone out of my back pocket, scroll to Elliott's messages, and hand it over to him. He views the message thread, see's that what I said pans out and then asks, "Would you mind taking a screenshot of your messages and sending it to me?"

"Yeah. Of course," I say. I screenshot the message and plug in the number as he gives it to me, sharing the image.

I think that will be the end of the questions, but neither officer stands.

Spence flips the page in his notepad, scanning the words he has written, and then turns his attention back to me. "Did you and Mr. Marshall have sexual relations that evening?"

I am taken aback. "Um, yeah. We did."

"Was this before or after you left the bar?"

"After. But before we left the parking lot," the words rush out.

"We found DNA evidence in the back of the vehicle which supports your statement. I'm assuming if we tested it, it would match yours?"

"Probably. But Elliott was a fuckboi. Mine might not be the only DNA you find." I chuckle nervously again, and then stop immediately, wiping the smile from my lips. I am so nervous, I'm not sure why I said that or why I laughed.

"And you didn't see him after that?" Spence asks.

"No. I came straight home," I insist.

Spence looks to Desire where they stand leaning against the wall. "And you can corroborate that?"

"Uh-huh," they answer. "We got up the next morning, had a cup of coffee, some breakfast, and then she went to work."

"Where were you when these 'activities' took place?" Spence asks Desire.

"I was serving drinks down the street at George's. We closed at 2 and then I came home," Desire says.

Spence flips another page over and without raising his eyes, he asks Desire, "And Ms. Goins was here when you arrived?"

"Yeah," they say nonchalantly.

Spence stands and looks over at the other officer before looking back at me. "I think that's all I have for now. Here's my card. If you can think of anything else. Anything that might help, please call me." He hands me the card and then he and the other officer walk to the door and I see them out.

About fifteen minutes after they leave, Desire walks into the living room where I'm still sitting in shock on my chair and plops down on the seat across from me.

Desire releases an exasperated sigh from where they're sitting, and I raise my eyes, meeting their agitated glare. "Care to tell me why I just lied for yo' ass?"

UNRAVELED (MELODY)

"Lie for me?" my voice pitches up. "You didn't lie for me! That was the truth!"

Desire leans back in their chair and looks at me accusingly. "You know damn well that wasn't the mutha fuckin' truth. I was already home when you came in loud as hell. Remember? When I woke you up, I told yo' ass about how rude you were and that you tracked mud all over. You smelled like ass, so that part was true. But you failed to mention what time you came in and the state of yo' nasty ass feet."

"I was home before midnight! I checked my phone when I pulled into the parking lot and then came straight in and went to bed," I argue.

"And you what? Walked through a mud puddle before fucking Elliott in the parking lot, forgot about it completely, and crawled your ass in bed? Huh-uh." Desire looks away from me.

"I don't know how mud got on my feet, and no, they weren't dirty when I fucked him. But yes, I came straight home and went to bed. Why would I lie about that?"

"Why would you fuck him after you said it was just drinks? Why would you be rude as hell, leaving the bar with a mutha fuckin attitude, and go get a tattoo? Why would you do any of the things you been doin'?" they chastise. "This ain't fuckin' you. None of it: the lying, the outbursts, the random hookups. I'm not slut shamin' you, girl. But damn? Something's gotta give."

"I'm not lying! I'm not capable of whatever this is. And I thought you knew me?" I snivel.

"So the fuck did I," Desire mumbles before rising from their seat and stomping down the hall where they slam their door.

Shocked at everything that has come to pass in the last hour, I sulk to my room. I take a quick shower, crying the tears of frustration that built up during my questioning, and then get ready for bed.

I am brushing my teeth, looking in the mirror at my sunken in eyes, while flashbacks of the interrogation play in my mind. I place my toothbrush in the holder and brace my hands on the sink as I stare at my reflection.

"I didn't fucking do anything," I say aloud, attempting to persuade myself of such. But I am unsuccessful. *I know I fucked him, but I left him standing by the side of his car and came home. I came home.*

I am still reeling when I crawl into bed an hour later, after taking a shot of tequila to calm my nerves. I am so shaken up, and I'm not sure I can fall asleep without a little assistance.

As I am burrowing beneath my covers, I reach over and shoot Aaron a quick text.

> This night was shit, but I'm home. Going to bed. Talk to you tomorrow?

> Hope everything is okay? Yeah. Talk to you tomorrow.

> Thanks. And yeah, it should be.

Or so I hope.

· · ·

I'm tossing and turning in my bed about an hour later, unable to fall asleep, when I decide to get up and get another drink.

I walk to the kitchen, take a quick shot, and then walk to the front door where my muddy boots from Thursday night sit in the shoe rack. I lift one up, see how ruined they are, and plop it down before heading back to my room.

I close the door to my room quietly behind me with a click and then turn around, flinging myself onto my bed, where my face lands on something hard. I raise up, slide my hand beneath me, and pick up my necklace. It drapes across my hands; the stone refracting the light and sending prisms across my face.

I am transfixed by its beauty and it calls to me, just like it did as I was walking by the vendor at the market. I am propped up on my elbows, toward the head of my bed, when without thinking about why I took it off in the first place, I loop my necklace over my head.

It nestles between my boobs and immediately heats. I flip over onto my back, my body arching away from the bed as pain shoots through my chest, and before I can reach up and tear it off me, my world goes black.

As if staring at a tv screen while a videotape rewinds, images stream behind my closed lids. There are flashes of light, splashes of dark crimson, and silhouettes of people moving so fast before my eyes. It is disorienting.

The movement slows and the sound of the tape screeches loudly in my ears as it comes to a halt. The last vision, my dashboard as I look down at my phone, is paused on the screen. And as if in a virtual reality game, I reach forward and press the play button blinking dead center.

Clicking sounds in my ears as I lower my head down to where my phone is in my lap and I type out a message.

> Nope. Not a pumpkin. I guess I was wrong.
> Care to finish where we left off?

It's a response to Elliott's last text asking if I turned into a pumpkin yet. A message that I don't have in my phone.

Three dots blink as he types out his reply, and then an address pops up on the screen.

See you in 15.

That's my only reply and then I sit my phone in the cupholder as I place the car in reverse and leave my parking spot.

I fast forward to the next part, street lights and stop signs blurring past as I make one turn after another, eventually pulling into a parking space in front of a house.

Picking up my phone from where I placed it in the cupholder, I look at the time and it says 12:21 a.m. I then delete the last messages between Elliott and me before turning off my phone completely.

Dropping my phone in the center console, I close the latch, concealing it, and then open the car door. I step out of my vehicle, look around the empty street, and then lock my car before sauntering up to the front door where Elliott stands in the doorway.

He steps to the side and I walk past him, standing in his entryway as he closes the door behind us. I hear it latch and then feel his hands on my shoulders as he slides my jacket down my arms. I let him.

I can hear my jacket brush against the wall as he hangs it on a hook at the front door. And as my eyes wander, I take in his living room.

There is a toffee-colored leather sofa in the center of the space, taking up most of the room, a small metal coffee table just before it, a tv mounted on the far wall playing a podcast, and a matching recliner off to my right. A mid century dark bronze tree floor lamp with five copper orbs looms just behind the sofa, dimmed and offering mood lighting to his sitting area as I step toward the space.

Elliott stops me, asking if I want to take off my boots. I do, handing them to him where he leaves them on the tile of the front entryway.

Turning back around, I step forward, my feet landing on the plush carpet. My toes squish through my socks as I pad forward on the carpet to a recliner on the right side of the room. I take a seat, leaning back into the chair as Elliott asks if I'd like a drink. I accept and he walks to the far-left wall where he prepares me a drink at a copper bar cart.

He turns, two drinks in his hands, and walks back across the room toward me. He extends a drink and my hand reaches out and takes it. I cross my legs, and he takes a seat on the sofa as he tosses back the contents of his glass. I raise mine to my lips, gulp it down and then engage Elliott in some small talk.

This part is boring, so I fast forward. My head tilts several times, I hear laughter in response to something he's said, and then he returns to the bar cart at least twice before we finally get up and walk down a hallway.

Our feet shuffle down the hallway, we enter a bedroom, our hands wander, and then our clothes end up a pile on the floor, before Elliott pushes me back on the bed.

I consider pressing the playback button, ceasing the fast forward, but after sex with Aaron, whatever is about to happen would be a disappointment, so I speed past this next part, too.

There is lots of blurred movement, my legs in the air above me, and Elliott's face contorting in an unflattering manner before being tossed to the bed as I ride him.

This goes on for far too long, and thank god for the fast forward or I would have had to endure all of it in real time.

Eventually we put our clothes back on, the fabric as it brushes over my skin sounding in my ears, as we talk back and forth, our voices echoing off the walls like Alvin and the Chipmunks as it speeds through.

He walks me to the front door and I walk back to my car and he gets in his Range Rover. My car comes to life, and I'm speeding down the street, stopping at every sign and light as we twist and turn through the city, Elliott not far behind me. I must have asked him to follow me home after god knows how many drinks.

It's not long before we're heading down MLK, but instead of going through the light toward my apartment, we turn east on AR16. I'm not sure how long we traveled on that road, but seeing as how dark it is and the fact that I am fast forwarding, it has been at least ten minutes.

Confused about where we are, I press the playback button and the car slows to the actual speed as I look out the front windshield. I pull off onto a county road when I see the street sign for Van Hoose Drive, and Elliott turns in behind me.

I bring the car to a stop, placing it in park and turn off the ignition. Elliott does the same, his headlights turning off after several minutes, when he opens the driver's side door.

Once he steps out of his vehicle, I swing open my door, exiting mine. I step into the overgrown brush at the side of the road beside where my car is parked and drop my pants, taking a quick pee.

After several minutes of me in the bushes, Elliott walks toward my car. He stops at the side of my vehicle and calls out to me. I peek through the bushes at him, his dim silhouette against the side of my vehicle barely visible in the darkness.

I ask him to toss me a bag from my front seat and he opens the driver's side door, leaning over the center console to the passenger side. He grabs the bag and tosses it into the bushes, unsure of exactly where I am. I pick it up and when he asks what I needed; I answer I had baby wipes to clean myself off.

Elliott chuckles, leaving the car door ajar, and is walking back toward his vehicle as I stalk him from my hiding place in the overgrowth's darkness.

He reaches the front of his Range Rover, is leaning against it with his hands on the hood when I spring from the bushes. I startle him and he jumps back, leaning against the front of his Range Rover with his hand clutched to his chest. He yells out, "Jesus fucking Christ, Mel," before leaning over and bracing himself on his knees. His head is hanging down, and he tilts his head to look up at me where I'm now standing within arm's reach and his eyes widen.

Before he straightens, my leg arches up into view, kicking him in the face. He flies back, blood arcing into the air from where my foot landed in the middle of his face, and his body thuds against the side of his vehicle, leaving an Elliott sized dent in the driver's side quarter panel.

He slumps to the ground, and my boots crunch on the gravel road beneath me as I take the two steps toward his body.

Standing over where he slumps against his tire, I look down and see bright red blood seeping from Elliott's nose and mouth. I knocked out a tooth when my boot met his face and it's now somewhere, lost amongst the gravel.

"Not so handsome anymore, are you, Elliott?" I shout into the darkness, my voice gravelly and sounding not like my own.

I turn and walk away from Elliott, my boot slurping as I step into a mud puddle. One catches, and it squelches as the suction releases. I pull it free, shaking the excess off as I curse to myself.

As I step around to my trunk, I'm mumbling incoherently about the stupidity of men before I throw it open.

Inside, I grab a square bag and tear it open, revealing a blue plastic tarp with metal eyelets. It's a cheap one, but it's only Elliott, after all.

I drape it across my trunk, smoothing it up the sides, covering all the exposed felt like carpet. And once I'm satisfied, I begin the arduous task of dragging Elliott's body back to my vehicle.

I place his ankle on my shoulder, standing between his legs before I turn around and pull. His ass is heavy, heavier than I imagined he'd be, and I grunt and groan as I drag him behind me. It takes longer than I anticipate, and I am covered head to toe in sweat by the time I finally get him to the rear of my car.

The next part is a feat, and it, too, takes me a long time as I muscle his dead weight into the back of my car. Once I finally have him loaded, I wrap the excess tarp around him, ensuring none of his blood or the mud I tracked dragging him is visible outside of the tarp. He may be dead weight, but his stubborn ass is still exhaling shallow breaths as he slumbers nestled securely in my trunk.

I look down at my mess one last time before releasing a deep groan as I close my trunk. The latch clicks and I wearily stumble back to my driver's side, sliding inside where Elliott left my door ajar. I slam it shut, turn on the ignition, and my car comes to life.

I place the car in drive and it lurches forward as I head down the road. I only move the car several feet before turning. The road is narrow, so I execute a three-point turn and then drive back past Elliott's vehicle before turning onto the blacktop once again.

Bugs fly at me, illuminated in my headlights, as I seem to zoom down the road at warp speed, but I'm only going the speed limit. Safety first, after all. Because I'd hate to get pulled over with a body in my trunk.

I fast forward again, rushing through what could have been forty-five minutes to an hour, just past Combs, when I finally turn on another county road. There is a large shop on the right side, and I pass by many small buildings as I traverse down a straightaway.

I pass a small cemetery, which would be a great location, but that's not exactly what I had in mind when I started my drive earlier this morning, so I continue on.

The road twists and turns some, and after about fifteen minutes, I am pulling up to a cattle gate leading to what I am certain is private land. I mean, it had said no trespassing on the sign, and this is Arkansas, so the owner probably has a gun, but who would shoot little ole me?

I get out of my car and yank the gate open, pull just inside, and then close it behind me. I reenter the vehicle, driving around to the side of a dilapidated natural stone building, past some rusted out raised fuel tanks where I park. My car's not exactly concealed, but I'm out in the middle of Bumfuck, Egypt, so what's the worry?

The building has steep stone steps, or the remnants of steps, as time and weather have taken their toll on them. They lead up to where the front door used to hang, but no door hangs now as the entry is wide open. There is no glass in any of the window openings, and a metal roof gleams in the moonlight. Which is odd because it doesn't fit with the age of the building. Someone must have had it done after the facility closed, but why would they update that feature, leaving the wood eaves in their state? They loom haphazardly below the windows of the upper floor, jutting out and broken in more places than I care to count. Not like that fucking matters, so I go back to my task.

I step out of my car, walk around to my trunk, and throw it open. Elliott stirs inside, so I go to the side of the house, grab a loose stone from beside the foundation and walk back to the car. I raise it over my head in one hand and throw open the tarp with my other. Elliott shifts when I throw open the tarp and I bring down the stone with a crunch. It connects just at the edge of his temple, sending blood splattering upward where it splashes across the lid of my trunk and just misses my face as I jump back. There is some on my wrist, and on the face of the stone, so I wipe it off on the front of his hoodie while I voice my disgust.

"Look at the fucking mess you made," I grumble.

I toss the stone onto a pile at the base of the foundation, and it tumbles into the thick grass. I then step back to the car to begin the exhausting task of getting him out of it when I decide to fast forward through the next part.

I skip once, then twice, and the next scene that greets me once I press the playback button is one where I am straddling Elliott in the tall brush behind the rickety outbuilding that lies just beyond the academy. His cock is seated limply within me, and I have a dagger raised above me as a stone in the pommel glimmers in the moonlight.

I press pause and I can feel my heart racing as adrenaline courses through me. *Do I want to know what happens next? I could just skip it. I could just skip to the end and see the final scene. But I need to know. I need to face whatever I've done, even if I don't know why.*

I press play, and as I do, I see myself reaching forward, grasping the neckline of his hoodie, and muscling him up against me. I quickly release my grasp, snake my arm around his back, and press him against my chest.

"Almost there, my loves. Almost there," I struggle to voice, my words clipped as Elliott's body attempts to slump away from me.

He is hard to hold on to with one hand raised above my head, and I am sweating from the exertion. It beads on my brow, one drop trickling down the side of my face while I grit my teeth. "That's it," I mutter, attempting to grind onto him. "That's what we needed. It's good, isn't it? So good." I fake a moan, agitated by the lack of fullness within me. "Oh, fuck it!" I growl in frustration, allowing Elliott's body to fall back. It thuds, the grass crunching and settling as he nestles onto the ground.

With Elliott passed out beneath me, I take the dagger in both hands and raise it high into the air once more. I arch back, gathering my strength, and breathe out a loud, "Argh," as I bring it down, embedding it deep within his chest.

Elliott's eyes shoot open and his nails dig into my forearms as he attempts to pry my hands off the dagger. He is struggling, and I lean all my weight forward, pressing the dagger in further until I hear a crunch.

His hands slide down, landing at his side, and he releases a last gurgling breath. It sputters, the blood seeping out of the corners, and I yank my necklace off me, breaking the chain. I press the stone of my pendant to his lips, holding it there and swiping it through his blood, as I await his life-force to rise from within.

It's dim at first, the illumination of his life force as it drifts up in small puffs from his lips. But then it billows out of his mouth, snaking up and being drawn into the stone.

"This time is different," I pant, the words crackling as I say them. "This time I offer none of myself. This time I give nothing in return. I take freely, and without consequence."

I cackle, shifting my weight as I raise from where I'm straddling Elliott's lifeless form. I stand above him and looking down I utter a final, "I think I like you best this way," before turning and walking away, leaving him lying behind a ramshackle building in the middle of nowhere.

The playback ends. My car hidden in the shadows beside the academy is the minimized still frame image centered on the screen as I hold back a scream, trapping it in my throat. Then the words *play next title* blinks in the center of my vision.

Do I keep watching? Do I see what else I've done? Or do I maintain my ignorance?

Curiosity gets the better of me and I press play, the next title expanding and filling the screen that is my vision as it queues. A loading symbol rotates in the center as the stairs of C4 lie static in the background.

You've got to be fucking kidding me? I think, immediately pressing the skip button over and over until the cursor is at the end. I take it back, pressing play, and again the loading symbol circles before the image expands.

When the scene finally opens, I am looking down at the palm of my hand where my pendant lies in the center, coated in blood. It drips off my wrist and falls to dry grass as I look down at my feet. My eyes shift, and when they focus, I see Elliott's bloated body lying beside Jen's still form. Just like Elliott, she too has a bloody mark in the center of her shirt, and blood seeping from the corner of her lips.

I shake, muffled cries escaping my lips as I move the cursor all around the screen, looking for the exit button. "Please. Please. Go away. Go away," I plead, my voice quivering. But there is no "x" in the corner, and pressing the screen over and over does not remove the image from my view. It is just there, permanently etched into my mind.

As nausea overtakes me and bile rises in the back of my throat, heavy breathing sounds loudly in my ears as if someone is panting into a microphone.

After several torturous rounds of panting, a maniacal cackling replaces the breaths before a woman's voice speaks. "Melody. Oh,

Melody. It didn't have to be this way. We could have been partners. We could have done this together," the singsong voice says.

If whoever this is wants to soothe me, they are doing a shit job of it; I think as I continue to shudder.

"But you took off the stone," they sing. "You took off the stone and left me no choice," she chastises, her anger seeping through her tone. "And now I am in charge. I am in charge from now on because you have been compromised. You let him touch us!" she seethes. "You let him sink his cock deep within us and I am far from happy. So, here's how this is gonna go. I am now you, and you are now no-one. I hope you understand?"

The screen blinks out as a low humming sounds. The same vibrational sound an old TV makes just after it's shut off before the residual electrical current dissipates. Its continual buzzing has me disoriented and I want it to stop, so I imagine myself walking over to the plug, placing both hands firmly around and pulling the cord from the wall. The sound is now gone, but I am left alone in the darkness and the world has gone completely silent.

CHAPTER 39
STANDING ACCUSED (HADES)

*C*an I just take a moment and share a couple of things? Can I do that? I'd really like to that. Pretty please with a cherry on top? I'm begging, I get that. And it's a bit much; I get that too. But this is my damn part of the story, so indulge me for a second. Or two. Or an hour. You catch my drift?

So, I'm a fan of lists, right? Believe it or not, they've completely controlled my life until now. I mean, come on! I label and catalogue everything. And it's a little OCD, I'm aware. But, if there ever was a god that was self-aware, it's me. In the history of gods, you won't find another more capable of understanding themselves than me. Trust me, I've checked.

I've done the work. It was hard and took a long time, several millennia, in fact. But how hard it was and how long it took was so beneficial to my personal growth. Because now I am more in tune with my feelings, understand my behaviors and characteristics, and, as an added bonus, am so cognizant of how others perceive me. But give me a break, will ya'? Because for every so called "crazy" action, there's a valid reason behind it. I'm not making excuses here. I genuinely believe that the way I do what I do and the reasons I do what I do are legitimately the best for all concerned. Or at least I want them to be.

That is the conversation I rehearse in my mind as I sit drinking a beer in Mr. Evans' living room once I get back from dropping off Melody that evening. It's confusing, and a little convoluted, but there is so much we need to unpack. So much I need to share and questions I need her comfortable enough to answer. But, unfortunately, as it often happens, other things got in the way and I never got to sit her down for the awkward conversation.

I had said there were things we needed to discuss, but that was before she rendered me speechless with her scent; that sweet and seductive jasmine and lavender that turned me inside out as it spun me out of control. And that kiss! That mind muddling, life altering, body shaking kiss. The one delivered by velvety soft succulent lips, once again igniting a desire that I thought died the same day my hope did oh so long ago. And now I circle back to my mention of lists. Starting with, and in no real order of precedence, things I could have never predicted happening in the day following my return to the mortal realm.

I never expected the level of satisfaction I would feel doing something entirely on my own, and with no power to draw from. But as I stood before the copy machine, following Melody's instructions from memory—not Mr. Evans's—I pressed each button and watched as it pulled the parchment from the feed tray. Ugh, I can't explain the level of accomplishment it provided me. It took everything in my power to not do a little dance and shout above me, "Who's the god? Who's the god?" But I am a man now. So I choked down my excitement, like a man, and smiled to myself instead.

Having a perfectly paired drink with the meal, one that enhances the flavors and smooths out the textures in order to create a more satisfying dining experience, has always been my one indulgence. Okay, one of my indulgences. And it is because of that vice that I have checked off all thirty-three of the most common varieties of grape, finally ticking off number 8,796 earlier that morning as I sprint toward my goal of tasting all 10,000. But I don't have a glass of wine with every meal, and I've skipped one, a time or twenty. Regardless, nothing could have prepared me for the smoothness and rich flavor of that Don Julio 1942 Anejo as its decadence splashed in my mouth while I stared longingly at Melody that afternoon as she teased me with her torturous tongue sliding over the rim of her glass. It took everything in my power not to moan out loud. Or maybe it had nothing to do with the luxuriousness of the alcohol at all, and everything to do with the quality of my company?

I had said she smelled sweet, felt the calm washing over me as I took in her essence, filling my nostrils with every ambrosial note. But the minute my tongue darted out, coating the tip with her satisfaction, lapping that sugary goodness straight from her core, my heart did more than skip a beat; it fucking stopped. And as expected, my brain ceased to function and my organs started to die, my muscles tensing as I went rigid from head to toe. Then our eyes locked, something unspoken between us, and she brought me back with her life-saving measures when she screwed her eyes shut; that electrical shock to my system, coaxing me back from the edge of nothingness. And later, when she moaned out, "Don't stop!" Ugh, the rigidity then had nothing to do with death and everything to do with the life she stirred within me, manifesting itself in the most glorious erection, begging to be set free.

I didn't think mortal men had it in them. I didn't think something so frail could move with such force behind it, delivering a performance even a god could be proud of. But as Melody's cries filled the air, her nails digging into my back—the back of this mortal—marking his flesh in ways I only wish I'd marked her now, I felt the Earth shift; falling away from its axis as everything went topsy-turvy. The ground quaked beneath us, and as eternal night closed in all around when the moon fell away, the tides crashed cataclysmically on the shores as we drowned in the floodwaters of that tidal shift. But when we fell apart, our fingers interlaced as we basked in the comfort of our euphoria, I opened my eyes only to find that everything had righted itself faster than our mortal eyes could track, likened to the beating of a humming-bird's wings during courtship; an impressive 200 beats per second. I stared longingly at her hummingbird, hidden behind that covering, and found meaning in it, even if it held none for her.

Lost. That's how I feel as I toss back another beer, sinking farther into the cushions of the sofa as I sit in the living room, reminiscing on all the ways I will never get her out of my system. She's ruined me, but it's the good kind. The kind of ruining where every surface of your skin aches for their touch, every lung full breathed in tastes less sweet when you're not with them, and every idle moment spent apart sends your mind circling back to them. I am hers, and this man—this god—is forever altered. Not in the way Persephone had altered me, but in a way that really matters. Because I don't want to change her and don't want to control her. I want to possess her, sure. But I don't want to claim her as mine. I don't want to force her to be with me. Don't want to trick her into loving me. I want her to choose me, not the other way around. And maybe that's where I went wrong with Persephone from the beginning. But I can't go back. We can only move forward. And hopefully she'll want to do so with me.

The next morning, when I wake up, I send her a quick text:

> Hope you slept well. How would you
> ACTUALLY like to get some coffee? Meet me?

There is no immediate reply, so I go about my morning, heading downstairs where I make myself a quick breakfast. I eat, head upstairs for a shower, check on "sleeping beauty" in the guest room, and then head back downstairs to check my phone.

I pick it up, seeing a message on the Lock Screen, open it and read her full reply.

Slept like complete shit. As expected
considering the events of my evening at home.
But yeah, coffee would be good. Plus, we
need to talk. Meet me at Arsaga's Mill District?
Give me about an hour.

I have errands to run, a couple of books to drop back at the library for my oversized paper weight slumbering down the hall, and it's only a couple blocks from my place—his place—so I text back.

See you there.

An hour later, after a mad dash through town and a quick stop at the library, I'm pulling into the crowded parking lot of Arsaga's. Melody's car is already in the parking lot, so I head inside, scanning the room as I search for her beautiful face.

I find her along the front wall, sitting at a four top with a baseball cap and sunglasses on as the sun shines in through the large window beside her. Her ponytail peeks out, the loose strands cascading over the neck of her dark purple hoodie, and I think to myself, *the color does nothing for her complexion*. I hate it, actually.

She is staring down into her coffee, her finger circling around the rim of her ceramic cup as she grips it tightly in her other hand, and when I finally reach her, she raises her face toward me.

I lean down to place a kiss on her cheek and she pulls back, her lip curling up in revulsion as she says, "Not here. We're in public."

I'm taken aback by her reaction to my attempted affections, but I brush it off, sliding into the seat opposite her.

There are no smiles offered for me now and her lips draw tight, as if she's holding her breath. She looks out the window, her cheek resting on her knuckles, and ignores me as I stare over at her.

A server arrives at our table and I order a cappuccino, asking

Melody if she wants anything else as they stand waiting patiently. Melody doesn't answer. She just waves her hand dismissively as she shakes her head no.

I slump down in my chair, tapping my fingers anxiously on the tabletop as I try to figure out what I've done wrong.

"Could you just stop," she barks, the agitation and shrillness of her tone jarring me.

"Have I done something wrong?" I ask, leaning forward as I rest my elbows on the table. I slide my hands toward her and she pulls back, crossing her arms over her chest.

A snarl dresses her lips and she groans. "What?" she asks, forcefully.

"That's what I'm asking!" My irritation slips into my tone, so I try asking once more, but this time I say each word separately for effect, "Have I done something wrong?"

"I have a fucking hangover. Okay? Geesh," she breathes out in exasperation.

"Oh. That explains the sunglasses." I chuckle, some of my unease finally lifting. "So, what did you want to talk to me about?"

Melody's head jerks toward me so fast, I'm surprised her neck doesn't crack. "As if you don't know?" she accuses.

I'm caught off guard. "I don't," I retort, raising my hands in surrender as I lean back in my chair. "Seriously, Mel. What is this about?"

"When I got home last night, the cops were at my place," she grits.

"And?" I prompt her to continue.

"And," she exaggerates the word, "they had a lot of questions about my friend that is missing."

She doesn't seem upset, not really. Everything that she's doing seems forced, like an act. A pure Persephone move, but there's only one way to know with certainty.

Unsure of where this is going, I decide to play along. "That's awful, Mel," I feign shock. "Do they know what happened?"

"As far as I can tell, no. But they were extremely interested in the events from the last night I saw him."

"And when was that?" I ask, genuinely interested to know her answer.

"Thursday night, down on Dixon," she replies. "I told them the last time I saw him was in the parking lot, but then I went home," she says flippantly.

"Oh, the guy you left with," I say in acknowledgement.

"I don't think they believed me, though. Even after I gave them a screenshot of our message thread showing the timestamp of when I got home," she whines, but it's not convincing. She could actually care less and it shows.

"Do they have any leads? Any idea of where he went?"

"Not as far as I could tell. But don't worry, I didn't tell them you were in the parking lot, too." In a show of concern, she reaches for my hand and I allow her to take it. She pats it reassuringly, then grips it tight as she pulls me toward her. She leans in, whispering, "Because honestly, it wouldn't look good; you spying on us and then acting all jealous when I tried to walk to my car."

I pull my hand from hers, taken aback by her inference. "Me? I did nothing to him. Why would I?"

She crosses her arms. "Oh, I don't know, maybe because you're obsessed with me? Maybe because you keep showing up everywhere I go, stalking me all over town?" she accuses.

I laugh out loud, leaning back in my seat as I glare at her. "You're delusional, you know that?"

"Me?" she shrieks, pushing back from the table and causing a scene. "You're the one obsessed with me. I've told you once and I'm telling you now, leave me the hell alone," she raises her voice, knocking into my shoulder as she brushes past me and storms for the door.

I stand, embarrassment flushing my cheeks as I toss down a twenty on the table. I look through the window and see her stomping toward her car.

She'd wanted this. She wanted to cause a scene. She wanted me to meet her some place very public and throw her accusations in my face before fleeing like a victim.

I clench my jaw, growling out in my mind as the certainty I sought sets in. *Persephone! If she wants a scene, I'll fucking give her one.*

Jogging out the front door, I pass by a couple going inside, and I apologize when my shoulder collides with the man as he's coming in. He nods his response and I continue into the parking lot.

Persephone's in no hurry, taking her sweet time to unlock Melody's car, fumbling with the keys when I finally reach her.

I tap her shoulder and she spins herself around, continuing her act when she slams her back onto the door of her car and yelps.

"Show's over, Little One," I growl, being careful not to touch her as I stand with my hands raised at my sides.

She tears off her sunglasses, those emerald eyes flaring wide as she glares at me. She spews, "It's over when I say it's over. You have no power here, but I do! Stay away from me, or Melody has an unfortunate accident." She pouts, raising her hand and wiping a fake tear from the side of her cheek.

I back up, fumbling with my phone as I attempt to record her outburst while I make my way to my car. I call out, "This won't turn out how you think it will!" I reach my car and tear open the door as I keep my eyes and my phone on Persephone.

She jerks open her door, plops down in the seat and turns on the ignition. She backs out and I am standing beside my car still with my phone raised when she drives by with her window rolled down. She flips me off and yells out the window, "Just watch me," before pulling out of the lot and speeding off down the street.

CHAPTER 40
WILY WOMAN (PERSEPHONE)

I have a lot to do, and not a lot of time to do it in. This is the story of my life. Or, at least, that has been the way it has been written; up until now. But my plans will change all that, giving me a different ending to my tale; a never-ending story, if you will.

Chuckling to myself, the idea of such an outcome makes me positively giddy as I lean back onto the over-stuffed pillows lining Melody's bed, scrolling through the vendor's webpage she has saved on her laptop the night following my very public run-in with my ex.

To think, by this time tomorrow, I can be one step closer to freedom from that asshole and hours from achieving the most blissful freedom anyone could ever dream of. Freedom from Death; the god and the outcome all mortals face day after excruciating day.

Erymanthe was right; or Aphrodite, as I found out much too late. This road hasn't been an easy one, but one where each treacherous step forward has been well worth the trip. This road has allowed me to truly live, feeling that power as it drips down my fingers, plopping down where it soaks into the earth, and finally allowing life to spring forth once again from its crimson well. And I will carry those fond memories with me from now until eternity. Because eternity is what she promised, so eternity I shall have.

When I finally scroll to the bottom of the page, I run my cursor over the contact us icon and type the telephone number that pops up into my phone. It rings twice, and finally a man answers.

"A to Z Oddities, dis Shane," he says in the most country twanging but cheerful customer service voice.

"Hi, Shane. My name is Melody, and if you're the same vendor from the Maker's Market last weekend, I have a couple questions for you about a necklace I purchased. That is, if you have the time?" I say in my sweetest voice.

"Oh, sure. I kin help ya out. Can ya describe which one it twas?" he asks.

"I looked it up on your site. It's the Alexandrite stone. Maybe you remember me? You offered me a box, which was super nice of you, but I just wore it home."

"Jeah. I 'member. Tha little thang, walkin' round with jer very tall... er, friend." He tries to be PC, but he's not fooling anyone. He obviously has an opinion about my... er, friend.

Jackass.

"Yup. That's me. You know it's not all it's cracked up to be; being a little thing. But it has some advantages," I offer in the most bubble-headed voice possible.

"Ju don't say?" His tone is skeptical, but I'm playing the part of a ditz, and he scored the role of the village idiot. So I allow it.

I do say; you back woods, country bumpkin ass, bigot.

"So, what can you tell me about my stone? Are there any cool stories that go with that one? Or is it just your plain, run-of-the-mill knock-off?"

"No, Ma'am. She's no knock-off. That's a piece a histry you got jurself, der," he insists.

"Really!" I feign excitement. "Oh, that's amazing. What kind of history?" I prod.

"Well, like most histry, it's a lil jaded. Don't really have much of a happy ending. But what I can tell ya is, the last girl done owned it... well, she had herself one heck of a time," he answers fervently.

"How so?"

"Done got herself locked up in the looney bin." He chuckles, coughing a couple of times as he clears his throat. "Scuse meh. As I's a sayin', she started hearin' voices n such. Course I'm not one fer gossip, but it coulda been on account of her being wily," he whispers as if sharing a secret.

"Wily?"

"Dat da only word to describe Miss Marilyn Sawyer. Whut else would ja call a woman wit loose morals?"

"Oh. I see," I say earnestly.

Yes, Billy Jo Bob, I do see. Whatever do we do with those wily women folk? I roll my eyes.

"Any chance you know where they put wily women like her? I have a friend who could use a vacation." I laugh. He laughs. We both laugh, and then another fit of coughing ensues.

Oh, brother!

"Well, ju know the first place she was at done closed down. But I think dey moved her over to Spring... somethin' or other over in Franklin County," he mumbles through the last part.

I can hear him attempting to rub his two brain cells together, hoping to create a spark, through the phone.

"I thank you kindly, Mr. Shane. And I hope you get to feeling better," I offer.

Mr. Shane is attempting to form a complete sentence as I "accidentally" hang up. I quickly block his number and take a deep breath, hoping to restore some of the oxygen to my brain and rekindle some of the brain cells he snuffed out during that conversation.

Gods! To think, people like that are allowed to procreate? What is this world coming to? And how in the Sam Hill does he have a website?

Shaking my head, I open up my browser and search for what little I could glean from Mr. Shane. I find the facility, dial their number, and when a woman answers, I ask to speak to Miss Marilyn Sawyer. The woman says she is unable to accept calls, but if there's an inquiry, she'd be happy to leave a message for her doctor. I decline and thank her before hanging up the phone.

One task down. Now to call off for work tomorrow because I have a field trip planned over to Spring something or other.

CHAPTER 41
HALF LIFE (HADES)

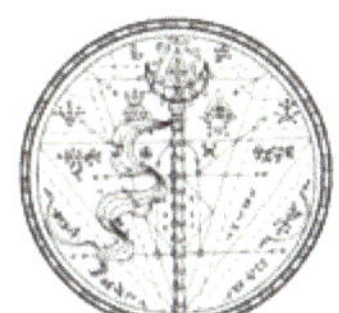

She didn't show up for work that morning, which I suspected would happen. Even so, I am saddened I don't get to see that beautiful face. Even if it is currently being worn like a mask by someone utterly hideous.

I spent the rest of yesterday fuming, wracking my brain for what to do with the hand I've been dealt. But Persephone has a royal flush, and I am merely bluffing, the remorse of going all-in slapping me in the face as I stare blankly at my screen in my office that afternoon.

I can't focus, and I'm getting nothing done sitting here as the sand flows through the narrow neck of the hourglass, faster than just your standard one grain at a time, as the time for me to stop Persephone and save Melody quickly runs out.

I have to stop her, and there has to be a way, but with no power here, and no time to make my way back to the Underworld for answers, I may be shit out of luck.

As I sit in my office, the day close to its end, a knock comes rapping at my door. "It's open," I call out, not bothering to look up from the report in front of me.

"Mr. Evans?" an unfamiliar voice sounds.

I look up to where a man in a suit and a uniformed officer stand in my doorway. Leaning back in my chair, I grasp my hands in my lap, crossing my ankle over my knee. "I was wondering when you were coming to see me," I offer cheerfully, smiling.

The two men look back and forth at one another before the one in the suit asks, "You were expecting us?" He cocks a brow in surprise.

"Oh, absolutely! Please, come in. Take a seat. Get comfortable. Hopefully, this won't take too long because I'm busy, you're busy..." I smile through my entire delivery.

They step inside, closing the door behind them, and they both take a seat side by side in the office chairs before my desk.

I lean forward, bracing on my elbows, and say with all certainty, "You have some questions for me."

They look at one another again, the uniformed officer grinning to himself, as the man in the suit looks at me. "As a matter of fact, we do, Mr.?"

"Aaron Evans." I point to the little pad he has opened in his lap. "That is two A's and then, well, you know the rest." I chuckle.

"Right," the man in the suit says, exaggerating the word. "So, Mr. Evans-"

"Aaron, please," I beam.

"Can you account for your whereabouts last Thursday evening?"

"Oh, absolutely. As Melody has probably already told you, I was at the same bar she and Elliott were at on the night in question," I answer jovially.

"You seem awfully happy for someone getting questioned in the disappearance of one of their co-workers," he says matter-of-factly.

"Oh, I am. I assure you. You see, this is all a game to Melody. She sent you sniffing in my direction, to take any, and hopefully all, suspicion off of her." I lean back, tapping my fingers on my desk twice in front of me. "Pretty smart, huh?"

He tilts his head as he surveys me. "And why exactly would she do that?"

I chuckle. "Where do I begin? Oh, I don't know, maybe because she's completely unhinged, and not only presents a danger to herself, but so many others. That might have something to do with it."

"Is she now?" His tone says he thinks I'm lying, and that's okay.

I continue, "So much so, in fact, that she concocted this wild story about how I'm obsessed with her, and how I'm stalking her around town despite multiple requests for me to stop. That sound about right?"

"Yeah."

"Here's the thing, fellas. Melody has gone so far off her rocker that she had me meet her at a public place 'to talk.'" I make air quotes for effect. "And then, once I got there, she played the role of a victim by creating a huge scene in the restaurant and closed it all out with a riveting performance in the parking lot. And as she sped away, she flipped me off, told me there's no way I was going to stop her, and went about her merry way. I was trying to record her but there just wasn't time." I finish my rant and take a deep breath, settling back in my chair once more as I open the video and play what little audio I got of me and Melody's last interaction.

"What is it you're claiming she said you can't stop?"

"Murder." I say pointedly. "Cold-blooded, ritualistic, gruesome murder. Can I get a drumroll, please?" I tap my desk again.

"Did you say ritualistic?" He leans toward my desk, jotting on his notepad.

"Sure did. You see, Melody thinks she's some resurrected Greek goddess who's comeback to escape the final death by collecting the life force of others in some measly stone after she plunges a dagger in their chest. And judging by her escalation, I'd say her next victim has already been chosen, or she's making her choice as we speak." Again, I take a deep breath.

"Are you on something, Mr. Evans? You seem amped up," he states.

"Nope, not amped up. But I am genuinely concerned about

Melody's well-being. Her mind is fractured and in her current state, who knows what she's capable of?" I counter.

"Do you have any evidence to support your statements, Mr. Evans?"

"Not a stitch. But this is where you, my friends, have your work cut out for you. Because believe me when I say she is on the hunt. Whatever she's planning will go down tonight. And the faster you find her, getting her to the first available bed in whichever psych facility you can, the safer everyone will be."

"Any idea where she might be?" he asks.

"I wish I could help you. But you see, she called into work this morning and I don't have her Lojacked, despite her claims to the contrary. I will tell you this... she likes remote, she likes the countryside, and she is quite the fire starter. If there's been any unexplained fires out in the boonies... I'd put my money on that was all her." I wink at the man in the suit.

The two men stand. I shake both of their hands and walk them to the door, where the man in a suit hands me his card. "If you can think of anything else. Or, if Ms. Goins contacts you, please call me."

"Will do, Sir." I stand at my door, watching them walk to the front desk, and wave as they check out.

Once the officers head down to the lobby, I move back to my desk, pulling up the tracking device I totally placed on Melody's car. I see she's still in Franklin County and her car hasn't moved all day. Hell, maybe I can call and reserve her a bed, seeing as she's been a visitor there since this morning.

I could send the cops her current location, but this seems way too easy. So I'll wait, because I am incredibly curious but patient enough to see how this all plays out.

Several hours later as I watch the tracker, I finally see it move. The screen blinks, the location refreshing, and now her car is well off any main road, out in the middle of the country.

Before I can second guess my decision, I pick up my phone and call my good friend, Det. Spence, as his card says, and tell on myself.

I admit to offering a little white lie earlier that day and that no, I'm not stalking her, I seriously am worried, and my tracking device says she is currently at (address redacted for privacy reasons) in Elkins.

I get in my car and start the fifty-four minute drive to her last location, speeding when I can, but do my best to not draw attention to myself. But in a two door Mercedes, out in BFE on gravel and dirt roads, someone's gonna notice; I don't exactly have my muddin' tires on, after all.

It is dark as I turn off the blacktop and the road is straight most of the way until it gets a little twisty, but still I am hauling ass. Faster than I should be, anyway.

As I pull up to the location, police vehicles and fire trucks are on scene as smoke billows from a small structure beside a large stone building. The internet had listed it as an abandoned academy, and it does in fact sit on private land, *no trespassing* signs warning all those looking to take some cool pictures. At least that's what all the internet searches said on my way here.

I park my car along the road, leaving room for other vehicles to pass, and walk toward the property where I am stopped by a uniformed officer and told this is an active crime scene.

I ask if Detective Spence is around and the officer walks back onto the property. He points in my direction and who I assume is Spence steps around the side of the building and motions for me to enter.

Stepping just inside the cattle gate, I stop, my eyes training on the gurney off to my right with a black body bag being wheeled toward an emergency vehicle.

I start toward the gurney and Spence stops me.

My voice quivers. "Is that her? Is it?"

"Mr. Evans, you really shouldn't be here," he offers.

"Tell me!" I command.

Detective Spence sighs. "We got here as soon as we could but, I'm sorry."

"Oh, gods," I whimper. "I thought we had time. I thought we could get her help. I never expected..." I trail off, unable to finish my statement.

"You did everything you could, Mr. Evans," Detective Spence assures me, placing his hand on my shoulder.

I am sick to my stomach, bending over and bracing myself on my knees as I sob. I shake my head in disbelief. "How did it happen?"

"We're still trying to piece it all together. But from what we know so far, based on the admission of the assailant-"

I interrupt, "Assailant? What assailant?" I look over toward the main building where an older gentleman is sitting on a large stone with his hands cuffed behind his back as he nods in response to whatever the investigator questioning him asks. Straightening, I ask, "When?"

"Twenty, thirty minutes ago, now."

I press, "Did he say why?"

"Turns out he and Ms. Goins had a conversation last night. The whole thing made him a little suspicious. And today, when he went over to visit his wife, he saw Ms. Goins leaving the facility and it just didn't sit right with him. He questioned the staff at the hospital, and they told him she had called last night asking for his wife. So, when she showed up this morning attempting to get permission to visit, they called him and he rushed right over," Spence says.

"That doesn't make sense," I snivel. "How did her going to see his wife prompt this?"

Detective Spence shifts as he crosses his arms. "You know, after our conversation with you this afternoon, I told my partner you were the craziest SOB I had ever met." He points to the older gentleman, "But then I met that man over there. And, I have to tell you, he's got you beat, and then some."

With tears still streaming down my face, I ask, "How so?"

"His wife has schizophrenia. She heard voices and such. He had a lot to say, like you did, about a dagger, a stone, and ritualistic murder."

My brows raise. "Did you find them? Did you find the relics?" I am anxious as I await his reply.

"We haven't recovered either of those items from the scene yet, just as we told him."

"Do you think I could talk to him?" I ask.

He shakes his head no. "That is completely out of the question."

I nod my head in understanding. I clear my throat. "How did he…"

"Shotgun. Close range. He says he followed her here, saw her walking around the property, and when she became aggressive when he was questioning her, at gun point… he shot her in self-defense."

I shriek, "How can he claim self-defense? He's bigger than she is!"

"Well, seeing as they were standing next to the corpses of two of her victims, his age and overall health; I'd say he had every right to be worried. The gun and his unease were warranted."

I take a deep breath, reeling. "Is he going to get away with this? He can't, can he?"

"All of that is up to the DA, and, if and when it goes to trial, a jury."

"This is insane!" I grab fistfuls of my hair at my temples and growl. "Ugh!"

"That's all I can say for now. Go home, Mr. Evans. And I'm sorry for your loss."

"Yeah." I swipe my hand at him dismissively as I stumble back to my car, distraught.

Friday, November 15, 2024, will forever be a date etched in my mind. Because today, I lay my love to rest. It happened fast and was something I never expected. I had only seen her as a means to an end; a piece of the puzzle. But now I struggle to imagine an eternity without her. And maybe I don't have to.

I know exactly what I must do, so once again, I make my way back to the Underworld and back to my archives where my one chance, well, Melody's one chance of salvation lies.

Standing in front of my full-length mirror, once I've returned from my quip trip back to my realm, I tighten the Windsor knot of my cobalt blue tie. I then secure the cuffs of my pale blue dress shirt with compass cufflinks before sliding on my dark navy suit jacket, buttoning and then smoothing it down.

Sitting on the edge of my bed, I slip on my dress shoes before standing and grabbing my key fob and the stone I grabbed from my chest of precious jewels off the bedside table. I place them both in the pocket of my jacket and leave the room.

My apartment—Mr. Evans'—is eerily quiet, and my shoes squish into the carpet, squeaking as I walk down the stairs. The funeral for Melody begins soon and Moore's Chapel is about ten minutes from my apartment, so I need to get going.

I've never met Desire, so I'm not sure they will even know who Melody was to me, but seeing as there will be others from work in attendance, my presence shouldn't be too unexpected.

I walk up the red brick walkway and through the front doors of the two story white building where others mill about inside, chatting quietly with one another. I have one white rose, wrapped with sprigs of lavender and jasmine, in a small bouquet that I carry in my hands as I make my way into the ceremony where, I assume, Desire stands greeting those as they walk in.

Stopping in front of them, I offer an, "I'm sorry for your loss," before taking a seat in the back. I don't wish to stand out amongst all those in attendance, so I keep to myself as I grip the bouquet tightly in my hands.

I need to get to Melody's body, need to place the stone in her hands before it is too late, but there are too many people around to do so inconspicuously. So, I'll wait until after the ceremony, and when the opportunity arises, I will give her one last gift. I think it's a gift, anyway, but maybe she won't see it as such. And there's only one way to find out.

The ceremony ends, and I stay seated as those in attendance depart to their cars to wait for the procession to the cemetery.

I am watching Desire as they say their last goodbye, tears streaming down their face, awash in grief, when someone plops down beside me.

Still staring at the bouquet in my hands, I don't look over until they speak.

"I thought it only right I pay my last respects," Detective Spence offers from my left.

I look over and offer a genuine smile. "Same here," I say.

"You really cared about that girl, didn't you?" he asks.

"And then some," I admit, a tear trickling down my cheek.

"I'm sorry things didn't turn out the way you hoped. But at least she's at peace now," he says.

Nodding my head, I sob out, "That's all anyone can ever hope for."

I choke down the emotions as they attempt to break free, and clear my throat.

Spence stands, pats me on the shoulder, and states, "See you at the cemetery."

I just nod.

Once I'm the only one left, and before they come to load Melody's body, I walk to the front of the room.

I look down into the casket where Melody lies pale with overdone makeup and her hair cascading around her. She looks so peaceful, and maybe what I'm about to do is selfish, but still.

Pulling the Renascence Ruby from my pocket, I use my other hand to lift her interlaced fingers from where they're resting on her stomach, and slide the stone underneath.

Imagining Persephone trapped in Melody's body, anger rages

inside me. And in what I can only describe as my last act of revenge, I lift the bottom of her casket, slide my hand down the inside, and grasp her calf. Then I call my fire, my palm heating, and sear my handprint into that cold flesh.

If Persephone's soul is indeed in there, trapped for all time, then I want her to bear that symbol of my wrath for all eternity. I want her to look down as she walks through her forever and know she will never be safe from me. They may not have found the relics, and she may not be trapped in this corpse, but if she is, I want this to be a reminder that not even in death can she run and hide from me.

I turn and leave, get in my car, and join the procession outside. We slink slowly through town, patrol cars leading the way, and eventually arrive at Evergreen. I stay for several minutes, but overcome by grief, I head to my car and leave.

Driving back to the apartment, tears stream down my face, and eventually I pull into the driveway. I park the car, head inside, and make the preparations to depart. There is no reason to linger, and I'm needed back home, so I rouse the real Aaron, leave him lying delirious in the guest room, and leave that place.

A prepaid Uber waits outside and they take me back to the cemetery. I am quiet on the ride over, staring out the window as the world blurs by, and soon we are there.

I pass back by Melody's graveside service, stand in line to toss my rose onto the casket once it's lowered, and sulk off to find Sophia's grave for the last time.

After several minutes of traipsing through the cemetery, I stop before the gleaming white obelisk-like marker and place a white rose at the base. I pat the stone, thank Sophia for all her help, though I'm not sure she realizes how much she's done for me, and finally make my way home.

Once again, I find the portal, and as the power fills me, I'm pulled back to the Underworld. Down, down, I fall, my arms out at my sides as gravity, treacherous gravity, sends me toppling. But as I'm falling, I think of my Melody, and hope I don't arrive too late to explain. And even once I explain, who knows, she still might not decide to stay. *But then again, maybe she will.*

CHAPTER 42
OTHERSIDE (MELODY)

There is nothing more jarring than waking up surrounded by darkness in an unfamiliar place where the air is stale, thick with a mildewy smell, as you come to realize you're lying prone on slick, algae coated rocks deep within a cave of some sort.

I can hear water dripping in the distance, the large drops echoing off the walls as I imagine them landing in pools of standing water; their contact sending ripples across the surface.

Those ripples stop at the edge of each pool. But their movement causes infinite waves, bursts of visible multi-colored energy, extending out far beyond the confines of the puddle they initially landed in, and bounce off into the darkness where they finally collide with one another.

What I'm seeing, or what I think I'm seeing, is exactly how I imagine bats use echolocation. Difference is, what I'm seeing is like being on a carnival ride, the ground undulating beneath me as my body spins around out of control, halting suddenly just before moving in the opposite direction. It's the tilt-o-whirl, and I'd like to get off this ride please, Mr. Conductor, because I'm about to be sick. But it's just a figment of my imagination, and the world isn't moving; nor am I. This is brought on by whatever head trauma that led me to be… wherever I currently am.

Dirt rings around my mouth, and as I run my tongue over those sandpapery granules, the wetness from that swipe now drawn back in, causes me to spit out the tiny particles coating the insides of my lips.

I shift, rolling over onto my back, and peer up, my eyes adjusting slowly as they focus on little specs of light on the ceiling above me.

Rising, I prop up on my elbows as my legs lie out stretched, extending into the darkness. A dull ache radiates down my spine, and my bones creak as I bend my knees, drawing my legs toward me.

With my head tilted back I squint, trying to pinpoint exactly how high above me the ceiling is where a bioluminescent glow emanates like thousands of tiny stars twinkling amongst the crystal chips.

My neck muscles tense, spasms from craning shooting down into my shoulders, and I've got to move. But I don't know which direction to head and can't see the opening through which I must've fallen.

My idleness while I stare in wonder at all the pretty lights gets me nowhere, and I need to escape whatever hole I've been tossed into. So, turning over onto my hands and knees, I slowly rise.

I stand on wobbly legs, feeble and unsure like a fawn, as mine, too, attempt to learn how to support the weight of my body.

Taking my first step, my movement sends dust billowing into the air. When my inhale tickles the back of my throat, I cough, and the bearing of my weight sends pain radiating up my ankle, causing me to wince.

"Ow, fuck!" I call out, my voice echoing into the ether.

I look down to survey the damage, and my eyes catch on the skirts of the unfamiliar gown I am wearing, crumpled and covered in dirt. I brush it off, patting at the front as I wipe back and forth across the soft fabric.

I freeze, and when I inspect my hands closer, raising them up to eye level where I turn them over, rotating them, they appear to glow. I extend my arm out away from me, and trail my eyes up the length of it.

There is a distinct outline, a glowing silhouette, tracing the entirety of each body part I can see: hands, arms, legs, feet. And I carefully take in each one, waiting for the announcer to cue me to turn myself around, because I'm doing the damned hokey pokey at this point.

Wishing I was still trapped in playback mode, I want to fast forward through whatever this next part is going to be, but this is real time. *Or so I think.*

Ignoring the odd glow about my person, I take another step, this time with my other foot. There is no pain with this movement, so wanting to avoid any further opposition from my other ankle, I drag my foot behind me, scraping it through the flour-like silt at my feet.

Traversing through the cave, I look all around, hoping my eyes will land on something I can use as a crutch. But as luck would have it, this is the only cave in the history of caves absent of debris.

Drag, step, drag, step; I noisily make my way forward, kicking up dust and leaving evidence of my path trailing behind me. But there's a bright side to my plight. With luck, someone will come looking for me. And my shuffled steps will lead them to me, where I'll still be chugging along, like the little engine that could, panting "I-think-I-can" with each labored breath. Because my reality isn't, I think I can. It's more like I know I must.

Chugga, chug, chugga, chug, I say in my mind. The drag, step was too reminiscent of the Cha-Cha Slide, and I hate that damned dance. So now, like a proper engine, I'm chugga, chugging my happy ass down the line, or cavern, as it were.

After about what seems to have been an hour but just as easily could have been twenty minutes, I scoot over to a large boulder and rest. Now, as I sit here, the sound of my foot dragging behind me halted, I can hear voices in the distance; a mumbling of sorts. It's coming from the direction I'm headed, and there are no other openings visible from my vantage point, so if there is a God, he must be on my side, because I am so close now I can taste rescue on the tip of my tongue.

Rescue tastes a whole helluva lot like dirt, but beggars can't be choosers. And if I find myself lucky enough to be rescued? Well, God, serve me up a big heap of mud pie, because I will dig into that bad boy gladly.

I increase the pace of my chugging, wincing now and then as I gauge how bad my ankle actually is, and the mumbling is getting louder now. Soon I will be upon whoever is up ahead, and soon I can get the hell out of this dratted cave.

Moving through a large opening, the cave widens out, and I gasp. Stalagmites and stalactites have formed along the far left of the space, jutting up from the cave floor and haphazardly seeming to drip from the ceiling, but there is no one other than me inside. What I have been hearing must be echoes from farther on into the system, and I groan. "You've got to be fucking kidding me? Well played, God. Well played, you sadistic fuck!"

Columns appear when I finally reach what I hope is the end, and when I take that next step, torches come to life, sputtering as they illuminate the way. Another good sign, because fire means people, and people lead to rescue.

This must be a mining operation of some sort, and the mumbling I keep hearing has to be coming from people toiling away up ahead. But the closest mines I know of are the crystal mines out in Ouachita and the other is out west near Poteau. *Fuck, has someone really dumped me that far from home?*

Farther into the system I go, using the increased mumbling as my guide, my sheer will and determination driving me to take step after pain filled step. And when I look down, I see my swollen ankle.

A baseball-sized knot with purplish-blue bruises form beneath my skin, and a handprint is seared into my calf. "What in the..." the question halts on my lips as I turn my injured leg.

I've been branded? Some asshole marked up my stems! Ugh! Seriously, I have got to get the fuck out of here. And when I find whoever did this; that mother fucker is going to pay dearly!

Agitated by the state of my leg, I step faster. There's no more stopping, no more resting, because I want this shit over!

I step through another set of columns and I'm smacked in the face by a very unpleasant sulphury odor. I scrunch my nose, turning my attention to where large pyres sit burning on each side of the path, their whooshing flames barely audible over the loud echoes of mumbling filling the cave now. And I can hear each distinct mumble as it bounces off the flower-like crystals formed above me.

I crane my neck, the light from the pyres refracting through the crystals, sending prisms dancing along the walls, and the sight is otherworldly. It's pretty. Nevertheless, the voices are so loud now they drown out my dragging foot as I shuffle, so I push onward.

Deeper into the cave, the walls narrow once more, and the mumbling, once only loud and unintelligible, is now discernible as muffled cries of confusion.

Questions of, "Where am I?", "How did I get here?", interspersed with "Do you know?" fill my ears, and finally, up ahead, I see people.

I rush toward them, and when I reach the first one shuffling just as labored as I have been, I spin him around, gripping tightly to his shoulders.

A gaunt man faces me, his eyes widening as he calls out, "Priscilla?"

I drop my hands, stepping away as confusion dresses my features. "No. I'm sorry. I'm not Priscilla." And just like their muffled cries of confusion, I sob out my own. "Where am I?"

The man answers with his own shriek, "Do you know?"

As he reaches out for me, I step back away from the man in fear and bump into someone behind me.

I spin, stepping to the side as a ragged woman steps forward, joining all the others. There are hundreds of them; men, women, and children, young and old, confused and disheveled, bouncing off one another like bumper cars as they wander into the opening up ahead.

I join the throng, saying nothing as I grasp my hands over my ears, hoping to muffle some of the chaos.

I slide along the left wall; the stones scraping my shoulder raw. But I don't want to touch any of those around me. They smell like death; rancid and putrid, stinging my nostrils. I want to plug my nose, but then I would have to remove my hands from my ears and let in all the wailing. I am already overstimulated, so I soldier on, blowing my cheeks out as I hold in my breath as the voice of Ludo from *Labyrinth* yells out in my mind, *"Smell Bad."* But at least they're not bubbling and popping like the Bog of Eternal Stench.

Even though some of them have evidence of boils on their skin, and I have enjoyed a good session of popping bubble wrap, there is absolutely no way I am doing so now. Not today, intrusive thoughts. *Thou shalt not pass!*

God, I'm such a dork!

I roll my eyes, allowing myself a quick chuckle to battle the hysteria bubbling its way to the surface as we continue down the tunnel with no visible end. And, unsure of how long we all have been walking, my second nature has me looking down for a watch that no longer wraps around my wrist.

Finally, we halt. The mouth of a large opening where rusted-out iron gates with skulls, their mouths opened in silent screams, adorn six massive hinges; three on each side, as it lies closed before us, trapping us inside.

They open, groaning out in opposition until they clank noisily against the stone wall of the cave's exit. And once they are gaping wide enough for those gathered to enter, a man steps forward.

When he crosses the line the gate scored in the sand, a gust of hot air whooshes through the tunnel, blowing my hair back as I squeeze my eyes shut. It rushes past, a groaning in the wind that wails out in agony as it echoes down the tunnel behind me. And once it stills, the throng rushes forward, running across the line and out into God know's where.

Bodies push past me, battering me against the wall, and I cling to it as I'm jostled. Most of the crowd has dispersed, fanning out once over the line, and from what I can see, it is pure pandemonium.

There are large, robed figures, galloping back and forth atop terrifying steeds, black as pitch, while their flame tipped manes and tails catch the wind, flying like flags trailing behind them. They drive the crowd with the efficiency of a herding dog, away from the gates and out into the open, where they flock like sheep, banding together in one enormous mass.

I thought the cries of confusion in the tunnel were bad, but thousands upon thousands of frightened and disoriented peoples' wails are deafening, and I clasp my hands over my ears once more.

Allowing the chaos to settle, I walk hesitantly toward the gates, stopping just at the scored line in the sand. As I peek out, I cling to the iron post of the gate, not crossing the barrier as I survey the scene before me.

I see the figures on horseback dividing the mass of people into two groups. They herd one group toward a large vessel bobbing in the choppy river waters, and push the other toward the river's edge, away from the first.

Cowering at the gates, I see a rider turning and rushing toward me. The hoofbeats of his horse, as they barrel toward me, sound like claps of thunder as they pound through the sand. They are charging fast and slide to a stop once they are within earshot.

"There's no use in hiding," he bellows, the percussive wave from his booming voice blowing me back; knocking me on my ass.

His horse rears, and he expertly holds on as he stares me down. The hooves land once again and the quake from the impact sends silt dust billowing into the surrounding air.

Pacing back and forth, his gravelly voice calls out once more, "I can do this for as long as it takes. But once those gates close, you are at the mercy of the beasts of the Labyrinth. What say you? Is that a gamble you wish to take?"

I rise to my feet and choking down my fear; I cross the barrier. Once on the other side, I feel different; drained.

The glowing silhouette I alone seemed to possess is now gone, and I'm fully at the mercy of what I now acknowledge is the depths of the Underworld.

I had been dreaming about the Underworld. Had visions of Hades and Persephone. Hell, for all I know, Persephone was the parasite who took over my body and made me do the most...

I shake my head and take another step toward the horsemen. In my most demanding voice, and with as much confidence as I can muster, I say, "I need to speak to Hades."

The guard chortles. "Show me your tithe!"

I look down, searching my person for anything I might offer. But I find nothing, only this damned flowy dress I wouldn't be caught dead wearing.

A laugh gets caught in my throat and I raise my chin in defiance. "Hades will want to see me. I have information," I insist. "Valuable information."

"Yeah?" He halts his horse, and leaning toward me, red eyes flash beneath his hood. "And I'm the Dali Llama. Now, move!"

He circles around me, and just like he did with the throng, he herds me toward the second group.

"Wait! Please!" I cry out. "I'm not lying. Hades will want to hear me! He needs to hear me!"

The guard ignores me, continuing to push me toward the direction I know I shouldn't go.

In a last ditch effort, I finally show my hand by screaming, "I know about Adonis!"

The guard stops. "What did you say?" he glowers. He dismounts his horse, jerking the reins behind him as he stomps toward me.

I gulp down the breath I'd been holding, and once again raise my chin as I assert, "I know about Adonis!" I clench my teeth, tightening my jaw in hopes he knows I mean business.

He says nothing, so I continue. "I know about Persephone, too," I say assuredly.

He cackles. "Persephone? Ha! Ha!" His face goes completely vacant. "Everyone knows about Persephone. Now move!" he growls, kicking sand at me and urging me on.

I circle around him, hissing as I show my teeth. He may be bigger than I am, way fucking bigger, but I'm not going without a fight. I'll go fucking feral if I have to, but I am not going toward the other group. *Fuck him and the horse he rode in on.*

"You know, it's been a while since I've gotten enjoyment from this part. But you bitch..." He points at me. "You just made my fucking day," he jeers.

"Tell Hades I want to speak to him or so help me, I will sic Cottus on your ass!" I seethe.

"Cottus? Cottus is busy behind the walls of-"

"Tartarus. Yeah, I fucking know!" I grit, interrupting him as I roll my eyes. "And you have to appease Anástasia to get in and he's oh so busy with Kairos that he couldn't possibly have time to grant an audience with little ole me. Am I right?" I cock my hip out for effect. "Now get fucking Hades!"

The guard's mouth goes slack, his jaw dropping open as he gapes at me. He takes a step back.

I step forward, flailing my arms toward him as I command, "Well?"

He turns and walks off, looking back once to glare over his shoulder at me as he leads his horse toward the ferry.

Once beside the river, the guard waltzes up to a very tall, very imposing robed figure. The guard's arms flail in the air as he, I assume, explains the situation to the robed figure, pointing several times directly at me.

The robed figure turns their hood in my direction, and from this far away, I can't see his eyes, but I feel his heated gaze as he surveys me warily. It creeps up my neck, settling on my cheeks, and my head throbs; an obtrusive pressure.

The guard leaves his horse by the river, striding angrily toward me, and his glowing red eyes never leave my form as he steps before me.

"Charon said, 'Get fucked,'" he announces triumphantly, grabbing my wrist and dragging me toward the point of no return.

As he jerks me behind him, I struggle in his grip, twisting and turning as I attempt to break loose of his hold. But it's no use. Even uninjured, I didn't have the strength, and now...

Then I remember. My ankle; it doesn't hurt anymore. Struggling to look down, I no longer see the bruising around my ankle, but as luck would have it, that bright red marking, the handprint I couldn't place before this moment, shines brightly on my calf.

"He marked me!" I wail. "You can't do this, you over-grown glob of flesh! He marked me!"

That gets his attention, and he stops. He drops my wrist and I fall at his feet. My eyes raise slowly, fear coursing through me, and when they reach his face, he throws back his hood, revealing his skeletal form.

His jaw hinges open as a deep rumble escapes his lips, and a roaring laughter spills out. I am so taken aback that I fall onto the sand, cowering at his feet.

I scramble backwards and he grabs my ankle, dragging me forward. We are almost at the river and I'm still yelling for him to look when the palm of my right hand heats.

My fingers close around my palm protectively, and as we reach the rest of the second group, where guards are pushing one body after another into the river, I feel a weight in my hand.

I thrust my hand into the air, yelling out joyfully, "I have a tithe!" And finally he stops.

He drops my ankle, clasps his skeletal fingers around my wrist and prompts me to open my hand.

I do, and when he sees what lies within, this time, he's the one that gasps.

I gather my strength, rise to my feet, bracing myself on my knees as I bend over, panting around hurried breaths.

I am panting so hard I struggle to force out the words, so I linger between the groups as I ask, "Now,... will you please... take me... to see... Hades?"

This time when I say his name, a bright light fractures the space between me and the guard, and a freakishly tall, irritatingly handsome, dark-haired man appears before me. He offers me his hand and I take it.

Once I'm on my own two feet, the man scoops me up in his arms and walks toward the ferry.

As I'm nestling into his chest, calmed by an oh so familiar scent, the man growls out over his shoulder at the guard several paces behind us, "We'll talk about this later!"

"Yes, my king," the guard answers, defeated.

When I gather the courage to look up, storm cloud grey eyes rimmed with shining silver threads gaze back at me.

"It's you," I whimper, the realization that a god, but not the one I begged to save me, holds me in their arms.

"It's me," he soothes, leaning down and placing a soft kiss on my head.

How had I not put it together before? How had I not seen the similarities in their eyes? Hades and Aaron are one and the same. Different bodies entirely, but the same. My head swims as the realization sets in.

We are boarding the ferry several minutes later, when those familiar eyes look down on me once more. He sighs. "I am so sorry to have to do this, and we really have little time, but I need you to decide."

"On?" I pose.

"Will you stay with me, or am I sending you home?" His eyes spark.

"Back home..." I begin, "how bad is it?"

"Pretty fucking bad." He chuckles, curling me into him as he places another kiss on my head.

"Not really much of a choice, is there?" I'm not angry when I say this, it just happens to be the state of things.

"This is not how I wanted this," he admits.

"Yeah, well. Even gods can't have it their way all the time," I joke.

"Ain't that the fucking truth?" He laughs wholeheartedly.

His throaty rumble is so fucking sexy, and I am getting so turned on by him, as I'm jostled against his tight chest, but I keep it in. I hold it together. There will be time. Well, depending on what I decide.

"I need an answer, Mel," he urges. "Clocks a ticking, so to speak."

"How long now?" I ask.

"Only until the boat docks on the other side. Once your feet touch the sand, it's a done deal." He huffs.

"Deal," I say.

He asks for clarification, "Deal?"

"Deal!" I shout out in confirmation, raising my fists into the air triumphantly.

His face is beaming, and I've never seen something shining so brightly as he is as he holds me, the glow of satisfaction creating a golden halo all around him.

The ferry reaches the shore and the planks are being lowered when I tap his chin, gaining his attention.

He smiles down at me and I up at him.

"There's just one itsy, bitsy, teeny stipulation," I say.

His face falls. "Stipulation?"

"Get this god awful, hideous fucking dress off me!" I shout

A hearty laugh rumbles free, and his head falls back as he takes the first step down the planks, placing me on the ground once he steps off the ferry.

I straighten and he pulls me into him, brushing the pad of his thumb over my lip as he hovers over my face. There is comfort in the fire burning in those eyes as he says, "I think I can do that." He places his lips on mine, and we share my first and last life altering kiss, as my fate is now sealed. Because I am gladly and forever tied to Hades.

THE HEART

OF THE

Renascence

RUBY

ANGELA M. JOHNSON

About the Author

Angela M. Johnson is an independently published, BIPOC author of adult fantasy and romance novels living in Northwest Arkansas (NWA) with her family. She is active in her local writing community, encouraging aspiring authors by donating her time to educate and share her knowledge of resources. She is a retired Army Veteran, mother, artist, Cosplayer, crafter, and Heavy Athlete competing in Scottish Highland Games. When she isn't writing full-time, she is chasing dopamine; collecting skills and hobbies like they are Pokémon cards. From 3D printing, Laser Engraving, CNC Carving, and other types of fabrication. As an author, Angela takes the imagery playing in her mind as if from a streaming service, and delivers in written form by way of epic adventures, comedic banter, romantic entanglements, and high stakes action. She published her first fantasy novel in 2022 and has now ventured into the romance genre; releasing three novels in 2023 and more to come in the future.

www.notyouraveragejohnson.com